An Ordinary Girl's Life

An Ordinary Girl's Life

RAE WETZEL

RESOURCE *Publications* · Eugene, Oregon

AN ORDINARY GIRL'S LIFE

Resource Publications
An Imprint of Wipf and Stock Publishers
199 W. 8th Ave., Suite 3
Eugene, OR 97401

www.wipfandstock.com

PAPERBACK ISBN: 979-8-3852-6835-1
HARDCOVER ISBN: 979-8-3852-6836-8
EBOOK ISBN: 979-8-3852-6837-5

VERSION NUMBER 01/14/26

Poem reprinted with permission from Paul Wiegel.

This book is a work of fiction. The names, characters, places, and incidents are the products of the author's imagination or are used fictitiously.

Dedicated to the memory of my mothers, May and Rosemary

Thank you to my siblings and family, from whom I've borrowed so much. I give a shout-out to all the kids and their parents who lived on Stadium Drive in the 1960s and 1970s. May God bless each and every one of you, and I hope to be reunited one day, possibly for the best block party ever!

For my husband, Robert, the love of my life and my inspiration

"CONVERSATION WITH THE MOON"

The moon is not as quiet
As it seems. You lean out
That upstairs window and look
Up on some summer night
Trying to decide how much the
Moon really knows about things.
Sometimes there are clouds,
But this nighttime visit
Is really about clarity.
Clear skies and clear minds
Can only come together
After the moon rises high enough
For you to see it there
While you lean on that sill
Wondering if there is anyplace
Else where the conversation
Is as good as this one.

PAUL WIEGEL

Acknowledgments

First, I would like to thank Tom Baxter, a former coworker, for introducing me to his mother, Jean Baxter. Jean is a talented author who propelled me forward. Her example and encouragement were the big pushes I needed to get going and write! She read many of my drafts from the earliest days forward and provided valuable critiques and helpful suggestions. I don't believe I could have done it without her. And, yes, she is still my friend!

Thank you to my loving husband, Robert Wetzel, for his thoughtful insight and suggestions, especially when a male perspective was necessary. You put up with many long days of writing and editing, looking at my back. You are my biggest and best supporter!

To the people who provided valuable feedback and assistance: my sister, Renee Smits; my daughter, Rachel Wetzel; my son, Michael Wetzel; my daughter-in-law, Sara Wetzel; and my friend Diane Hayes. To Heather Walter, your meticulous review of an early draft is much appreciated. To my older brother, Craig Yakel, who answered many questions, especially about our grandparents. To my younger brother, Curt Yakel, who prefers to be surprised. I hope I did you all justice. And to a special someone who changed one word.

Thank you to Laurie Bannow and Mary Dollar for their help with the history of their local businesses, Bannow's Arena Handi-Mart and Rola Rena.

I also give a big shout-out to the Green Bay Area Writers Guild. Many members listened to me read and offered valuable feedback.

Thank you to the wonderful team at Wipf and Stock Publishers.

Finally, and most importantly, thank you, Jesus! I absolutely could not have accomplished this without you! For I can do all things through Christ who strengthens me (see Phil 4:13).

CHAPTER 1

MARLEE ASCENDED THE STAIRS on her way to bed. It was a warm summer evening, and she stopped briefly in the first bedroom at the top. It stood vacant. She walked the width of the room and peered out the open window, the night air pleasant. Searching for the moon, she smiled when it met her eyes and marveled at its beauty. Glancing across the street, she remembered herself fifty years earlier as a curious twelve-year-old girl alone in her bedroom, gazing out into a summer night in this same familiar way.

Many evenings throughout her childhood, Marlee often lost herself in thought as she knelt on her bed, pressed tight against the bright pink walls, her forearms folded and propped on the sill, scanning the darkness.

Transported back to another era, Marlee recalled the sound of crickets that serenaded her then, too. A flurry of memories flooded her mind. She yearned for the carefree days of her youth.

Growing up, the girl did not understand that her family was one of the few blended families on their street. She reached adulthood before that realization fully hit. There were three others at their end of the block alone, one on each side of them and one kitty-corner to the east. That was the sixties and seventies, long before the concept of *yours, mine, and ours* was in vogue.

Sixty-two years had come and gone, and Marlee had never truly relocated. Since leaving her childhood home, she circled the small town where she'd resided for her entire life, living in a few apartments, one duplex, and two houses. For the past twenty-five-plus years, Marlee lived south of her childhood home by mere blocks. She admitted not knowing how to count city blocks but knew the colonial two-story home she and her husband owned sat less than a mile from the small ranch where she'd grown up. Her mind tried sliding back to that neighborhood, but a gentle breeze snatched her thoughts. She sighed and raked her hands through her dark, short hair. After one more look at the moon, she reluctantly pulled herself from the window and shuffled down the hall to her bedroom.

"Marlee?" her husband asked.

"Yes," she whispered.

"Where've you been?"

"I'm too nostalgic for my own good," she told him, slipping under the crisp sheet close to his warm body, inhaling the fresh, sunny scent of the bedding that had hung outside to dry.

"Huh?"

"Go to sleep, hon. We can talk in the morning."

Marlee closed her eyes and listened for any soothing sound to help quiet her mind. Reflecting on the past always seemed to stir her brain. If she wasn't careful, she might give in and plunge headlong down the rabbit hole of memory lane.

The soft whirring of the ceiling fan directly above the bed, with the steady movement of air pleasantly floating down, successfully lulled her, and Marlee staved off insomnia in favor of welcome, blissful sleep.

CHAPTER 2

OCTOBER 24, 1954. MARLEE stood at the end of the hall in their small house and looked at her reflection in the full-length mirror. Standing less than three feet tall, feeling sad and unsure, she clung to her mother's hand-made, scarlet-colored skirt. Anne took one last look at herself and, with her manicured hand, reached up and smoothed her dark, shoulder-length hair. A whiff of powder prompted tears from her daughter. Anne snuggled her youngest tight to her side, hoping it was enough to comfort her.

"Oh, baby girl. Don't cry." Anne bent down and kissed the top of Marlee's head, breathing in her clean scent.

Marlee did not want her mother and father to leave. She did not want a babysitter that Saturday evening. And unbeknownst to her, it would be the last time she would know her mother's presence because Anne Becket died that night in a tragic single-car accident, leaving behind her husband and three small children. Marlee was the youngest at three and a half, and her mother was just thirty-one when life went dark for the Becket family. Since that fateful day and for a big portion of her early life, Marlee struggled to comprehend why her mother had to die. Different people said it was God's will. Understanding, more than acceptance, eluded her.

Happily married for thirteen years, Marvin and Anne Becket were often seen as an attractive, fun-loving couple. It was common for them to be out with their friends and neighbors, Duane and Meredith Wenz, who lived down the street. On that ill-fated night, the two couples enjoyed dinner and dancing at a supper club thirty minutes out of town. Unfortunately, none of the four returned home that evening.

Six o'clock the following morning, ten-year-old Todd Becket woke before anyone else in his home. He rubbed the slumber from his eyes and ambled down the hall, stopping short when he found Mr. Milner asleep in the living room. April Milner, their teenage babysitter from up the street, apparently had been replaced by her father. Todd quietly turned on his heel, hurried to the end of the hall, and saw his parents' bedroom door wide open, the bed still made. Directly across the hall, his sisters slept in their shared bedroom. He shook Melanie awake and, speaking softly, said, "Come here." Without questioning, she scooped their rustling sister from the adjacent twin bed and swung her onto her hip. They followed Todd to the living room, where they observed Mr. Milner reclining on the sofa. The little bit of hair on his head jutted out at odd angles.

"What is he doing here?" whispered seven-year-old Melanie.

"I don't know, but Mom and Dad aren't home yet."

Mr. Milner's eyes opened, and he jolted upright at the sight of the children. He did not immediately speak.

Todd led the girls to the big, boxy, orange chair across from the sofa. The three kids packed into it, and Todd swiveled it around to face the bay window. Marlee rubbed her eyes, and the sisters waited for their brother or Mr. Milner to say something. Nothing came. The children watched, void of understanding, as cars suddenly began to pull into the driveway, with more parking on the street in front of their home. Todd knew something was seriously wrong, and instantly, his insides twisted in fear.

People entered the house without knocking or ringing the bell. Some stayed in the kitchen, while others crowded into the living room. There were an aunt and an uncle, as well as neighbors, including Mrs. Milner, who joined her husband and two men whose identities the children did not know. They spoke in hushed tones. Bernice Becket appeared, and weeping, she dropped to her knees before her grandchildren seated in the orange chair and pulled them to her, group-hugging them. Melanie cried, too, but didn't know exactly why. Sam Becket stood stone-faced behind his wife.

Bernice took a deep breath, quickly summoned the necessary fortitude, and told the children about their mother and father. They heard that their parents, along with Mr. and Mrs. Wenz, were on their way home from their night out when an accident had occurred. And their mother was dead. As if losing her was not enough, numbing them to their core, they learned that their father lay in critical care. He suffered severe trauma and had undergone multiple surgeries. He, too, may not survive. Those were inconceivable words for them to hear.

Unfortunately, Mr. Wenz also perished that night. Sadly, Mrs. Wenz was in serious condition but, thankfully, was expected to recover from her injuries.

The heinous event unraveled over the ensuing days and weeks, revealing disturbing details. It was 1:10 a.m. when the car the two couples were traveling in missed a curve and clipped off a utility pole, careening 277 feet out of control down an embankment through trees before landing on its roof. A man driving behind them witnessed the car leave the road, and he stopped in the driveway of a nearby residence. After startling the homeowners awake, they called for help. The driver told the authorities what he saw: red taillights that dove off the side of the road, turning vertically before disappearing. He later wondered how many times the car would have rolled before landing with a terrible thud, its roof crushed and its wheels spinning frantically.

Anne Becket had been brutally flung from the vehicle, one arm severed, torn from her body above the elbow, and her chest crushed, just like the car roof, her contorted body thirty feet away. Killed instantly, they said. A blessing, many suggested.

Marvin Becket had also been thrown from the vehicle, and as he skidded along the ground, his throat filled with dry leaves and brown dirt that blocked his air passageway. Barely alive and with his body badly broken, he lay unconscious.

Meredith Wenz had painfully pulled herself up from the cold earthen floor, her mind muddled. Her eyes darted wildly through the smoldering, eerie darkness. Silent with hysterical terror, save for her heavy breathing, she found Duane, her husband of seventeen years, pinned beneath the wreckage, any sign of life violently stomped out.

Both Duane and Anne were pronounced dead at the scene. Meredith and Marvin were rushed to the nearest hospital in separate, screaming ambulances.

Marvin had undergone a tracheotomy on the way. He suffered multiple head injuries, broken bones, and internal damage, and the days slowly passed with no one certain whether he would ever come out of his coma. Then, during the night of the twenty-eighth, Marvin regained consciousness but was confused. He did not know what had happened and wondered why Anne was not at his bedside.

Someone moved about the dimly lit room, and Marvin croaked, "Where's Anne? Where's my wife?"

"I don't know," was all the nurse replied before quickly leaving to inform the night supervisor that her patient was awake.

The following day, a doctor matter-of-factly informed Marvin that his wife had died. Marvin did not remember an accident. And the possibility that Anne was dead never occurred to him. Not once. The situation was difficult for him to fathom, compounded by the shocking reality that she was already buried. He scarcely could take in that detail. Grief filled his entire being, nearly suffocating him.

Duane Wenz had recently undergone care at the Mayo Clinic in Rochester, Minnesota. He sought treatment for sporadic blackouts. At the time of his death, the cause was still unknown. Some deduced that he may have suffered one of these blackouts behind the wheel the night of the accident. Interestingly, an autopsy was neither required nor performed.

By the time Marvin Becket had regained consciousness, Meredith Wenz had been released from the hospital. Never having had children and being an only child herself, she relied on the attempted comfort of her parents and Duane's only sibling, his bachelor brother, Ralph. Devastated and afraid, she felt alone.

Neighbors of both the Wenz and Becket families paid their respects to Meredith at her husband's funeral. And because she had been unable to attend Anne's funeral, it was the first opportunity since the accident for most of them to see her. Fortunately, no one pressed her for details of the awful night. All they knew was what they had heard or read in the newspaper.

Roughly twelve hours after the deadly crash, the Becket children were whisked away to their grandparents' house, one hour north in Suring, Wisconsin. With Sam and Bernice at their sides, they had mourned their mother at her funeral under curious scrutiny, and with their father's future hanging in the balance. Everyone's lives were turned upside down, and immense adjustment was demanded of all. Todd and Melanie were enrolled in the small town's only elementary school. All three children struggled with the permanent absence of their mother and with the hopefully interim absence of their father. Bernice had shuddered at the thought of her son passing.

None of the children visited their father in the hospital. In later years, no one remembered why. Maybe it wasn't allowed. Melanie had written one brief letter. It read, "Dear Dad, I love you. I hope you get better. I hope you get out of the hospital. Grandmother said you will get out of the hospital in a week. In school, I draw. Marlee is a good girl." She signed it, "Melanie, Todd, and Marlee."

Marvin and the kids were finally reunited on November 15. His hospital release came three weeks after the accident, exactly twenty-one long, grueling days later.

Sam and Bernice hadn't told them about their father's impending release but instead played it safe, making sure it happened and opting for it to be a surprise. That November day, they anxiously worked with the kids outside in their sprawling yard, raking leaves and stacking sticks and branches for burning, when a vehicle pulled into the half-moon drive-way. From the front passenger side, Marvin exited. Noticeably thinner, he steadied himself against the car. He smiled. His children stampeded toward him, yelling and crying, "Dad!" "Dad!" "Daddy!" He lifted them with his left arm, his right still in a cast. Sobbing emanated from the en-twined bodies, but it was the happiest of bleak days.

Everyone was glad to have Marvin home at last. The kids' demeanor reflected that sentiment more than anything they said. The sisters stayed close by, often playing at his feet, and when not at school, Melanie re-mained attentive to Marvin's every need, insisting that he take it easy.

Todd's persistent, serious expression, especially when observing his father, did not go unnoticed by the adults. And there was plenty to be concerned about.

Marvin suffered mightily, both physically and mentally, and grieved over the death of his young wife. But with encouragement mainly from Bernice, he persevered and focused on his family and required physical rehabilitation. With Marlee nearby watching, he completed his daily regi-men using pages of illustrated exercises given to him at the hospital. The girl giggled when her father grimaced, not realizing he was in pain, and told him he made a funny face.

Although Marvin would be forever grateful to his aging parents for their selfless love and care, he wanted to return home as quickly as pos-sible. It was important to him that he be well enough to take his children home in time for Christmas. That was his hope. As a widower, he had life to figure out and thought it best to move forward.

With a headache threatening, Marvin pinched the bridge of his nose and shifted in his chair to get more comfortable. Tentatively bringing his fingers up, he ran them across his forehead and felt the length of a deep and ugly gash still healing. It ran diagonally from his hairline to his brow.

He sighed deeply, knowing he would have a telltale scar and a permanent reminder of the turning point in their lives.

"What's wrong?" Bernice asked.

"It's time," Marvin announced. "Christmas is around the corner. I want us to forge ahead with our new . . ." He paused, cleared his throat. "Normal."

"Marv. What will you do?" his mother asked, wringing her hands. "My gosh, you certainly can't go back to work yet. Not in your condition. Who will help with the kids?"

"Oh, Ma," he said, averting his eyes. "I don't know. I suppose I'll have to look for a girl to come in and help with Marlee while the other two are in school. However, I need to return to the office. I'm going goofy." He shook his fists in frustration. "Maybe I can go back after the first of the year. At least for half days." His voice caught with trepidation, "You've seen Melanie. She will be a big help to me."

With the matter quickly settled, Bernice Becket visited the school the following week and explained that Todd and Melanie would finish their seven-week stint at Suring Elementary before the start of Christmas break. Everyone had hoped from the beginning that it would be a temporary arrangement. Thankfully, it worked out that way.

Todd shared that he looked forward to returning to his buddies in Sister Sylvia's fifth-grade class. Melanie didn't say anything about school, but when she talked about going home, she cried, wondering what it might be like without her mother. She wept whenever her thoughts settled on Anne. She missed her greatly. They all did. Marlee's level of comprehension was challenging to decipher. Bernice said her youngest granddaughter sometimes seemed confused or perhaps sullen, while at other times she was amiable. Everyone coped the best way they knew how.

Marvin hired a young woman he heard about from a neighbor. Patty Wilson seemed fine, a bit on the shy side. He hoped she would open up more with the children. He soon realized, though, that Patty's presence did not enthrall Marlee. She regressed and became disagreeable.

"Marlee, sweetie, please put your clothes on for Daddy. *Please,*" Marvin pleaded. For three consecutive days, his daughter had refused to wear the clothing he set out for her. Having got down on one knee, he patiently persuaded her to cooperate.

In addition to watching Marlee, Marvin hired Patty to wash clothes and cook supper for the family before leaving for home each afternoon. One day, he was surprised to discover she had also boldly rearranged the living room furniture. He thought that was odd, and it unsettled him. If Patty found herself bored, he certainly knew of other jobs she could do around the house.

At the supper table one evening after Patty had gone, Marvin said to the kids, "I don't know about you, but I've had my fill of crummy hot dogs and Jell-O."

Todd laughed. Patty did cook hot dogs a lot, though she proved inventive by preparing them in at least four different ways. Her specialty was slicing and tossing them with buttered noodles, which the kids enjoyed. She also split them in half by cutting them the long way and fried them with sauerkraut, fixing them with a creamy white sauce—possibly Alfredo—and, of course, the tried-and-true classic method, serving them on a bun with catsup and mustard.

"I'm sorry, but there's no disguising a hot dog, no matter how hard one tries, and I am sick of hot dogs," Marvin grumbled.

Todd chuckled. "At least we get baked beans once in a while. Beans, beans, the musical fruit, the more you eat, the more you toot," he sang. The girls giggled.

"Not at the table, Todd," their father frowned.

When Marvin began working full days, Marlee spent more time in Patty's care. Each afternoon, when Patty plunked herself down on the sofa to watch her program on TV—her soap, she called it—she paid very little attention to Marlee.

One mild, sunny winter afternoon with the snow melting and water flowing freely down the gutter in the street, Melanie and Todd got off the school bus and trekked up the driveway. They entered the house through the breezeway and let the screen door bang shut. Seeing no sign of their younger sister, Melanie asked Patty, "Where's Marlee?"

"Ah, she's um . . ." Patty stammered, surveying the room. "I don't know. Marlee?" she called.

For all her seven years, Melanie glared at Patty, then rolled her eyes at Todd. He checked the bedrooms, thinking their sister might be asleep. Melanie went outside, stepped off the front porch, and hollered, drawing it out, "Marrrleeee!"

In a panic, Patty jumped up off the sofa and practically flew out of the living room through the breezeway door into the backyard. "Marlee?" she called. She looked around. "Marlee!" she hollered.

Melanie, hearing no reply, headed down the street toward Mrs. Wenz's house, where she saw her sister huddled in the corner on the front stoop. Marlee was not yet four, and Melanie knew she should not be there alone. "Marlee," she said as she approached. The child threw herself at her big sister, wrapping her arms around her waist, knocking Melanie backward.

Patty ran, worried and gasping for breath as she reached them. "Oh, Marlee!" she said, sounding exasperated. "Why did you come down here without telling me? You can't just leave like that." She splayed out her arms. "What the heck?"

Marlee buried her face in Melanie's side.

"Don't you ever do that again! You scared me half to death," Patty scolded angrily, and turned toward the house.

Melanie took her sister's hand, and they followed.

"I found her on Mrs. Wenz's porch," Melanie reported to Todd. He shook his head in disbelief.

Three days later, Meredith pulled into her driveway after work and discovered Marlee alone on her front steps, fully aware that the child had been there just a few days ago. Stopping the car short of the garage, Meredith got out and left the door open. With arms extended, she steadied her voice, feeling an ache deep in her chest, feeling sorry for Marlee.

"Marlee, honey, what are you doing here?" Meredith gathered the child into the fold of her embrace. Marlee clung to a tattered blanket and clutched a lime-green plastic sand pail. Full of a young girl's treasures, the pail held a small doll with a dirty face, a pink rubber ball, two purple bottle caps, and one smooth, flat rock. Marlee whimpered. Meredith did not speak; she could not trust her voice at that moment.

She carried Marlee into the house and set her on the kitchen counter, where they were eye to eye. Clearing her throat, Meredith asked, "Marlee, does Miss Patty know where you are?"

"I don't know," Marlee shrugged meekly.

"Well, let's . . ." Meredith began, then stopped. She reached for the rotary dial wall phone. "I'm calling Patty. She needs to know you're here."

Meredith began spending more time with the Beckets, and they often found themselves happily at her home. Marlee liked to nuzzle Meredith's cat, Fanny—a soft, mellow, gray tabby who tolerated the girl toting her around. Todd and Melanie chose to sprawl across Meredith's living room floor, playing checkers or watching TV. Marvin and the children also ate considerably better since Meredith frequently invited them for supper, and he repeatedly complimented her cooking.

She laughed, "Oh, Marv, I don't think it takes much of a cook to drum up something fancier than hot dogs and macaroni. Besides, it's no fun cooking for myself."

After dinner, Marlee enjoyed sitting with the adults for a bit, curled up on Meredith's lap and sharing her black coffee with a casual sip. Marlee disliked the taste of the dark, bitter liquid but savored the closeness.

Meredith also began accompanying the family on their Sunday morning road trips to visit Marvin's parents, Sam and Bernice. That went on for weeks, which stretched into months. They would head north after church, and occasionally after the noon meal, they would drive a bit further north to visit Meredith's folks at Anderson Lake before returning for supper with the elder Beckets. The kids were thrilled when they visited Alvin and Ruby Simon because the couple raised and sold poodles. They usually had several puppies eager to be cuddled.

Meredith's mother gave long, silly names to their own two pups. A white one Ruby named Cinderella Princess Snowball, but they called her Cindy for short. The other was Sheila Sweet Maiden Belle, though the dog answered simply to Sheila. Marlee said Cindy and Sheila were not your usual dog names, for she had grown accustomed to the kind of names she typically heard for dogs—her Grandpa Becket gave his dog the name Cocoa, and there were two canines in the neighborhood named Champ and Brit, the latter being a Brittany spaniel.

"Cindy and Sheila are people names," Marlee once told her dad. "Someone ought to tell Ruby—I mean, Mrs. Simon—that." He chuckled.

On Sunday evenings, after watching *Walt Disney's Wonderful World of Color*, Meredith Wenz and the Becket family bid goodbye to Bernice and Sam and departed for home. The children commonly fell asleep on the ride. Marvin always carried Marlee into the house, set her on the toilet to tinkle, and then changed her clothes, gently slipping a nightgown over her head before tucking her into bed. She feigned sleep, peeking at her father through the thin slits of her partially closed eyes. When Marlee grew up, she realized her father probably had always known she was awake, and she loved him for going along with it and caring for her in such a tender way.

In early March, shortly after Todd turned eleven, he woke in the backseat and heard the adults quietly talking. They sounded different, serious.

"I don't care what anyone thinks. It's *none* of their business anyway. It doesn't affect them."

"You're right, Marv," Meredith said softly, "but it might be too soon. It might be awkward or even uncomfortable for some."

"Maybe so," he agreed, "but not for us. They will have to get used to the idea."

A moment passed before Meredith spoke again. "Well, I guess we've decided—May then." She felt almost giddy and smiled at Marvin across the bench seat. His grin was visible in the twilight. He reached for her hand and squeezed.

CHAPTER 3

"You know," Meredith began, "this feels right. Not long after you and the kids returned home from up north after the accident, the holidays were over, and we were all doing our best to adjust to our new lives— us without our spouses and the kids without Anne. Then we started to spend more time together . . ." Marvin cocked his head but let her continue. "It was hard. I saw three young children who desperately needed a mother. Remember Marlee on my porch? That broke my heart." She frowned. "Then you suggested we get married. It seems natural. Right. I guess because I want to be more than just your wife. I want to be Marlee's and Melanie's and Todd's mother. And now . . ."

"It's not going to be easy," Marvin said, holding back a smile, but he liked her way of thinking. "It's a big thing taking on someone else's children."

"Oh, I know. I've thought about this a lot, Marv." Meredith cleared her throat. Bravely pushed on. "I do have one condition I need to share with you if we're to move forward."

"Oh?"

"I'm sorry," she said, "but I will not—cannot—live in another woman's home." She hesitated but only momentarily. "Anne was my friend, and I loved her dearly. And I admired her. I miss her still. But I want to stay here, in my home. I'm sorry if that's not what you want to hear."

He took a deep breath. "I understand, Mer. I truly do."

"Does that mean you're willing to live here? In my home? Are you saying you and the kids would be okay moving in with me?"

"I am if you will have us," he winked. "I think the kids will be, too. We'll find out soon enough, though, won't we?"

Relieved, Meredith smiled. Marvin reached for her, and she hugged him tightly.

"I want you to be happy, Meredith. If staying in your home makes you happy, I'm good with that."

"I'm so glad."

He appreciated her candor and was grateful they'd settled the matter easily, assuming the children had no objections. He didn't expect a problem. They loved Meredith. And he trusted that moving into her house would be a sound financial decision since she had received a death benefit from Duane that paid off the mortgage.

"Hey. What do you think if we rent out my house?"

"It seems you've thought about this." Meredith nodded. "You'd be a landlord."

"Technically, *we* would be landlords."

"Technically, *I* would be a landlady."

They laughed.

A week before the nuptials, the family planted three lilac bushes in the northeast corner of Meredith's backyard. The number signified two families forever changed by tragedy that came together boldly to form a new third family—one filled with strength and hope, for it is well known that there is strength in numbers.

So, less than a year after the accident—seven months to be exact—Meredith Wenz and Marvin Becket were united in marriage. They chose to wed on Meredith's birthday. Of all possible days, May 31 fell on a Monday. Marlee and Melanie were flower girls and wore pretty lavender dresses, the bride's favorite color. They scattered purple and white flower petals as they strolled the church aisle to where their father stood in a black tuxedo at the front near the priest. Marvin smiled proudly at them.

Todd trailed behind, wearing a black suit, a crisp white shirt, and a bow tie, which he grumbled about. He carried a small, white, shiny satin pillow with rings tied atop it. Meredith looked regal in her beautifully simple, slimming, off-white gown and shoulder-length veil of creamy white illusion.

The couple pledged their love to one another, speaking the traditional vows, and afterward celebrated with a small group of family and close friends, eating fried chicken with all the fixings.

The newlyweds spent one night alone in a local motel before traveling to Canada for two weeks and taking the children and Sam and Bernice Becket with them for what everyone called *the family honeymoon.*

Meredith's mother, Ruby, explained to Marlee that kids and grandparents usually do not go on honeymoons. "But this is a special honeymoon, and it's allowed this one time," she said. "Your new Grandpa Alvin and I will be waiting for all of you to return. Besides, fishing's not our thing. And who would take care of Cindy and Sheila? And the puppies?"

It turned out that fishing was neither Marlee's nor Melanie's thing, either, but they were glad for the trip. They had loads of fun. They jumped off the roof of an old shack tucked away on the side of a hill, back from the beach, shaded with trees. They jumped repeatedly, landing on smooth, chilly white sand—until Melanie landed near a garter snake. The girls screamed and ran. Then they pretended to be castaways and made stone and pine needle soup.

The family ate cold ham sandwiches with potato salad almost every day for lunch and freshly caught fish with bread and baked beans practically every night for supper.

In the evenings, the sisters bathed together before dressing in matching baby-doll pajamas their new mother had set out for them.

The cabin they rented had only two bedrooms. The newlyweds slept in one, and the rest of the family piled into the second room with two double beds. Marlee complained it wasn't much fun sharing a bed with *both* of her siblings.

Bernice told Marlee to quit her bellyaching. "Some people don't even have a bed," she stated.

Marlee didn't believe her but didn't say so. Instead, she quipped, "Well, Cocoa and Fanny and Cindy and Sheila all have their own beds and don't have to share. And they're dogs," she added.

Todd scoffed, "Fanny's a cat."

"I wasn't talking to you."

"Stop it, Marlee," Bernice scolded, "and go to sleep."

On the morning of the big relocation, Marvin and the children completed the move to their new home when the bulk of their possessions were hauled one hundred yards down Stadium Drive to Meredith's house, the new Becket residence. Marvin had borrowed a company truck from his employer, and a few neighbors helped with the heavy lifting. Todd worked alongside the men and put things wherever they made the most sense. It was a chaotic, fun-filled day for the kids. Marlee and Melanie reveled in all the action, especially setting up their new bedroom. Instead of twin beds with matching bedspreads, they shared a double bed with a brand-new purple-and-white floral summer coverlet.

That first night after everyone went to bed and Marvin's breathing had slowed, simmering just below snoring, Meredith slid out from underneath the sheet next to him. She tiptoed to the living room, pulling her lightweight cotton bathrobe closed. Two previously unoccupied bedrooms now had sleeping children nestled in. She sat, exhausted but happy, thinking about how quickly life had changed for all of them. The kids openly showed their love for her, and Marvin told her she was a blessing to them. She vowed to be a loving wife and a loving and caring mother. The plan was that she would legally adopt the children; they had an upcoming court date they viewed as a formality, for she would be more than a stepmother, although that word was *never*—not once—uttered aloud by any of them. It was never discussed, but happened naturally. Meredith was their mother. It was as simple as that. She had become one of them—Meredith Armelis Becket.

After seventeen years of marriage, she had accepted that motherhood was not in the cards for her, but then she married Marvin, and voilà, just like that, she became an instant mother to not one but three growing children. She shook her head. Smiled. But Marvin never had the chance to attend his wife's funeral, and she could scarcely fathom that. Now he had her, his new wife.

The kids left their home, the only home Marlee had ever known. They immediately began to call her *mom*. She wondered how that felt for them, especially Todd and Melanie. Meredith believed it had somehow been easier for Marlee. Being so young, the girl seemed almost hungry for another woman she could call her own—another loving mother.

Fanny meowed at Meredith's feet. She moved to the side to make room in the chair, patting the space beside her. "You're seeing some big changes, too, aren't you, girl?" The cat instantly purred. Scratching Fanny's ears, Meredith closed her eyes and let everything sink in. She was hopeful for their shared future.

Marlee sat on the red vinyl step stool in the kitchen and worked a ball of blue Play-Doh between her hands. Her mother prepared jars for canning, and a crate of fragrant peaches waited on the counter for her attention. Marlee threw the Play-Doh ball in the air, caught it, and repeated that process numerous times. She questioned her mother about everything from why she canned peaches, to how she didn't have any brothers or sisters, to how the tooth fairy knew when a kid had lost a tooth.

Meredith answered most of Marlee's questions, save for one or two that she artfully dodged.

"Why are you inside on this beautiful, warm day? You should be out playing."

"Eloise had to go to the dentist," Marlee stated matter-of-factly, "and I didn't feel like playing with anyone else." Eloise White and Marlee Becket were best friends, just eight months apart, and their families happened to live next door to one another.

Marlee's line of questioning began again, and so did her Play-Doh tossing. Meredith had grown weary and decided against another round.

"Marlee, you've got to stop. I need you to sit in that chair there." She pointed to the big gray chair in the living room. "Sit there and be quiet, please, no fidgeting and no talking for at least five minutes. You need to sit still. I'll put the stove timer on five," she said.

"What?" Marlee asked, puzzled.

"You're badgering me."

"What does *badgering* mean?"

Meredith sighed, "Later, now go."

Marlee huffed her way to the chair but did as she was told. Meredith glanced at her daughter, dwarfed by the large chair. She realized that a stranger observing the child for the first time, sitting calmly, quietly, and sweet-looking, with her hands folded in her lap, may have described her as angelic. Marlee appeared the part, with her head tilted slightly to the right, perhaps with a hint of a smile, her medium-brown hair flipped up perfectly above the white Peter Pan collar of the red dress she wore, with bangs that lay straight across her forehead, short enough to showcase wide-set, hazel eyes. All of it might make one think of a serene angel. Meredith was slightly amused.

The kitchen timer signaled the end of five minutes. "You're free to get out of the chair," she told Marlee. "And that wasn't so bad, sitting quietly for five minutes, was it?"

She shrugged.

"You have to get better control over yourself," Meredith explained.

They heard Melanie wheel into the driveway. She hopped off her bicycle and leaned it against the concrete steps. Entering the kitchen through the side door, she announced, "I'm thirsty," and filled a tall glass with tap water, gulping it down.

"Where've you been?" Meredith asked. "Do you know where your brother is?"

"He's at the park. Playing baseball. I was there, too, but I need to go to the bathroom, plus I'm thirsty."

"Marlee's bored without Eloise. How about you take her back to the park with you?"

"I guess."

"I'll get my bike," Marlee said enthusiastically.

"Okay, I'll be right out."

"Be home for supper. Your brother, too," Meredith called from the side porch as the girls pedaled away together. Marlee tried to keep up on a hand-me-down bicycle with training wheels, which she adamantly insisted she no longer needed, though no one, as yet, had taken the time to remove them.

The two girls joined the others on the ball diamond. Melanie shared a glove with a girl from the other team, but Marlee had to be content with fetching bats when someone got a hit.

Chris Curtain hit the second pitch thrown to him, and the ball sailed into right field, but he didn't just drop the bat; he chucked it, hitting Marlee in the shins.

"Ow!" she cried, falling to the dirt and clutching her right leg. Tears stung her eyes. She moaned and rubbed her shin.

"Marlee!" Todd shouted from his position at shortstop. He ran to his sister. So did Melanie from the outfield.

Chris rounded first base and stopped at second. He stood on the bag and looked toward the backstop. "Sorry!" he hollered.

The game halted. Todd and Melanie helped Marlee to safety on the grass behind the fence. A few kids huddled around.

"Curtain clobbered her with his bat," said a girl.

"Not on purpose," sneered a boy.

"You're gonna have to hang on, Marlee," Todd told her. "We gotta finish the game."

"I can't ride my bike home," she cried.

"Just hang on. I'll help you," he told her.

"Play ball," called an outfielder.

Instantly, an egg had formed on Marlee's shin, and wincing, she ran her hand over it. Sniffling, she wanted to bawl, and she wanted her mom, but she wasn't willing to hobble home alone, so she was forced to wait.

Todd's team lost 4–1 to Chris Curtain's crew.

"Get on," Todd told Marlee, squatting next to her. He carried her home by way of piggyback. "I'll get your bike later."

He didn't have to; someone dropped it at the house, as it was discovered in the front yard under the birch tree after supper.

The Beckets packed both their car trunk and their boat full of camping supplies, and Marvin tied down the canvas cover.

"We can't afford to lose anything," he explained to his children as he tightened the ropes. "I would hate to see a life jacket or a pile of beach towels go flying down the road in our wake."

"Yeah, that wouldn't be good, Dad," Todd agreed. "Hey, we learned knot-tying in Scouts this year," he added.

"I should have had you put your skills to work. Next time. Remind me, okay?"

"How about for the trip home?"

"Sure. Remind me."

"Okay, Dad."

"Will we get a campsite by the water again this year?" Melanie wondered.

"We always get one by the water," Todd stated.

"Not always," Melanie said.

"That's right," Marvin agreed. "We don't always get one on the water, but the last couple of years we have, and I think—no, I'm sure of it—it's because we've been going up on a Thursday night." He pulled down hard one more time on the rope. "Okay, we're ready. Let's go, kids, get in the car."

They did secure a nice campsite on the water, not far from the water pumps or the bathrooms. Everyone pitched in to set up the tent and inflate the air mattresses underneath the sleeping bags. Todd helped his father put the screen tent over the picnic table while the girls helped their mother arrange the inside of the tent.

"I'm sleeping between Todd and Melanie," Marlee informed them.

"I figured as much," Meredith acknowledged.

Melanie followed her mother's lead and laid their suitcases and duffels at the foot of the adults' cots. When they finished, Marvin told the kids they could play or explore. Todd and Melanie wandered toward the lake.

"Be careful," Meredith called after them.

Marlee watched her parents unload a cupboard from inside the boat. Marvin had built it years ago, and it came in handy, perched on one end of the picnic table, housing their food and supplies. Marlee chose to stay close to her mother and straightened the contents that shifted on the drive.

"Remember always to use the hook to keep the cupboard closed," Meredith said. "We certainly don't want raccoons getting in."

Marvin gathered kindling. Marlee gathered, too, then watched as he started a campfire. The sun went down about an hour later. Everyone was worn out from the long day and didn't talk much. Instead, they watched the orange flames flicker and the smoke rise. It wasn't long before the girls crawled into the tent to curl up in their sleeping bags.

Marlee zipped hers almost to her chin, relishing the soft, cozy confinement. The campfire and the familiar scent of the tent heightened her awareness, and she thought of the thin canvas separating her from the outdoors. The various night sounds brought comfort—quiet voices, the crackling fire, the hoot of an owl, and the wind rustling the tree leaves. Contentment made her smile. She drifted off to peaceful sleep but woke in the dark to rain pelting the roof. That, too, was pleasant. By morning, the air mattress needed to be reinflated.

The family ate a simple breakfast of cereal, fruit, and venison sausage. Afterwards, the kids took turns brushing their teeth at the makeshift wash station—a white, red-rimmed enamel bowl atop a tree stump. Melanie glanced at her reflection in an old mirror they'd hung above the basin on a nail in a tree. That fogged oval aided their father each morning when he shaved the stubble that darkened his cheeks overnight.

Marvin told the kids they could play for an hour before he would put the boat in the water. Marlee grabbed a stick and hummed while she drew pictures in the dirt. Todd and Melanie wandered away with empty coffee cans.

Forty minutes later, they returned to the campsite. Todd strode in, holding his can above his head.

"We got tadpoles!" he announced.

"And lots of them!" added Melanie.

"Let me see." Marlee craned to see inside Melanie's can.

"Can we bring them home?" Todd asked.

"That's up to your mother."

Meredith caught her husband's eye. "Ah, well, not all of them. Maybe just a few."

"Only a few?" Todd grumbled.

"Todd," Marvin warned.

"Let's decide at the end of the week," Meredith suggested.

"Wait till our friends back home see these," Melanie grinned.

Marlee hung on Todd's arm and peered into his coffee can. She fired off questions. "Where'd you get 'em? Were they hard to catch? Will you take me there? Show me," she said.

"We found them in the little swamp by site twenty-seven. Yeah, I'll take you there when I go back."

"Let's go now," Marlee suggested.

"Later," Todd said. "I saw a boy hanging around twenty-five. He was kinda watching us. I'm gonna head over and hope to talk to him."

"Don't be long. We'll probably be out by the water when you get back," Meredith said. "Bring your new friend if you want."

Todd hopped on his bike and left the campsite for the second time that morning.

The girls helped haul chairs and sand toys to the beach and played beneath the hot sun. Melanie's blond hair would be a shade lighter by the end of the week—butter blond, their father liked to call it.

Todd showed up roughly twenty minutes later and shared that he'd met the boy from site twenty-five. "He's from Oshkosh," Todd informed them. "We're gonna hang out later. His family is hiking to the fire tower now."

"Well, get your suit on. Marlee's in the boat, chomping at the bit. Dad is ready to take you kids water-skiing."

"Be right back," Todd said.

Meredith eventually lit the camp stove to warm a kettle of chili. She set a Tupperware container of corn bread on the picnic table before briefly returning to the water. She watched Todd drop a ski and begin another lap around the lake. Melanie quickly waded into the knee-deep water to retrieve the ski and dropped it on shore.

"When they get back," Meredith called to her, "tell them lunch is ready."

It was mid-afternoon when a tall, skinny boy wearing only swim trunks and a towel around his neck walked through their camp.

He waved. "Hey, Todd."

Meredith sat up straighter in her lawn chair. Marvin rose to his feet.

"Hey, you found me," Todd said. He turned to his parents. "This is Brian, who I told you about, from twenty-five."

"Hi, Brian," they said simultaneously. Marvin offered his right hand. Brian shook it.

"Sir," he nodded. "Nice to meet you," he said to both parents.

"Those are my sisters," Todd gestured to the girls.

"Hi," Marlee said. Melanie waved.

"Hi," Brian smiled.

"We're gonna take off," Todd said, and the boys ventured down the tree-rooted trail along the back of several campsites to the main beach area. Todd returned alone about an hour later.

"Where's Brian?" Meredith asked.

"He went to his campsite."

"Did you have fun?"

"Yeah."

"Good," Marvin said.

"We'll fix supper soon," Meredith announced.

After a full day of tadpole catching, swimming, boating, and waterskiing, the family gathered around the picnic table in the screen tent and assembled pudgy pies. Meredith laid out rye bread across a clean, vinyl flannel-backed tablecloth patterned with yellow and white daisies. Melanie spread softened butter on each slice. Meredith carefully placed one slice of bread, butter side down, on one half of the iron cookers. Marvin and Todd added corned beef and sauerkraut, and Meredith squirted a dollop or two of Thousand Island dressing. They entrusted Marlee to place a piece of Swiss cheese on top of each before Marvin finished them with buttered bread, clamping the irons shut. Everyone cooked their own pudgy pie over the open fire.

"I'm glad we all have an iron," Melanie said.

"It is handy," Marvin agreed.

"Kids, be careful not to burn yourselves opening your irons. Use the oven mitts," Meredith instructed them. "And don't burn your mouths," she warned. "Marlee, I'll help you with yours in a minute."

They followed the pudgy pies with juicy watermelon and honey cookies.

"I can't wait to make dessert pudgy pies," Melanie said.

"That'll be with another meal. Maybe tomorrow," Meredith suggested.

After cleaning up, Todd and his father stoked the dying campfire back to life. Smoke floated throughout the campsite. Meredith and Marvin stretched out on matching webbed chaise longue chairs. Marlee scrounged around, scraping the dirt with a small, sharp rock. The two older kids volleyed a shuttlecock back and forth with badminton racquets.

Early in their relationship, sometime before they were married, Marvin told Meredith how important it was for his children to maintain a relationship with Anne's family.

"Of course, they know she's gone," he had said, thinking it was somewhat of a stupid thing to say, though, and continued, "but I want them to see all her family—their family—as they had before she . . ." His words trailed off.

"I wholeheartedly agree, Marv. Nothing needs to change there. Nothing at all."

So it was. Novak relatives arrived at Boulder Lake for a day visit— two of Anne's sisters with their husbands and families. The men hauled coolers from which the women extracted various cold dishes. One contained Marlee's favorite potato salad, topped with sliced hard-boiled eggs, and a classic tuna macaroni salad with peas.

Betty appeared suddenly flustered. "Where's the coleslaw? Jim, I don't see the coleslaw," she shrieked at her husband.

"It's there," he said, assisting his wife. He pulled a container out from under the ice at the bottom of the green metal Coleman cooler, and it seemed as though everyone felt Betty's relief.

The men grilled brats and hot dogs, though Marvin would not eat a hot dog; he would enjoy a brat. Betty and Alma cut the buns. Meredith set the food out, buffet style. She produced a fruit salad and opened a big box of potato chips. Alma brought a pan of gooey, seven-layer bars for dessert. Everyone enjoyed lunch, and when they were sufficiently stuffed, they burned their paper plates and napkins in the smoldering fire. Marlee watched the plates curl in the heat.

Once they cleared the picnic table, a deck of cards showed up. Each man took his place with a pile of coins before him. The women and children headed to the beach. Marlee walked arm in arm with her cousin

Julia. The women relaxed in lawn chairs in the sun. Meredith poured a round of Tom Collins drinks, and they visited while the kids played. The women refereed a petty squabble when the boys splashed the girls.

"We told you to knock it off!" Susan yelled.

"Mom!" Melanie hollered.

"You've got to be kidding!" Todd grumbled. "You're already wet; you're swimming, for crying out loud." The boys laughed.

"Todd . . ." Meredith warned.

"Joseph, stop bothering the girls," Alma said.

"Yeah, Joseph," his sister mocked in a cloying voice.

"It was an accident," he protested, defending himself and the other boys.

"You kids play nicely and get along," Alma insisted.

Todd swam away from the girls. "Come on, Joe. Come on, Pete. Let's get away from them."

"Whiney babies," whispered one of the boys.

Eighteen-month-old Trina played with toys at the women's feet.

The men's deep voices carried through the scant trees separating the campsite from the beach, providing little privacy. It sounded like they were enjoying their card game. Playful ribbing and hearty laughter floated out.

The ladies eventually brought out the leftover salads as the afternoon rolled into the supper hour. Meredith added a plate of cold cuts, a loaf of bread, and a jar of mustard.

After they ate, everyone gathered around the campfire, and Uncle Harry led the kids in singing silly camp songs. "Little Bunny Foo Foo," complete with hand gestures, was followed by a raucous rendition of "John Jacob Jingleheimer Schmidt" belted out at the top of their lungs. Then they took turns around the wide circle telling jokes.

Marlee asked, "What did one strawberry say to the other?" Barely giving anyone time to venture an answer, she blurted out the punch line, "If you weren't so sweet, we wouldn't be in this jam." She laughed, holding her belly. A mix of groans and giggles followed.

When darkness threatened, the relatives said goodbye, hugging and shaking hands, and piled into their cars, exhausted and sun-kissed.

The Becket children slept well that night.

Two more fun-filled days were spent at the lake before the family broke camp, packed everything back into the car and boat, and took off for home. Another memorable week at Boulder Lake was in the books. It might have felt odd or even sad, although no one spoke of it, but it hadn't seemed a whole lot different that year with Meredith instead of Anne.

CHAPTER 4

SHORTLY BEFORE SCHOOL STARTED, Meredith told her husband she was pregnant. At thirty-nine years old and with child for the first time, she would be three months shy of her fortieth birthday when she gave birth. The newlyweds decided to keep it under wraps for a bit, as Meredith wanted to wait, aware that things could happen in the early stages, especially at her age.

Six weeks passed, and Meredith told Marvin she was now comfortable sharing the big news. The kids were surprised, and they cheered; the girls did, anyway. Todd was quieter, as he seemed to be processing the news.

"The baby's expected to arrive by the end of February," Meredith offered.

"After my birthday?" Todd perked up. His birthday was the nineteenth of February.

"We believe so. It could even be the first part of March," she explained. "We have to wait and see."

"I hope it's a girl," Marlee said.

"I'm outnumbered," Todd said, "so I hope it's a boy. I should have a brother. Don't you hope it's a boy, Dad?"

"We hope it's healthy."

"I'm going to be twelve when this baby is born. That baby will be twelve years younger than me," he announced.

"We're aware," Meredith said.

"I can't wait," Melanie smiled. "I don't care what it is. I can't wait!" She grinned from ear to ear.

"We're happy you're excited," Marvin said. "You all go easy on your mother now, okay? Help her out more. Todd, you carry the heavy stuff."

"Marvin, I'm fine."

"I know. And we want to keep it that way. You kids help your mother out," he reiterated.

"I won't be the youngest anymore."

"That's right, Marlee. Soon, you won't be the baby of the family." Meredith smiled.

"You'll always be a squirt to me, though," Todd teased, pretending to punch Marlee as if they were in a boxing ring.

November ushered in the gun deer hunting season, with the coveted few inches of snow blanketing the ground.

"Boy, was I glad to see that snow falling yesterday," Sam Becket said. "It'll sure make tracking easier, and you gotta like that."

"You betcha," Buzzy agreed.

The entire Becket family, which included the families of Marvin's brother and sister, congregated in Suring at the elder Beckets' home for the first weekend of the annual deer hunt. Everyone had crammed into the house and taken their places in the assigned bedrooms. There were four cousins on Marvin's side, two each in his brother's and sister's families, and much to Todd's chagrin, all were female. Three were older than he. He was outnumbered by girls whenever the Becket side of the family came together. Thank goodness for the thirty-two cousins on the Novak side of the family, where there were always plenty of boys to play with.

The six girls shared one bedroom upstairs, three to a bed, across the hall from their grandparents. Todd bunked on the floor next to the pull-out couch that Marvin and Meredith slept on in the large dining room off the kitchen. Marvin's brother, Buzzy, and wife, Francine, slept on a second pull-out couch in the adjacent living room. Marvin's sister, Judy, and husband, Bill, always used the bedroom on the first floor when the whole crew showed up at the house. As a bonus, they had easy access to a newer bathroom with a shower stall after Sam had built an addition a few years back.

Marlee liked using the added bathroom because it afforded more privacy, and she slowly wandered through the bedroom, looking at her aunt and uncle's belongings. She knew it was a nosy thing to do but didn't care. Once, she snuck a peek inside her aunt's open purse, sitting in plain view on the vanity. An adrenaline rush warmed her as she boldly looked inside and saw a small notebook, a wallet, and what she assumed to be a crumpled tissue. Marlee wondered how much money might be in Aunt Judy's wallet. The idea crossed her mind to check, but she didn't dare.

Judy and Bill's daughters were Lisa and Dana. Dana was one year older than Marlee, and they played well together. Melanie would join them when they pulled out their grandmother's round, metal, silver button box, rimmed in faux black leather, full to the brim with buttons of every size. They sorted through them and found mostly black, white, and clear, but got a little excited each time they discovered a pretty red or bright blue, or even better yet, one with an acrylic jewel in the center.

The older cousins played checkers or cards with Todd when he wasn't off with the men somewhere. Whenever he decided to haul up the giant Carrom game board from the basement, all the cousins played together until their fingers were sore from flicking the striker piece.

Buzzy and Francine's daughters were Nancy and Bobbie—short for Roberta.

Bobbie liked teasing Dana and Marlee, which usually didn't go well when the adults caught on to her shenanigans. She was also known for being a prankster, and because of that, she and Todd meshed well. Together, they guaranteed trouble, often conspiring to pull off pranks.

One time, Bobbie made a fuss while she pretended to swat at a nonexistent fly. "Where did this grimy fly come from?" she asked loud enough to arouse her cousins' attention. "It's nearly winter. They should all be dormant or dead by now." Then she feigned trapping the so-called fly under a napkin. "Well, looky here." She held it out for a split second before popping it into her mouth and chewing.

A chorus of "Eww!" and "Gross!" erupted from the other girls.

Bobbie's older sister, Nancy, tattled, "Mother, Bob ate a fly!"

"A fly? What on earth . . ."

Todd and Bobbie laughed. "Settle down," Bobbie said to her sister and cousins. "It was just a raisin. I ate a raisin."

"It was not. It was a fly. I saw it," Dana proclaimed.

"It was a raisin." Her sister, Lisa, defended Bobbie.

Aunt Francine shook her head.

Dusk descended as the men returned home from the hunt. Two dead deer lay in the bed of Sam's pick-up truck. He backed up to the rear door of the honey house where, on other days, in a pristine front room unsullied by blood and animal carcasses, he and Bernice extracted honey from the comb their bees produced. That day, in the back room, reserved for this kind of job, Marvin, Buzzy, and Bill hung the deer from the rafters and gutted the pair—a decent-sized six-point buck Marvin shot and a spike buck Sam brought down.

Bill admitted to taking a shot at a deer. "But I missed the damn thing. I think it was too far," he scoffed.

Buzzy only saw a doe with two fawns. "I know we have a doe tag," he said, "but I didn't want to use it on day one, not for a doe with two fawns by her side."

"I don't blame you," Marvin agreed.

The women visited the honey house to see the deer but quickly retreated to the warm kitchen, where they had begun preparing the meal.

The men finished up and made their way to the house. They removed their outer clothing in the breezeway before entering the kitchen. Buzzy set about making brandy old-fashioneds for most of the adults.

"Those were nice-sized deer you shot," Meredith said.

"Yeah, not bad," Sam said. "I couldn't be choosy, though. Hell, that was all I saw, that lone spike buck, and it was late in the afternoon, besides."

"Yeah, not much activity out there today," Bill echoed.

"Tomorrow we try again," Sam said. "Hell, we have three tags to fill plus the doe tag. Ma, are you coming out tomorrow?" He turned to his wife. Usually, she hunted with them, and Meredith would have joined them, too, but not that year, being six months pregnant.

"I plan on it," Bernice nodded.

"We'll head further west and hope to see more." Sam moved to the dining room.

The family sat down to a hearty meal of roasted pheasant, boiled potatoes, carrots, and corn from the garden, the corn previously cut off the cob and frozen, along with freshly baked bread, and for dessert, chocolate cake with chocolate icing so smooth it looked like brown ice you could skate across.

The kids pulled out the convenient leaves from the underside of a red-and-white enamel-topped table to eat in the kitchen. The adults occupied the dining room, gathered around a large wooden table Bernice's father had built when she was a baby. A table that Bernice had surgery on as a young girl when her appendix risked rupturing. She liked to say that she still remembers the day it happened. Marlee always found the story fascinating.

"Pass the toothpicks," requested Sam as he vigorously swished warm tea in his mouth.

Thanksgiving 1965 was a new experience, especially for Meredith. She and Marvin hosted her folks and his for the traditional meal, and she found herself cooking for a small crowd. It was different from previous years when she and Duane hosted only his brother and her parents. Meredith was relieved when Ralph begged off.

A welcome tradition began when Bernice offered to bring her homemade dinner rolls.

Meredith prepared a feast that wouldn't vary much over the ensuing years, featuring a twenty-two-pound stuffed turkey with all the usual fixings. Everyone poured her rich, lump-free gravy over creamy mashed potatoes and herb dressing. The classic green bean casserole and orange Jell-O with mandarin oranges became favorites with the children. Her candied yams had just the right amount of brown sugar added. The cranberry sauce revealed the shape of the tin can it slid out of. Marlee got a kick out of that. Meredith baked two pies for dessert—one pumpkin and one apple, with homemade whipped cream.

The men gathered around the black-and-white Zenith in the living room to watch the Baltimore Colts take on the Detroit Lions. Todd chose a spot on the floor about five feet from the TV. The women cleaned up the kitchen and washed dishes before visiting around the table, sipping their coffee. The girls colored using brand-new Crayola crayons in new coloring books from Grandma and Grandpa Simon.

"So, Ralph didn't want to join us today?" Ruby asked.

"It didn't surprise me," Meredith admitted. "He wasn't big on coming for the holidays when Duane was alive."

"I'm guessing you two don't talk often?"

"That's right, Ma. Less as time goes on."

"I think that's sad," Bernice weighed in.

"I do, too," Meredith agreed, "but I've tried."

"He's always been a loner, hasn't he?" Ruby acknowledged.

"Pretty much. He and Duane hadn't been close since, oh, I'd say, since maybe high school. We never could figure it out."

After brushing her teeth, Melanie waited in bed while Marlee put on her pajamas. Their parents entered the bedroom. "Did you say your prayers?" Meredith asked.

"Not yet," Melanie admitted.

"Remember to pray for your other mother and Duane, and don't forget Great-Grandma Hall." Marvin's maternal grandmother had passed recently.

"We will," Marlee said, jumping into bed.

"Good night, sleep tight," Meredith said, leaning down to kiss each girl and crossing their foreheads in blessing.

Marvin followed suit and tucked them in. "Don't let the bedbugs bite," he teased.

Meredith turned off the light. Pulled the door nearly closed, leaving a gap.

"Keep the hall light on," Marlee reminded her.

"Yes," she replied.

After praying, Marlee exhaled. "I'm not very tired."

"Let's talk," Melanie suggested.

"Okay. Um, what are you going to ask Santa for?"

"I haven't given it much thought yet. What about you?"

"I would like a doll."

Melanie wanted clarification: "A baby doll?"

"Yeah."

"I would like a doll, too, but I want another Barbie doll—Midge or Skipper, maybe."

Marlee yawned.

Her sister noticed. "Are you tired *now*?"

"I guess." She rolled to face the wall.

"Good night, Marlee."

"Night, Melanie."

Todd helped his father get their Christmas tree into the house. They'd cut a seven-foot evergreen from Sam and Bernice's property up north. And the family returned home earlier than usual from their Sunday outing.

Marvin struggled to secure the tree in the metal stand. "Hold it straight, doggone it!"

"I am," Todd insisted.

"Well, try harder!"

Todd sighed.

Meredith entered the room just then, possibly diffusing the mounting frustration. "We'll trim the tree after supper," she announced. "The girls and I got everything down from the attic. Remember to water it."

"We will," Marvin said.

"We tested the lights," Meredith added.

"Great," Marvin grunted.

After eating, Marlee went to the living room. She inhaled deeply. "It smells like a forest in here."

"That's one of my favorite things of the season," Marvin said, walking in behind her.

He picked up the star, tossing aside the tissue paper wrapping, and placed it on top of the tree. Next, he strung multicolored bulbs while savoring the fresh pine scent filling his nostrils, hoping it would carry into the new year. Todd helped Meredith and Marvin decorate the top third of the tree with small, shiny glass baubles. The girls trimmed the lower two-thirds with larger balls. After Meredith finished with the tree, it dripped with silver tinsel.

The couple sat in the living room that evening, content, admiring their beautiful, shimmering Christmas tree.

The kids woke early on Christmas morning and rushed to the living room. Marvin counted to three before switching on the floor lamp, illuminating three separate, distinct piles of unwrapped gifts, presumably left by Santa Claus. There were alternating girl/boy/girl piles that made it obvious which pile was for whom. Each child muscled their way to their individual swell. Marlee squealed with delight at a giant toy stove. A boxed set of plastic Corning Ware dishes sat atop it. Upon closer inspection, she also noticed a doll.

"I got Barbie's little sister," Melanie said when she saw Skipper, "and oh my gosh, loads of Barbie clothes and a record player!" She also received a less exciting hair dryer.

Todd grinned when he saw the Rock 'Em Sock 'Em Robots and an electric football game but shouted, "Thank you!" when he noticed a BB gun that had been on his list every year since he was eight years old.

Marvin and Meredith laughed, delighting in the children's reactions.

When they worked their way through the unwrapped toys from Santa, the kids noticed several wrapped presents under the tree. Meredith asked Melanie to read the tags. "You can pass them out. They're from your father and me." Each girl opened boxes containing a soft flannel nightgown and a pair of furry slippers.

"Can we put them on?" Melanie asked.

"You sure can."

The girls carefully made their way over the toys and out of the room. Marlee returned, twirling in a tight circle, modeling her pink and white flannel gown.

"Don't you look sweet." Meredith said. "What do you think?"

"I like it." Marlee ran her hands down the length of her body and slid her bare feet into her new slippers. "I love these," she said.

"They're so soft," Melanie said, as if speaking for her sister, referring to both the slippers and the nightgowns.

Todd opened a new pair of buckskin gloves and a gray hooded sweatshirt.

"Thanks," he smiled at his folks.

"Those gloves are from my deer hide. The one I shot this year," Marvin explained.

"I like 'em," Todd said, checking the fit by making fists with leatherclad hands. "I needed a new pair."

"I noticed," his father agreed.

Meredith and Marvin quietly exchanged gifts while the children busied themselves with their new toys.

"What's that, Mom?" Melanie asked.

"Your dad surprised me with a beautiful pearl necklace and matching earrings. Look," she said, holding them up.

Meredith gave Marvin an expensive black car coat.

"Pretty snazzy," he said, trying it on. "Fits perfectly."

"It looks nice on you."

"Thank you." Marvin kissed his wife. Then, shifting gears, he said, "All right, everybody. It's time to get ready for church."

The family scrambled to get dressed for Mass.

"Can I bring my new doll?" Marlee asked.

"No," Meredith replied. "It will be here when we get back. Bring your church book instead."

"I always bring that book," she grumbled.

"It's that or nothing."

"Fine, I'll bring the book. Can I bring my yellow blanket?"

"No, you cannot," Marvin interjected. "You're not a baby. You're a big girl."

Marlee accepted his answer, and soon, the family was out the door. The living room looked like a bomb had exploded.

After returning from church, Meredith donned an apron and began preparing food.

"Marvin," she called. "Can you and one of the kids add the leaves to the table, please? Our folks will be here soon. Todd, please bring up chairs from the basement."

Alvin Simon drove both sets of grandparents to the Becket residence in his big, comfortable Buick. The kids did their best, waiting patiently for them to arrive. When they finally pulled into the driveway, the two oldest hurried outside to help unload the car. Grandma Becket brought dinner rolls and surprised Meredith with lemon meringue pie. Grandma Simon carried a large, flat box with scrumptious-looking rosettes.

"Merry Christmas," Ruby said. "And Meredith, these aren't necessarily for dessert today. They're part of your gift. I left a box just like it at Sam and Bernice's."

"Okay, Ma. Thank you. They're beautiful, as always. You have just the right touch for making rosettes."

"And here's your honey." Sam plunked a jar down on the counter next to the pie.

"Good timing. We were getting low," Meredith said.

"Don't yous ever run out 'cause I know me a good beekeeper," he chuckled.

Meredith chuckled with him. "Never, Sam. I won't ever let that happen. And thank you." She pecked his cheek.

The children and Alvin carried in the last of the packages from the trunk.

"Melanie!" Todd exclaimed, hanging back a little, "I've never seen this many presents all at once."

"Me neither!" Her eyes were wide with excitement.

Marvin came up from the basement. "Merry Christmas," he greeted his in-laws and parents. "Sorry it took me so long," he said to Meredith. "I helped Todd clean up after he tipped over a box and broke an empty jar."

"I was wondering," Meredith said, scrunching her nose. "Todd didn't say anything."

"Big surprise." Marvin shook his head.

"Excuse me," Meredith got everyone's attention, "and I'm sorry to disappoint you, kids, but the food is almost ready, so we're going to eat before opening gifts. It'll be maybe another fifteen minutes or so."

"Aw," complained Marlee. She didn't care about eating just then; she wanted to know what was in all those colorful packages.

"You can wait," Sam teased. "I'm hungry." He nuzzled her cheek with a whisker rub. She wiggled away. Whisker rubs weren't her favorite.

Marvin mixed an old-fashioned for his father.

Bernice moved closer to Meredith. "How are you feeling?"

"Big." The women shared a chuckle.

"That baby will be here before you know it."

"Oh, I know. I'm nearly ready."

"What names are you and Marv tossing about?" Ruby inquired. "Or maybe you've already decided."

"When the baby's born, Ma."

"Oh, Meredith," she grumbled. "You can tell me. I'm your mother."

"No, sirree!" Meredith shook her head.

Ruby Simon had as much fun watching the kids rip the wrapping paper from their packages as they did ripping it, and she laughed heartily, basking in her role as a new grandmother, bearing gifts for her first Christmas with the trio. They opened a variety of things. There were books, clothes, stuffed animals, the game of Operation, travel bingo, a remote-control car, a football, three paint-by-number kits, a baby doll—complete with a package of diapers, Barbie accessories, and a "poodle" desk lamp for the girls' bedroom. The children had never seen such gifts as they experienced that first Christmas with Grandma and Grandpa Simon. It turned out that the Simons were generous gift-givers in general, but there was nothing quite like that first Christmas. Todd especially liked his new jacket. It had patches on the sleeves.

Before turning in for the night, Meredith and Marvin sat quietly in the glow of the Christmas tree lights—the only lights illuminating the room. The Shiny Brite glass ornaments collected over the years by two families filled every square inch of the evergreen. With the tinsel glinting, the whole thing sparkled.

"We really do have a lovely tree," Meredith smiled.

"We do," Marvin agreed. He stood and offered his hand to his wife. "Let's go to bed."

January and the first few weeks of February proved agonizingly long for the kids as they awaited the baby's arrival.

"How many more days?" Marlee inquired more than once.

"What do you think it is, Mom?" Melanie asked, "And don't you just want to see him or her already?"

"I am definitely to that point," she admitted.

"What do you think you're having?" Melanie asked again.

"I want a girl!" declared Marlee, thrusting her arms in the air.

"We know, Marlee," Meredith said. "You don't have to shout. And like your dad always says, we want a healthy baby."

"I hope like heck it's a boy," Todd said.

Meredith chuckled. "We have to wait and see."

Marvin and Meredith planned for Todd to share a bedroom with the baby, whatever the gender, at least for a little while.

"Not an ideal situation, I know," Marvin told his son after Christmas, explaining the new sleeping arrangements. "But I have an idea, and your mother agrees. We're going to build a bedroom in the basement for you."

"For real?"

"For real," Marvin said. "Don't get too excited. It won't happen right away. It's going to take time, you know. And I'll have to do this mostly on the weekends."

"I can help," Todd said.

"I'm counting on it."

"I can't wait to get started!"

Friday, February 25, arrived, welcoming a vibrant baby boy, born in the morning to Meredith and Marvin Becket. Children were not allowed on the maternity floor at St. Mary's Hospital, and they were sorely disappointed that they couldn't visit their mother and meet their new baby brother. As a result, Marvin drove his kids to the hospital where they gathered proudly outside at the edge of the snow-covered lawn, three stories below their mother's window. She waved down at them, smiling. They enthusiastically waved up at her. Marlee jumped and shouted, "Hold the baby to the window!"

"She can't hear you," Marvin said.

"I wanna see him."

Meredith called home that first evening to speak to the children. "Thank you for coming to see me. I wish you could have come up. I guess they have rules against it."

"Mom!" they shouted, all vying for control of the phone. "What's his name?"

Meredith giggled. "Keeping with Becket tradition, we chose *M* names for a girl and *T* names for a boy. We've narrowed it down to Travis or Troy."

It was momentarily quiet, then Todd and Melanie said, "I like Troy," and they laughed.

Sheepishly, Marlee said, "I like Troy, too."

"What's wrong, my Marlee?" Meredith asked.

"I was still hoping for a baby sister."

"What would her name have been if it were a girl?" Todd thought to ask.

"Tell them, Dad," Meredith prompted.

"Probably Maureen," he said.

"Whoa!" Todd snorted. "I like Troy way better."

Meredith laughed. "Well, Dad, what do you think?"

"I've chosen names thrice before; you may have the honor, my lady."

"Oh, Marvin." She paused briefly, then announced, "Troy, it is!"

A chorus of cheers erupted. Meredith pulled the phone away from her ear and shook her head, then smiled. She was still getting used to the sudden exuberance of three children.

The hospital released Meredith and her infant son on Monday afternoon, and she patiently waited for Marvin to arrive to bring them home. A baby that just a short time ago, she could not possibly have imagined. Meredith cuddled Troy's tiny body tighter to her chest, breathing in his sweet smell. A pleasant shiver ran up her spine. An intense, all-consuming love filled her.

Marlee had spent the day playing next door with Eloise in the care of her mother, Joanna White, while Marvin worked and Todd and Melanie were in school.

The Whites were another blended family on the street. And Eloise's much older brother, Jerry, was from their dad's first marriage. Marlee thought Jerry and Eloise looked alike with their big, smiling eyes and blond hair. But Jerry White was not often around.

The family details weren't well-known to all the neighbors, but the Beckets knew that Jerry's mother lived on the East Coast, far from where the Beckets and Whites resided in the Midwest in a small town called Ashwaubenon—a suburb of Green Bay, Wisconsin.

Historical archives claim the town got its Native American name nearly a hundred years ago, in 1872, when it was named after As-ha-wau-bo-my, the son of a powerful Ottawa chief.

The town's north border adjoined the City of Green Bay, home of the Green and Gold, the now-storied championship Green Bay Packers. And the Whites' and Beckets' backyards, along with their neighbors on the north side of the street, butted up against the stadium's massive gravel parking lot—the famous Lambeau Field. A measly four-foot-high chain-link fence was the only thing separating them from the hallowed grounds.

Marvin sprang into action when he received the call that his wife and newborn were ready to go home, and he happily cut his workday short to pick them up.

A little later, when Mrs. White informed Marlee that her parents and new baby brother had arrived home, the girl nearly burst, "Really? Wow! Okay, I gotta go!" She jumped up from the floor where she'd been playing. "Thanks for having me," she politely told Mrs. White. "See you later, Eloise!" Marlee grabbed her jacket, slipped into her boots, and practically flew out the door and floated down the driveway, not cutting across the lawns as there was still too much snow.

"I'm home!" she announced, noisily entering.

"Not so loud, Marlee." Her father sounded almost annoyed. "Your mother's got the baby in our bedroom. Let's see if he's awake."

He was awake. And Marlee could hardly believe her eyes. She peered in for a closer look but didn't touch him, such a little bitty thing, she thought.

"He looks Chinese," she said decisively.

"He does not," Meredith said, caressing his soft, fuzzy cheek.

"Yes, he does."

"Marlee, that's enough," Marvin said. "He looks like a baby."

"A Chinese baby."

"Marlee!" her father scolded. She wrinkled her nose at him.

Todd and Melanie had rushed home from school, eager to meet their baby brother for the first time.

"Hey, Troy, hi, little man," Todd cooed, admiring his newest sibling, swaddled in the bassinet.

"Ooh!" Melanie sounded breathless. "He is the sweetest little guy. I love him already. Look! He's got my finger!"

Todd smiled. "I remember that with Marlee."

"Yup. That's a reflex," Marvin explained. "All babies do that."

"He's amazing!" Melanie gushed.

"I think we got the wrong baby," Marlee grumbled. "He looks Chinese."

"Stop saying that," Meredith snapped. "We do not have the wrong baby."

Marvin shot Marlee a warning look.

"He is cute, isn't he?" Melanie smiled.

"I couldn't agree with you more." Meredith beamed. "He is precious."

The supper table was set, and Melanie had the Bible opened on her plate, the purple satin ribbon marking the page. She waited for her family to gather before reading a brief passage. With their heads still bowed, they recited their meal prayer, then passed the dishes around.

According to Marlee, Meredith Becket was a great cook, and that night she'd prepared pork chops with bubbly, crisp fat. Marlee loved the fat.

"Dad," she said, reaching for him to take her plate. "Please cut my chop for me."

That was about the extent of words spoken by any kid at the Becket supper table. But it wasn't a bad thing. It wasn't as if the children were seen and not heard in the home. Not at all. Their father needed to unload his mental stress, and they obliged by being respectful. They ate quietly while their father relived his workday at the office for their mother. She listened and asked smart questions.

Marlee pondered what to do after supper. Todd had been teaching her to play checkers, and she decided to corral him for more one-on-one lessons.

"May I be excused?" Todd suddenly requested.

"Already?" his mother asked.

"Yup, I'm done."

"All right then, bring your plate to the sink."

And sure enough, Marlee observed an empty plate that would have earned her brother a *clean plate button*. That, though, happened before her time. She'd often heard about the clean plate buttons—which weren't actual buttons—that her older siblings earned when they were younger, before she was old enough to partake. It had been something their dad made up using small, multicolored plastic discs he collected. In later years, neither recipient could remember where they'd come from, if they ever knew in the first place, but Todd and Melanie had competed to see who could amass the most "buttons." A quart jar full of them stood on each of their dressers. Marlee didn't know when or why the practice ended, but it did, and that was fine with her. She understood it had been a ploy to get them to finish the food placed before them, but she didn't need encouragement. Marlee gobbled up her mother's cooking.

On Saturday, Marvin and Todd worked together again in the basement. The space they diligently labored in for weeks had begun to take shape, resembling a bedroom. They trimmed out the built-in paneled closet, and by the end of the day, the only thing left to do was lay the carpet and move the furniture in. Todd proudly admired their work.

"I have the whole basement to myself," he announced.

"Not exactly," Marvin said. "Your mother's washer and dryer are around the corner, and of course, the playroom's still there." He gestured to his right. "It's hardly what I would describe as having the space to yourself."

"I know what you meant, Todd," Meredith said, "and I quite agree. You will have a lot of privacy down here."

"Don't abuse it," Marvin stated.

"What does *abuse* mean?" Marlee asked.

"It means he shouldn't misuse the privilege of having space to himself."

"What does *privilege* mean?"

"The right to something. Todd shouldn't misuse the right to have his own space," Marvin clarified.

"Oh," Marlee said and skipped away.

"It's so dark down here," Meredith commented out of earshot when Todd left to retrieve something from upstairs. "I don't like that he doesn't have a window."

Marvin agreed. "Yeah, I worry a little since there's no way to escape. Pray nothing happens."

"Don't even *think* it," Meredith shuddered, her voice edgy. With that, she held Troy closer and kissed the top of his head.

Todd bounded down the stairs. "When can we move my bed in? And my clothes and the rest of my things?"

"Well," Marvin said, "we can't move the bed in until the carpet is laid. So, I'm going to say next weekend."

"Okay." Todd sounded disappointed.

Meredith asked, "Is there any reason he couldn't move his hanging clothes and fill the drawers under the closet?"

"It doesn't matter to me." Marvin shook his head.

Eloise's mother had given birth to her brother Devin in November, just after Halloween, almost four months before the arrival of baby Troy.

"We both have baby brothers now," Marlee told Eloise one afternoon as they played house in the Becket playroom. They each had their favorite baby dolls, and that day, they pretended the dolls were boys. That was a new development, as the friends were always mothers to sweet baby girls.

"What should we call them?" Eloise asked.

"I'm going to call mine Charlie, like Charlie Brown." Marlee smiled.

"I think I'll call mine David."

"Why David?"

"Why Charlie?"

"I like Charlie."

"I like David."

"It sounds too much like Devin."

"It does not," Eloise defended her choice.

"Well, they both start with the same sound."

"So?" she challenged.

Meredith carried a pail of diapers to the basement to wash in the machine. She heard the girls and what sounded like a quarrel. Out of sight, she stood near the playroom door. Being a mother was still relatively fresh, so she took the opportunity to listen and learn. She couldn't help but wonder why neither girl named their baby after their new brothers. She thought she may have done that as a child. But she didn't have a brother or a sister, so what did she know about it?

Eventually, the friends decided they needed a snack break and marched up the stairs.

Marlee noticed the radio playing in the kitchen but found her mother around the corner, dusting the living room. Troy lay in his bassinet nearby.

"Can we have a snack?" Marlee asked, peering over the edge of the wicker basket. "Hey, Troy's awake."

"I know, and yes, you can have a snack. We have peanut butter cookies in the jar on the counter, or you can have raisins." She cut to the chase. "Let me guess. You want cookies?"

The girls looked at one another and nodded in agreement.

"As I thought. You can have two each."

Marlee opened the bottom drawer and stepped on its side edge, attempting to reach the cookie jar.

Meredith didn't like that. "Get down, I'm coming. I'll get you both a small glass of milk if you want."

"Please," said Eloise.

"Such nice manners." Meredith smiled.

Marlee suddenly shrieked, "I love this song!" And she belted out the chorus of Nancy Sinatra's recent hit, "These Boots Are Made for Walkin'."

Meredith sang along, smiling at the girls as they danced, holding hands in the kitchen, twirling until they were dizzy.

CHAPTER 5

EASTER MORNING ARRIVED, AND Mother Nature cooperated with a burst of glorious springtime weather. The sun shone brightly on a balmy sixty-three-degree day in northeastern Wisconsin. The daffodils had sprouted along the front of the house, up about four inches.

The children woke early to jellybean trails that snaked from their bedroom doorways to the living room, to where their Easter baskets sat.

Following the trail, Melanie noticed more candy sprinkled about the room. "Hey, there are jellybeans everywhere." She scooped them off the end tables and from the bookcase shelves.

"This is great!" Todd said. He stuffed the colorful beans in his pajama pocket.

Marlee didn't catch on right away. Bright yellow Peeps and trinket toys filled her basket to overflowing, capturing her attention.

"The Easter bunny must have spilled the jellybeans when he hopped around the house," Todd said, grinning wickedly.

Marlee's head snapped around. "He was hopping in *here*?" She looked skeptical.

"How do you think your basket got filled, dodo?" Todd asked.

"Don't call your sister a dodo," Marvin said.

Melanie tilted her head, looking puzzled. "I never thought about that before."

"I wish I had seen him." Marlee emptied the contents of her basket onto the floor.

Twenty minutes passed before Marvin halted the fun. "Okay, kids, you can play later. It's time to get dressed for church."

"Already?" Melanie asked.

"Yes, it's time."

Marvin whistled at his daughters as they exited the house. "Well, aren't you girls dressed all fancy-like? I like your spring bonnets."

Marlee held out her right leg, wiggling her foot. "How do you like my new shoes, Dad? Mom says they're patent leather."

"They are patent leather and so shiny you can almost see your reflection in them."

"Aw, Dad, they're not that shiny."

"Well, almost," he teased.

"We'll have to take pictures after," Meredith stated matter-of-factly. "We need to go."

The church was packed with standing room only, and everyone had dressed in what looked like new clothes, nicer than their usual Sunday best. Some women wore orchids pinned to their dresses, and Easter lilies decorated the sanctuary. An usher motioned Meredith forward. People squeezed in toward the middle of the pew to make room for her and the baby. Marlee tagged along, and they squeezed in even tighter.

After Mass Marvin commented, "Packed in like sardines, they were."

Marlee waltzed into the house cheerily, singing, "Alle-Alle-Alle-lou-ooo-yah! Alle-Alle-Alle-lou-ooo-yah!"

Meredith caught her husband's eye. He shook his head, and they smiled.

The children were instructed to remain in their church clothes until at least the grandparents arrived and could see them all gussied up.

"Don't spill," Meredith warned. "Marlee, tuck a napkin in your collar before you eat your cereal."

"Aw," she scoffed.

"I hope they get here soon. I want to get this monkey suit off," Todd complained.

"You look handsome," Meredith smiled. The girls giggled.

The grandparents arrived, and Ruby brought more sweet treats for the children, as well as a tall, fragrant Easter lily for Meredith.

The festive holiday meal consisted of ham, scalloped potatoes, boiled carrot coins, steamed broccoli with herbed butter sauce, orange Jell-O with whipped cream, and Bernice's fresh dinner rolls. For dessert, Meredith made a rich carrot cake with cream cheese frosting. As if that were not enough, the children raided their baskets, eating malted milk eggs and hollow chocolate rabbits.

Everyone went outside to soak up the sunshine, and the adults watched the children play. They hauled out jump ropes, a basketball, and a hula hoop. The bikes also made an appearance. Todd passed his grand-father a baseball glove.

"Will you play catch?" he asked Grandpa Becket.

"You bet. Toss me the ball." Sam moved away from the lawn chairs. "Put her there," he said, pounding his fist into the glove.

Ruby and Bernice took turns cuddling Troy to their chests. He sported a light blue knit cap, which was Meredith's handiwork. Marlee admitted she didn't think her baby brother looked Chinese anymore.

Instantly irritated, Meredith huffed. "He *never* looked Chinese."

Changing the subject, she praised her eldest daughter. "Melanie's been a big help with Troy. She likes to tote him around. That gives me more time to get my work done. She's started changing wet diapers, too."

"That's a good girl," Bernice said. "Melanie's always been helpful. I bet she's real good with the baby."

"Oh, she is," Meredith agreed.

"Your birthday's coming up in a few weeks, Melanie," Ruby stated. "What would you like Grandpa and I to get you?"

Melanie blushed. She glanced at her mother.

"Go ahead. She asked. You can tell her what you want."

"Umm," Melanie stammered. "I would like a straw purse or a flow-ered suitcase." She shyly shrugged.

"Have you seen those?" Meredith asked both grandmothers. "The small, colorful canvas suitcases for girls? Melanie spotted a pretty floral one at Montgomery Ward."

"Well, how about that?" Ruby marveled. "If today wasn't Easter Sun-day, we could head on down the road and I'd get it for you today, for your birthday. That would have been fun, wouldn't it?" she said.

Melanie's ninth birthday turned out just as she had hoped. On Fri-day, April 29, she woke to the delectable smell of her favorite breakfast—and on a school morning, no less! Her stomach rumbled. She quickly dressed in a pale yellow blouse and plaid jumper she had settled on the night before and went to the kitchen. Her mother was lifting a fluffy car-amel-colored waffle from the steaming iron. Bologna sizzled and popped in a pan.

"Good morning, birthday girl," Meredith said. "Pull up a chair. You've timed it perfectly."

"Happy birthday, Melly." Her father kissed the top of her head.

"Thank you."

"You are one special girl to have breakfast fit for a queen on a school day. Did you thank your mother?"

She beamed. "Thanks, Mom. It smells good."

Todd slid in next to her at the table and shoved her gently. "Happy birthday, sis."

The night before, Meredith frosted twenty-eight red velvet cupcakes with white icing for Melanie to take to school for a birthday treat.

Her class presented her with a pink construction paper card artfully decorated with a colorful kite on the front and the words *Happy Birthday*. Everyone had signed it.

That afternoon, Melanie returned home from school with a song in her heart. She discovered four neatly wrapped presents on the kitchen table, alongside a cake decorated in pastel-colored icing, her name written in pink cursive. It looked almost the same as the cake her mother had made for Todd two months earlier, except for the different-colored icing. Nine balloons tied to the backs of the kitchen chairs floated about. That is when Melanie spotted the small bowl of leftover creamy frosting.

"Hello," Meredith smiled, rounding the corner. "I saved that for you. And it was no small feat. Your sister tried to eat *all* the extra frosting. She was sorry she missed you this morning. The little sleepyhead."

"Happy birthday!" Marlee bear-hugged Melanie. "Do you want to know what's in the packages?"

"Don't you dare," Meredith warned.

"I won't. I was teasing."

"That's right, you were."

After Melanie's supper of choice—roasted pheasant, mashed potatoes with gravy, and creamed corn—she opened her gifts. She received a pot holder loom with rainbow-colored cotton loops and a straw purse with three ladybugs stitched in the grass under a ball of sunshine. "This is perfect! Oh, thank you! Just what I hoped for," she gushed. A flat box contained a soft, pale orange sweater set she said was pretty, and lastly, she tore the wrapping from a rather large box that turned out to be a typewriter in a matching turquoise case. "How cool. Wow! Thank you for everything," she enveloped her mother's neck and jostled her.

"Be careful of the baby," Meredith reminded her, holding two-month-old Troy. "And you're welcome, honey. You deserve it."

"You're welcome," Marvin echoed as he caught her up in a big hug.

"There are some greeting cards here addressed to you," Meredith said, handing Melanie a short stack. Two were from her grandparents. A third one came from her godparents—Uncle Buzzy and Aunt Francine, who lived in Milwaukee. A crisp five-dollar bill fell out when she opened that one.

"I bet you'll get more gifts on Sunday when we see the grandparents," Todd said.

"I would guess so," Marvin agreed.

Fifteen days later, déjà vu settled on the Becket home. On Saturday, May 14, Marlee turned five. She'd requested the same fluffy waffles for breakfast as Melanie had, but with bacon instead of fried bologna.

Todd took Marlee outside after so Meredith could clean up the breakfast mess. When Melanie called them in, Marlee saw her birthday cake on the kitchen table alongside five multicolored balloons bouncing about, tied to the chairs. There stood a neat stack of brightly wrapped gifts. Melanie had made a sign that read, "Happy 5th Birthday, Marlee!" Marvin taped it to the wall.

"Holy cow! How fun is this? When's everyone coming?" Marlee wanted to know.

"About noon," Meredith answered. "You need to change your clothes."

Marlee shed her play clothes in favor of a brown sleeveless dress patterned with purple, orange, and white geometric shapes. Her brown hair had grown to shoulder length, and Meredith told her that if she wanted to continue growing her bangs, she would need to keep them pinned back. So, she wore plastic barrettes—one purple and one orange—on the sides of her head.

"What do you think of my birthday outfit?" she asked.

"You look pretty hip." Twelve-year-old Todd snapped his fingers.

"Like something from *American Bandstand*," Meredith added. "Get a brush. I'll put the barrettes in again."

"I already put them in."

"It looks like it." Todd wrinkled his nose.

"Mom," Marlee whined.

"Come here," Meredith said. "Your hair just needs to be smoothed down a bit. That's all."

Melanie occupied Troy while her mother and father bustled about preparing for the party.

Marlee had requested venison for her special meal, but Meredith told her it would have to wait until another day. There were too many people to cook for, and she didn't want to spend all that time in front of an electric skillet, frying and turning so many small venison pieces.

As a result, Marlee agreed to barbecue chicken on the grill, with her all-time favorite potato salad and homemade baked beans.

Marlee's godparents—Anne's sister Carol and husband, Ed—arrived with cousins Eddie, Wade, and Katie. Eddie and Todd were the same age and in the same grade. It was the same for Wade and Melanie, although Katie was one year older and one year ahead of Marlee in school.

"Carol and Ed," Meredith said in greeting. "I'm happy you could come."

"It worked out well," Carol smiled. "I had hoped you'd have a party."

The grandparents arrived together in Alvin's Buick. Ruby happily held Troy while Meredith put the finishing touches on the meal. The men sipped their drinks and watched Marvin grill the chicken. The children enjoyed the warm day outside, running and playing until they were called in to eat.

They took a break after the meal, before cake and ice cream, while Marlee opened gifts. Carol and Ed gave her three Little Golden Books. From her parents, she got four tiny dolls called Liddle Kiddles with a car-rying case for twelve. She also opened a pair of turquoise-colored pedal pushers—or clam diggers, as Meredith called them—with a matching top and a Suzy Homemaker toy hair dryer. Bernice and Sam gave their granddaughter a small handmade quilt and a paint-by-number kit of a sweet-looking kitten.

"I made the quilt for your baby dolls," Grandma said.

"It's pretty. Thank you. Can I paint the kitty gray like Fanny, even if it's brown striped on the box?" Marlee asked anyone who might answer.

Meredith spoke, "You can if you have gray paint."

"I hope I do. Thank you, Grandma and Grandpa."

Marlee unwrapped a floral canvas suitcase from Ruby and Alvin. "It's just like the one you gave Melanie."

"It is. I thought maybe your mother could braid different-colored yarn ties for the zippers so you can tell them apart," Ruby suggested. "Open it up."

Marlee found a pair of light blue baby-doll pajamas, a Liddle Kiddles locket doll, a six-pack of white ruffled socks, and a package of underpants.

"Days of the week underpants," Melanie giggled.

Todd snickered. "You'll have to learn how to read to know what pair to wear."

A chorus of laughter erupted among the kids. Marlee flushed with embarrassment.

Meredith came to her rescue. "I think it's time for cake."

That summer, Marvin Becket purchased a newfangled color television. Meredith's first husband, Duane, had worked as a TV repairman for Zenith, so they consciously chose another Zenith, never considering another brand.

The delivery men arrived on a Thursday afternoon while Marvin worked. The children were excited beyond belief when the truck finally arrived. Two men carried the heavy television in a large wooden cabinet through their front door into the living room. Marvin cleared a spot on the carpet the night before by relocating the previous black-and-white to the bedroom.

"I can't wait for Saturday cartoons—*Jonny Quest* in color!" Todd exclaimed.

One of the men who had *Howard* stitched on his shirt told the children they would be amazed. To Mrs. Becket, he said, "You won't know how you ever lived without it."

"I don't know about that," she politely replied. "I'm sure it will be a treat, though."

"That it will," Howard said. "My wife enjoys her soap operas in color."

"Our mom doesn't watch soaps," Marlee offered.

"No?" Howard asked.

"No, she thinks—"

"Well, thank you, gentlemen," Meredith interrupted. "I think that's it."

"We need to turn on the set, ma'am. Make sure it's working properly," Howard's helper, Doug, told her as if she should have known.

"Of course," Meredith nodded.

Doug powered up the set. They watched a commercial advertising Clairol hair color.

"It doesn't work. The TV doesn't work," Melanie protested.

"Not everything is in color yet, especially commercials," Howard explained. "If we wait a bit, you'll see the program in full color."

They waited with something close to bated breath. And sure enough, after the commercial break, *Days of Our Lives* came to life in amazing color.

"That's so cool," Todd marveled.

"It works," Melanie said with relief.

"Can we watch it?" Marlee asked.

"Not now," their mother said. "We'll watch something this evening."

Marvin packed a pint-sized crib in the trunk, specifically purchased for camping. Ruby Simon had told her daughter she was nuts to want to take a five-month-old baby along.

"It'll be fine," Meredith assured her.

"But not much fun for you."

"It'll be fine," she said again. "We want to go camping, and this is our family now. We don't want to miss out because of Troy."

"I'll watch Troy for you," Ruby offered. "I would enjoy it."

Meredith hesitated. "Hmm. Why don't you and Pa come to see us one day, maybe our second-to-last day, and you can take Troy home for one night? We can pick him up on our way through. What do you think of that idea? It would make packing up easier for us."

"Absolutely," Ruby said joyfully. "Any day of the week."

Boulder Lake met the Beckets in the summer of 1966 with all the fun of previous years; however, two things threatened to mar their week.

While the family lounged on the beach, Troy asleep in the shade in his playpen, Marlee played in the water and planted her hands on the sandy bottom, doing handstands until she was dizzy. Disoriented, she panicked and swallowed a mouthful of water. As she resurfaced, sputtering, coughing, and crying, her mother came to her aid and helped her to her feet.

"I was drowning," Marlee gasped.

"Did you get dizzy practicing handstands?" Meredith asked.

"Uh-huh," she nodded, her little heart beating wildly.

"You might not want to attempt so many next time."

"It scared me."

"I can see that. But you're okay now."

"I'm glad you're here."

"Oh, me too." Meredith cuddled her.

The second mishap occurred the day relatives came to visit. It frightened everyone, though for Marlee, not more than her struggle in the lake had. That shook her up pretty good. But she hadn't been in any real danger. She just thought the lake would swallow her up.

It happened after lunch. Melanie and her cousins, Susan, Linda, and Bethany, ventured out to the fire tower, licking orange sherbet Push-Ups.

Rumblings began roughly an hour later when someone said they thought the girls should be back. Betty suggested the older boys walk to the tower to find them.

"Or the men could go?" Alma offered.

"They did have their swimsuits on," Meredith noted. "Maybe they stopped at the other beach."

"We'll run and check, Dad," Todd offered. "Pete and I will go."

"Quickly, Todd," Marvin said. And the boys took off running.

"The tower's about a twenty-minute hike from here," Bethany's father told them.

"Yeah, I would agree, George," Marvin nodded.

"Linda knows her way around this camp," Gerald said, hoping to ease the tension. "She's been coming here since the kids were little, and we've hiked to that tower a dozen times over the years."

"Maybe they didn't lose their way," Alma added to the drama. "Maybe something else happened."

"Oh, dear God," Betty uttered under her breath.

Minutes later, the boys ran into camp. They stopped short of the adults and bent at their waists, hands on their thighs, needing to catch their breath.

"They weren't there," Todd said, standing up and clutching his side.

"Okay." Marvin blew out a breath. "Let's head to the fire tower."

Marvin and his brothers-in-law, Harry, Gerald, and George, left to search for their daughters and nieces. Jim stayed back; he had a bad leg. Todd and Pete wanted to accompany the men but were denied.

About a mile down the winding, black-topped campground road, Harry spotted the girls approximately a hundred yards out. They were leaving a dirt path for the pavement, walking toward the men.

"Susan, Melanie!" Harry shouted. All the girls raised their arms to wave, like they didn't have a care in the world.

Closing the gap, Susan called, "Hey, Dad. Are you going to the tower?"

"We were looking for you."

"How come?" she asked.

"Where've you been?" Gerald asked. "They're worried," he said, referring to the women at the campsite.

"The tower. We took a wrong turn on the way back." Linda shook her head. "I don't know how we missed it, Dad."

"You have to pay closer attention," he said.

"Your mothers will be happy to see you," George breathed. "They thought you might be lost."

"Or worse," Harry stated.

"Bethany and Melanie did start to get scared," Linda tattled.

"I tried not to be scared," Melanie told her father.

"Oh, Melly." Marvin tousled her hair.

"Mostly because I was sort of in charge," she added.

"In charge?"

"You know, like a hostess. They all came to visit, so I felt like I should be in charge, you know?"

"I suppose," he chuckled. "Come on, your mother will be relieved." He corralled Melanie around the neck. "But you probably need to hone your hostess skills."

"Aw, Dad, cut it out."

As summer wound down, Meredith treated her daughters to separate days of school shopping and lunch. Marlee would be in kindergarten soon, and she nearly jumped out of her skin, beyond herself, with anticipation. The new shoes she chose thrilled her—sky-blue Mary Janes. Meredith had tried, to no avail, to convince Marlee to get a sensible brown pair, telling her the blue wouldn't match with everything.

"*Please*, can I get the blue ones?" Marlee had begged. "Brown is boring."

Meredith caved, "Oh, why not?" It wouldn't be long before she'd outgrow them.

Meredith introduced the girls to The Terrace Room downtown. The restaurant sat atop the multilevel H. C. Prange Company department store and boasted a magnificent view overlooking the city and the Fox River. Their neighbor, Jean Curtain, worked as a waitress there. Marlee thought Mrs. Curtain was somewhat of a local celebrity. She wore a crisp, pristine, cream-colored uniform and apron, and her hair was expertly styled in a smooth French twist. She was poised yet speedy as she walked back and forth in the dining room doing important work. Marlee proudly noticed that Mrs. Curtain had addressed her and taken her order with respect generally reserved for adults. She liked that.

As the final goodbye to summer, a weekend-long Labor Day celebration took place in Suring each year, and all three adult Becket siblings and their families descended upon their childhood home.

On Saturday, Marvin gave his kids three dollars each for games and rides. "When that's gone, you're done," he informed them. "Don't ask me for more. It should last you a while."

The adults accompanied the children to the carnival. Buzzy, Judy, and Marvin agreed it felt like a high school reunion. Many of their former classmates returned with their families for the big shindig. The surrounding communities were well aware of the festive celebration in Suring, and people came from near and far. There were two solid days of fun—rides, games, a talent show, and a polka band on Saturday evening, capped off with a parade on Monday morning.

Marlee rode the Ferris wheel with Todd and Melanie, and it reminded her of The Terrace Room restaurant. So much of the town could be seen from the top. Coming down, the ride tickled her belly. She squeezed her sister's leg, and a squeal escaped.

Bobbie asked Melanie and Todd to ride the giant wheel with her. Waiting in line for their turn, Bobbie leaned close to Todd, whispering something in his ear that she didn't want anyone else to hear. Todd snickered. The ride went as the two had hoped, stopping to let riders on and off, and when they rocked gently at the top, Bobbie reached into her shoulder bag and pulled out a screwdriver. She pretended to tighten a screw in the safety bar. Todd kept his composure.

"You don't have to worry, cuz," Bobbie told Melanie. "You won't fall out. Todd's got you."

"Wh—, wh—, what are you doing? Why do you have a screwdriver?"

"It's nothing. I need to fix this, tighten this loose screw," Bobbie said.

Melanie stammered again, the rising fear evident in her voice, "Wh—why? Why are you doing that?"

"I work on all the rides."

"That's just stupid! Stop it, Bobbie!"

Todd laughed, causing the bench seat to rock even more.

"It's not funny, you dumbass jerks!" Melanie shouted, on the verge of tears, and clinging onto the bar for dear life. "I'm telling Dad!"

"If you live to tell." Bobbie bubbled with sinister laughter.

"Shut up!"

"You'd better knock it off, Bob," Todd warned. "She's gonna tell."

Bobbie elbowed Melanie. "Aw, don't be such a wuss. Gee whiz."

Breathing a sigh of relief, Melanie exited the ride down the ramp, seeking out Marlee, staying with her and Dana for the rest of the day. She figured there would be no stupid, scary shenanigans with them. The three played the duck pond game. They leaned over a long oval metal tub that Melanie said reminded her of an animal trough. Each selected a yellow plastic duck and turned it over to read the number on the bottom.

"A prize every time," quipped the carnival worker.

Judy rolled her eyes at Meredith, "It's all junk," she whispered.

Melanie won at the ring toss table, and a carny gave her a clear bag containing a single goldfish.

"Can we trade that for a cherry soda?" Meredith promptly asked. The carny was kind enough to switch them out.

"Why is that always a carnival game prize?" Judy asked.

"I think because goldfish are cheap."

"Why couldn't I keep the goldfish, Mom?"

"I didn't want to deal with it, Melanie. I'm sorry."

"Can I drink the pop now?"

"Sure."

Meredith whispered out of the side of her mouth to Judy, "Nor did I want to deal with a broken heart when that fish would undoubtedly die two weeks from now."

Judy giggled. She took the stroller from Meredith. "Troy has gotten so big," she said. "I just love his eyes. They're so brown they're almost black."

"I know what you mean."

On Monday, a crowd lined the streets for the annual parade featuring the high school marching band, a fire truck complete with several candy throwers, clowns, and several horses with riders waving miniature American flags. Veterans of all ages and branches saluted when the color guard marched by, presenting a full-sized American flag. Typically, at least two floats were entered. The local 4-H club could always be counted on, and Stangle's grocery store usually had representation. It would not be the Suring Labor Day parade, though, if they did not have four guys dressed as old, buxom women wearing calico frocks and aprons, whose boots were nailed to two long planks. It was comical watching them in wigs and with hairy legs "walk" down the street. Each year, the kids looked forward to seeing "The Grannies," as they dubbed them, and they were rewarded again for their patience. Everyone got a big kick out of them.

Shortly after the parade, Buzzy and Judy left for home with their families. They'd waited for the road to finally clear before heading out. Marvin and the family ate an early supper with Sam and Bernice before leaving. They did not stay to watch *Walt Disney's Wonderful World of Color*. The children needed to wind down earlier than usual. School was starting the next day, and Marlee's first day of kindergarten awaited. She would attend class at the local high school due to persistent overcrowding. Construction of a new elementary school across town was underway.

"Good luck getting that one to sleep," Bernice said to her son, referring to Marlee, as they hugged goodbye.

As always, Sam and Bernice stood in the driveway, waving as they drove away.

CHAPTER 6

MARLEE WOKE EARLY, READY to dress for school.

"You don't go until after lunch," her mother pointed out. "Put some play clothes on for now. You can change later."

Marlee barely touched her breakfast, partly because she was anxious but mostly because she talked nonstop. "Tell me again," she said to her mother, "how do you say my teacher's name?"

"En-ge-bret-sen. Miss Engebretsen."

Marlee repeated it, enunciating every syllable correctly.

"And did you say I get a snack there?"

"Yes, I did."

"And I just raise my hand if I need to go potty?"

"That's right."

"Will any of my friends be there?"

"I'm sure you'll make friends, and there'll be kids from the block. You may have some in your class," Meredith explained.

Marlee exhaled, and Meredith could almost see the wheels turning in her daughter's head, but distracted by her siblings on a busy morning, it seemed Marlee forgot her next question.

"Make sure you bring everything," Meredith reminded the older kids.

"I wish I could go with them," Marlee said.

"Next year."

Todd looked up from reading the wall of cereal boxes lined up before him and slurped the last of the milk in his cereal bowl. "The bus is coming for you," he stated. "You get a ride to school, plus you can sleep in every day, you lucky bum."

"Yeah," Melanie echoed.

"I wanna go now."

"Come on. Let's take Todd and Melanie's picture." Meredith ushered them outside. Todd and Melanie stood together, smiling. "I'll get you later," she told Marlee.

"Bye," they waved.

Marlee puttered around, staying close to Meredith, every so often asking when it would be time to go.

"Soon enough," was always her answer.

Marlee ate a cold meatloaf sandwich without her dad, who hadn't yet come home from work for his noon meal. The radio was on, and Marlee listened intently as Paul Harvey told a story. The man had a way of capturing her attention.

"Hey, you need to change your clothes," Meredith interrupted.

Marlee popped up from the table, hurried to her bedroom, and returned wearing a pale pink dress, bought specially for her first day of school, and her new blue shoes.

"Well, don't you look cute. Hold still." Her mother clipped a silver barrette into her hair, and the two went outside for Meredith to snap a photo.

"Let's watch for your bus," Meredith suggested.

"Dad's not here to see me go."

"I can't help that."

Marlee hugged her mother tightly before skipping across the street to wait with the others. Boarding the bus, she chose a window seat to see Meredith. Marlee waved wildly at her, a big smile on her face.

Three-plus hours later, the same yellow bus rumbled down Stadium Drive, the second time that afternoon. Meredith and the other mothers stood on their front porches or at the bottom of their driveways, watching for their children.

Meredith smiled when Marlee came around the front of the bus to cross the street. The child beamed with an ear-to-ear grin.

"Well, tell me all about it," Meredith said, grabbing Marlee's hand.

"Oh, it was the best, Mom! And I did make friends, just like you said."

"I knew you would."

"Miss Engebretsen has the coolest toys—way cooler than ours!" She already pronounced her teacher's name like an old pro. "We took turns pedaling a big toy car outside, and we got to set up a bunch of wooden road signs that we had to obey. Do you know what a *yield* sign is? I do," Marlee proudly stated. "And we had to lay down for a nap after snack time. *Nobody* told me that would happen." She wrinkled her nose with disgust.

"What did you eat for a snack?"

"Graham crackers and milk. We all got a tiny carton. I wanted to keep mine, but the teacher said I couldn't. If we didn't drink the whole thing, we had to dump it in a bucket. I drank mine."

"Good girl."

"Are Melanie and Todd here? I want to tell them about kindygarden."

"Not yet. And it's *kindergarten*."

"I know—kindygarden."

"I bet you can't wait to go to the liberry, either," Meredith teased. The comment went over Marlee's head. It seemed to Meredith that most kids mispronounced those two words.

On Saturday after supper, Marlee hoped to play Kick the Can outside with any number of kids in the neighborhood until the streetlights popped on. When she finally ventured out, she noticed a group of kids in a front yard, two houses up, on the left. In those days, there was no such thing as a shortage of playmates on Stadium Drive. During its heyday, the block had a whopping eighty-six kids ranging in age from toddlers to teenagers.

At least a dozen rowdy kids chased after one another, playing tag. Marlee joined the fray and quickly shed her sweatshirt. Older kids showed up and organized two dodgeball teams, though back then they called it murderball. As the younger ones were systematically eliminated from the game, they resumed zigzagging through the yards, avoiding tags and tagging one another out.

Suddenly, Marlee bolted home. She did her best to hold her shirt together. The back had been ripped clear from the neckline to her waist, connected only by the hem.

Meredith met her at the side door. "What on earth happened to you?"

The words tumbled out in an amped-up, whiny voice, "We were playing tag, and that nasty Dennis Meyer ripped my shirt when he pulled me down!" The floodgates opened, and tears streamed down.

"Oh, honey, it'll be okay. I wish Dennis didn't play so rough, though." Assessing the damage, Meredith said, "Well, I can't salvage this shirt, so go grab another one. This one's headed for the rag bag."

"He's such a dink!"

"Marlee!" Meredith said. "Where on earth did you hear such a word?"

Using the back of her hand to wipe her nose, she shrugged, "I don't know."

"We don't talk like that. That's not a word I want to hear come out of your mouth again. Do you understand?"

She nodded.

"Now get a new shirt on and go back out and play."

Marlee regained her composure and wandered back up the street, but was still mad. She stuck her tongue out at Dennis. He made a face at her. His sister Becky thrust her tongue out. They made her so angry. She wished she could smack them. Instead, she rolled her eyes and turned her back on them, kicking one foot behind her as if to cast them off.

Later, before it got dark, the yards and street had cleared of nearly everyone when Mrs. White poked her head outside and called to her children. "Kyle, Eloise, *The Wizard of Oz* is on in thirty minutes, and you need baths."

Just like almost everyone else, the Becket children looked forward to watching that classic each year. That evening's viewing proved extra special for the Becket family because of their new color TV. With amazement, they watched the famous switch from black-and-white to color. Oz and the yellow brick road came alive like never before!

Nearly an hour into the movie, Marlee hunkered in close to her older brother and slid under his arm, outstretched across the back of the sofa. It fell around her shoulders.

"Are you cold?" their mother asked.

"Marlee doesn't like this part," Todd informed her.

The girl closed her eyes. "I don't like the flying monkeys."

Melanie passed her sister the popcorn bowl, and Marlee stuffed handfuls in her mouth, happy for the diversion.

Late one morning, before Marlee left for school, Meredith noticed that the cookies she was saving for her husband's lunch were gone, the plate empty. "Did you eat the cookies?" Meredith asked Marlee, holding the plate.

She shook her head no.

"They were on the counter this morning after everyone left. Since then, it's just been you and me, and Troy, home. I didn't eat them, and I know Troy certainly didn't, so who does that leave?"

Marlee looked down at her stockinged feet. She said nothing.

"Well?" her mother probed. "I was saving the last three peanut butter cookies for your father to have for dessert today. Those weren't for you, young lady. Not only did you not ask to eat them, but you lied to me." She pointed down the hall. "Go! Go to your room."

"I'm sorry," Marlee halfheartedly mumbled.

Twenty minutes later, Meredith entered the girls' bedroom and found Marlee stretched out on her bed, looking up at the ceiling, fiddling with some trinket toy.

"Why did you lie to me?"

"I don't know."

"Yes, you do. Why did you lie?"

"I guess because I wasn't supposed to eat the cookies."

"And what? You didn't think I would notice?"

"I don't know."

"Marlee, you didn't think about it at all. That's your problem. You often do whatever you want without thinking about anyone else or the consequences of your actions."

"*Consequences*? What does that mean?"

"The importance of what you've just done," Meredith answered. "You can't lie, Marlee. It will catch up with you every time. Maybe not right away, but it will. Trust me. A person needs to turn away from making poor decisions—turn away from the devil. You need to fight the devil in life, Marlee. Every day, you must choose good over bad. Next time, ask, and no more lying. Got it?"

"Got it."

"Get ready for school."

After bedtime prayers, Marvin and Meredith kissed their daughters. "Don't let the bedbugs bite," their father teased, leaving the room.

In the bed she shared with her sister, Marlee promptly rolled onto her belly and rose to her knees. She punched her pillow violently.

"What are you doing?" Melanie shook her head.

"I'm fighting."

"Your pillow?"

"Yup," Marlee replied, winded.

"Why?"

"Because Mom told me I always have to fight the devil." She socked her pillow harder.

"I'm pretty sure the devil doesn't look like your pillow."

"Well, I've never seen him," Marlee said. "And I never want to!"

Melanie sighed, "Just lie down."

Giving in to her sister, Marlee stopped punching and rolled onto her back, her breathing ragged. She stared at the ceiling and thought about what her mother had told her.

The afternoon school bus stopped one house west of the Becket residence, and five excited kindergarteners prepared to exit. It had barely halted when Dennis Meyer pushed past Marlee, knocking her into a seat, to scramble down the stairs ahead of her off the bus. She raced after him. Without a word, she grabbed him by the wrist and, with all her might, chomped down and bit his arm through the vinyl jacket he wore. He screamed. She bolted across the street.

It seemed only moments after greeting her mother that they heard a knock at the front door. Marlee scrambled to answer it with Meredith on her heels. Mrs. Meyer and her son stood on the front porch. They did not look pleased. Marlee noticed Dennis had red-rimmed eyes and no longer wore his ugly vinyl jacket. Mrs. Meyer held her son's arm out for Meredith to see.

"Look what your daughter just did to my boy!" she hissed. "All because she selfishly wanted off the bus first."

Marlee stood frozen. No one could deny the distinct pattern of bite marks on his forearm that matched exactly Marlee's two bottom-front, crooked teeth. She flushed with shame and anger and desperately wanted to slam the door shut in their faces.

"Marlee did that to you? Just now?" Meredith asked Dennis. Turning to her daughter, she saw Marlee look away, which told her all she needed to know.

"Yes," Dennis nodded.

"Why on earth . . . I am *so sorry*! What do you have to say for yourself, Marlee Becket? Apologize to them. Now!" she ordered.

"I'm sorry." It didn't exactly sound heartfelt.

To Marlee's horror, Meredith grabbed her right arm and held it out to Dennis. "She needs to learn that biting is unacceptable. You can show her how it feels. Go ahead." Meredith encouraged him.

He looked up at his mother, and she nodded ever so slightly. Dennis stepped forward and took hold of Marlee's arm. She flinched. He bit down, not nearly as hard as she had, but Marlee gritted her teeth against the pain, though she did not cry. Dennis backed away, feeling awkward, and looked toward his house.

"I can assure you this will never happen again," Meredith said apologetically.

"I should hope not," Mrs. Meyer huffed, stepping off the porch. She grabbed Dennis by the wrist and left.

The front door clicked shut, and Marlee immediately felt the sting on her backside. Meredith landed three firm spankings.

"That ought to teach you. I don't want to hear or see that you have bitten anyone else. Ever again! Do you hear me?" Meredith boomed.

"He shoved me!"

"That's no excuse."

Marlee stomped to her room. She felt betrayed and tried to fight back tears, but failed; she could hardly believe her mother had him bite her. Immediate hatred boiled in her for Dennis Meyer, and something short of that simmered for her mother. No one asked why she had done it. But she knew, deep down, like her mother told her, there was no acceptable excuse for her behavior. But did anyone care about rotten Dennis Meyer shoving her to cut in line so he could be the first one off the bus? They did not. He was the selfish one. The whole thing was his fault.

No one breathed another word about it, at least not to Marlee. If her father knew, which Marlee felt certain her mother would have reported what happened, he hadn't let on. It was better that way. It embarrassed her. She shouldn't have bitten Dennis even if he deserved it. Biting was something babies sometimes did, and she, most certainly, wasn't a baby anymore. But Marlee had grown to dislike Dennis Meyer something fierce.

One morning, before Marlee had to leave for school, Meredith squeezed in a visit to the Ninth Street Library. It was one of the girl's favorite places to go. Upon entering, Marlee instinctively inhaled the familiar pleasant smell. Nothing compared to the library, she thought. She could be blindfolded, twirled in circles, and if someone walked her into the Ninth Street Library, she would surely know it by its unmistakable scent. The woodsy, earthy smell was both defining and satisfying.

Meredith always allowed her daughter a tall stack of books. *Harold and the Purple Crayon* made the cut every trip. As did *Blueberries for Sal.* Marlee knew just where to find them on the shelves.

"I think it would be a good investment for us to own copies of those two. Don't you agree?"

"What does *investment* mean?"

"It would be a good value for us to purchase some of your favorite books. The ones you repeatedly check out, again and again."

Marlee shrugged her shoulders and resumed making her selections.

"I wish I could go blueberry picking with Sal and Little Bear," she suddenly declared.

"You don't even like blueberry picking, Marlee."

"I think I might if I could go with Little Bear."

"You very well might."

Five Dr. Seuss books, *Madeline*, and *The Littlest Angel* by Charles Tazewell were included in the tall stack to take home.

"You chose a Christmas book?" Meredith questioned, putting the pile on the desk to be stamped for checkout.

"Yup."

"I'm certain we own *Green Eggs and Ham*."

"It's okay."

"All right then." Meredith shifted Troy to her other arm. "Grab your stack."

Each fall, Sam and Bernice Becket, with their adult sons, made an annual trip to South Dakota for pheasant hunting. They usually departed west soon after school started. Meredith, herself a hunter and angler, planned to accompany them.

Alice Bogart toted her burgundy hard-backed suitcase and a bulging green purse up the two steps to the side door. Marvin got her name from a family friend, and he hired the middle-aged woman to stay with the three oldest children while he and Meredith were away.

"I would have carried that for you," Marvin apologized as he opened the door. He reached for her suitcase. "Come on in."

"Not to worry. I'm used to doing for myself."

"Hello, Alice," Meredith smiled with Marlee at her side. "You remember the children."

"Yes, yes. How are we today?"

"A bit apprehensive," Meredith admitted.

"No need to be. We'll get along just fine." She winked at the kids.

Marvin took the suitcase to his and Meredith's bedroom, and Meredith hung Alice's coat in the hall closet, talking the entire time, giving instructions. She directed Alice to a large notepad on the kitchen counter listing the phone numbers of where they were staying and other details they had previously discussed.

"And here are the house and car keys, if you need our vehicle for any reason." Meredith handed over a silver ring. "We're all packed," she quickly added. "Do you have any questions?"

"No. You've been very thorough. Thank you."

Meredith reached for Todd to hug him first, and he dodged her kiss that landed instead on his cheek.

Melanie said goodbye without any fanfare, but Marlee started to whimper.

"We talked about this, Marlee. Come on now. Mom and I need you to be a big girl." Marvin scooped her into a bear hug. He whispered something into her ear. Whatever he said seemed to satisfy her.

Meredith followed with a hug, and Marlee hung on for dear life.

"It's just a week, honey," Meredith cooed. "It's going to fly by, and you'll have such fun with Alice here."

Marvin peeled Marlee off her mother, and the girl hugged him again before stepping back between Todd and Melanie. Everyone went outside. The children stood in the driveway with Alice and waved goodbye. Marlee swallowed a lump in her throat.

Alvin and Ruby Simon had driven to Green Bay the day before, a fine autumn afternoon, and picked up Troy. They—more Ruby than Alvin—were thrilled with the opportunity to have young Troy to themselves for an entire week. Marlee wished she could have left with them, but her parents wouldn't release her from school. She'd asked.

Alice Bogart had a gruff manner and was not necessarily the type of woman to whom the children had grown accustomed. Marlee found herself alone with Alice each school morning. As a result, she became more familiar with her than her older siblings had. That didn't mean much except that the girl knew best how to push Alice's buttons. And Alice had no qualms about disciplining Marlee for her infractions.

Once, Marlee failed to remove her shoes before walking across a freshly mopped kitchen floor. For that, Alice said, "Go sit in the living room and think about what you've done."

Marlee didn't do it on purpose.

Another time, while Marlee and Eloise played outside, Alice called Marlee several times before she finally responded. The woman huffed and said, "Go to your room." Another fifteen minutes alone was her punishment.

Marlee never learned why Alice had called her.

Despite all that, Marlee thought Alice, who insisted she not be addressed as Miss Bogart, wasn't terrible. She could cook a decent meal—nothing like her mother's, of course, but tasty enough—and she always kept a pan of Rice Krispies treats on the counter.

Alice insisted that the children play outside every day after school for a good solid hour before basically allowing them back in the house. One rainy day, she even opened the overhead garage door to back the car out and told them to play in the garage until she summoned them inside. Todd and Melanie had to postpone their homework until after dinner every day that Alice stayed with them.

"You young'uns need your fresh air," she liked to say.

"I don't think she's used to having kids around," Todd said one afternoon as they raked leaves into piles to jump in.

"Yeah," Melanie agreed.

"I can't wait for Dad and Mom to come home," Marlee complained.

"Oh, you," Todd shoved her into the growing pile. He completely covered her with leaves.

Marvin and Meredith returned home on Saturday morning. They came with pheasants galore for their freezer, plus three small gifts—one each for Todd and the girls—and little Troy in the flesh.

"Oh my gosh, he grew!" Melanie extended her arms. "Can I hold him?"

"He's all yours." Meredith handed him over.

"I missed you, birds," Marvin said, hugging his children tight. "Pun intended," he chuckled.

"We missed you!" Marlee said.

Alice spoke very little but acknowledged that all had gone well. "Oh, your phone messages are there on the notepad."

Marvin gave Alice an envelope with her payment for the week. He and Meredith thanked her, and she, in turn, thanked them.

"Goodbye, children," she patted each on their shoulder.

"Goodbye," they said.

Marvin saw her out the door.

Both girls received a coin purse with a colorful pheasant stitched on the front, and Todd received a pheasant key chain.

"Mom thought you could use it for the key to your bike lock," Marvin said.

"Good idea. Thank you."

"How did it go with Alice?" Meredith wanted to know.

"Fine," Melanie offered.

"Yeah, fine," Todd echoed, shrugging his shoulders.

"Alice can be a grump sometimes," Marlee told them.

Meredith stifled a giggle. "Do you care to elaborate?"

Marlee cocked her head.

"Anything you want to tell us?" Marvin inquired.

"I guess not."

Everyone laughed.

On second thought, Marlee held up her pointer finger. "Well, she does make us play outside every day when we get home from school."

"Yeah," Melanie agreed.

"What's wrong with that?" their father asked.

No one said a word about the day it rained, when Alice backed the car out of the garage, shooing them out of the house.

Marlee dressed for Halloween in her brand-new Casper the Friendly Ghost costume. Todd dressed as a pirate, Melanie as a witchy-looking woman, wearing a long black wig with a thick white streak. Todd ditched his sisters to trick-or-treat with friends. The girls went out with several neighborhood kids. They trick-or-treated for several blocks, even crossing one busy street, and were gone for hours.

Marlee returned home hot, sweaty, and exhausted. She flung her mask off and dumped her filled plastic pumpkin on the living room floor. She perused her candy, following the example set by her brother and sister, and sorted her treats by type. Todd traded his small chewy candy for her mini chocolate bars.

"Don't let him swindle you," their father warned.

"Trick or treat!" The girls jumped up at the sound of the familiar chant and raced to the front door. A large, costumed group of kids greeted them. Melanie dropped a treat in each vessel presented before her. A couple of older kids held out pillowcases.

"Thank you," they called in unison.

"I get to do it the next time someone comes," Marlee insisted as the kids retreated.

"It should be coming to an end soon anyway," their mother noted. "It's getting late. Todd, will you please check to see if our jack-o'-lanterns are still lit?" They were glowing yet, now just short, stubby candles after burning all evening.

They heard the chant twice more, and Marlee was thrilled when Melanie gave up, letting her pass out the candy.

"Let's turn off the outside light," Meredith finally suggested to Marvin. "Please make sure the candles are extinguished. And these kids need to dress for bed and wind down. Pronto," she told them. It was Monday, and the school week had just begun.

On Sunday, November 6, 1966, the Green Bay Packers hosted the Minnesota Vikings. A small party of adults arrived at the Becket home for pregame festivities before heading to the stadium. Located so close, Marvin and most of his neighbors parked cars on their front lawns for five dollars apiece. They generally filled quickly, especially since the town prohibited street parking that close to the stadium on game day. Also, the Packers charged more to park in the lot.

Pointing at each car on the lawn, Todd counted aloud, bobbing his head, "Five, ten, fifteen, twenty, twenty-five, thirty, thirty-five, forty. Forty dollars! Eight paying customers," he said to no one. The other cars belonged to friends who parked for free. Not a hard way to earn a buck or forty, he thought. He wondered if his father would let him park cars for the next home game and keep the money, or at least part of it.

"Luann Curtain will be crossing the street soon, in about fifteen minutes—to babysit you rascals," Meredith informed the children.

"Oh, come on! I don't want a babysitter. I don't need anyone to watch me!" Todd protested.

"*You* may not, but the other kids do. Luann will cater mostly to Troy and Marlee," Meredith stated. "Besides, you're usually off gallivanting somewhere anyway."

Home game days were always exciting, whether Green Bay won or lost. The crisp autumn air smelled of dry leaves and grilled bratwurst. A small airplane could be heard overhead circling the area, trailing a banner advertising one thing or another, and you heard cheers when the Packers scored a touchdown or kicked a field goal. "People watching" was fun, too. Some women wore long fur coats when the weather turned colder. Marlee wanted to run her hands down the length of every fur coat she saw. A lot of the men dressed nicely, too, especially those accompanying the fur-clad women. They donned tweed sport coats, dress shirts with ties, and long, wool, camel-colored coats. Occasionally, you would see a man wearing a fur cap. Binoculars hung from the necks of many fans.

The kids had to wait until the adults left for the game before they could eat the leftover snacks Meredith had served. They had more than the typical chips and dip to munch on, feasting on shrimp cocktail, cheese and sausage with crackers, and mixed nuts—not just plain peanuts. Marlee picked out the cashews but left the Brazil nuts.

Their father was not pleased when, after the last home game, he observed an empty jar of maraschino cherries on the counter by the sink, the cover cast aside, and the glass jar two-thirds full of only the remaining sticky red liquid.

"Those cherries weren't meant for you kids," Marvin had said. "I use them for cocktails. They're off-limits. Do you hear me?" The guilty trio nodded.

Everyone was understandably disappointed whenever the Packers lost. And when that happened, the guests returned to the house but did not stay as long as they did when celebrating a victory. Instead, they claimed their vehicles and headed out into a sea of red taillights, impatient to merge into traffic and head north or south onto the congested Oneida Street.

The Packers had a bye before hosting their rival, the Chicago Bears, on the third Sunday in November. The bye was due to the league's expansion to fifteen teams, allowing the Atlanta Falcons in. They were the first National Football League franchise in the Deep South.

Todd convinced his father to let him help park cars. For his efforts, Marvin gave him ten dollars. It was not the entire forty-five they earned, but it was ten dollars more than he started the day with.

The usual crowd had descended on the Becket home for their pre-game party. That day, Meredith served a large kettle of chili with corn bread and apple pie for dessert.

"I like it better when we have snacks. We can eat chili any old day of the week," Marlee grumbled.

"We can't have a bottle of pop any day of the week," Melanie told her.

"Whoopi ding dong," she replied.

Melanie looked sideways at Marlee before reaching for the bottle opener. She knew they equally enjoyed the soda treat.

The Packers defeated the Bears 13–6. The friends who returned to the Becket home and the fans who poured down Stadium Drive seemed exceptionally jovial on that game day. They laughed loudly, rehashing the game, reliving the big plays. The men were animated and talked using their hands, waving their arms. Some fans even sang.

Every year, the H. C. Prange Company—better known as Prange's—dazzled onlookers with its Christmas window displays. The Becket children were always truly captivated. They oohed and aahed over the detailed, colorful scenes. The animated mechanical people and woodland creatures twirled about their houses and forests. The unveiling of the windows marked the unofficial start of the holiday season and stirred nostalgia and a sense of magic among the horde of visitors.

Walking back to the car, Melanie said, "My favorite window was the cozy kitchen with the old-fashioned wood stove, just like the one in Grandma and Grandpa Becket's basement."

"I liked that one, too," Marlee agreed. "The cookies looked real, didn't they? But I know they weren't. And the girls' dresses were fancy. Did you see that cute kitten?"

"I saw it swishing its tail," Meredith smiled.

"I liked the forest scene best with all the animals. The doe and her fawns were pretty cool," Todd said.

"So cool!" Marlee gushed.

"Who wants to stop at Kaap's for a hot chocolate or an ice cream sundae?" Marvin asked.

"I do, I do, I do!" the children shouted.

"I scream, you scream, we all scream for ice cream," their father joked.

Meredith ordered decaffeinated coffee, and everyone other than Troy was served a sundae with toppings. Meredith offered Troy a taste of whipped cream on the end of her pinkie finger. He licked it and shook his little arms, squealing with delight. The waitress came by with a dollop of cream just for Troy.

"That's kind of you," Meredith smiled.

"I could see the little guy enjoyed it." The waitress winked.

"He did at that."

"Hey," Marvin elbowed his daughters next to him, one on each side, seated in a giant booth. "I notice you all have your *own* maraschino cherry."

"Yeah, so you don't have to swipe the ones he saves for cocktails."

"What are you saying, Todd? You helped empty that jar on game day."

"I had one. Here." He held out the cherry from the top of his sundae. "Who wants it? I don't like 'em anyway; they're way too sweet."

Nobody accepted his offer.

"Put it in the cup," Meredith said, reaching toward Todd.

Meredith began her holiday baking after St. Nicholas visited the house on the fifth of December, the children fast asleep in their beds. They woke on the morning of the sixth to find their stockings filled with candy canes, chocolate Santas, and chocolate bells wrapped in colorful foil. And if they were good, they received a small toy or two.

But the best treats of the season came from Meredith. Her various cookies and candies were delectable. Marlee especially liked the sweet-and-salty combo of the white chocolate–covered pretzels. Her mother made a large batch and filled a round Christmas tin, using wax paper to separate the layers. Meredith probably should have hidden the goodies, but she did not. She set them on a chest freezer in the basement against an outside concrete wall. Copious treats were stored there—a risky thing for her to do because an unrelenting sweet tooth plagued Marlee, and she frequently raided the different tins and Tupperware containers. Her mother's divinity fudge melted in your mouth, and you couldn't beat her creamy peanut butter balls. Marlee suspected she was not the only one sneaking treats, but her mother never let on if she knew.

The kids decorated cut-out cookies in every shape imaginable. Meredith made colored icing—not just plain white—which enhanced the fun. Marlee liked decorating trees and stars the best. A messy explosion of sprinkles and colored sugar on the kitchen floor under the table was evidence of their creativity. Melanie swept, but it seemed someone always found a runaway candy ball here and there that escaped her dustpan.

Marvin sat with the kids while they watched the first of many animated Christmas shows on television—*A Charlie Brown Christmas*, one of their favorites. Meredith seized the opportunity to hole up in the bedroom and wrap gifts.

As they watched *How the Grinch Stole Christmas!*, Marlee announced that their neighbor, Lisa Boland, looked just like Cindy Lou Who.

"She does!" Todd screeched. "That's so funny."

"I think it's cute," Melanie nodded.

"What's cute?" Meredith asked as she entered the room.

"Marlee said Lisa Boland reminds her of Cindy Lou Who."

"No, I didn't. I said she *looks* like Cindy Lou Who."

"Same difference," Melanie scoffed.

"She looks *exactly* like her!" declared Todd.

"Lisa Boland is a cute little thing if I do say so myself. And I'd have to agree—she does resemble Cindy Lou Who," Meredith said.

"Who? Get it? Who wants to look like a cartoon character?" Todd guffawed.

"I bet you wouldn't mind looking like Jonny Quest."

"Oh, that's good, Melanie," their mother chuckled.

"I don't want to look like Jonny Quest, but I wouldn't mind *being him.*"

"You realize you're talking about cartoon characters here?" Marvin shook his head. "You all sound ridiculous."

For her sixth Christmas, Marlee received an exceptional gift. Grandpa Becket built her a child-sized kitchen cupboard. With a laminated countertop, it looked like a mini version of the real thing. There were two small upper cabinets for toy dishes, two drawers for utensils, pot holders, a gingham apron Grandma Becket made, and two bottom cabinets for larger items.

"Wow, Sam, that's quite the gift." Meredith tenderly touched his arm.

"It was nothing."

"Yeah, Dad. That's really nice," Marvin said, admiring the piece. "Marlee will have fun with it."

"I liked making it."

"Will you take our picture?" Marlee asked, hopping up and down. She posed next to the wooden cupboard with her grandparents, sporting a big smile.

The family spent the evenings during the week between Christmas and New Year's Day visiting relatives. They drove to Kewaunee, about thirty-five minutes east, to see two of Anne's sisters, a brother, and their families, going from house to house. Meredith explained to Marlee that besides visiting, they wanted to see everyone's Christmas trees and the gifts they received. Marlee didn't really care why they did it; she was just glad they did. It was always such fun getting together with the cousins.

A night or two later, everyone reciprocated by coming to Green Bay to visit them and Ed and Carol. Another night, the whole gang headed south to Appleton, thirty minutes away, to see yet another of Anne's sisters and her family.

Anne Novak Becket was the youngest of nine children and sadly the first to pass into eternal life.

"This week between holidays makes it rough trying to keep my girlish figure," Meredith complained after dressing to see relatives for the third time in five nights. "I suppose I could exercise better self-control, but then I wouldn't have an easy New Year's resolution to make." She laughed at her own joke. "But I've got to say, the amount of tempting food put out so late in the evening is nuts. Absolutely nuts, I tell you. I understand the sweets and drinks, but a Crock-Pot full of sloppy joes or a platter of hot beef sandwiches making their appearance at eight or nine each night is something I don't think I could ever get used to."

"Aw, c'mon, Mom, the food's great!" Todd beamed.

"Oh, to be young."

"And don't forget," Marvin reminded his wife, "we're going to my sister's for noon on New Year's Day."

"I didn't forget."

"Will Grandma and Grandpa Becket be there?" Melanie wanted to know.

"Of course," Marvin said. "Uncle Buzzy and Aunt Francine, too."

"How about Bobbie and Nancy? Will they be there?"

"I expect so," Meredith piped in.

"I love this time of year," Melanie grinned.

"So do I!" Marlee shouted.

New Year's Day at Judy and Bill's house presented a welcome surprise for the three eldest Becket kids. They would join the adults at the big table for dinner. A highchair set at one end of the table awaited Troy.

"You mean there's no *kid table*?" Marlee asked Aunt Judy, incredulously searching for another place to eat.

Judy chuckled. "We have plenty of room to seat everyone."

"That is a giant table," Marlee acknowledged.

"You do have a nice, big area here to accommodate all of us," Meredith commented. "We could certainly use the space at our house."

"It must be like a damn dance hall in here when your table's not humongous!" Buzzy roared. He liked to kid his sister. "Do you and Billy dance a jig after dinner?"

Todd laughed at his uncle. He thought any occasion with Buzzy was fun and boisterous.

The men retreated to the living room to watch the NFL championship game in Dallas, Texas. Their beloved Packers beat the Cowboys by a score of 34–27. The Kansas City Chiefs, meanwhile, easily defeated the Buffalo Bills in New York in the AFL championship game, 31–7.

"You know what this means?" Marvin said, smiling. "The Packers will take on the Chiefs in two weeks for all the marbles."

Hopeful, Todd asked, "Will they play at home?"

"They'll play in Los Angeles."

"Why is that?"

"It's a neutral site. Neither team has an advantage of being at their home stadium."

"Hmm," Todd mused.

Two weeks later, on January 15, 1967, the Green Bay Packers beat the Kansas City Chiefs, 35–10, in the first-ever AFL–NFL World Championship Game.

Todd nearly went crazy when Willie Wood intercepted a Len Dawson pass, returning the ball fifty yards to set up the ensuing touchdown. Bart Starr deservedly was named Most Valuable Player.

February meant the arrival of the Becket brothers' birthdays. Todd celebrated his thirteenth birthday by going ice fishing at Chute Pond with his father and grandparents. Meredith and the three younger children remained at Sam and Bernice's house. She baked and artfully decorated an angel food cake for Todd. And later, the family dined on freshly caught fried fish for supper, with reserves Bernice had thought ahead to thaw, had they not been as successful.

Todd received a new hunting jacket from his grandparents and planned to wear it that fall when they traveled west for pheasant hunting in South Dakota. He was over the moon when his parents told him they had already decided he could accompany them that year. Sure, it was seven months away, but the thought of being pulled out of school for a week in October to hunt was enough for him. His parents did, though, surprise him with a guitar he'd been pining for since before Christmas.

Meredith baked two cakes for Troy's first birthday—a tiny one for him and a larger one for everyone else. He smiled proudly when the candles were lit and the family sang "Happy Birthday."

Strapped in his highchair, Troy looked at his cake. "Go ahead and eat," Meredith encouraged him. "It's all yours." She took hold of his little finger, swiped it through the smooth chocolate icing, and brought it to his lips. He grabbed a mitt-full. Everyone laughed. Troy gobbled cake while kicking his little legs excitedly against the chair's metal footrest, causing a racket. He managed to cover his face and head with chocolate.

"He likes it," Melanie clapped.

"Look at his hair!" Marlee made a face. "Oh, and his ears. Eww." She scrunched her nose. "He looks like he fell in a mud puddle."

Ruby Simon happily snapped photographs. "He's having so much fun."

"I should have made a white cake with vanilla frosting," Meredith said.

"The cleanup's the same," Bernice noted.

"I suppose you're right."

"He has some in his ears!" Marlee shouted, as if no one else could see that.

"It'll be okay," Meredith told her. "We'll get him washed up."

Troy sat on his mother's lap while she helped him open gifts. Todd helped Grandpa Simon carry a spring-loaded rocking horse into the house. They set it in the middle of the living room, and Marvin put the birthday boy in the saddle. He held him, gently bouncing the horse back and forth. Troy squealed with delight.

"He is so darn cute," Melanie gushed.

"Is he ever!" Ruby beamed at her grandson.

CHAPTER 7

THEY HAD TO PUT down Meredith's old gray tabby shortly after Easter. Marlee was saddened to lose her little furry sidekick, and she cried.

"Fanny got old and sick, sweetie. She got tired. It was time for her, that's all," Meredith gently explained.

"Was it time for Fanny just like it was for my first mama? And for Duane?" she asked as an afterthought.

Marlee's candor stunned Meredith. "I—I guess it was," she replied softly.

"Did Fanny go to heaven?"

"I think so, and now she has your other mama and Duane to love her up."

"Fanny won't be sick or tired anymore?"

"No, she won't be. Remember, we talked about heaven. Everything is perfect there—no sadness or pain—only happiness."

"I like heaven."

"Me too, Marlee."

"Do you want to go to heaven, Mama?"

"Someday, but not for a long, long while."

"I don't wanna go for a long while either. But I would like to see my first mama."

"I know. I would like to see her, too." Meredith's eyes misted over as she tenderly pulled Marlee to her chest, cradling her head.

Sunshine filled a clear, perfectly blue sky on a warm spring day between Melanie's tenth and Marlee's sixth birthdays. Alvin Simon's gold Buick glinted in the sun as he drove into the Becket's driveway.

Meredith called for her husband. "Marvin, my folks are here. Hurry!" She ran outside to meet them.

Alvin set a box down on the grass. A periwinkle blue towel concealed its contents.

"Hello, Ma. Hello, Pa," Meredith quickly hugged her mother and then her father.

Marvin saw his family huddled around a box. The children questioned their grandparents about its contents.

A tiny nose poked out of the box as Ruby lifted off the towel. A small, fluffy white puppy looked up and clumsily wagged its hind end. The children dropped to their knees.

"Oh my gosh, it's adorable!" Melanie raved. "I've never seen anything so sweet in all my life!"

Many hands reached in to pet the toy poodle.

Troy giggled.

"Is it a boy or a girl?" Todd asked.

"It's a girl," Ruby stated.

"It figures. Sheesh, I'm always outnumbered."

"Can we take her out of the box?" Marlee wanted to know.

"Can I hold her?" Melanie asked.

"Can I hold her?" Marlee echoed.

"Let Grandma lift her out," Meredith said. "Oh, Ma, she's so little. I hope I don't regret this."

Alvin laughed and cheerfully slapped his son-in-law on the back.

The tiny poodle wagged its tail, trying to climb onto Melanie. Melanie brought her face down to the little ball of fluff and met a wet nose. She giggled. The excited puppy wriggled about the circle that enclosed her. She dropped her hind end and tinkled on the grass.

"She's going potty," Ruby said, and the kids instinctively widened the circle. "I can tell she's delighted to meet you."

"Is she ours?" Todd asked.

"She is," Ruby smiled.

Todd looked at his mother. She winked.

Ruby spoke, "I've been calling her Crisco, but you name her what you want."

"Crisco, like the shortening?" Marvin asked.

"One and the same," Alvin replied. "Grandma thinks this pup is fluffy and white just like shortening."

Everyone took turns holding the little dog. Troy squealed whenever she got close to his face.

"Aww, does the puppy tickle you?" Meredith reached out to pet her. "I have to say, Ma, she is awfully sweet."

Alvin went to the car. He returned carrying a water bowl and bed, among other pet supplies.

"Someone want to put water in here?" He held the bowl out.

"I will," Todd offered, grabbing the dish. He took both steps of the side porch in one giant leap. He reemerged with fresh water.

Marlee lay on the grass next to the puppy, watching her drink from the bowl.

"I can't believe we have a dog." Melanie shook her head.

"Well, believe it," Marvin said. "You know, I had a dog when I was a kid. I called him Pal."

"What kind of dog, Dad?" Marlee inquired.

"A mixed breed of some sort. He was also white."

"Was he fluffy?"

"No, Pal had short hair."

"I think I may have been crazy when I agreed to this," Meredith worried.

Alvin let out a belly laugh.

"It'll be an adjustment, but a fun one," Ruby said.

"Pal, huh?" Marlee pondered. "I guess I like the name Crisco."

"Do you, honey?" Ruby asked.

"I like Crisco, too," Melanie agreed.

"Todd?" He turned to look at his mother. "What should we call the dog?"

"I can't think of another name for her since Grandma said Crisco."

"Does that mean you like it?"

"Yeah, it fits her."

"That was easy," Marvin said.

Marlee's birthday fell on a Sunday and coincided with Mother's Day. The family prepared to go to Suring to celebrate. Marlee complained that she couldn't open even one of her gifts before they left.

"Come on! I want something to do. I need something to keep me company on the ride," she persisted. "Can we bring Crisco?"

"No!" Her parents were firm.

"And your argument's weak," Marvin noted. "You have a car full of people to keep you company."

"How about just that small pink one?" she pressed, pointing to a box peeking out from the top of a brown grocery bag that Todd carried to the car.

"Marlee, what did your father say? You know you would've had to wait to open your gifts if your grandparents came here."

She sighed in defeat.

An hour later, they found Sam outside in a lawn chair, turning the crank on an ice cream maker.

"Reinforcements," he said when the car doors opened. "It's about damn time." He wasn't angry.

"Do you need someone to take over?" Meredith asked.

"Sure would be nice. My arms are 'bout ready to fall off."

"Hi, Grandpa," Marlee ran. "You're making ice cream?"

"I am. Say, a little birdie told me it's your birthday. Does that birdie know what she's talking about?"

"Yeah," a smile spread across her face.

"What flavor are you making?" Todd asked.

"Vanilla."

"We have chocolate sauce," Bernice announced, coming from the house with a stack of bowls and a handful of spoons.

Marlee ran to her grandmother.

"How's our birthday girl?" she asked, hugging her.

"I'm good."

"Chomping at the bit to open her presents." Meredith shook her head. "Happy Mother's Day, Bernice."

"Happy Mother's Day to you."

"Ma! Happy Mother's Day." Marvin handed her a rectangular box tied with a gold ribbon, which she knew was her favorite fine chocolates. That box would last a month, with her and Sam each enjoying one piece a day until they emptied it. She could always count on her son to bring Kaap's Old World Chocolates.

"Thank you—my favorite," Bernice said warmly. "We can sample it later. Say, Meredith, your folks called about ten minutes ago. They're on their way."

"Perfect."

"We have a box of chocolates for Grandma Simon, too," Marlee offered.

"She'll be happy about that," Bernice said.

"Do you know what we got for Mom?" Marlee asked her grandma. "A big bunch of flowers!"

"A beautiful bouquet." Meredith smiled.

Marvin took over for his father and straddled the ice cream maker, cranking away.

Alvin and Ruby pulled into the half-moon driveway, honking the horn. Marlee did a little dance and ran to greet them.

"Happy birthday, buttercup," Ruby pecked Marlee's cheek.

From the back seat of the car, Alvin retrieved a purple bicycle complete with a basket, bell, and silver streamers flowing from the handlebars. He wheeled it directly to Marlee.

"Happy Birthday!"

"For me? You got me a big bike? No training wheels!"

"They fell off," Alvin teased. "Ah, your mother told us you're good to go now. You don't need training wheels anymore."

"I don't!" she proudly shouted.

"Hop on," Sam said. "Take her for a spin, see how she rides."

Marlee hiked up her light blue seersucker dress and peddled up and down the long, curved driveway, smiling like a Cheshire cat.

"Sound the bell," Ruby hollered.

The girl did as Grandma ordered before braking hard. "A big-girl bike. Thank you!"

Everyone laughed.

Todd elbowed Melanie. "I bet she couldn't care less about what's in that pink box anymore."

"Probably not, but I would like to know."

The box held a little watch. "To help you be on time for supper," Marvin said.

"Now you just have to learn to tell time," Todd teased.

"She's working on it," Meredith defended her.

Marlee treasured all of her gifts. "I can't wait to show Eloise everything I got. She's going to love my new bike. Hey Dad! Will my bike fit in the trunk?"

"It will."

"You sure?"

"Yup, no problem."

"Whew!" Her relief sounded like a whistle.

Meredith suspected she was pregnant again but planned to confirm it before telling her husband. She didn't know whether Marvin would be pleased.

Several days later, they sat alone in the living room. The children were in bed, and the ten o'clock news had just wrapped up. *The Tonight Show* with Johnny Carson was on deck.

"I saw the doctor yesterday."

Marvin turned to his wife. "Oh?"

"I suspected but now I'm certain. I'm preg—"

"You're pregnant?" he interrupted, the surprise obvious in his voice.

"I confirmed it earlier today."

"How far along are you?"

"Eleven, twelvish weeks."

"Oh, goodness."

"Is that a *good* 'oh goodness'?"

"Yes. Yes! You took me by surprise, is all."

"It took *me* by surprise. I'm due in December."

"December, huh? Well, I'll be darned." He rose from his chair, walked a few feet to where she sat, and took her hands in his. She stood and fell into his embrace.

"You're happy, then?" She pulled back to get a good look at him when he answered.

"I am. Are you?"

"Yes."

"Are you sure?" It was his turn to lean back and assess her face.

"I'm still getting used to the idea."

Marvin tenderly kissed her. "How've you been feeling?"

"Good."

"Wow."

"I know."

They sat silently for several minutes, each with their thoughts, staring at the television, half listening—or not at all—as Johnny Carson interviewed his first guest.

"Ready for bed?" Marvin asked. "You are sleeping for two," he teased.

Meredith shook her head. Smiled. "Let's go."

He turned off the TV, and they shuffled down the hall together. Meredith laid her robe on a chair. She got in bed and moved to the middle to rest her head on her husband's chest. They both thought about the baby, but neither spoke. It was a while before Marvin gave in to sleep.

The couple celebrated Meredith's birthday and their second wedding anniversary with a romantic dinner at a local supper club. But before they left home, Meredith used the vase from her Mother's Day bouquet to arrange a large bunch of fragrant lavender roses and baby's breath that Marvin had given her. Over dinner, he presented his wife with a stunning but simple pair of emerald earrings—her birthstone—from Rummele's Jewelers.

"These match last year's pendant necklace. They're beautiful, Marv, and extravagant." She admired the deep green hue before looking up again. "Thank you." Smiling, she reached across the table and took his hand. "You're so good to me. I'm afraid all I got you is a card. I thought we agreed no gifts."

"I don't know what you're talking about."

"Marvin, you do, too."

"It's not my birthday," he winked.

"But it is *our* anniversary."

"I wanted you to have them. You make me happy, Meredith."

"And you make me happy, and I love you."

"I love you," he smiled.

They ate in silence for several long moments before Marvin spoke. "I've been thinking I should look for a new job to earn more money, with the baby coming and all."

Meredith met her husband's eyes but said nothing, knowing he had more to say.

"You're aware that I've been approached in the past by some companies—competitors in the trucking supply business. Now, I've been thinking that I should put my feelers out—reach out to them."

"What companies?"

"Specifically, a supplier in the Twin Cities area?"

"As in Minnesota?"

"Are you opposed to that?"

"I guess not."

"You guess not?"

"It would be a big change."

"It would," Marvin agreed. "But I think I need to earn more money. And I probably need to go elsewhere to do that, to a larger market."

"It won't hurt to look," she said approvingly.

Meredith reconsidered her Father's Day gift for Marvin. She had planned to give him another tie to add to his growing collection, one of which he wore every day to the office. Instead, she decided the children should give their father the earth-tone tie, and she opted to surprise him with a pair of leather golf shoes. He had recently taken up the sport but hadn't yet purchased the appropriate shoes. She chose brown and cream-colored saddle shoes with an optional fringe flap over the laces.

"What could this be?" he asked when she gave him a rectangular box. "It's about the size of a bread loaf but too heavy," he joked.

"Aw, Dad," Marlee said. He set the box aside briefly to accept his children's offering.

"Open ours, Dad," Melanie coaxed him.

The kids huddled around, anxious to see if he liked their gift.

He tore the paper off a long, narrow, flat box, and the cover came with it. "A tie! And a nice one at that. I'll wear it to work tomorrow. Everyone will ask me about it. Thank you."

"Do you like it, Dad?" Marlee wanted to know.

"I sure do. Did you pick it out?"

"Mama did," she admitted.

"I thought that might be the case. Your mama's got good taste, doesn't she?"

"Open the package from Mom," Todd encouraged him.

Picking up the gift again, he looked quizzically at it. He unwrapped it and lifted the lid, laughing heartily. "Golf shoes! These are great, Mer. Come here," he planted a kiss firmly on her lips. "They're perfect. Thank you!"

"You won't know if they're perfect until you try them on."

Marvin slipped into them, tightening the laces. He stood, wiggling his toes about. "Yup, perfect."

"I'm glad," Meredith said. "Happy Father's Day." Marvin kissed her again, surprising her with a spontaneous dip. The girls giggled. "Oh, Marv," she playfully scoffed.

Melanie helped her mother quickly tidy up the kitchen by stacking the breakfast dishes in the sink.

"I hate to leave these." Meredith balked. "But we need to get on the road." After Mass, she had made blueberry pancakes and fried bacon. The pancakes were one of Marvin's many favorite breakfast entrees, and making a hearty meal was a small thing she could do for him, knowing he would take pleasure in it.

"We do need to get going," Marvin agreed. "Come on, kids, let's roll." And they were off for their weekly visit up north. They had a bottle of brandy packed for Sam and a bottle of bourbon for Alvin. Alvin wasn't much of a drinker but desired an occasional glass of good bourbon on the rocks. Over the years, he often said he preferred to pour for others rather than indulge in one himself.

Marvin remembered many of Meredith's stories from when she was a young woman in the forties, when her father owned the Fern Room, a tavern in downtown Green Bay. Alvin sat quietly whenever Meredith retold the tales—stories that alluded to occasional visits from gangsters up from Chicago passing through to a place in the north woods. He remained mysteriously silent as she spoke, neither confirming nor adding to her words.

After supper, Marvin and Meredith took Troy across the busy Oneida Street to watch Todd play baseball. The ball diamond was in a large empty lot next to the Green Bay Packers' outdoor practice field. It wasn't a great ball diamond with its portable backstop and bases and two wooden benches plunked down in the dirt for the players, but it sufficed for league play. Parents and fans occupied a small, metal, portable bleacher stand, while some spectators brought lawn chairs and others sat on blankets on the hard ground. A few of the dads paced about. One shouted at his son to keep his eye on the ball. Neighborhood kids chanted, "Hey, batter, batter, batter, batter, batter, batter, batter . . . *swing*!"

Melanie and Marlee were allowed to go to the game on their own since they lived only three houses up from the corner. Oneida Street was one of the busiest thoroughfares in town, so they were cautioned to be careful when they crossed the road. (Years later, that huge lot became a massive indoor practice facility for the Packers known as The Don Hutson Center.)

Instead of going to the ball game, Marlee walked next door to see if Eloise could play, not knowing whether her family was even home. Stepping out of the air-conditioned house, it felt warm outdoors. As the sun sank lower in the western sky, descending to sunset, the evening temperature held steady at a sticky seventy-five degrees. Marlee pulled her thin navy cardigan over her head and realized she could see through it. "This is pretty neat," she breathed, leaving it on her head as she walked the worn grass path between the two houses. Stumbling, she fell into the corner of the Whites' concrete steps. Her scream split the air, and blood spurted from her head. Touching it, her fingers reddened through the fabric. Crying, she struggled to free herself of the sweater.

Marlee didn't stop at home to get help from her sister, as she probably should have, but instead went straight to the ball diamond where her folks were. Through blood and tears and a throbbing head, she did her best to look both ways before crossing the busy street. The fans sat with their backs to the road, so no one saw Marlee approach until they heard her cries, over the traffic and noise of the game.

Her parents were stunned when they turned and saw her holding a blood-soaked sweater to her head.

"What happened?" They both asked.

"I tripped on Eloise's porch," she sobbed.

"Oh my gosh!" Meredith lifted the sweater and assessed the damage. "Oh," she gasped. "We need to take you in; that looks nasty. I think it needs stitches."

Those words triggered Marlee, and she wailed louder.

"Let me take a look," Marvin said, getting closer. "How'd this happen? Where's your sister?"

"I tripped!"

Someone offered them a clean towel and a first-aid kit.

Marlee shrieked when her mother dabbed at the spot with the towel.

"I'll run home for the car," Marvin said.

Meredith calmed Marlee as best she could, but it didn't help when Troy cried.

Marvin pulled up next to the curb. "You stay here with the boys," he instructed Meredith. "I'll take Marlee to the emergency room. Melanie's home."

"I want Mom!" Marlee clung to Meredith as she tried to get her into the car.

"Mom's staying here. It'll be okay, Marlee."

"I want Mom!"

Meredith looked longingly through the open car window.

Marvin took control. "It'll be okay, Meredith. I've got you, Marlee. Keep that towel pressed to your head." He left his wife with Troy, whimpering in her arms.

Approximately two hours later, Marvin and Marlee returned home, the game long over, but everyone was thankful for summertime when the kids' bedtime stretched to ten o'clock or later. Marlee hustled through the kitchen ahead of her father, a bandage above her left eye. Meredith sat in the living room with the two older kids. She set the newspaper aside and met them as they rounded the corner.

"How's our girl?"

"She's a trooper."

"I got seven stitches," Marlee stated proudly.

"The doctor said that's two more than she may have gotten had the cut been elsewhere. They called in a specialist to close it up since it was on her face. And you'll have to make an appointment, take her to the doctor in a week to get the stitches out. She needs to keep the area dry for the first two days and shouldn't go swimming until the stitches are removed."

Meredith carefully lifted the bandage to peer at the doctor's handiwork. Marvin read her mind.

"The surgeon said it shouldn't scar, but the cut goes right through her eyebrow, so she may permanently be out a few brow hairs. Not a big deal."

Todd asked, "Did you cry when they stitched you up?"

"A little," Marlee admitted. "It stung."

"She cried more when they cleaned it. Whimpered when they numbed the area to sew it up."

"Did they give her any kind of pain reliever?" Meredith inquired.

"No, they said we could give her baby aspirin."

"Okay, wow," Meredith clasped her hands together. "Well, we're glad you're back and thankful it wasn't more serious. Let's get you in some pajamas. Oh, but those dirty feet."

"Yeah, she's at least in need of a foot washing. Those are some filthy toes." Marvin pointed to Marlee's feet in rubber thongs. "Though she has something she needs to tell you first."

Meredith glanced at her husband before meeting Marlee's eyes. "What?"

"Um, I . . . I . . ."

Meredith tilted her head. She couldn't imagine what Marlee had to say.

"Spit it out," Marvin said.

"I had my sweater over my head," she said, looking at her dirty feet.

"When?" No sooner had Meredith voiced her question than it hit her, and she realized what Marlee meant. She waited.

Marvin nudged Marlee for more. "I had my sweater over my head when I . . . when I fell and hit the porch. But I could see through it!" she quickly added, defending her decision.

"You walked with your sweater over your head?"

"Yeah," she answered sheepishly.

"Why were you walking with your sweater on your head?"

"We've been over all that," Marvin said. "Just a dumb move, right, Marlee?"

"A dumb move," she agreed, her eyes downcast.

Meredith shook her head and winced, "That's a painful lesson to learn." She touched her daughter on the shoulder. "Come on, let's get you cleaned up and ready for bed. It's also time for you two to get to bed. Let's go," she said to the older children.

"Okay," Todd groaned. "Good night."

"Good night," Melanie echoed.

"Sleep tight," Marvin said.

Together, the Becket and White families walked up Stadium Drive. At the last house on the right at the top of the hill, they took the pea-gravel path over to Lambeau Field. The kids were giddy, and the adults welcomed the camaraderie of the warm Fourth of July evening.

Marlee and Eloise skipped ahead.

"Dad, there's Terry and Chris," Todd said. "I'm going with them, okay?"

"Be home when the fireworks are over. And behave!" Marvin shouted after him.

Melanie walked beside her mother, willing to help with Troy, although she would have rather liked to find her friends. She didn't think her parents would allow it, insisting she was too young and the crowd too large.

Joanna White and Meredith chatted without pause as they made their way. One would bet they hadn't seen one another in a long time when, in fact, the complete opposite was true. They often talked over the fence separating their backyards when they hung wash out or in the early evenings as they sat together in lawn chairs, relaxing while supervising the younger children.

The women pushed strollers, and with Devin White four months shy of two years old and Troy Becket sixteen months, the boys had a lot in common, so the mothers often found themselves discussing and comparing their toddlers.

"Devin has regressed a bit and is not sleeping through the night."

"Do you remember that with the others?" Meredith asked.

"I do. And if I remember right, it was usually due to teething."

"Ah, the dreaded teething."

"Nonstop for two years," Joanna bemoaned.

"How's Devin with food? Is he a good eater?"

"He's picky. It's always interesting figuring out what their preferences are. How about Troy?"

"Look at him," Meredith chuckled. "He's not a bit picky. There's a reason my mother nicknamed him Pudgy." Both women laughed.

"Stick together," Joanna called to the children.

As always, the fireworks did not disappoint; they were, in fact, spectacular and dazzled the crowd, about one-third of the stadium's capacity. The color exploded against the night sky, and the kids' jaws dropped in amazement. Everyone enjoyed the warm, patriotic evening.

The buzzing of the tight, energetic throng made leaving the stadium a little challenging. Eloise's older brother, Kyle, threw his arm in the air, waving when he was separated from the group.

"I see you, Kyle," his father called.

"I wish he had taken your hand," Joanna told her husband.

As people reached the exits, they dispersed into the wide-open parking lot free of vehicles, due to possible falling firework remnants. Branching out in all directions, everyone breathed easier.

The girls shared their favorite blasts. "I like the ones that sizzle and rain down."

Meredith noticed Eloise's use of the word *sizzle* and thought it very appropriate.

"I like those and the ones that change color," Marlee said.

"Oh, me too," Eloise agreed.

Melanie offered her two cents. "I like the displays on the ground. When you can see them take shape, it's fun to watch them come together and reveal the whole message."

"We can't read all that," Marlee scoffed.

"Don't be rude," Meredith scolded. "I like those too," she nodded at Melanie.

"I liked the grand finale best," Marvin said.

"Oh, yeah, that is the bestest," Marlee agreed.

"It's the *best*," Meredith automatically corrected her.

"It sounds as if you liked everything," Eloise's father chuckled.

"I did!"

"Me too," he said.

A veil of smoke hung in the air. The smell of spent fireworks lingered.

The month of July didn't only mean fireworks; it also meant Boulder Lake had summoned the Beckets during the dog days of summer. They went for their usual week. Much company visited—the usual grandparents, aunts, uncles, and cousins. Ed and Carol, along with their kids, Eddie, Wade, and Katie, surprised them when they arrived. Meredith noticed that Marlee had been in her glory through the steady influx of people and shared her observation with her husband.

"Marlee really enjoyed the family this week."

"Yeah, that one's always up for a shindig," he agreed.

Besides Todd being stung by a bee, the week went smoothly. Once again, the family headed to Green Bay more sun-kissed than when they arrived.

On the drive home through the Nicolet National Forest, the kids squealed with delight as their stomachs flipped when their father sped up over the succession of rolling hills. Meredith wasn't crazy about him driving like that to entertain the children while hauling a boat. She told him it made her nervous.

Marvin dismissed her concern, "Ah, there's nothing to worry about."

"Until the boat goes airborne," she said, meant only for him.

"That could happen?" Melanie asked.

"That's not going to happen," he assured them. "Your mother's a worrywart."

The neighborhood park program hosted an end-of-summer hobo parade. Meredith assembled costumes for the three bigger kids using a combination of old, mostly discarded clothes. She saved a meat bone to tie in Marlee's hair—her inspiration modeled after Pebbles from *The Flintstones*. She tied red bandanas to the ends of sticks to serve as makeshift hobo sacks and found an old pipe for Todd to hold between his teeth, then photographed the kids. She could hardly wait to eventually show their father, whenever the roll of film was full and ready to be developed. She'd done well with their outfits.

Troy napped, and Meredith refused to wake him. She realized that she would most likely miss the parade but stepped outside to see some costumed kids on their way to the park. Other mothers also apparently took the hobo parade seriously since all the kids looked as if they had just stepped off the tracks.

Marlee startled Meredith when she suddenly showed up at home, alone and crying, carrying the meat bone, her hair in an awful mess.

"What on earth happened? Where are your brother and sister?"

"They're still up there. But people were laughing at me. They hurt my feelings."

"You're crying because someone laughed at you? Who laughed, other kids or people watching the parade? Was it even over, by the way?"

"No, it wasn't over, but *everyone* was laughing at me."

"Oh, Marlee, they weren't laughing at you. They wanted to laugh with you. I'm sure they thought you looked cute. Your costume is good— if I do say so myself."

"Well, I didn't like them laughing at me."

"So, you just left?"

"Uh-huh."

Meredith sighed. "You shouldn't have dressed up then. Take it off."

Marlee handed her mother the bone. "I'm gonna change and go back to the park."

"No, you're not. You wait here for the others."

"What! Why? Why can't I go back?"

"Quiet down before you wake your brother." Meredith hoped the box fan in Troy's bedroom would muffle the racket.

"Why can't I go back?"

"Because I said so, that's why."

Marlee huffed away, catching the screen door so it didn't slam.

"Where are you going?" Meredith asked from the kitchen window.

"To the swing set. Geez."

"Don't *geez* me. And don't you even think about sneaking off back to the park."

Marlee made a wise decision not to talk back.

Over supper, Meredith and Marvin announced that they were expecting another baby.

"Really?" Todd asked.

Meredith nodded.

"Are you kidding? You're not kidding!" Melanie's voice pitched an octave higher. "For real?"

"It just has to be a girl this time," Marlee insisted.

"You're having another baby?" Todd asked again.

"Yes," their father confirmed.

"Does that bother you?" Meredith asked.

"No. Why would it bother me?"

"You don't sound happy about it."

"It's not that," Todd said. "I'm just surprised."

"Caught off guard?" Marvin offered. Us, too, he wanted to say.

"When will the baby be born?" Melanie wanted to know.

"December."

"It's so exciting!"

"I'm glad you think so." Meredith smiled.

"*Please* make it a girl," Marlee pleaded, her hands folded in prayer.

Marvin piped up, "A boy would be fun for Troy."

"That's enough," Meredith teased. "You don't get to pick."

"But there is one more thing we need to tell you." Marvin scanned their faces.

"You're having twins!" Todd shouted.

"Two babies this time?" Marlee's eyes bugged out of her head.

"No! I'm not having twins," Meredith said, exasperated.

"But we are moving," Marvin interjected. "I have a new job in Minneapolis that I'll be starting in October."

"We're moving! When? It's August. I'll be in eighth grade in like three weeks," Todd said.

"We're moving?" Melanie looked inquisitively at her folks. It was hard to believe. She needed confirmation.

Meredith sighed.

Marvin spoke, "I'll admit the timing is a bit unfortunate. It would have been nice to have all of this settled so you kids could start the school year there, but your mother and I have yet to find a house."

"We're moving to Minnesota," Melanie mused aloud.

"We are," Meredith said. "What do you think of that?"

"There's no way I'll be a Vikings fan!" Todd stated emphatically. His parents laughed.

"Me neither," Marvin looked to his wife.

"Nor I," she said.

"It's exciting!" Melanie shrieked.

"What about you, Marlee? What do you think?"

She jumped up from the table, did a little dance, swinging her arms over her head. "I think it'll be fun."

Meredith raised her eyebrows at Marvin.

"What about Eloise?" Todd asked Marlee.

Without skipping a beat, "Oh, she'll come to visit."

Both Becket girls saw Mrs. Curtain again, on separate occasions, downtown at The Terrace Room when they stopped for lunch with their mother after shopping for school clothes. For Marlee, school shopping signaled the end of summer. Meredith knew she would miss bringing the girls to The Terrace Room and realized she would need to find another special place in a new city to treat her daughters. She also realized it probably wouldn't be too difficult in Minneapolis.

The event that sealed summer's fate was the annual Labor Day celebration in Suring. That year, Buzzy, Francine, Nancy, and Bobbie were no-shows. They attended a wedding in Chicago. Francine's nephew—her sister's son in the Navy—came home on leave to get married.

Marvin announced that Meredith was pregnant and they were moving to Minnesota. He would have to make a long-distance call to Buzzy.

As expected, Bernice and Sam were happy about the baby but not about the move.

Bernice sighed. "That'll end our Sundays together."

"I'm sorry, Ma."

"You'll still come for deer hunting?" She sounded hopeful.

Marvin looked at his wife. "It all depends. We'll have to see how Meredith's feeling."

Bernice's eyes watered. Sam chastised her, "Oh, don't start blubbering. It won't change nothin'. Not a damn thing will it change."

Judy hugged her mother. To her brother, she said, "Of course, we wish you all the best."

"It's not terribly far away," Marvin said.

"Halfway to bird hunting," Bernice grumbled.

"True statement. I'm sorry, Ma."

"We'll pick 'em up on our way to South Dakota," Sam said. "Let 'em live their life. It is what it is, woman."

CHAPTER 8

MEREDITH THOUGHT THE CHILDREN looked sharp in their new, crisp, never-before-worn clothes. She took the traditional first-day-of-school picture in the driveway after breakfast. Marlee proudly joined her sister and the other big kids on the mile walk to school. Todd and a group of even bigger kids headed off in a different direction toward the high school, which housed grades seven through twelve that year. At least kindergarteners weren't there taking up residence anymore, with the new elementary school built across town.

Marlee got Mrs. VandenLangenberg as her first-grade teacher. Meredith knew the name *Engebretsen* had been a mouthful for Marlee the previous year, so she was relieved to learn the children could address their new teacher simply as Mrs. Van.

That afternoon, Meredith glanced at the clock, and almost as if on cue, the door opened and her daughters entered the kitchen. They took turns telling her about their first day.

"We don't get rest time in first grade even though we're at school *all* day," Marlee informed her mother as if she didn't know those facts.

"You must be bushed."

The girl looked at her quizzically.

"Tired. You must be tired."

"Nah. But I am hungry." She perused the cabinets, looking for something to eat.

"How was your day, Melanie?"

"Good. It's a little weird, though, having a man teacher."

"It is different for you."

"I have homework," Melanie stated. "Our assignment is to write three paragraphs about ourselves and our family."

"That shouldn't be difficult."

"I'm going to write about us moving and having another baby."

"Hmm. Did you girls see one another during the day?"

"Not once," Melanie said.

"Will it always be like that?" Marlee wondered aloud.

"I would think you would occasionally, at some point during the week, anyway."

"Oh," Marlee remembered to tell her mother, "I want hot lunch all week. Mrs. Van read the whole menu, and I want to try all of it."

"That's fine. What about you, Melanie?"

"Hot lunch for me, too, please."

During the second week of school, Meredith didn't feel well. She was cramping and, since nine that morning, felt as though she might be in labor. It worried her. It would be much too soon. She called Joanna White. Her neighbor thankfully agreed to watch Troy. Holding hands with Devin, they walked over.

"I'll feed the boys lunch and do my best to get them to nap. You call me if you need anything. I hope you feel better," Joanna said.

Meredith telephoned her husband at the office. She told him about the pain and cramping.

"I'm coming home."

"Thank you," she said and closed her eyes, gritting her teeth against the escalating pain.

Meredith made her way to the toilet when a sudden, sharp pain down below gripped her. It did not let up. A moment later, she knew her water had broken. Reaching down over her swollen belly, she felt something unusual. Gasping, Meredith began to cry, and her body shuddered involuntarily. Several minutes passed before Marvin came through the back door.

"Meredith?" he called out.

"The bathroom," she groaned.

He discovered his wife on the toilet.

"Get a mirror."

"What?"

"I need a mirror," she cried.

Marvin reached for a hand mirror in the cabinet and quickly passed it to his wife.

"The baby's coming," she sobbed, not needing to look at her reflection after all.

"I'm calling an ambulance." Meredith did not object, and that frightened him.

Thirty-five minutes later, the doctor at the hospital confirmed the baby was gone. "We don't know why these things happen," he said.

Meredith clung to her husband and wept. Marvin ached for his wife and baby, and he, too, cried.

The doctor tried earnestly to convince the couple that this was probably for the best. "I believe the development of the baby was abnormal; who knows, there may have been a chromosomal abnormality or a heart defect. Unfortunately, this is one of those things we can't know for sure."

Meredith looked blankly at him; her mind and body were numb. Marvin held her hand, his heart heavy.

Eventually, he called Joanna. She gasped. "Oh, Marvin, I'm *so sorry*."

"Thank you," he said. "Are you able to keep Troy until I make it home?"

"Absolutely."

"Would you please watch for the older kids to get home from school?"

"Don't worry about a thing here. What do you want me to tell them?"

"Ah, tell them I took their mother to a doctor's appointment. Try not to say more. And Joanna," he hesitated, "thanks."

"I'm sorry, Marvin. Tell Meredith."

"I will."

The hospital released Meredith at four in the afternoon. Despite the bright sunshine, she told her husband she felt a familiar darkness. "And I feel as if I've been hit by a Mack truck."

Marvin cleared his throat but said nothing. Instead, he reached across the bench seat and took her hand. It felt lifeless to him. Meredith turned toward the window.

Arriving home, he helped her into bed. She instructed him to fetch the children. "Bring the kids to me. I want to get this over with." A high-pitched, singular, mournful cry escaped her battered being and broke her husband's heart.

"We don't have to tell them right away, Mer," he said. "I'll tell them you're not feeling well."

"No," she shook her head emphatically.

He kissed her forehead. "I'll be right back."

Marvin knew that the kids sensed something wasn't right. They walked behind him, and oddly, only Todd asked a question and just one at that.

"Is Mom all right?"

"No," he replied matter-of-factly.

They followed him into the bedroom—a room typically off-limits. They observed their mother, propped with pillows, her face pale, tears pooling, and somehow, looking older. A gut-wrenching sadness filled the room. She beckoned them with outstretched arms. The older ones hugged her. Troy squirmed in his father's arms.

"Let him come to me."

"What happened?" Todd asked. Goose bumps surfaced on his skin.

Marvin held Troy by Meredith's side, but the boy tried to climb over her to the middle of the bed.

"Gentle," she breathed. Marvin lifted him over to her other side. He saw his wife failing in her quest for strength.

"The baby died," she said, and her eyes spilled over.

"No!" Melanie wailed.

Todd stood dumbfounded. Marlee wept, clutching her belly, feeling as though someone had punched her in the gut.

Marvin's heart hurt as he watched the moments unfold.

"Mama," Marlee cried. "How did the baby die?"

"He tried to come too early."

Marlee didn't understand but refrained from asking more.

Melanie covered her face. Her sobbing wracked her.

"He?" Todd asked, giving in to tears.

"It was a boy," Marvin stated. "We . . ." His broken voice trailed off.

Everyone stayed close to Meredith on the bed, filling every inch of space across the double mattress. Their presence seemed to infuse her with strength. Several minutes passed before Marvin told the kids to go to the kitchen.

They plodded down the hall in silence. Marvin warmed three cans of Campbell's chicken noodle soup and tossed a loaf of white bread on the table. Melanie set out the butter dish and took it upon herself to bring a jar of canned cherries up from the basement. They ate a measly meal without comment or complaint. They cleaned up after themselves without being asked. No one went outside to play. Instead, they sat together in the living room, each equally subdued. There was no bickering about what to watch on TV, and Melanie kept Troy content, helping him build tall towers with wooden blocks.

Because of the late miscarriage, plans quickly changed for the Becket family, and they stayed put. It was 1967; Marlee was six years old and disappointed. Losing her baby brother was sad. So was the missed opportunity to start again in a new school. She wanted to be the new girl but had no idea why. She wasn't unhappy. In her young mind, relocating meant adventure and excitement.

Pheasant hunting in South Dakota had been delayed a week. Ruby Simon suggested it, and everyone agreed it was a good idea. When the time came, she and Alvin went to Green Bay to gather Troy and his things. Meredith wrote a note to the school requesting that Todd be excused, as he would finally join the adults on their fall hunting trip.

The year their mother died, the three children had traveled west with the adults. Anne wasn't a hunter, so it worked well, as she kept the children from getting underfoot. They'd stayed at a property owned by a wonderful family whom Sam and Bernice knew from previous hunting trips. They had private accommodations, but Marvin still told Meredith he wouldn't be in favor of taking *all* the children hunting ever again. It had been too much, he admitted. And now, he said, they would have no one to watch the children.

Alice Bogart agreed to care for the kids for a second year for the same amount of money; however, she would have the responsibility of two girls rather than three children.

The sisters found Alice as they remembered her, complete with Rice Krispies treats and mandated time outdoors every afternoon after school.

Marlee looked forward to watching *The Early Show* during "Elvis Week," but because the girls had to play outside, she, unfortunately, missed Monday's movie, *Fun in Acapulco*. That did not sit well with her, so she devised a plan and defied Alice. Aware that the woman liked to recline—her afternoon siesta, as she called it—Marlee watched and waited outside until she saw Alice through the bedroom window, drawing the shade against the afternoon sun. Seizing the opportunity, Marlee quietly entered the house against Melanie's advice. She tiptoed to the living room, clicked on the TV, cringing at the sound, and looked over her shoulder. She kept the volume low and sat on the floor, not four feet from the television.

"What, young lady, do you think you're doing?"

Marlee jumped, and she snapped her head around. "I—I always watch *The—The Early Show* if I like what's on. My mom lets me."

"Your mother, young lady, is not here. Now, is she? You know my rules. Outside."

"I want—Al—Alice, please. I want—"

Alice silenced Marlee with her arm extended, her palm in the girl's face, warning her to stop. "I won't listen to your complaining. I'll call you in for supper. You kids need fresh air for a good night's sleep. I keep telling you that."

Marlee could hardly believe it. Anger boiled in her veins. Tears stung her eyes. She wanted to tell Alice to go home, to pound sand—like her dad sometimes said. And she vowed, then and there, to tell her folks what a mean old lady Alice Bogart turned out to be. And she would ask if they could *please* find someone different to stay with them the next time they left for South Dakota.

"Told you so."

"Shut up, Melanie!"

The following morning, the phone rang shortly after ten. The school secretary summoned Alice to pick up Marlee. The child didn't feel well.

"I'm on my way. I'm not far." She sounded flustered. "I'll be there momentarily."

Alice found her way to the office. "What's wrong? Does your belly or head hurt?" she asked Marlee.

"My belly," she lied.

"When we get home, I'll fix you a mug of warm chicken broth if you think you can manage it. In the meantime, I want you to get into your pajamas and crawl into bed."

"Can I go on the sofa?" Marlee asked, hoping to be there still when *The Early Show* aired.

"I don't think that's best."

"Aw, c'mon! Why not?"

"That's enough," Alice scolded.

Marlee was mad and refused the broth and everything else offered to her. She didn't leave the bedroom except to go to the bathroom. It nearly killed her when Alice forbade her, a second time that day, from watching the Elvis movie.

"I don't think she gets it," Marlee complained to Melanie later. "Tell her how much I like to watch Elvis."

"It sounds like she's made up her mind."

"You're not even gonna try and help?"

"It's not that big of a deal, Marlee."

"Maybe not to you, but dang it, it is to me!"

Melanie glared at her. "I think you need to forget about it."

Marlee huffed, "Go away!"

Meredith had asked Alice to accompany the girls to watch the high school homecoming parade on Friday, even though they only had to walk to the corner to view it. The route went south down Oneida Street. Alice suggested they bring lawn chairs. The girls declined, insisting they'd rather stand, so the elderly woman sat alone, wondering why she needed to be there.

The girls enjoyed the four floats the freshman through senior classes constructed, especially the one with a giant kettle "cooking" the opponent's mascot—a redbird flailing about. Marlee thought the homecoming court couples waving to the crowd from atop the backseats of convertible cars were neat. It looked like something she might want to do one day. The volunteer firemen threw candy—black and orange–wrapped chewy peanut butter kisses—while sounding a bell on a vintage fire truck. The girls collected plenty, and Alice accepted a piece Melanie offered her. The high school band played the school song as they marched by.

"Can we go to the homecoming game tonight?" Melanie asked Alice.

"Football? Your mother didn't say a word to me about taking you girls to a football game."

"We might go if our parents were here."

"I'm sorry. I'm neither interested in football nor want to sit on wooden bleachers."

"They're not wooden," Marlee noted. "They have metal stands."

"It's all the same to me. I'm sorry, no."

"It's all right," Melanie shrugged.

Marvin and Meredith returned home, rejuvenated by Mother Nature. Todd gushed continually about the trip. He'd bagged his share of birds.

Todd selected off-white crewneck sweatshirts in three sizes for his parents to give to his siblings, each featuring an identical proud pheasant on the front with *Aberdeen, South Dakota* stitched in red cursive.

The Simons brought Troy home on Sunday morning after the rest of the family attended Mass. He arrived with a stockpile of new clothes, toys, and even cold, hard cash—probably a pound of coins in a worn-leather drawstring bag.

"How's my boy?" Meredith beamed, nuzzling him under his chin, causing him to belly laugh.

"He sure missed all of you," Alvin offered.

"I imagine I'll have to undo the spoiling you and Ma doused him with. Am I right? Probably as soon as this evening—hmm? Bedtime, I'm guessing. You probably held him, Ma, every night until he fell asleep?" Beseeching her mother's eyes, she dared her to answer honestly.

Ruby laughed guiltily. "What are grandparents for, if not for spoiling their grandchildren?"

"I wonder if a week with you and Pa is worth it," Meredith teased.

"By the looks of the clothes they bought him, yes, definitely worth it!" Marvin chuckled.

"Says the parent who will go to work tomorrow, leaving me with all the dirty work."

"It can't possibly be as bad as all that," Ruby dramatically rolled her eyes.

"Oh, yes, it can. Trust me, Mother."

"Hey!" Marlee exclaimed.

"Straw's cheaper," Marvin quipped. Meredith groaned.

"You guys want to know something?" Marlee said. "Awful Alice wouldn't let me watch *The Early Show*! Can you believe that?"

"Awful Alice?" Meredith raised an eyebrow.

Melanie tattled on her sister. "Yeah, Marlee snuck in once when we were supposed to stay outside. She turned the TV on when she wasn't supposed to. Alice got mad."

"Yeah!" Marlee felt the disappointment all over again. "Next year—"

"You little sneak," Marvin interrupted, suppressing an urge to laugh. "Alice *did* report that you came home from school one day when you didn't feel well. She said you thought you could lie on the sofa all afternoon watching television." He did not let on that he saw humor in her antics.

"Yeah!" Marlee scoffed. "But she didn't let me do that either. That woman frustrated me!" The adults laughed. "Can you get someone different next year?"

"That's a long way off," Meredith told her daughter.

"Please! I won't be able to stand it."

"We'll talk next fall." Marvin hoped she would forget.

Marlee struggled with the transition to first grade. Her parents recognized this when Meredith began receiving phone calls after a few weeks of school starting, asking her to pick up their *sick* child. The teacher also called and spoke with Meredith. "Marlee frequently gets discouraged with the worksheets she's expected to complete daily in class," Mrs. VandenLangenberg explained. "I'm afraid the concepts aren't clicking."

"How can we help her?"

"I'll send home extra worksheets if you could reinforce the concepts."

"Yes, please do that," Meredith said, encouraged. "We'll work with Marlee each evening."

"Excellent. I'll start immediately. I'll also update you periodically. We can discuss it further at parent–teacher conferences."

Two days later, Marlee complained at the breakfast table that she felt sick. Her parents exchanged a knowing look.

"What are you feeling?" her mother asked.

"My belly hurts."

Marvin cleared his throat. He approached his daughter as she rose from her place at the kitchen table. He exhaled. Getting down on one knee to face her at her level, he gently took hold of her arms and looked directly into her eyes. "Marlee, do you remember when I explained what it means to be nervous or anxious?"

"Yes," she said, frowning. Standing close to the table, she heard her Rice Krispies snap, crackle, and pop in the milk inches away from her head. She knew with each passing moment that the cereal was getting soggier.

"Okay. Well, you need to stay at school today, all day—every day. Do you understand me? You cannot have the school secretary call your mother again to fetch you unless you are ill. And you've not been ill, not really, have you? You get nervous, Marlee, but the way for you to work through this is to stay at school. It will get better. I'm sure of it." He paused. "Can you get that?"

She nodded, tears welling, threatening to spill over.

"I know first grade is different from kindergarten," Marvin acknowledged compassionately, "but that's how it is now. You're older; this is what's expected, and everyone goes through this."

"They do?" Her bottom lip trembled.

"Yes, to one degree or another. But it'll get better. I know it will. Believe me when I tell you this." Marvin rose to his full height. Kissed the top of her head. "Finish your breakfast."

Marlee's appetite was gone. In its place were knots, and her nose started to run. Meredith passed her a napkin.

"I'm not hungry, and my cereal's soggy."

"I know, sweetie," Meredith nodded sympathetically. She reached for the abandoned bowl and rinsed the remains down the garbage disposal.

Todd snatched the last two purple grapes from Marlee's fruit bowl and plopped them in his mouth.

Meredith had a heavy heart watching the children leave. She felt for Marlee, and to take her mind off things, besides tending to Troy's needs, she immersed herself in household chores. Both times when the telephone rang, she jumped, feeling leery. The first call came from a pleasant-sounding woman soliciting homemade goodies for an upcoming church bake sale. Her husband also called.

"I want to remind you that I won't be home for lunch. Remember, I'm taking a customer out." Meredith suspected he also wanted to check whether anyone from school had phoned. But he didn't ask, and she didn't offer.

"I remembered," she smiled to herself. "Enjoy. I'll see you after work." Meredith did not need a reminder whenever her husband would not be home for lunch. It was something a wife did not forget—being free to do as she pleased. If she wanted a slice of cheese or a folded-over peanut butter sandwich rather than preparing an actual meal for two, that was her choice. Sure, there were days when Meredith only warmed up leftovers, but other days she put forth real effort.

She turned to Troy. "What should we eat?"

"Coco Puffs," he smiled.

"What's your second choice?"

"Tony Tiger."

"Frosted flakes? How about something other than cereal? I'll tell you what. I'll give you some choices. Would you like a bologna or liverwurst sandwich, or soup?"

"Iverwurst," he said, mispronouncing the word.

Meredith scooped up her son. "Iverwurst it is," she giggled, strapping Troy into his highchair.

The telephone remained quiet the entire afternoon, and for that, Meredith was grateful. While Troy napped, she did something she usually saved for the evenings. She read a book—a cheesy Harlequin Romance. Joanna White loaned her paperbacks faster than Meredith could keep up. She usually managed maybe five or six romance novels a year.

The girls returned home from school, and Marlee tore off her coat and hat.

"It's hot in here," she said.

"It's cozy," Melanie smiled.

"I have a roast in the oven," Meredith explained. "How was school today?" She specifically looked at Marlee, thankful she'd made it all day. And Meredith refrained from pointing that out as she wanted to hear what Marlee had to say without her influence.

"Same as yesterday," Melanie reported.

"Yeah, same as yesterday," Marlee echoed.

Meredith raised an eyebrow.

"I have homework," Melanie offered.

Still nothing more from Marlee. Interesting, Meredith thought. But she would let sleeping dogs lie.

The radio played "Oh, Pretty Woman" by Roy Orbison. Meredith hummed to the music. "Your mother loved this song."

"What?" Melanie snapped her head around.

"Pretty Woman," she said. "That was Anne's—your mother's—new favorite song."

"It was? Really? I *love* knowing that!" Melanie smiled widely.

"It's my favorite song, too."

"Right, Marlee."

"It wasn't on the radio long be—never mind," Meredith shook her head.

"Long before what?" Melanie probed.

"Nothing."

Melanie tilted her head questioningly. "Tell us."

"It was a newer song. That's all." Meredith hesitated momentarily. "Yeah, Anne liked it." A weak smile turned up the corners of her mouth.

The sisters shared an ambivalent smile. That was the type of random fact about their first mother they searched for repeatedly throughout their lives. And they gladly accepted any nugget offered that could help them better discover the precious woman they longed to know. They especially liked it when someone—often a stranger to them—told either girl, "You look like Anne." It usually happened at an event where they were introduced to someone who knew her. And they beamed with that knowledge. A couple of older cousins regularly told them that, too, especially as the sisters grew up.

Cousin Maria frequently gushed about their mother. "Aunt Anne dressed so cool. She made many of her clothes, you know. That's what my mother told me," Maria had happily informed them. "I remember her wearing short shorts, halter tops, and sundresses. She always painted her fingernails red. So fashionable she was. With the times, you know." The sisters were all ears. "Your mother was the baby of her family. Did you know that? My mother was one of the older ones. I looked up to your mom."

Melanie's eyes had filled with tears.

"Oh gosh, I don't mean to make you cry," Maria said sadly.

"It's okay. I like to hear it. We both do."

Meredith entered the girls' bedroom as they crawled into bed for the night. She sat on the edge of the mattress, listened as the two prayed their rote bedtime prayer.

Marlee closed her eyes and continued, "God bless Mom and Dad. Melanie, Todd, and Troy. God bless Grandma and Grandpa Becket and Grandma and Grandpa Simon. And please, God, bless our other mom and Duane, and Grandma and Grandpa Novak." She squeezed her eyelids tighter. "Amen," she said.

"You know," Meredith began, "God never gives you more than you can handle."

"Really?" Marlee asked.

"Really." She crossed her daughters' foreheads and kissed them. "Sleep tight, sweet dreams." She pulled the door partly closed behind her.

A beef stew supper in the oven had an hour to go. While they waited, the Becket children watched television. Meredith recognized the opening theme song to *Gilligan's Island*. She knew the time without looking at the clock. "Marlee," she called, "let's get your worksheets and flashcards done."

Together, they read and reviewed the reading comprehension pages.

"Where is Dick going?" Meredith asked Marlee, pointing to each word as she read.

"Apple picking."

"Good. Who is Dick going with?"

"Jane."

"How many apples do they need?"

"Eighteen."

"Why do they want apples?"

"To eat and for Mother to make a pie."

"Very good. Let's review your flashcards. See how many words you recognize."

Marlee rattled off words: "And, the, for, I, see, you, look."

Meredith interrupted, "I need to shuffle these. Okay, start again."

"Sat, dog, my, look, boy, and, cat, I, the, you, how, see, girl, me, for, from, did." Marlee took a deep breath.

"Nice." Meredith smiled. They finished the stack. "Now, read this whole sentence."

Marlee followed with her finger, reading carefully not to miss a word, then hurried to the end, "I—see—the—cat—and—my—dog—Spot—sees the cat."

"Good." They read more sentences before Marlee practiced rhyming words. It was clear to Meredith that Marlee liked the rhyming exercises best. When they had done enough, Meredith excused her daughter. Marlee skipped to the living room, singing, "Cat, hat, sat, sat, hat, mat, dog, hog, log, log, hog, dog . . ."

"Shush. We can't hear," Melanie complained.

The first weekend of the annual deer hunting season seemed like a carbon copy of the previous year. Because of the Packers' schedule, Marvin went north alone early Saturday morning for opening day, leaving before sunrise and returning home that evening after bagging a four-pointer.

Sunday, the San Francisco 49ers came to town to take on the Green Bay Packers. The Packers shut them out, 13–0.

The family traveled to Suring for Thanksgiving Day. Alvin and Ruby joined them. Bernice prepared traditional dishes with one dessert change-up. In addition to the usual pumpkin pies, she whipped up a delicious bread pudding.

"This pudding's tastier than mine," Ruby complimented Bernice.

"Nice of you to say. I had a hankering, so I thought, why not?"

"Why not, indeed," Ruby agreed.

Meredith sat in the woods on Friday morning for almost five hours and decided she'd had enough. A deer never crossed her path, but she had heard plenty of shots, which may have explained why she saw nothing.

The deer tags were all filled by Saturday before lunch, so most adults gathered around the large dining room table in the afternoon for several hands of cards, mostly Schafkopf. Laughter and a bit of playful bickering filled the room.

"You gotta be cheating!" Buzzy accused his brother.

"I guess you're just not very good," Marvin said.

"Seriously, how do you do it?" Buzzy poured another martini and lit another cigarette.

"You better water it down," Sam teased, "or he'll surely whip your ass."

"Ah, everyone knows it's just the luck of the draw."

Marvin laughed.

After church and breakfast on Sunday morning, Buzzy and Francine left for Milwaukee. Everyone else gathered around the television to watch the Packers take on the Bears in Chicago. Marvin knew his brother would listen to the broadcast on the car radio. Green Bay prevailed in a close game, winning 17–13.

Meredith and Marvin hosted friends for the NFL championship game between the Packers and the Dallas Cowboys on December 31, 1967. The New Year's Eve temperature was a frigid thirteen degrees below zero. The Becket kids watched the adults dress for the weather in their kitchen and living room, adding several layers of warm clothing before they ventured out to Lambeau Field. No one left any earlier than necessary, and they took thermoses of hot coffee with them.

Luann Curtain walked over to babysit. Todd and two of his buddies left for the stadium shortly before kickoff. Without tickets in hand, they scaled a fence and landed on the other side, obscured from view by a parked trailer. The boys cautiously surveyed their surroundings.

"We're in," Chris said.

Many people still walked on the concourse, making their way to their seats. Todd figured that played in their favor, and there was less chance of them being seen by security.

Terry and Todd soon realized they had been spotted.

"They see us!" Terry shouted.

Todd grabbed Chris by his jacket. "Run!" he yelled and led the way, threading them through the crowd to the nearest bathroom.

"Wow, that was close!" Terry said, catching his breath. "That ticket taker saw us. I knew he couldn't get us, though. He was fat," he laughed.

The boys waited in the warm restroom for several minutes, hoping not to be noticed when they left.

"Let's walk out one at a time," Todd suggested.

"And go where?" Terry wanted to know.

"My parents sit in the south end zone, first row. How about we meet there?"

"Sure," Terry agreed.

"Okay," Chris nodded.

Todd tried to disguise himself by pulling his hood over his hat. Chris left first, then Terry, then Todd, his heart beating fast. He didn't want to get caught and thrown out of the stadium before seeing a down.

The boys made their separate ways to the south end zone. There wasn't room to sit with Marvin and Meredith. Everyone had seemingly shown up, bundled up, and filled every inch of the bleachers. Todd, Terry, and Chris squeezed together in a corner section of the end zone, many rows up, to watch their team. It wasn't a bad vantage point. But then again, there weren't really any bad seats.

"Damn, it's cold," Terry complained with a puff of breath, moving his booted feet, trying to keep his blood circulating.

After fumbling twice in the first half, Green Bay held the lead, 14–10. Neither team scored in the third quarter. But now, late in the fourth quarter, the Packers trailed by three. Less than five minutes remained on the clock. The Packers' offense marched downfield to inside the one-yard line. A time-out was called with just sixteen seconds left to play. Coach Vince Lombardi was not interested in a game-tying field goal to go to sudden-death overtime. He told his players to run the ball. Dallas Coach Tom Landry told his defense that Green Bay would have to throw the football. If they ran and didn't score, they would be out of time and couldn't attempt a game-tying field goal. The crowd held its collective breath, awaiting the snap. Bart Starr decided to keep the ball on a quarterback sneak. He plunged into the end zone, scoring a touchdown in the waning seconds. The crowd erupted in cheers. Fifty-thousand-plus people, cold and some undoubtedly frostbitten, went wild. The Packers kicked the extra point to defeat the Cowboys 21–17.

Fans stormed the field. Several climbed the goalpost, including Todd and his buddies. Grown men worked together, rocking it back and forth until it snapped. Todd and several gloved fans hauled a large section of the gold upright out of the stadium, and he told them they could cut it up at his house. He led them east down the parking lot along the back of the houses on Stadium Drive.

"That's my house, the green one!" Todd shouted as they got close. "Go through the gate!"

Surprised to see a group with a chunk of goalpost, Marvin, having arrived before they did, retrieved two hacksaws from the garage. In the backyard, the men sawed the hollow stem into roughly eight-inch pieces and distributed them to hovering fans who strode away jubilantly with their souvenirs. A five-foot-long piece remained. Todd and Chris carried it into the garage to finish cutting it later. The boys had yet to claim their portion of the authentic goalpost.

In all the excitement, Terry said he forgot how cold he was. "But man, I gotta get inside, get these boots off. My toes are frozen!"

History dubbed that memorable football game *The Ice Bowl*. And Lambeau Field earned the catchy, fun nickname *The Frozen Tundra*.

The defending NFL champion Green Bay Packers met the AFL champion Oakland Raiders on January 14, 1968, in Miami, Florida. The Packers dominated most of the game, putting it away when cornerback Herb Adderley returned an interception sixty yards for a touchdown. The Pack won 33–14 and, with that victory, became three-time World Champions. The following year, that final game of the season officially became known as the *Super Bowl*. In effect, the Green Bay Packers won the first two Super Bowls.

Most of the city and much of the state, just like the Beckets, rode the high of the Packers' success throughout the gray winter Wisconsin days. Day after day, the newspapers were chock-full of sports and human-interest stories related to the Green Bay Packers. It seemed to be all anyone could talk about.

The good luck felt around the area may have been passed on to Marlee. At least, that's what her father suggested. But truly, luck had nothing to do with it. The girl did better in school thanks largely to her mother's dedicated tutoring. As a result, Marlee grew to like school and looked forward to going. Marvin and Meredith were thankful that her earlier hiccup seemed behind them. Her report card reflected all the hard work put in, as she mostly earned satisfactory marks. Two U marks indicated unsatisfactory performance. Those came due to a lack of class participation and inconsistent conduct.

Meredith told her husband, "I'll have Marlee continue with the extra worksheets until the end of the school year, and I'll encourage her to raise her hand. Participate more in class. See if she can't bring that grade up. What's your plan to help improve her conduct grade?"

"Prayer," he answered.

"She is a work in progress. I guess we all are."

"Maybe she'll outgrow it. Todd did."

"Oh?"

"He was rambunctious, too. Had similar temperament at her age."

"I would not have necessarily thought that."

"He did."

"Hmm," Meredith mused. She wondered when he had outgrown it and how long she'd likely have to wait for Marlee.

CHAPTER 9

WINTER PASSED SLOWLY. TODD and Troy celebrated their fourteenth and second birthdays. Todd received mostly money and some clothes as gifts. Troy received more toys than anything else.

Easter came and went. And Melanie and Marlee celebrated their eleventh and seventh birthdays. Melanie especially liked a gift she'd received from her godparents—her Aunt Francine and Uncle Buzzy—via the United States Postal Service. A small package arrived containing a five-dollar bill wrapped around a glass tube of lip gloss. That was a surprise since sometimes when they sent a gift, it was a pretty sweater or blouse from the Boston Store, where Francine worked part-time. Marlee was partial to a hot pink rain slicker she'd received from Grandma and Grandpa Simon. She loved the sheen of the waterproof fabric.

One spring afternoon, she ditched her rain jacket when the sun came out, and she and Eloise played with some kids from the top of the block. They lined up six across on their bicycles and raced down the street. Marlee remembered Brett signaling the start of the race.

"On your mark, get set, go!"

But that was the last thing Marlee remembered before finding herself in a crumpled heap on the faded blacktop beside her bike, just fifteen feet from the starting line. She shook her head and tried to mount her bicycle. Feeling woozy, she opted to walk the bike to where Eloise stood at the bottom of the street. The friends met partway up the hill.

"What happened?"

"I fell."

"How?"

"Heck if I know. I just did." Marlee flung her leg out to show Eloise the scrape on her right knee.

"I bet that stings."

"Yup. Let's go to my house. I need a band-aid. Who won?"

"Danny."

"Figures."

The end of the school year finally arrived. Mrs. VandenLangenberg distributed report cards just minutes before the dismissal bell rang. Marlee saw that the sealed envelope was addressed to "The Parents of Marlee Becket" and written in neat cursive penmanship. She tucked it into her book bag. That meant she would not see her marks before her parents did.

Melanie met her sister at the bike rack. Marlee watched her pull out a key strung on a piece of worn brown leather from the inside of her blouse. She opened the padlock that locked their bicycles together and coiled the plastic-coated chain around the stem beneath her seat.

"We cleaned out our desks, and I have all my stuff," Marlee told her. "Then we sponged them down. That part was fun."

"We had to clean ours out, too, except I don't have much to bring home today. The garbage can got passed around the room, and I dumped most of my stuff. Mr. Bird said not to burden our mothers with junk."

"We got Smarties for a treat."

"We had cupcakes that Sharon Nelson's mom baked."

"Aw, you lucky duck." Marlee pedaled after her sister. It was a short ride home, and she felt free and happy.

Melanie parked in the garage. Marlee set her kickstand by the porch.

The pair found their mother in the backyard. Troy played in the sandbox, scooping sand into a lime-green pail.

"Mom!" Marlee shouted. "I got my report card!"

"Well, hello to you, too. How was the last day?"

"Open it," she insisted.

"I'll wait for Dad."

"Aw, c'mon!"

Melanie held out her report card.

"We'll look at them after Dad gets home."

Melanie plopped down on a wooden triangular seat near Troy and ran her fingers through the cool sand. "We mostly cleaned our desks and helped Mr. Bird tear down his bulletin boards. Sharon Nelson brought cupcakes, and Bonnie Derks brought fruit punch. Mr. Bird let us listen to the radio."

"That sounds nice."

"Yeah, it was all right," Melanie agreed.

"Can I get Eloise?" Marlee wanted to know.

"Go ahead. But change your clothes first," Meredith reminded her.

Eloise and Marlee played hopscotch with Sally VandeGarde. Eloise had just tossed her stone when Marlee saw her dad's car turn the corner. "Gotta go!" she said, dropping her stone and galloping across the road.

Marlee accosted her father as he stepped from the car. "Hey, Dad!" she jumped into his arms.

"Hi, Marlee. Hey, you're too big to carry." He set her down before they reached the porch.

"We got our report cards. Mom said we had to wait for you."

"How was your day?" Marvin kissed Meredith on the cheek.

She leaned into his kiss. "Fine. Yours?"

"Not bad."

Troy raised his arms to his father. "Uppie."

"You I can handle. How's my boy?"

"The girls brought home their report cards. I told them we would wait for you."

"So I heard. Let me get this tie off first." He put Troy down and knelt on one knee before him.

"Melanie!" Marlee yelled, "Dad's home. He just took off his tie."

Melanie scampered into the kitchen. The kids watched their father as he waved his hand over the Windsor knot.

"Hocus, pocus, dominocus!" The knot released with a singular pull as if by magic. His little performance never ceased to wow them.

"We got our report cards," Melanie announced.

"That's right, last day of school. Look out! The Becket kids are free."

"Aw, Dad," Marlee said. "All the kids are free. For the whole dang summer."

"Woo-hoo!" he cheered. "Okay, well, let's see how you did. Gimme those report cards."

Meredith opened the envelopes before passing them to her husband.

"Let's see." He silently perused Melanie's grades before clapping her on the back. "Nice job, Melly." He read aloud, "Reading—A. Arithmetic—B. Science—A. Social Studies—B+. Language—B. Spelling—A. Penmanship—A. Art—A. Music—B. Phys. Ed—B. And Conduct—A. Whew! All As and Bs. You did well. Way to go," Marvin beamed. He reached for his daughter and squeezed.

Meredith agreed. "You earned a good report card, Melanie."

"Thank you," she smiled shyly.

"Okay, what does Miss Marlee's say?" Marvin silently read both the front and back. "Well, Marlee, you did all right. You improved in three areas for sure. No big fat Us."

"None?"

"Hmm," Meredith pursed her lips.

"Nope. You earned mostly Ss, even an S+ for Effort. You got an S– for Conduct. Not terrible. It's an improvement. You do have an I for Class Participation, however. I means," he searched for the key. "I is for 'Improving, but not as yet satisfactory.' Your teacher wrote a comment: 'It was a pleasure having Marlee in class and getting to know her. Her extra work paid off. Marlee is promoted to the second grade.' How about that?"

She jumped up and hugged her dad. "Good job," he said.

"Your hard work did pay off, Marlee," her mother acknowledged. "Of course, there's always room for improvement."

"For sure," Marvin nodded. "What do you say we go for ice cream after supper?"

"Yes!" shouted his offspring.

"Where's Todd? Did he bring home a report card?"

"He's at baseball practice," Melanie informed him.

"I believe his report card will arrive in the mail," Meredith noted.

Two weeks after school let out, the Beckets woke early and drove south, headed to Florida for a ten-day vacation. Marvin said he always wanted to swim in the Atlantic Ocean.

"Except you never swim," Todd shrugged his shoulders.

"Well, that's about to change," Marvin pointed at him.

"Do you even own a swimsuit?" Melanie asked.

Ever since the accident, Marvin had been self-conscious of his body. He bore a long, ragged scar down his belly.

"You don't even wear shorts, Dad, ever," Todd said.

"No one wants to see my bowlegged sticks. But I am going into the ocean. Mark my words. Your mother bought me a swimsuit."

"I would call it a swim outfit."

"Outfit? You have an outfit?" Todd roared.

Melanie's eyes widened, and she bust a gut, too. Everyone laughed, even Troy.

"Having fun at my expense, are you?"

"I'm sorry," Meredith said teasingly. And to the children, she explained, "It's not that crazy. It's a tank top and a pair of shorts sewn together, an all-in-one swimsuit."

"I can't wait to see you, Dad," Marlee grinned. "Will you wear it to the pool tonight?"

"Nope. It's for the Atlantic Ocean only—a one-time deal."

"We'll have to take his picture," Melanie chuckled.

"Oh, we will," Meredith agreed, with a little chuckle of her own. "We definitely will."

Marvin planned to drive for a full day, reach Kentucky before nightfall. They had reservations at a Holiday Inn in Louisville.

Earlier in the day, they stopped at a wayside to eat lunch. Their Coleman cooler contained meatloaf sandwiches, carrot sticks, milk, and more food for future meals. They also ate potato chips and homemade chocolate chip cookies and shared two thermos bottles of tepid water.

The kids busied themselves on the ride with books and travel bingo. They liked it when they found vehicles with out-of-state license plates. They had their share of squabbles, too.

"Stop jabbing me in the side!" Todd complained to Marlee.

"I'm just colorin'. Geez!"

Meredith turned to the backseat, where Marlee sat in the middle. "Why don't you move closer to your sister?" she suggested. "Give your brother more room."

"I need it for colorin'."

"Move!" Marvin demanded loudly.

His unexpected command startled her. It startled everyone. She glared at Todd. Moved an exaggerated distance from him.

Everyone was hungry when they arrived at the motel, the supper hour upon them. After checking in at the front desk, they lugged their bags and cooler to room 212. Meredith commented on the weather, saying it was muggy. The air-conditioned burger joint next door, with its flashy neon sign, beckoned.

The menu featured milkshakes—a real treat—with hamburgers and French fries. Marlee chose strawberry, Melanie chose chocolate, and Todd decided on banana. Troy happily sampled all three flavors.

After eating, the kids changed into swimsuits, grabbed towels, fins, and swim goggles, complete with plastic breathing tubes, and tromped to the outdoor pool. Their parents followed behind. Marvin blew into a small Donald Duck inflatable ring.

The kids played, swimming and splashing for an hour. Todd and Melanie dove off the diving board. Marlee bounced before leaping feet first. Meredith let Troy dabble near the steps in the shallow end.

Later, back in the motel room, the boys shared a double bed—one side banked with rolled blankets for Troy's safety. The girls slept on the floor, taking the first night in the sleeping bags. Sufficiently exhausted, everyone fell fast asleep without complaint.

The following morning, the family ate breakfast in their motel room before Marvin drove them a short distance to Churchill Downs Racetrack. The Kentucky Derby took place over a month ago, on the first Saturday in May. The American Thoroughbred, Dancer's Image, won the race but was disqualified after failing post-race testing. Officials had discovered prohibited drugs in the stallion's urine. He was the first winning horse to be disqualified in the history of the Derby. Todd had a copy of the *Sports Illustrated* magazine in the car, where the cover story drama unfolded on the inside pages. Following the disqualification, the second-place finisher and favorite in the race, Forward Pass, was declared the Derby winner.

The family strolled the grounds.

"It's not much, is it?" Meredith commented. "A big dirt track with paddocks and fences."

"Where are the horses and all the little, short people who ride them?" Marlee asked.

"They're called jockeys, you imbecile."

"Todd!" Meredith scolded. "That is an awful thing to call your sister. You will not do that again." She turned to Marlee. "They're jockeys. Now you know."

Marlee frowned at her brother. He shook his head.

"Yeah, where are the horses?" Melanie asked.

"We're too late to see them training," Todd explained.

"We should have gotten here before breakfast then," Marlee grumbled.

"No," Marvin said. "I think your brother is trying to tell you that we may have been able to see the horses train in the days before the derby. I don't know that they're here anymore."

"They're not," Todd said.

"It would be something to see this place on race day," Meredith commented. "Wouldn't it be fun to see the flowers and all the big, crazy hats?"

"Those twin spires are cool, though, huh?" Todd looked up at the grandstand, taking it all in. "I'm glad we came."

Troy toddled around the grounds, his little legs working hard to keep pace. Marvin scooped him up onto his shoulders, and he squealed. He liked his new vantage point.

They visited the gift shop, and with some of their allowance money, the girls purchased small resin horses. Melanie selected a sleek black one. Marlee chose a brown horse. Marvin bought a commemorative pint glass for behind the bar in the basement. Meredith considered a plastic toy horse for Troy but set it back in the bin. He didn't know the difference.

"You're not getting anything?" Meredith asked Todd.

"Nah, I'm saving my money for something later. I have the magazine. That's kind of like a souvenir."

They grabbed lunch at a local sandwich shop. Marvin raved about his choice—shredded smoked pork on a chewy roll. Meredith said the pimento cheese she ordered was delicious, with just the right amount of spice. The kids were less adventurous in their selections—simple ham and cheese and roast beef on plain white rolls.

"Everyone needs to use the restroom again before we leave," Marvin insisted, "because our next stop is the Grand Ole Opry in Nashville—about a two-and-a-half-hour drive."

Troy crawled across the front seat to sit between his parents. The three older kids settled in the back. Melanie looked out the window at the passing scenery. Marlee played with a Barbie doll, flipping it haphazardly. Todd read a comic book.

"Oh, ugh!" he suddenly groaned. Meredith turned around. Todd brought the back of his hand to his face like a shield. "Did you fart, Marlee?"

"Todd! What have I told you?" Meredith vehemently shook her head. "You're *not* to use that word. It's vulgar, and I don't want you kids talking like that. I've said this before. This isn't new." She sounded frustrated.

"Sorry," Todd rolled his eyes. "Who let a *stinker*?" He made fun of the last word.

Melanie giggled. She pinched her nostrils shut.

"I couldn't help it," Marlee admitted.

The smell must have wafted to the front because Marvin cracked open his window.

"Silent but deadly," Todd groaned.

Meredith stifled a chuckle. Marvin laughed outright.

Fart was one of three *F* words forbidden in the Becket home, not including the king of all *F* words—no one dared to even think of *that* one, the one that rhymes with "duck"! But undoubtedly, *fart, fem,* and *fag* were unacceptable, and Meredith was adamant they would not become part of the kids' vocabulary.

The stop at the Grand Ole Opry amused the adults more than the kids. They weren't overly interested in country music and were unfamiliar with many artists.

Meredith loved country singer Patsy Cline, and she had mourned her death five years earlier when the singer perished in a small plane crash. Patsy's orange-colored *Showcase* album cover pictured the pretty brunette seated, one leg drawn up to her chest and her feet clad in gold, glitter-like booties. The album stood first on a rack full of records in the Becket living room, next to the stereo. Meredith often swayed while she listened to Patsy belt out her hits. "I Fall to Pieces" and "Crazy" were two favorites. The kids heard those songs enough times that they could sing along.

"I would give anything to see Johnny Cash and June Carter Cash sing their duet," Meredith told her husband. She liked the song "Jackson."

"How about seeing Glen Campbell or Roy Clark?"

"Any one of them would be a thrill."

"Are there any singers here now?" Melanie asked.

"There's a variety show on stage this week, but it's in the evening. We just came to see the auditorium where so much great music is sung," Meredith explained.

"Exciting place," Todd whispered to Melanie. She elbowed him in his ribs. "We're striking out—first no horses and now no singers," he said.

They toured the country opera house and received a cardboard handheld fan that pictured the Grand Ole Opry. A tongue depressor–type stick glued to the back served as the handle. An up-and-coming country singer they did not know introduced himself and autographed it. His signature was illegible. It may have been signed by a Billy something or other.

"Let me see that," Marlee said to her mother, reaching for the fan. Instead of handing it over, Meredith fluttered it lightly over her daughter's face. "I want to see it," she said again.

"Your mother wants to keep that as a souvenir," Marvin said knowingly. It was chintzy, but Meredith liked to save that type of thing.

"I want to tack it up on the wall in the barroom by your glass from Churchill Downs."

"Good idea," Marvin nodded.

The kids' pace quickened when their father announced they needed to get going.

"Are we gonna stop later for something to eat?" Todd inquired.

"There are snacks to tide you over," Marvin stated. "We're going to drive to Atlanta before we stop for the night." Another Holiday Inn had a reservation in their name.

Meredith accessed the cooler in the trunk. On their way out of town, they noshed on cheese and sausage, crackers, venison jerky, and grapes.

"How far to Atlanta?" Todd tapped the back of the front seat.

"Three-and-a-half to four hours," Marvin replied.

"Will we be able to swim when we get there?"

"You should have time."

"Maybe we can order a pizza for delivery," Meredith suggested.

"Where are we going tomorrow?" Melanie wanted to know.

"We'll continue to Florida," Marvin said.

"What does that mean?" Todd asked. "Will we stop to see anything in Georgia?"

"Not planning on it. We'll have breakfast in the room and stop somewhere for lunch, but tomorrow's a day of driving."

"How much driving?"

"Six, seven hours, more with gas and food stops," Marvin told them. "We'll get to Daytona by late afternoon."

"Can we swim in the morning before we leave?" Melanie inquired.

"We'll see how the morning goes."

They arrived in Daytona a little weary and a bit testy from the long ride. They stopped three times—once for lunch and gas, and twice more for gas and bathroom breaks.

The next day, the children could hardly wait to see and experience the Atlantic Ocean up close and personal. Marvin warned them it would be different from what they were used to. "Remember, it won't be like swimming in Boulder Lake. The ocean is salt water, and let me tell you, if it gets in your eyes, it can sting something fierce."

"I'm gonna keep my eyes closed." Marlee bebopped about the motel room in her swimsuit and terry cloth cover-up. Troy fed off her excitement and did his own little dance around the room.

Meredith gathered two canvas bags with towels, sunblock, hats, sunglasses, goggles, and sand toys. Marvin and Todd filled the cooler with fresh ice and beverages. The girls grabbed two beach blankets.

It was a short drive to the ocean, and they could not have asked for better beach weather—sunny, humid, a hot eighty-seven degrees.

Marvin disappeared into a clapboard-sided changing station.

"Where's Dad?" Todd looked around.

"In there." Meredith pointed to a small building with a sign that read *Restrooms and Showers.* "Don't you dare laugh at your father when he comes out." She sounded serious.

Marvin emerged wearing a green-and-blue-striped one-piece swimsuit. The kids sized him up. Melanie clapped her hand over her mouth.

"Dad." Todd did his best not to smirk.

"Your legs are white," Marlee announced innocently. That was all it took. Everyone busted a gut, Marvin included.

"Yeah, yeah," he said. "Take a good look," he waved his hand through the air down the length of his body, "cause *this* ain't happening again."

Meredith shook her head and regained her composure. She had a camera strapped around her neck. "Get together for a picture," she said.

Marvin corralled his youngest son to stand before him, effectively hiding his legs in the photo.

After a few camera clicks, he asked, "So, is everybody ready?"

Meredith took Troy's hand and walked to the water. Todd blew by them, running full speed into the surf. The girls exchanged glances and squealed. Melanie grabbed her sister's hand, and swinging their arms, they counted, "One, two, three!" and took off for the water. Marlee remembered her dad's warning about saltwater and tightly pressed her eyelids closed before plunging into the ocean.

Marvin wiggled his toes in the shallow water, stirring the sand. He scanned the obscure horizon over the vast Atlantic Ocean. "This goofy getup's worth it," he smiled at his wife. Then he waded into deeper water and dove in, even getting his hair wet.

At some point, each family member touched their damp fingers to their lips, tasting salt. "How weird," Todd mused.

Marvin knew it would not be a trip to the ocean without at least one child tortured by saltwater. First, and in full dramatic fashion, came his youngest daughter.

"Oh my gosh! I can't see! It's burning! My eyes are burning!" Marlee cried angrily, pumping her right leg up and down in the sand.

Marvin grabbed a jug of water from the cooler. He poured a steady stream over her eyes. She jumped.

"That's freezing!"

"But it's fresh and will flush your eyes."

"Oh gosh!" she moaned, mashing the heels of her hands into her eye sockets.

"You'll be okay," Meredith assured her, passing a towel.

Marlee buried her face in the warm, soft terry cloth. She recognized the familiar scent of laundry soap.

"That was rough, huh?"

"I think I'm done." She plopped her butt on a blanket and reached into the cooler for an ice cube, circling her eyes with it until it melted.

Meredith sat down next to her. "Yeah, good idea—take a break."

Melanie and Todd also managed to get salt in their eyes—no surprise with all the jumping and splashing they did.

"Yeah, that stings," Todd agreed.

Melanie flushed her eyes and dabbed them with a dry towel. "I don't think I could get used to this," she said.

"You could wear goggles," Todd suggested.

Almost miraculously, Troy avoided getting any saltwater in his eyes. For that, Meredith was thankful.

The next day, the family traveled an hour to tour the Kennedy Space Center and Cape Canaveral. Marvin supported President John F. Kennedy and his efforts with the space program. He admitted that seeing the spacecraft and launch pad was thrilling. "To be here on blast off . . ." he mused. "I can only imagine what that must be like." He dreamed of talking with astronauts Alan Shepard, the first American in space, and John Glenn, the first American to orbit Earth.

Marvin Becket was not a big man—he stood five feet eight inches tall—but he appreciated the little-known fact that NASA required astronauts to be less than five eleven so they could comfortably fit in the spacecraft.

"Don't you find all this fascinating?" he asked his family.

"I don't think I could be an astronaut," Marlee said.

"Why not?"

"That stimulator thing—"

"*Simulator*," Meredith interrupted. "It's called a simulator."

"Yeah, that's too small."

"Yeah," Todd agreed. "I bet you can't be an astronaut if you're claustrophobic."

"You have a point there." Marvin nodded.

After leaving Cape Canaveral, the family stopped at a roadside stand and bought fresh, delicious citrus. They spent the better part of their last day in Florida eating oranges and grapefruit and soaking up the sun before beginning their journey home to Green Bay.

They drove for long stretches and finally stopped to sightsee in Illinois. Abraham Lincoln's large, historic home in Springfield took them a bit out of their way. Todd and Melanie, in particular, found the stop interesting. As expected, the kids studied Honest Abe, George Washington, and many presidents in school. It intrigued them to learn that despite updates and additions to the house, it never had indoor plumbing.

"That is some bold wallpaper," Meredith noted in one of the bedrooms. "I wonder what your folks would have to say."

"They don't hang paper that crazy—not in Suring anyway."

"I would like a house like this," Melanie smiled, "and to think a president lived here!"

"The sixteenth president," Todd offered.

"The home was eventually deeded to the State of Illinois in 1887 for one dollar," Marvin read aloud from a posted sign.

"One dollar?" Marlee scrunched her nose.

"Yup. One whole dollar."

History captivated Todd. He purchased a book on the American Civil War to read on the ride home.

The Beckets spent the night in Illinois at another Holiday Inn, the family motel of choice. After an early supper at a local restaurant, the children were antsy to get in the pool. They were the only people swimming. The older three wasted no time jumping into the deep end, where they enjoyed a curved slide.

Marvin scooped a towel from the tile floor to throw it over a chair, and when he stood and turned, Troy was no longer at his side. He immediately surveyed the whole room. The boy was gone. Marvin hurried to the pool edge. Realizing his worst fear, he saw his young son splayed out on the bottom. Terror seized him. He dropped to his chest, his heart hammering. With all his might, Marvin reached into the water, grabbed hold, and heaved Troy up and out by the seat of his swim trunks.

Todd surfaced from his first plunge. "Dad!"

Meredith turned. She saw the awful hold Marvin had on Troy. "What? Oh, dear Lord!" she screamed.

Marvin thumped Troy on the back. He coughed violently, and water shot out. He sputtered, expelling more water, then cried. Marvin's face had drained of all color, and he appeared breathless. With wide, frightened eyes, he dared to meet the face of his bewildered wife. She reached for Troy.

"What happened?" she trembled.

Troy coughed again. They pounded his back, and he cried. Meredith cradled him, and shaking, she sobbed.

Several seconds passed before Marvin found his voice. When he spoke, he stoically stated, "He was at the bottom of the pool."

Melanie hugged Marlee to her side, their jaws slack. Both girls burst into tears.

"I don't know," Marvin muttered, shaking his head, his pallid face contorted with an unusual mix of horror and relief.

Troy stopped crying. He gulped air and laid one cheek against his mother's chest; his head fell forward onto her arm. An odd sound escaped. She held him with a tortured expression.

"Troy?" Marvin said.

"Is he going to be okay?" Todd wanted to know.

The boy's bottom lip quivered.

"He's scared," Melanie said, wiping tears from her cheeks.

"Was he drowning?" Marlee asked softly.

"Oh, Marvin," Meredith's face crumpled, and she sobbed again, her mind and body navigating a roller coaster of emotions.

He reached for his wife. They hugged one another, with Troy caught in the middle. "I'm sorry," he said, closing his eyes.

"Oh God, me too!" she cried. "I've never been so frightened in all my life. I can't believe how fast . . ."

Melanie reached for Troy. She wanted to bring him close, but Meredith didn't give him up. "Were you scared?" his sister asked.

"Yah," he croaked. At two-and-a-half years old, he did not possess the necessary vocabulary to offer any sure explanation had anyone tried to ask for more.

Meredith sat back in a pool chair. She exhaled and ran a hand over Troy's wet head. The kids stood, staring.

Marvin pulled a chair up. "That was damn close, scared the crap out of me."

"Go and swim," Meredith curtly told the others. Turning to her husband, she shook her head. "I'm thankful you saw him when you did." Tears welled again as anguish studded her face.

Marvin blew out a breath, "Yeah. You okay?"

"I will be."

Troy squirmed in her lap. "Me down," he said, and surprising them all, he toddled toward the pool.

Watching, Marlee gasped.

Todd quickly swam over, hoisting himself up and out of the water beside his brother. He looked at his parents. His mother nodded, "It's okay." Todd lifted Troy into the pool. He turned circles with him, slowly at first, then as he giggled, spun him faster. The giggling soon morphed into miraculous belly laughter.

"Maybe you ought to take it easy with him," Meredith called out.

"Okay," Todd said, slowing down.

To think that only moments before, the family escaped tragedy.

The following morning, after a hearty breakfast of eggs, toast, pancakes, and sausage, the family traveled the final leg of their trip. They drove the remaining six hours home, interrupted only by gas and bathroom breaks. They endured a single minor traffic jam near Chicago, which delayed them twenty minutes. Marvin flirted with stopping in Milwaukee to visit Buzzy and Francine, but it was unanimous to continue onward. Somewhat surprisingly, there was no squabbling to speak of. It was as if everyone recognized the precious cargo they carried and how close they had come to losing Troy the day before.

Arriving home twenty-four hours ahead of schedule—one full day—Marvin was pleased. He relished the thought of an extra day to regroup before returning to work.

CHAPTER 10

CHERRY PICKING BEGAN IN Door County in mid-July. The family plucked their share of the plump, ruby-red, tart fruit. Eighteen quarts later, plus more that filled their bellies, they chalked it up as a productive afternoon.

The girls helped their mother pit cherries until their fingertips colored purple. One did the job using a paperclip, the other was lucky enough to use a pitter attached to the top of a pint jar. Meredith made two pies and canned several quarts to get them through the winter months. She passed on a batch of cherry bounce. The remaining fruit sat in a colander in the refrigerator, and they would be lucky if it lasted a week.

Tart cherries and Georgia peaches were Marlee's favorite summer fruits, although it wasn't easy to narrow them down. All the colorful berries tied for third, with watermelon fourth on her list. The Concord grapes that grew in their backyard from a slip of her Grandma Simon's vine also ranked high. Suffice it to say, Marlee relished all fruit.

Boulder Lake summoned the Beckets once again for their annual camping week. Marvin and Meredith did not need a reminder to keep a closer eye on their offspring, especially Troy. They would never forget the scare in the motel pool.

Todd and Melanie ventured off together on day one and met the Redmond family from the Fox Valley area. They had four teenagers—all seventh graders and up—two boys and two girls. Tom, the oldest, was sixteen, and the second and third were fourteen-year-old boy-girl twins, Alex and Addie. The youngest sibling was Janelle. The teens bonded with Todd and Melanie almost immediately. Melanie admitted to Marlee that she had an instant crush on Alex.

"Don't breathe a word of that to anyone. I'm trusting you're not a baby anymore."

"Does Todd know your secret?"

"No! And you better not tell him."

"I won't. Maybe he's crushing on Addie," Marlee suggested.

"It wouldn't surprise me in the least. She's super cute, just like her adorable twin."

The next afternoon, Tom and Alex visited the Becket campsite. They walked through to where the family gathered on the beach.

Todd spotted them, "Hey, guys!"

Tom waved. "Hi! We came to ask if you and Melanie want to come over after supper tonight? We can hang out by the fire."

Melanie's stomach flipped at the sight of the boys.

"We'll pop popcorn and roast marshmallows," Tom said.

Todd turned to his parents. "Is it okay? Can we go over after supper?"

"Where are you at?" Marvin inquired. "You're sure it's okay with your folks?"

"Twenty-eight," Tom said, "and yeah, it's okay, it was my ma's idea."

"Sure, you can go," Marvin said to his kids, with a glance at his wife, not expecting any opposition.

"What can they bring? Some pop or juice?" Meredith offered.

Melanie's stomach flipped again, and giddiness bubbled up when her mother used the word *they*. She had thought it would be a minor miracle if her folks allowed her to go.

"What time?" Todd asked.

"How about we come for you when we're done eating?"

"We'll send beverages," Meredith said.

"Okay, see you later, then," Tom waved.

"See ya," Todd waved.

Tom had done all the talking, but Alex had met Melanie's hazel eyes while she sat on a towel with a *Tiger Beat* magazine open. He'd smiled. She'd smiled back and watched him walk away.

"Come on!" Melanie pulled Marlee by the elbow and grabbed a big inner tube. The sisters paddled out into deep water. Melanie looked as though she had died and gone to heaven. A mega-watt smile filled her face.

"Oh my gosh! I can hardly wait!"

"I wish I could go."

"Yeah," Melanie replied, but really couldn't have cared less.

Marlee broke out in song, "Melanie and Alex sitting in a tree, k-i-s—"

"Shush!" Melanie cut her off. Marlee roared with laughter. It wasn't easy for her to rile her older sister.

The family sat at the picnic table and ate a supper of grilled ring bologna, fried potatoes, and cold sugar snap peas in the shell. Melanie spoke very little and consumed nearly nothing, pushing her food around on an orange plastic plate. She helped clean up before disappearing into the tent to change out of her swimsuit and into her best outfit. She counted to one hundred while brushing her long blond hair, thinking about the Redmond family. Meredith suggested the kids take sweatshirts with them.

"It cools off after the sun goes down," she said, stating the obvious.

"How long can we stay?" Melanie dared to ask.

Meredith looked at Marvin. "Ten o'clock," he answered, "unless they boot you out sooner."

"Remember your manners," Meredith reminded them.

"How come they didn't invite me?" Marlee frowned.

"You've not been playing with them," Melanie told her.

"Yeah, 'cause I wasn't never asked."

"I *wasn't* asked," Meredith corrected Marlee.

"Yeah."

"This is just for the big kids. You and Troy have Dad and me to yourselves."

Marlee rolled her eyes.

Tom, Alex, Addie, and Janelle strolled in, almost on cue.

"Hi! You guys ready?" Tom asked.

"Take your flashlights," Marvin said, pointing to the table.

"Got 'em," Todd nodded. "Well, see ya."

"Yeah, see ya," Melanie echoed, accepting the flashlight and sidling up to the girls, beaming with a big smile.

"See ya," Troy waved. Meredith smiled. That little guy warmed her heart.

As soon as they left, Marvin suggested they walk to the water pump and fill their large water jugs. When they returned, Meredith and Marlee made a pitcher of lemonade. And they played Old Maid.

Later, two bouncing beams of light announced the kids' return.

"Right on time," Meredith said, leaning over to read her husband's glow-in-the-dark watch. "Did you have fun?"

"Boy, did we ever," Todd said. "John and Lou are pretty cool."

"Who are John and Lou? I thought there were four kids."

"There are four," Melanie confirmed. "Their folks said we could call them John and Lou."

Meredith shook her head. "What did you do over there?"

Marlee had been dozing on and off in a chaise longue, wrapped in a beach towel, but perked up to take in every detail.

"We sat around the fire, ate popcorn, and roasted marshmallows. Oh, we had one bottle of pop left, so I just left it there," Todd added.

"Were *John and Lou* by the fire with you kids?" Meredith wanted to know, emphasizing in her tone that the children called the adults by their first names. They all knew she was not thrilled with that.

"Part of the night. They mostly sat in their camper," Todd said.

"Hmpf," Meredith muttered.

Marlee followed Melanie into the tent.

"What do you want?" Melanie grinned.

"Tell me what happened tonight."

"There's not much to tell. We sat around, talked, and told jokes."

"I guess it's okay I wasn't asked."

"Oh, you." Melanie lowered her voice to a whisper, knowing their voices could carry straight out to everyone at the fire. "Alex did sit next to me, though, in the circle around the fire."

"Did you like that?"

"Ah, yeah . . . what do you think?" Melanie pulled on her pajama pants.

Whispering, Marlee probed, "Does he have a crush on you, too?"

"How should I know?"

"Ask him."

"I'm not doing that!"

"You want me to ask him for you?"

"No! Don't even think about it."

"Are you going to bed?" Marlee asked.

"Nope. I'm going back out by the fire."

Marlee followed her.

"Marlee?" Marvin said, surprised to see her. "I thought you went to bed. You could barely keep your eyes open, waiting for your brother and sister."

"I don't want to be in the tent alone."

"You wouldn't be alone. Troy's in there," Meredith stated.

"I know," Marlee said, plopping down on the chaise longue anyway, covering herself with the beach towel.

The night sky sparkled with starlight. Melanie tipped her head back and halfheartedly sought out the Big Dipper, her thoughts on Alex Redmond. She inhaled, filling her lungs with crisp air.

A car pulled into the campsite the following morning just after Meredith finished putting away the breakfast dishes. The four Redmond teenagers tumbled out, along with, presumably, their parents.

"Hi, I'm John Redmond. This is my wife, Lou, and of course, you've met our kids."

"Hello. I'm Meredith Becket, and this—" She turned to introduce her husband, but he was gone. "Marv?" she said. "He was here a minute ago." She wondered if the Redmonds' arrival meant something had happened the night before that Todd and Melanie conveniently failed to mention. "Thank you for hosting the kids last night."

"They had fun," Lou offered, "gauging by their laughter anyway."

John nodded. "We just got back from town and want to boat across the lake. Lou and I have friends staying at Echo Valley. We were wondering if the kids want to join us. They can go swimming. There's a big raft they can dive from."

"Marvin," Meredith called. He came from behind the tent. "This is my husband, Marvin. Honey, this is John and Lou Redmond."

"Nice to meet you." The men shook hands.

"Same here," John nodded.

Lou tipped her head, smiled, and gave a small wave. "Hi."

Meredith spoke. "They're boating to Echo Valley and wondered if Todd and Melanie want to go. The kids can swim."

"We have friends over there," John added.

Alex bent down by Troy, playing with trucks in the sand. Tom picked up a football. Though there wasn't much space, Todd backpedaled and threw up his hands, inviting Tom to throw him a short pass.

Marvin said to his wife, "I'm okay if they go. What do you think?" She nodded her assent.

"Excellent," John said. "We'll swing by in the boat, say, in an hour. We'll feed them lunch. If we're back by, say, two-ish, does that work?"

Marvin looked at Meredith. "That'll be fine," she smiled. "Thank you."

"Great. We'll be back in about an hour to grab them." John called to his teenagers, "Come on, gang."

As they drove away, Meredith turned to her husband. "What, they don't have enough kids? They want two more?"

"Yeah, that's something, huh?"

"I bet they have the house where kids always gather."

"You're probably right. The family seems nice enough," Marvin said.

As John promised, they returned just past two in the afternoon. Marvin helped Melanie out of the boat.

"Did they behave themselves?" he asked.

"You've got good kids, you do," Lou smiled. "Well-mannered."

"Thank you. I hope they weren't too much trouble."

"Not a bit."

"Thank you again," Melanie beamed. "I had a lot of fun."

"Yeah, thanks. I'll see you guys later," Todd raised his whole arm in a single wave.

Melanie tugged on her sister's top. "Walk to the bathroom with me."

"Be back." Marlee fell in step.

"You're never going to believe it!" Melanie exclaimed.

"What?"

"Alex kissed me!"

"For real?"

"For real," Melanie giggled. "We were all swimming and laying out on the raft and had so much fun. After lunch, I was the only one in the trailer. I told Janelle I had to go to the bathroom."

"Just like we're doing now."

"Oh geez, Marlee. Anyway, when I came out, Alex was standing there. I think he waited for me."

"And he kissed you?"

"Well, not that very second. He asked if I was having fun, and we talked about how school would be starting soon. He and Addie will be freshmen."

"What's a freshman again?"

"A ninth grader."

"Yeah, that's right."

"And he told me he was glad they met us, Todd and me. And then he—he kissed me."

"Did you see stars like they do in the movies?"

"No, you goof! You're thinking of cartoons. They see stars when they get bonked on the head. I didn't see anything, but my stomach flipped." The girls giggled.

"Did you like it? Was that your first kiss? Are you gonna tell Mom?"

"No, I'm not gonna tell Mom. I'm only telling you. Keep it to your-self, will ya!"

Marlee began to sing, "Melanie and Alex, sitting in a tree, k-i-s-s-i-n-g. First comes love, then comes marriage . . ." Marlee threw her head back with wild laughter.

"Knock it off, Marlee," she chuckled and shoved her, grinning like never before.

The camping week wrapped up after relatives visited. Todd and Melanie had introduced their cousins to the Redmond kids. The girls agreed that Alex Redmond was a cutie.

"His older brother's the real hunk," Linda declared.

Melanie scrunched her nose. "I think he might have a girlfriend back home," she said.

"Do you think you'll ever see Alex again?" Susan wanted to know.

"Maybe next summer, up here again."

Linda laughed, "You wish."

"You're right!" Melanie smiled.

Marlee got Mrs. Whaley as her second-grade teacher. She knew Mrs. Whaley had a daughter one grade below her and thought it would be weird to have your mother as a teacher at your school.

Thankfully, Marlee's problems in first grade indeed appeared to be behind her. That made it easier for Meredith to head west for pheasant hunting. Ruby and Alvin had claimed Troy for nine days, and Alice Bogart had come to spend the week with the three oldest. Marvin and Meredith had agreed not to pull Todd out of school for hunting.

"This being your first year of high school, and you're playing football, and well, it is homecoming again while we're gone—your mother and I think it's best if you stay here," Marvin explained.

"Yeah, I get it, but I'm still bummed about not hunting."

"I'm sorry to miss your game," Meredith said.

"It's no big deal, Mom; I'm not on varsity or anything. Nobody cares about freshman football except the players and, I guess, our coaches."

"That's not true. Your father and I care."

"She's right. But now you can help with the girls," Marvin said.

"Oh, great."

Alice seemed to have mellowed over the past year, or so Marlee thought, and she said it aloud to Todd and Melanie.

Todd chuckled, "Good for you it's not 'Elvis Week.'"

"Don't remind me!"

"I think Alice is different, too," Melanie told Todd. "I think it might be because you're here."

"What? Why?"

"Maybe she's not used to having a man around."

Marlee scoffed, "Todd's not a man."

"Almost. I almost am."

Todd sat in his father's spot at the supper table that evening. If anyone noticed, they chose not to comment.

The holidays were approaching, and Marlee lay on her bed on a lazy Saturday afternoon. Christmas music reverberated from the living room stereo. It sounded like Perry Como. She felt a deep longing for her mother—her first mother.

Marlee pictured Anne in heaven, seated on a tall stool with her arms crossed in front of her, resting on a whitewashed windowsill from which she leaned out. Her hair might be longer now, and she pictured it billowing in a light breeze. She imagined her mother could look down on Earth and watch her. Watch her life unfold without her. See her grow older. A wistful sadness filled Marlee, and yet she felt oddly comforted. The corners of her mouth slowly curved upward. It didn't seem right, but as much as she didn't want to own it, a smile formed. It warmed her heart to think of her mother that way—that she may be able to look down and see her. The girl's reverie was rudely interrupted when Todd hollered her name.

"Marlee! Telephone."

"Coming. Who is it?"

"Who else?" He rolled his eyes, "Eloise."

"Hello? Hold on, I'll ask. Mom! Dad! Can I go play with Eloise?"

"They're in the basement," Todd told her.

"Go ask 'em if I can play with Eloise."

"Go ask them yourself."

"Hang on, Eloise." She frowned at Todd and set the phone on the kitchen counter before bounding down the stairs to the basement. "Hey, Eloise is on the phone. Can I go over and play?"

"Hay is for horses," Marvin said.

"Go ahead," Meredith answered.

Marlee lifted a second phone receiver from the paneled wall at the bottom of the stairs. "I'll be right over, Eloise."

It sounded like her father grunted, earnestly engaged in some project, but Marlee took no notice of what occupied her parents.

"See you later," she called to them.

"Goodbye," Meredith replied.

Eloise waited at the door for her best friend. "Leave your shoes here, my mom mopped today. I'm all set up for us to play Barbies, and guess what?" Eloise didn't wait for Marlee to guess anything. "My mom gave me a tiny evergreen tree from her Christmas decorations, so now Barbie has a Christmas tree! Isn't that cool?"

"Do you think we can decorate it?"

"We'll have to find stuff to use." The girls scavenged for supplies. Eloise swirled a silver curling ribbon around the little tree.

"Let's pretend that's tinsel," Marlee suggested.

"It looks more like a string of garland."

"Yeah, garland! I like that."

They used a one-hole punch from a junk drawer to cut tiny circles out of colored construction paper and, with tape, stuck the "ornaments" to their tree. The friends admired their work. "I like it," they said simultaneously.

"Hey, we should put presents under the tree," Marlee suggested.

"Good idea. We can even wrap them." Joanna gave her daughter scraps of wrapping paper, and the girls used miniature Barbie accessories as gifts. The two played until supper.

Girls weren't allowed to wear slacks to school except under their dresses when the weather turned colder, and then they were required to remove them before entering the classroom. One January day, Marlee hung her pants on a hook and noticed the familiar smell of mimeographed worksheets wafting into the hallway. Entering the classroom, she breathed in deeply, savoring the unique scent. She knew it probably meant they were having a timed test of basic math facts. Marlee regularly practiced her flashcards at home but thought it unfair that they should have a timed test first thing in the morning, after walking to school. Despite wearing mittens, her fingers were still too cold and stiff, and she knew she would struggle to work her pencil as fast as she'd like.

After reciting the Pledge of Allegiance, Mrs. Whaley instructed the first person in each row to pass back the purple-printed worksheets.

Marlee brought the warm stack of paper—hot off the press—up to her nose and closed her eyes briefly before taking one and passing the rest back. She waited, with the worksheet face down, for the signal to flip it over and pick up her yellow no. 2 pencil.

Mrs. Whaley fixed her eyes on the wall clock above the door, and when the second hand met the twelve, she called out, "You may begin." A steady scratching of graphite sounded throughout the room. Marlee willed her fingers to move quickly down the columns.

"Time!" It always startled Marlee. "Put your pencils down."

A chorus of frustrated groans escaped from many children, Marlee included. She'd run out of time. Unable to complete two easy math problems. "Dang it!" she complained.

"Pass your worksheet to the right, and we'll score them."

Marlee's neighbor answered one problem incorrectly, but the last four were left blank.

That evening at supper, Marvin explained to his daughter that the timed tests were to challenge them. "If you keep practicing, you'll improve. I guarantee it."

"Well, I'm going to practice my flashcards after I eat."

"After dishes." Melanie clapped her sister on the back. "It's your turn to dry."

"Do I have to?"

"Yes," Marvin met her eyes.

Meredith added, "It won't take long."

Marvin clanked his butter knife against an empty coffee cup, alerting Melanie to fetch the pot. Marlee didn't know how that routine came about, but she hadn't forgotten the look Eloise shot her once when she ate over, observing the practice for the first time. Her raised eyebrows surprised Marlee. When they were alone, Eloise questioned her about it.

"I don't know why he does it," Marlee told her friend. "I guess it's just his way of asking for coffee."

"Well, I think it's rude."

"You take that back! My daddy's not rude."

"He's not normally rude, but clanging his cup for coffee seems rude to me."

Marlee clammed up but not before she said, "He always says thank you."

The two friends played side by side without speaking to one another for quite a while.

Todd's fifteenth and Troy's third birthdays were celebrated in the usual Becket way. And because Troy now understood birthdays better, it made it more fun for everyone. Plus, the little guy got so excited over any gift, whether he received a pair of socks or a Tonka truck. He was even old enough to request his favorite meal: beef stew, buttermilk biscuits, and warm applesauce. Marlee applauded his choice.

Todd had asked his parents if they would buy him a car for his next birthday when he turned sixteen and got his driver's license.

"Why don't you simply enjoy *this* birthday?" Meredith suggested.

"We're not going to buy you a car, Todd," Marvin stated. "I don't know where you got that harebrained idea."

"I was just asking, is all."

"You know," Marvin began, "maybe you could use the small inheritance you got from Grandpa Novak. Put it toward buying a car."

Todd, Melanie, and Marlee each received a small amount of money from Anne's father after he passed away. He died at the age of seventy-three, two months before his daughter perished in the horrific car accident. And his estate had not been settled by the time of his youngest daughter's death; therefore, her inheritance was divided into three shares for her surviving children.

"How much do I have?" Todd inquired.

"You each received $368. I put it in a bank account for you. Of course, it wouldn't have earned much interest yet, but I thought it could go toward purchasing a car or for school if you decide to go on."

"You mean college?"

"Yes, or technical school. You could learn a trade."

"I'm not going to college."

"Maybe not, but it's too early to make that decision."

"I think I'll use it to buy a car."

"Maybe, but not until next year at the earliest."

"There'll be more interest earned by then."

"A little," Marvin admitted.

CHAPTER 11

FIRST HOLY COMMUNION PREPARATION in the spring of 1969 was underway, and Marlee attended weekly catechism classes focusing on the Sacrament. Meredith planned for Marlee to wear her sister's white dress and veil. Two weeks after Easter, the night before the big event, Meredith realized she had not considered Marlee's shoes. She had checked that the dress and veil were clean and purchased a new pair of white tights and lace-covered gloves but never thought to check her daughter's shoes.

"How could I let that happen?" she lamented to her husband. "When Marlee wore her black shoes for Easter, it should have dawned on me that the girl needed a white pair."

Marvin sympathized with his wife but didn't know how to help. He figured Melanie's shoes would be too big, so he never mentioned trying them for size.

"No one will even notice what's on her feet," he ventured.

"Darn it anyway," Meredith balked, ignoring his comment. "She will have to wear her black patent leather. That's all there's to it."

"Or her blue ones," Marvin suggested.

"She's going to be so disappointed."

"Ah," Marvin scoffed. "She won't know the difference. Give her a choice between the black and blue, and it is what it is."

"What are you talking about?" Meredith suddenly remembered the old blue Mary Jane shoes Marlee used to have. "Oh, those," she said out loud. "Those haven't fit her for a long while. I gave them away. Kids grow, Marvin."

On the important day, Marlee donned her black shoes with the white dress and accessories, never mentioning them, though Meredith immortalized the look in a black-and-white photo. After Mass, Marlee posed with their neighbor, Larry Traeger, but the two did not stand close as their mothers had requested. In fact, when the women tried to coax them closer together, they did the opposite, leaning away from each other in mild embarrassment.

The Beckets invited a few relatives to the Swan Club for a family-style chicken dinner to celebrate. All the grandparents came, as did Marlee's godparents, Carol and Ed, and their children, Eddie, Wade, and Katie.

After enjoying the delicious, deep-fried, powdered kneecaps for dessert that helped make the Swan Club famous, Marlee opened gifts at the table.

She received a dainty silver cross necklace, a pale pink rosary in a round pearl-white box with a screw-top lid featuring Our Lady of Grace, a Mass missal, a prayer book, and twenty dollars in cash.

Meredith offered to put the necklace on Marlee. As she clasped it, she gave unsolicited advice, "Remember always to keep Jesus in your heart."

Marlee turned and hugged her mother. "I'll try, Mama."

Having used the entire roll of film, Meredith promptly brought it in for processing. When picking up the pictures more than a week later, she immediately noticed Marlee's black shoes and couldn't help but cringe. They stood out like a sore thumb. She felt as though she'd failed her daughter but realized then that on Communion Day, Marlee, rather uncharacteristically, hadn't seemed to care. Perhaps she never noticed that she was the only girl wearing black shoes with her pristine, white dress. Unlikely. Maybe she had more on her mind than what she wore. After all, she received Jesus that day.

Alvin and Ruby Simon drove to Suring on Sunday for a family dinner at Sam and Bernice's house. Together, the two grandmothers conspired—for no reason other than they could—to surprise Melanie on her upcoming twelfth birthday, just two days away. They sneakily gave the gifts they had initially planned to give her that day to her parents, not letting on to Melanie that they knew her special day was fast approaching. Bernice and Ruby also decided they would telephone Melanie on her birthday. And that is what they did.

Bernice dialed long-distance on her rotary phone using the shared party line. After a quick hello, Marvin handed his daughter the telephone; she heard her grandmother sing, "Happy birthday to you, happy birthday dear Melanie, happy birthday to you."

"Grandma?"

"Hi, sweetie. Here's Grandpa." Bernice passed the phone to Sam.

"Happy birthday, Melanie girl."

"Thank you."

He quickly gave the phone back to his wife.

"Melanie?"

"Hi, Grandma. You never called me before."

"No. But we thought we would surprise you this year. Did you open your presents?"

"Not yet. We just finished supper."

"Okay, well, I suppose Grandpa and I will let you get to it." Long-distance calls were expensive.

"Thank you for calling."

The telephone rang again. This time, Meredith handed her daughter the receiver.

"Hello?"

The whole family heard what came next. Ruby and Alvin sang, "Happy twelfth birthday, Melanie!"

She laughed. "Thank you."

"Did you have a nice day?" Ruby inquired.

"I did, and thank you for the locket."

"Aww, you're welcome, honey. We hope you like it. I wish we were there to celebrate with you."

"It's okay. I love the locket. I can't wait to pick out pictures to put in it."

"You'll have to show us. Did you think we forgot your birthday when we were all together on Sunday?"

"Maybe a little bit," she fibbed. She thought they'd *completely* forgotten her birthday, and she had been disappointed because she'd expected to open gifts that day.

"We could never forget you, Melanie. Your other grandma and I wanted to do something different this year. That's all."

"I was surprised to get gifts from everyone, especially since none of you are here."

"Well, it worked then. I hope we added to that surprise with our telephone calls."

"You sure did! No one's ever called me long-distance before."

"There's a first time for everything."

"I guess so."

"Enjoy the rest of your party, honey, and have a piece of cake for me," Ruby chuckled. "Please pass me back to your mother."

That night, Melanie fell asleep, smiling, remembering to ask God to bless everyone.

When the family celebrated Mother's Day in Suring a few days before Marlee's eighth birthday, Ruby told Bernice she wanted to surprise Marlee the same way they had surprised Melanie.

"But we'll be in Green Bay on Wednesday to pick up our paint order at Baldwin's," Bernice informed her. "We're stopping at the house after." Sam and Bernice were self-employed painters and wallpaper hangers.

"So, you'll pop in and surprise her on the actual day—you lucky dogs. And Alvin and I will telephone."

"Or you could ride into town with us," Bernice offered.

"What a wonderful idea!" Ruby exclaimed, happy to be included in the fun.

Marlee rolled out of bed on her birthday and flirted with skipping morning prayers. She thought better of it and dropped to her knees with her hands folded on the crumpled bedding. Her eyes fluttered closed. She prayed the bare minimum, focusing solely on herself, first reciting the "Guardian Angel Prayer." Then she added, "Oh, and Lord, you know it's my birthday. I hope I get everything I want. Thank you! Amen." She quickly dressed.

Passing the living room, Marlee noticed a stack of wrapped gifts but saw no cake in the kitchen. Her mother bustled about, preparing a special breakfast—one of her favorites—fresh rhubarb muffins with venison sausage.

"Good morning, birthday girl!"

"Good morning, Mom," Marlee smiled. "Um, Mom. I don't see a cake. Will you decorate a birthday cake for me today?"

"I most certainly will. I'll get started baking as soon as you kids are out the door. You weren't worried, were you?"

"Nah, not really. Save me the extra frosting, please?"

"I always do."

Marlee carried homemade honey cookies to school to share with her class.

At the end of the school day, the bell rang, and the sisters met at the flagpole out front to walk home. They caught up to other neighborhood kids waiting with the crossing guard, and the friendly mob made their way to Stadium Drive, meandering through Skyline Park. Marlee bid Eloise and her brother, Kyle, goodbye at the bottom of their driveway. She skipped the rest of the way.

"We're home," Marlee announced. Sure enough, in the center of the kitchen table sat an angel food cake, decorated specially for her.

"Shh," their mother brought a finger to her lips. "Troy's still napping."

"I like my cake," Marlee smiled, counting eight candles.

"Good," Meredith said. "Share this with Melanie." She gave Marlee a small, brown melamine bowl with pink and yellow frosting globs.

"Yum," she licked a spoon. "What about the beaters?"

"I gave those to Troy."

"The grandparents are here!" Todd said, bursting into the house. He set his books on the counter and returned to help the adults carry whatever they brought.

"Already?" Meredith glanced at the clock, thinking Troy was sure to wake up now.

Marlee bounded out of the kitchen, outdoors, soaring over the porch steps. "You're all here!" she shouted.

"We sure are," Ruby replied.

Todd held the door open to bring the party inside.

"They came for my birthday!" Marlee smiled widely.

"I know," Meredith nodded. "Did they surprise you?"

"Boy, did they ever!" She tilted her head. "Did they surprise you?"

"They did," she admitted, which was not a lie because she had not expected them for another hour.

Marlee roared with laughter, "How fun is this!" She grabbed Melanie and spun her in a half circle. Melanie lifted her sister off the ground, the two giddy.

Marvin arrived home from the office earlier than normal, quickly shedding his coat and tie.

Meredith was roasting two chickens and had prepared Marlee's favorite potato salad. She also made a crock of homemade baked beans using dry beans that soaked overnight—another popular dish with the birthday girl.

After eating, a thrilled Marlee tore open gifts and proclaimed that a red pogo stick was exactly what she wanted. The adults watched as the kids took turns bouncing on it. Not surprisingly, Todd showed the most finesse. He counted to fifty before hopping off.

Marlee bounced and counted to four before losing her balance. She tried again, reaching twelve, and on her third attempt, got to fifteen before falling. She vowed to do a lot better by the weekend.

"I'm going to get to fifty, too," she told Todd.

"Sure, but I'll be up to a hundred by then, 'cept I won't want to count that high."

"Bragger."

"Ooooo . . . testy, are you?" he teased.

"No!" she snapped.

"Time for cake," Meredith called. Marvin lit the candles. "Let's sing."

Marlee grinned proudly at her family gathered around. She made a wish before blowing out the flames. The adults sipped coffee with their cake and ice cream around the kitchen table. The kids took their dessert outside.

One day, Troy wanted to try the pogo stick. "There's no way you can pogo. You're way too little," Marlee told him.

She occasionally complained that her brother could sometimes be a pain in the butt, though she loved him. And liked him well enough, except when he decided to be her shadow, following her everywhere. Marlee often told Troy he didn't need to hang around her and Eloise because he had Devin and other boys to play with. Eric Johnson was always available. Same with Larry Traeger's baby brother, Oscar.

And what kind of name is Oscar? Marlee often wondered. It made her think of a wiener.

"*Please*, Troy, go find Devin or someone. *Anyone*," she pleaded. Eloise and Marlee were setting up Barbie dolls, and playing with them would fill the entire afternoon. They were busy choosing outfits, accessories, and what little furniture they had to pick from. A tiny, colorful comic extracted from Bazooka bubble gum was Barbie's Sunday newspaper.

It always seemed the girls spent hours making selections, setting up their homes, and dressing their dolls before they did any actual playing. And they grumbled when they had to pick up, which happened that day when Kyle summoned Eloise home for supper.

"I'll see you later," Eloise said after cleaning up.

"Yeah, see you tomorrow."

Marlee helped her mother with meal preparation. She set the table, washed two Macintosh apples for a lettuce salad, and made a pitcher of grape Kool-Aid before she and Troy were free to mill about the yard, waiting for their father. Kool-Aid was allowed as a mealtime beverage only during warm months.

Marvin generally arrived home from work shortly after five. They usually sat down to eat almost immediately upon his arrival.

Troy pushed a yellow metal Tonka dump truck through the sandbox, mimicking the sound. Marlee wandered about the backyard, counting the wooden cutouts sprinkled throughout that Grandpa Simon had made and painted. Her favorite was the little boy fishing in their clay birdbath. His line with a small wooden fish hung barely above the water, as if he were reeling it in. She also liked the little girl wearing a pink-and-white polka-dot dress and holding a watering can positioned to look as though she were watering flowers.

Marlee heard her mother calling them. "Come on, Troy," Marlee said. "It's time to eat." It surprised Marlee that she hadn't noticed when their father arrived home. She impatiently waited for Troy. "Come on. Let's go," Marlee said again. "Dad's home." She brushed the seat of his pants clean before he got out of the sandbox.

That night was Marlee's turn to read a short Bible passage before supper, and the family bowed their heads in prayer. The odd thing was that they did not read it in order. Whoever's turn it was could select a random verse from any book or chapter, though they usually stuck with one of the four Gospels.

As the meal progressed, Marvin and Meredith discussed preparation for their upcoming annual camping week. Usually, it was the highlight of the summer, although the couple had recently begun looking at buying property up north, and if they bought a place, the kids feared camping might end.

Marlee thought about waterskiing on Boulder Lake, where she and her siblings learned to ski, and how Melanie had once broken her eardrum. "Dangerous sport, isn't it?" Grandma Becket had asked. No one bothered to acknowledge her comment. If you were active, it was just that way—sometimes someone got hurt. Marlee knew it would be at least a couple more years before Troy was old enough to learn how to water-ski, and she wondered if he would get the chance at Boulder Lake.

"Will we still be able to water-ski if you buy a cabin in the woods?" she asked.

"Sure. We'll still have our boat. We may have to haul it to water when we want to go," Marvin told them.

"Will we ever go camping again?"

"Probably not if we get a place." His comment all but confirmed her fear. Marlee didn't want to hear that. Neither did her siblings.

On Sunday, July 20, 1969, the family gathered around the television in Sam and Bernice's living room. They watched live, gray, grainy coverage of the Apollo 11 moon landing. And listened to CBS News anchor Walter Cronkite as astronaut Neil Armstrong stepped out of the lunar module onto the moon, the first human in history to do so. Armstrong then spoke the words that are famously quoted: "That's one small step for man, one giant leap for mankind."

Chills ran up Marvin's spine. The image of a man walking on the moon took his breath away, and the view of the Earth from outer space— so much blue water and swirling white clouds—was amazing. He wished he could've made out the continents. But the surreal pictures of the moon's surface looked otherworldly to him.

Astronaut Buzz Aldrin joined Neil Armstrong, and they took photos of one another and collected moon rocks to bring back home.

"Remember the spaceships, the rockets we saw last year in Florida?" Meredith asked the children.

"Yeah, at Cape Canaveral," Melanie clarified.

"This is pretty wild!" Todd marveled.

"I know! I agree," Marvin said, glued to the television. "It's crazy to think they're walking on the moon. And boy, would I like to see one of those moon rocks up close. How about the views? But I don't know if I could rocket into space."

"Why do you think about stuff like that?" Sam asked his son. "You'll never get the chance."

"Even so, it's something to ponder."

"Landing on the moon might be worth thinking about," Sam conceded, "but whether *you* could go up in space is not because it's never gonna happen. Hate to tell ya."

"I know," Marvin muttered, keeping his eyes on the coverage.

Bernice glared at Sam, but he didn't notice. She disliked his comment.

"We are witnessing history," Marvin said to his children. "Don't you forget it. These names, these astronauts—Neil Armstrong and Buzz Aldrin—will forever be etched in history. And kids will be learning about them in school forever. You can thank President Kennedy for that. It's a shame he isn't alive to witness it."

Packers training camp rolled into town. Todd especially looked forward to that. He and his buddies usually rode their bikes to the stadium in the morning and, with a horde of other expectant boys, gathered outside as players exited the locker room to walk to the practice field across the street, about a quarter mile away. The kids offered the athletes the use of their bicycles, and if they were lucky, the players would let them ride on the handlebars. Otherwise, they happily jogged alongside. A boy felt honored if he had the same player every day for the trek across the big parking lot.

Parents occasionally showed up at the beginning of training camp to take pictures of their kids posing with the players. Autographs were not always requested back then, but it was terrific when they got one.

Boyd Dowler pedaled Todd. The big man played wide receiver. Ten years earlier, in 1959, he'd been named NFL Rookie of the Year. He was also a Super Bowl champion and was later inducted into the Green Bay Packers Hall of Fame. He stood six feet, five inches tall and weighed 220 pounds. Todd looked at the man with awe, and his bike nearly buckled under their combined weight.

Todd burst into the house after practice the first day he met the big wide receiver.

"You probably won't believe it, but Boyd Dowler rode my bike today!"

"No kidding?" Meredith smiled.

"I can't wait to tell Dad. He'll know who he is."

"I know who Boyd Dowler is," she scoffed. "What's he like?"

"He's tall, that's for sure. Basketball tall."

"What did he have to say?"

"He asked me my name and how old I am. I pointed out our house. Oh yeah, I almost forgot. He said now that he knows where I live, he might stop over some night for supper."

Meredith laughed.

"Do you think he would ever do that?" Todd wondered.

"I would guess he was teasing you when he said that. And if not, I would appreciate some forewarning."

"What?"

"Nothing. That was my attempt at teasing."

Marlee accepted an invitation to stay with her cousin Lori for a week in Mountain, Wisconsin, not far from Boulder Lake. Lori's parents, Gerald and Lorraine, worked each summer and deep-cleaned the school—the very school Marlee's beloved mother Anne had attended as a child. Marlee tried to picture it.

The two girls played in the classrooms while the adults scrubbed and polished floors. Playing in an *actual* school with giant chalkboards and using real desks elevated the experience to a new level. The only thing they wanted but didn't have were real live students. They were forced to use their imaginations.

"Okay, class. I'm Miss Engebretsen," Marlee smiled at Lori, sitting in the front row. "Can we say that together? Miss En-ge-bret-sen," she enunciated, remembering how difficult it had once been for her. "By the way," she explained to her cousin, "that was the name of my real kindergarten teacher."

"Mine was Mrs. Moser."

"Pay attention when I'm talking, please," Marlee tapped a desk with a pointer. "Pick up your reader and turn to page one." The girls used textbooks they'd found in a closet.

"What grade is this?" Lori wanted to know.

"Third grade."

"We'll be third graders this year."

"That's why I said it." And attempting a more mature voice, Marlee went an octave lower, "Please begin reading."

Lori perused the first paragraph. "You know what. I don't want to read."

"Okay. Put the book away then. Let's do some math," Marlee suggested, switching it up. "Take this chalk," she passed a piece to her cousin. "Please come up and write math facts on the board."

Lori started with basic equations. Soon, they heard her mother calling.

"Girls, come and eat."

They ate a simple lunch of peanut butter sandwiches with sugar snap peas and carrot sticks and paged through a school annual they'd found dated 1961, the year they were born.

"Look at their hair," Lori clapped a hand over her mouth. "It looks like a helmet!"

"Like what the astronauts wear," Marlee laughed.

"How about this one!" The cousins pointed at photos and snickered.

"I bet my sisters are in here." Lori flipped through the book to find their pictures and outdated hairstyles. Just one sister and her only brother were in the old annual. The girls laughed when they saw them.

There were five kids in Lori's family. Besides her sister Linda, who was twelve, Lori had three older siblings—a brother and two more sisters, all of whom were married. Linda was the same age as Melanie, and she went to Green Bay to stay with the Beckets while Marlee bunked with Lori. The two cousins essentially traded places for the week.

When they finished eating and poking fun at photos in the annual, the girls had the idea to check out the kitchen. Lori took several sectioned trays stacked nearby and lined them up on the counter. The girls squeezed dish soap from an industrial-sized bottle and ran hot water, creating a mountain of suds. They pretended it was goulash and served it to make-believe students. Then it dawned on Lori, "Hey. I don't want to be a lunch lady. I want to be a teacher. How about we go back upstairs to the classrooms? But we have to clean this up first."

The girls spent the afternoon playing school, taking turns being the teacher.

For Marlee, one of the best things about staying with Lori's family was the animals they owned. The barn cat always seemed to have kittens—this time, three of the sweetest, tiniest, striped felines you ever wanted to cuddle. Their fine, razor-sharp claws oftentimes got the better of Marlee, although she didn't let that deter her. She hugged them until they wiggled free. The only other farm animals they kept were chickens and goats. Marlee loved scattering chicken feed to watch the hens cluck about the yard. She also got a kick out of the silly goats that were full of mischief and climbed atop a picnic table near an old rusty car in the tall grass off the dirt driveway.

One night, Gerald and Lorraine treated the girls to hamburgers at a tavern on the main drag in town. They ended up staying to watch a horseshoe competition and, because of that, didn't get back until after dark. Gerald barely turned onto the drive of their property when he said, "Looks like we have a visitor."

Marlee gasped. She couldn't believe her eyes. On the stoop stood a humongous black bear.

"Oh, goodness!" Lorraine exclaimed.

"It's not like we've never had a bear here before," Gerald said to his wife.

"But we've got Marlee."

"And so, we'll wait."

The bear raised its head as the truck approached, then resumed pawing at the underside of the wooden step.

"Something's under there, and that bear wants it," Lori said for Marlee's benefit.

Gerald honked the horn. He blasted it. The bear snorted, shook its massive body, and lumbered away. They watched into the darkening night until they couldn't make him out anymore. Gerald waited a few minutes before hustling out of the truck to open the house door. He left the headlights on high beam, exposing both the garden and the left side of the barn. He flicked on the outside light above the house door and disappeared. Suddenly, a light illuminated the front yard. Moments later, he reappeared at the side door, "All clear," he hollered. With a big, long-handled metal spoon like the girls used in the school kitchen, he banged on the bottom of a large aluminum kettle, creating a racket.

"Okay, girls, run!" Lorraine instructed.

Marlee's heart wildly thumped as she followed Lori, jumping from the truck door closest to the house. It wasn't far—less than fifteen feet, although, to Marlee, it seemed a mile away. She moved fast, covering the distance to safety.

"Oh my gosh!" Marlee breathed, crossing the threshold with a rush of adrenaline coursing through her body. She grabbed hold of her cousin. "Did he bang on the pot to scare the bear?"

"It doesn't scare the bear so much as it lets him know we're here," Lorraine explained. "Bears don't like people."

"That's right," Gerald confirmed. "If you ever encounter a bear in the wild, don't scream because it might think you're there to hurt it. It may go into full defense mode to protect itself. Instead, you should raise your arms." He reached for the ceiling. "Try to appear larger and, like you mean it," he slammed his fist on the table, "shout, *Leave!*" Marlee jumped.

"Wow! Were you scared, Lori?" Marlee wanted to know.

"A little bit."

"I just didn't want anything to backfire," Lorraine said, shaking her head.

"I can't wait to tell my friends!"

Later in the week, Lori and Marlee rode one bike into town, taking turns sitting on the handlebars while the other pedaled. It was not an easy task for Marlee. The bike wobbled terribly. Lori was strong and thus better able to steady the bike. Nonetheless, they skidded off the road when the tires met gravel. Marlee pitched forward into the ditch, and Lori ended up on top of the bicycle on the shoulder of the road.

Lori started to laugh. Marlee wanted to cry. Her shorts and tennis shoes were wet with dirty water, and her right knee and palm stung with road rash.

Lori realized Marlee didn't laugh, but noticed she didn't cry exactly, either. Her face contorted in pain, or to avoid tears, perhaps both.

"I'm sorry, Marlee. Your knee's bleeding."

"My hand, too," she flipped her palm up. "And I'm wet."

"I guess it was dumb to ride like that, huh?"

"Yeah."

"Do you want to go back?" Lori asked.

"Yeah. I want dry shorts."

Lori turned the bike around, and the two walked on the side of the road.

"My chest hurts a little," Lori stated, although her shirt showed no signs of wear and tear.

Lorraine was surprised to see the girls so soon after they'd left, walking the bike no less. "Aw, what happened to you, Marlee?" Lorraine cleaned the abrasions, applied Bactine, and covered the scrapes with bandages.

The two ventured out again, this time on foot. Each held a stalk of fresh-picked rhubarb and a small, handy disposable paper cup that Lori pulled from the bathroom dispenser, with a good two inches of sugar for dipping. They passed the spot where they tumbled off the road, and Lori successfully coaxed a laugh out of her cousin.

Marlee carried her allowance money in her pocket, intending to spend it at the general store. There were knickknacks galore for sale. And though it was hard to choose, she settled on two tiny animal figurines, each less than two inches tall—one a raccoon, the other a spotted deer curled in a sitting position. Marlee kept those trinkets into adulthood—great childhood memories of her time up north with Lori.

CHAPTER 12

A RADIANT SUN BROKE through a fresh, vibrant blue sky to greet the Becket family on the first morning of a new school year.

Looking thoughtful and serious, Marlee cleared her throat and announced, "I am no longer a little kid."

"Hmm, how do you figure?" Marvin wondered, eyebrows knit together.

"Have you seen third graders? They're huge!"

Genuine laughter erupted from Meredith. "But you're not huge."

"No," she replied cavalierly.

"How does she come up with this stuff?" Meredith quietly asked her husband.

"Your guess is as good as mine."

"Who did you get for a teacher?" Todd asked.

"Mrs. Nielson. Did you have her?"

"Nope, but Mr. Nielson is the high school band director."

"Who's Mr. Nielson?"

"Mrs. Nielson's husband, you dope."

Marvin reentered the kitchen, straightening his necktie. "Who are you calling a dope?"

"Me," Marlee sneered.

"No more," Marvin warned his son.

"I didn't have her either," Melanie offered. "But I heard she's nice."

"Is everyone ready for a picture?" Meredith asked. "Let's go outside. Grab your things." Just like in previous years, the three older siblings lined up from tallest to shortest.

"Cheese!" Marlee smiled widely, holding her toothiest grin, to which Troy belly laughed. "Cheese!" she said again, charging him. Troy let loose another hearty laugh. It reminded Meredith of when babies first begin to laugh, and once you've done something to bring that out, you continue doing it until it wanes.

"Well, I hope you all have a great day," Meredith said. "I'll see you after school." She and Troy waved.

Marlee would be without her sister at the grade school for the first time as Melanie and a gaggle of girls headed to the high school for junior high. Eloise waited at the curb, and the best friends fell in stride. Kyle ran ahead to catch up to the Traeger brothers. Todd crossed the street to hitch a ride with Chris Curtain.

"Hey, CC, you ready?" Todd greeted his friend.

"Yup. Hop in," Chris said.

One of the guys on the football team liked to call him Drape. Chris rolled with it. When Meredith first heard the nickname, she doubled over laughing and said it was hilarious.

Chris recently passed his road test and got his official driver's license. Over the summer, occasionally, the Beckets observed him with his father in the Packers stadium parking lot, learning to drive the family sedan. Todd acquired his learner's permit, known among the kids as their "temps," and practiced in the wide-open lot, too. Over the years, many parents took their teens there for the all-important rite of passage.

As Meredith watched the kids go, she thought about the future, aware that in a couple of short years, Troy would join his siblings in going off to school. She wondered how it would feel but dismissed those thoughts, giving them the bum's rush. There was no need for that nonsense now, she thought.

"Crisco!" she called. Troy scooped the dog into his arms and carried her into the house.

The Becket family went apple picking at a local orchard. They filled two bushel baskets. Meredith preferred Macintosh for making applesauce and baked goods but liked the firm Cortland for eating out of hand.

"Can I bring Mrs. Nielson the biggest apple we picked?" Marlee asked.

"Absolutely," her father replied.

"She'll like that," Meredith added.

Marvin bought a ten-pound bag of "seconds" to use up north as deer bait, with bow season just two weeks out. He was not traditionally a bow hunter, but having decided to forgo pheasant hunting that year, he thought he would try it again.

They elected not to go to South Dakota mainly because Todd had invited Nita Fischer to homecoming, and Meredith had not been keen on them missing their son's first official dance. Another reason they didn't go was that Todd played football; however, as a sophomore, he would not suit up for varsity and take the field for the big homecoming game. Nonetheless, Marvin and Meredith liked watching him play on junior varsity.

Todd and Nita double-dated with Chris and his girlfriend since his buddy had recently bought a car.

Chris took Todd to pick up Nita and, after pictures at her house, went back to the Beckets' house for pictures before the dance. Meredith commented to her husband that Todd and Nita made a cute-looking couple. Marlee thought they acted goofy, but Nita was pretty and sweet with a soft, high voice.

"It's nice to meet you, Mr. and Mrs. Becket," she said in her honeyed timbre.

"You as well, and you look lovely," Meredith told her. "Your dress is beautiful."

Nita wore a baby blue, dotted Swiss maxi dress with a square neckline and an empire waist. She and Todd exchanged flowers and pinned them on one another. Marlee learned they were called corsages for ladies and boutonnieres for men.

"How about we take pictures over here?" Meredith gestured for the young couple to stand in front of the bookcase. Chris and his date also posed for a photo.

"We're probably going out for burgers after the dance." Marvin heard Chris say.

Marvin slipped his son a ten-dollar bill. He didn't know if Todd planned on that. Curfew was 12:30, and Marvin wondered if the kids would have enough time to stop for food. He didn't offer a later curfew but knew immediately he would allow a little leeway.

"How long does this shindig last?" Marvin asked.

"The dance concludes at 11:30 p.m.," Nita primly spoke.

Concludes? What is that? Marlee wanted to know but didn't ask. Everyone must have known what Nita meant because no one questioned the strange word she used.

The teenagers left, and Marlee ran to the living room and knelt against the back of the sofa to look out the bay window at them. Todd opened the car door for Nita. Marlee noticed that she'd slid across the backseat but stopped in the middle. Todd practically sat on her. Chris's date sat smack dab next to him on the bench seat in the front, and Marlee thought they all looked ridiculous.

Troy dumped a can of Lincoln Logs across the living room floor, and Marlee flopped beside him. They built cabins while watching *Family Affair* on television. Marlee commented that she wished her hair were like Buffy's, saying the signature ringlet pigtails were adorable. She also coveted the unique Mrs. Beasley doll Buffy had and shared that Cissy looked like Nita Fischer.

"She does resemble her," Meredith agreed.

Marvin chuckled, "You have a good eye, girl."

Marlee received the iconic Mrs. Beasley doll from Santa that Christmas, and for the next several months, she was rarely seen without it by her side. Mrs. Beasley even accompanied the family on most of their car trips. Todd had never said it out loud but found himself wondering who had come up with the idea of such a doll. And the dumb things she said when someone pulled the cord.

In February, Todd turned sixteen and went completely gung ho to road test for his driver's license. Unfortunately for him, it was an emotionally fraught six weeks because spring arrived before he finally passed. He endured two frustrating failed attempts at the motor vehicle department and often grumbled to his parents, "I just want my license already so I can ride a motorcycle."

"Well, you need to know how to drive a car before you can operate a motorbike. Where did the examiner dock you?" Marvin wanted to know.

"A little bit everywhere," he frowned.

"Well, you'll have to get out and practice more."

"It's driving me nuts."

"Pardon the pun?" Marvin laughed. "Driving—get it?"

Todd didn't appreciate his father's sense of humor at that moment. He rolled his eyes.

"It's simple, Todd. You need to show the examiner that you can drive. You need to pay attention to all the little details, everything you've learned."

When he finally obtained his license and subsequent motorcycle permit, Marvin allowed his son to use his inheritance from his maternal

grandfather to purchase a small motorbike. Todd chose a Honda 90. And
to get a bike, he also had to buy two helmets.

Bringing home the Honda 90 proved interesting to Meredith and
fun for the neighborhood kids, as the Becket driveway became a popular
hangout for teenagers. All the boys wanted to take the motorcycle for
a spin, and having boys hanging around meant teenage girls came by.
A few of Todd's classmates who owned motorcycles added to the scene
when they showed up, revving their bikes.

"Is this some sort of secret club I've never been aware of?" Meredith
wanted to know.

"It's a guy thing, almost like an early taste of manhood," Marvin
noted.

"That scares me."

"Nah," he scoffed. "I'd compare it to getting into your first real
fistfight."

"Well, that's a relief. I thought you might compare it to losing your
virginity."

Marvin laughed. "It doesn't rank quite that high."

"I just hope no one gets hurt."

After supper, Melanie worked on her Girl Scout Cooking Merit
Badge. She baked and frosted a spice cake she planned to bring to her
aunt's funeral luncheon. Anne's second-oldest sister, Lydia, died after
a yearlong battle with breast cancer—the same dreaded disease their
mother had succumbed to at the age of fifty-two, one year longer than
Lydia was afforded.

During cleanup, Melanie sliced her hand on a tin can. The cut did
not need stitches, but it bled for a while, so Marlee assumed washing duty,
something she rarely had the opportunity to do.

In a rather peculiar turn of events, just months before Lydia passed
away, she had convalesced at the Becket home for a few days. She rested
on the sofa, and Marlee curiously looked in on her aunt after school. They
didn't talk much, but Lydia would share her Dots gumdrops with her
niece. It was a small thing, but in years to come, Marlee fondly remembered her aunt whenever she saw a colorful box of chewy gumdrops. That
often happened around Halloween.

The whole visit had felt a bit odd for Meredith, but she welcomed
Lydia, who was Anne's kind sister—Anne, of course, having died years
earlier in the accident. But Lydia and her family lived forty miles north of

Green Bay, and that may have influenced her request to stay with them, as her cancer treatments were in the city. Another possible reason could have been a goodwill gesture on Lydia's part—it may very well have been her way of atoning for the horrible treatment Meredith had suffered at the hands of at least one extended family member around the time she and Marvin announced they were getting married.

Unfortunately, Meredith had been the woeful recipient of two nasty phone calls from a male caller whose voice she was 99 percent certain she could identify. He addressed her with awful, mean-spirited names, the worst being *murderer*, before hanging up. At the time of the calls, it unnerved both Meredith and Marvin. But Meredith knew how strongly Marvin felt about the children continuing to see Anne's family. As a result, she tamped down her feelings and dismissed the offender and his insulting names. Fortunately, the calls ended, making it easier to forgive.

Many years later, the culprit confirmed it was he when, under the influence of alcohol at a family wedding, of all places, he admitted to and apologized for his cruel behavior. His mouth formed a perfect O as Meredith told him she knew, all along, that he was the one who had telephoned her. Extending an olive branch, she said, "Let's not talk of bygones." Smiling sheepishly, he mouthed *thank you*. Meredith felt grateful and could finally put the ugly incident to bed once and for all.

Lydia passed away two days before Marlee's ninth birthday, and her funeral was scheduled for the day after. The family drove forty-odd miles to church, with Marlee riding in the front seat between her parents and Troy in the back, nestled between his brother and sister, the frosted spice cake in a covered pan on the floor.

"There's a red line going up my arm," Melanie announced nonchalantly.

Meredith spun around to inspect her daughter's outstretched limb. She reached over Marlee, who also turned around for a close-up look. Meredith saw the red streak that snaked halfway up the pale inside of Melanie's forearm, starting underneath the bandage on her hand covering the tin-can cut.

"Does it hurt? Is it hot or warm to the touch?" Meredith tried to sound unalarmed.

"Not really," Melanie said in response to both questions.

"Marvin, we've got to get her to a doctor."

"Okay. We'll stop and ask where to find one."

"What's happening?" Melanie wanted to know.

"It needs to be looked at," her mother stated.

As it turned out, they were only a few blocks from the small-town clinic where the doctor could see Melanie immediately. He removed her band-aid and washed and cleaned the cut.

"You have blood poisoning," he stated matter-of-factly. Then he applied a medicated gel before re-bandaging the hand. He told Melanie she needed to be brave while he gave her a Tetanus shot since Meredith couldn't recall when Melanie last had one. The girl winced at the needle poke.

"Here's a prescription for an antibiotic. This will make that streak disappear. You caught it early, and there's no pain, so that's positive. Where'd you say you're all from?" the doctor asked, shifting gears abruptly.

"Green Bay," Marvin said. "We're on our way to my sister-in-law's funeral."

"I hope you won't be late."

"No. We probably missed the entire showing, but we'll make the funeral."

"In town here? May I ask who died?"

"Lydia Stonewater."

"Ah, yes, Lydia. Sad, leaving behind six children and her husband like that. I paid my respects to the family last night at the funeral home. You have my sympathy," he said kindly. "I didn't know Lydia or Douglas very well, but this is a small town, and as I'm sure you're aware, we all know who everyone is."

"Yes, well, thank you for your condolences. What do I owe you?"

"Nothing. Be on your way."

"I need to—"

"I'm glad I was here to help. You don't owe me anything. Be on your way now, shoo," the doctor escorted them to the door.

"You're very generous," Meredith smiled.

"Yes, thank you," Marvin agreed. "We appreciate it."

"Thank you," Melanie echoed.

The good doctor nodded. "You don't want to be late. Goodbye now."

Incense from the funeral Mass caused Marlee to sputter through a coughing jag, and after, at her aunt and uncle's house, she gulped down a glass of water. She stood at the kitchen sink, watching her aunts fill two tables with casseroles, scalloped potatoes, sauerkraut, salads, buns, cheeses, pickles, and pickled beets. A Nesco roaster held a mound of sliced ham. The dessert table showcased a variety of bars, tortes, kolaches, cakes, cookies, and Melanie's spice cake. There appeared to be enough food to feed a small army.

Of course, the Novak family resembled a small army whenever they came together. Anne had been one of nine children, and those nine children produced thirty-five first cousins, including Todd, Melanie, and Marlee. That figures to 3.8 children each per the nine couples, although Anne's eldest sister gave birth to an only child, a son who went on to play in a rock band that produced a one-hit wonder. Several of the oldest cousins were already married and had kids of their own, ranging in age from one to seven years younger than their youngest cousins. It made for fun, albeit loud, gatherings.

Whenever the Novak sisters got together and laughed, it produced a cacophony like nothing you have ever heard. It became one of those things that Marlee and Melanie often reminisced about when they were grown, remembering occasions spent in the company of their many maternal aunts. People sometimes say they wish they could go back in time and experience something again. That laughter was one of those things. If the Becket sisters could hear that distinct, joyful sound again, it would surely bring forth smiles full of tender nostalgia, a longing for celebrations past.

Melanie hugged her cousin, eight-year-old Grant. She had a pretty good idea of how he felt. Although his mother had been sick and her death was not unexpected, like her own mother, she knew there sat an empty cavern in his heart. It seemed so unfair.

Grant, Marlee, Lori, Katie, Teddy, Johnny, Julia, and others sat on the carpeted step of the sunken living room. For some unknown reason, they talked about where they thought babies came from. Their innocence prevented any of them from knowing the truth. The boys convinced themselves that babies came out of their mother's buttocks, to which the girls reacted with total repulsion. They surmised babies came from a woman's belly button. Katie, the oldest of the bunch and in fourth grade, vowed to ask her mother before the cousins would be together again.

"Who knows when that will be?" Lori wondered.

"Well, I'm going to ask anyway because I cannot believe a baby comes out of a lady from where she poops."

Even Grant, in his deserved sullenness, laughed with the others.

Lori and Marlee bowed out to grab another dessert. They came upon Melanie sitting with Grant's only sister, Maria, who was almost twenty years old. Maria talked about how pretty Aunt Anne had been and how hard her mom, Lydia, took it when Anne died.

"That was her baby sister, you know, and so shocking for everyone."

"You're telling me," Melanie stated.

"And now your mama died," Marlee frowned.

"Yes, though I'm so much older than you two. I absolutely cannot imagine what that must have been like for you, to be so young and lose your mum. My mother's death now at my age seems unbearable," Maria lamented.

"Well, Grant can," Melanie offered. "He's eight. I was seven."

"It's all so terrible."

"Maybe your dad will get married again."

"Oh, God, I hope not. I'm too old for a stepmother."

Grant may want one, though, thought Marlee, leaving the words unspoken.

For her birthday, Marlee had received a locked diary she wanted and a zipped, satin, floral autograph book. Aloud, she wished she'd brought the autograph book to the funeral luncheon to get all her cousins' signatures.

"I think it worked out better that you didn't bring it," her mother said. "It may have been in poor taste."

"What do you mean, *poor taste*?"

"Inappropriate," Meredith simply answered, which satisfied Marlee.

School recessed for the summer, and Aunt Lorraine again invited Marlee to stay with them for a week. A lot of summertime, though, would be lived before that happened.

Marlee met the new parkies at Skyline Park, where each year, two teenagers—one male and one female—ran a summer program for the neighborhood. Everyone knew the quality of the parkies determined how much time the kids spent at the park.

They introduced themselves as Dot and Tony, and the older girls were initially disappointed in Tony, judging him on his physical attributes. They deemed him low on the cuteness scale.

It took the parkies just one week to win over most kids with games and activities they'd organized. Competitive rounds of Simon Says played with a big group proved loads of fun. Marlee tried her darnedest to be the last one standing. During each new game, she held her own for a long while until some older kid beat her in the homestretch. Elimination usually happened as her confidence sneakily edged higher after every successful follow-through until she got cocky and slipped up, touching her ear, hopping on one foot, or something similar, and executing the command without first hearing the required "Simon says . . ."

"Ugh!" She stamped her feet in frustration then quickly recovered, remembering she needed to be gracious. If she acted like a sore loser, Troy might report her to their parents, and being a poor loser was something they despised.

Dot presented several craft projects, the coolest being colorful plastic bracelets that they braided. Most girls tied them on their wrists or ankles and wore them all summer. A few boys braided the plastic strands and gave them to their mother, or so they said.

"Let's use the same colors," Marlee suggested to Eloise. They chose Kelly green, bright blue, and white. When they finished, Dot tied their new creations on their skinny wrists.

Melanie settled on orange, yellow, and red. "It's very summery," Dot commented.

The hot sun beat down on the backyard, and with their mother's permission, the kids dragged the sprinkler out of the garage after lunch, attaching it to the garden hose. Marlee didn't mind getting her new bracelet wet when she ran through the sprinkler to cool off. After all, it was made of plastic. She and Troy liked to hop over the metal bar, timing it to avoid the water spray, and they chased one another through the yard, around the swing set, and under the clotheslines, squalling when tagged on the back.

"Be careful out there!" Meredith warned from the kitchen window. "You kids already broke one birdbath this summer."

They didn't heed their mother's caution, and only moments later, the terra-cotta basin toppled off its pedestal, crashed to the ground, and broke into three large chunks. Before they saw her, they felt her wrath as the blows landed, stinging their thighs.

"Look what you've done!" she thundered. "What did I just say?" Their mother smacked their backsides, catching their thighs with a new, sturdy paint stick—the easiest thing for her to have grabbed off the kitchen counter before flying out of the house.

Marlee stood stunned as water dripped from her body. Four-year-old Troy clutched his leg, bawling, as Meredith towered over them, shaking her weapon of choice.

"What is the matter with you? Now your father has to buy *another* birdbath! Why can't you kids listen? I told you to stay away from the darn thing!"

In Marlee's mind, she reciprocated her mother's rage, thinking she was too old to be spanked. And what the heck! They didn't do it on purpose.

"Stop crying and get that broken clay into the garbage can."

Marlee turned from her mother and picked up two pieces. Troy followed his sister to the garage, carrying the third chunk and sniveling.

"You're done in the sprinkler, too," Meredith called after them. "Gosh darn it! If you can't listen, well . . ." Her angry voice trailed off.

The kids retrieved their beach towels and spread them in a sunny spot on the hot concrete driveway. They air-dried their bodies, each not daring to set foot in the house for a while. Neither kid acknowledged it, but both avoided their mother.

The Becket family traveled west during the last week of June. They visited the famous Mount Rushmore and beheld its granite magnificence. They also saw the unfinished Crazy Horse Memorial in the Black Hills of South Dakota. Driving further to Yellowstone National Park in Wyoming, all were mesmerized by the breathtaking aquamarine hot springs and steamy geysers. Old Faithful erupted about once every hour and was an impressive spectacle.

On the drive there and back, they crossed the panoramic Mississippi River—another beautiful slice of nature. Other than crossing the river, the route was boring. Marlee held Mrs. Beasley on her lap and read her book, *Pippi Longstocking* by Astrid Lindgren, which thoroughly engrossed her. She identified a wee bit with the nine-year-old, pigtailed girl whose mother died when she was a baby, although not the part about her father, who supposedly vanished at sea. Pippi's adventures made for captivating reading and helped Marlee pass the time quietly. Everyone appreciated that.

The family savored their traveling experiences and, one month later, fell into the familiar when they went camping. Marvin and Meredith hadn't yet purchased a place up north. The kids were perfectly okay with that. Following a fun-filled week at Boulder Lake, Marlee was dropped off in Mountain at her aunt and uncle's house. She and her cousin Lori would spend the next six days together.

Lori and Marlee stayed with Lori's older sister Louise and her husband, Don, for one night. They had a daughter three years younger than the girls. Lori couldn't help but think of Tami as more of a cousin than her niece. The three got along well.

Don and Louise operated a dairy farm. Early in the evening, Don asked the girls to bring in the cows. Marlee decided not to ask but could not imagine how they would accomplish that task. Instead, she followed Tami and Lori to the barn.

The girls pulled on knee-high rubber boots and slogged through the muddy, fetid pasture. The cows appeared to be made of stone, refusing to move. Lori and Tami tried different things. Using a branch, Lori prodded one, and the heifer began mooing and lowing, causing other cows to respond. When the cattle decided to go, it happened quickly. Marlee hurried to get out of the way, but it wasn't easy to run while wearing loose-fitting boots. Closing in on the fence and realizing she couldn't stop because of the slick pasture, she grabbed the taut wire strung horizontally before her. An electric current coursed through her entire body. Terror engulfed her; she'd heard about people being electrocuted and was sure it would kill her! When, finally, seconds later, the current unlocked her contracted muscles, allowing her to release her death grip on the electric fence, she screamed bloody murder.

"Lori!! Oh, my God, I'm gonna die!! Am I gonna die?!" Marlee sobbed hysterically.

Lori threw back her head and clutched her stomach. Unrestrained laughter bubbled up and out.

Stunned—twice—in the last minute and with tears streaming down her face, Marlee stood trembling, gaping at her cousin.

Catching her breath, Lori managed to say, "You won't die. It's not high voltage. I mean, it's a low current."

"Not high voltage!" Marlee shrieked. Her crying caught, and it sounded like hiccups. "My fingers are tingling! My arms feel weird! My chest hurts!" she bellowed.

"Yeah. That will get better."

"How do you know?" Marlee shrieked again, feeling certain she was having a heart attack.

"I've seen it before."

Tami ran to fetch her mother. Louise rushed to Marlee. Unlike Lori, sympathy flooded her face.

Louise hugged her young cousin. "Oh, Marlee! I'm sorry."

"Am I gonna die, Louie?"

"No, honey, you are not going to die, but I bet it scared you something awful."

"I'm not gonna die? Are you sure?" Marlee shivered with fear and disbelief.

"I'm sure. Come on. Let me help you get those muddy boots off and get you inside."

Lori followed behind, attempting to contain the remnants of her laughter. Louise shot her a look that told her she'd better succeed. Marlee's reaction troubled Tami. She'd never seen that happen to anyone.

Louise drew a warm bath for Marlee, and the girl soaked in Epsom salts. Afterward, Louise kept a close eye on her cousin, huddled on the couch, staring at the television with a glazed look, obviously physically and mentally spent. Louise was secretly glad it would be her mother, not herself, who would have to explain to Marlee's folks what had happened. But knowing Uncle Marvin as she did, she wasn't overly concerned. He was easygoing. Hopefully, Aunt Meredith was, too.

Thankfully, Marlee bounced back quickly, and upon her return home to Green Bay, she proudly recounted the story of her electrocution to anybody willing to listen. The experience helped her gain a healthy respect for all things electric.

The Becket sisters and Eloise White joined forces to set up the Becket backyard for a penny carnival. They bothered Meredith for a supply of wooden clothespins, a glass milk bottle, and a few old bed sheets. They dragged up three metal card table chairs from the basement, hauled out the floral TV tray tables, and found a small, empty tackle box to use for cash. Melanie gave Todd money to go to the grocery store and buy candy for them to use as prizes.

The girls hung the bed sheets on the clothesline and created separate game stations. They made signs using white butcher paper to advertise their carnival. They taped one sign to the White family mailbox and another to a wooden sawhorse at the end of the Becket driveway. Melanie eventually asked Kyle White to round up customers.

A bowl of clothespins sat on the grass beside the half-gallon glass milk jug. The kids would drop the clothespins approximately twelve inches above the jug, landing as many as possible inside. At another station, they used duct tape to mount a pin-the-tail-on-the-donkey poster—attached to Styrofoam—on the garage wood siding, where one of the girls would blindfold and spin the carnival-goer. They set up a bean bag toss, ring toss, and a short obstacle course using sand pails, hula hoops, and jump ropes.

Joanna White offered to make popcorn and mix a pitcher of lemonade.

Sally VandeGarde, from across the street, wandered over. She was more interested in seeing what games they came up with than playing them. Troy and Devin invited Larry Traeger, his brother, Oscar, and Eric Johnson to check out the carnival. Todd did his sisters a favor and rounded up more kids from the top of the block. Marlee turned up her nose when two of the Meyer sisters showed up with Dennis trailing in their wake. Becky Meyer waved when she walked into the backyard as if they were all best friends. Hiding behind Eloise, Marlee made a face, crossing her eyes and twisting her mouth.

"Hey, they're paying customers," Melanie pointed out.

Marlee shook her head, "Don't be so sure."

Eloise greeted Becky with a proper hello. Marlee offered a lopsided smile.

Each game cost carnival-goers a penny to play, and the obstacle course seemed to be a favorite among many. Troy and Devin turned out to be two of their best customers. Between them, they had a private competition, especially with the clothespin challenge. They aimed and dropped the pins again and again, groaning or cheering appropriately.

Sally ended up helping the girls with the games since so many neighborhood kids showed up. "I don't need to play," she said, "but I can help." And she agreed to forgo any profits.

Marlee tied a navy bandana exceptionally tight over Dennis Meyer's eyes. Then she spun him in circles twice as long as anyone else. Facing him toward the garage, she jumped out of his way so he wouldn't touch her. He staggered, reaching out in front of himself before he found the poster. Dennis pinned the paper tail in a space below the donkey's butt, then lifted the bandana to see how well he'd done. Marlee clapped a hand over her mouth, stifling a laugh, but snorted. The tail looked like a fat turd about to plop on the ground. Dennis was not amused. He huffed away and joined some boys tossing plastic rings.

"Hey! You can't cheat," Oscar warned his brother, Larry.

"I'm not cheating."

"I saw you tip the ring onto the post."

"I never did, you little rat!"

"Who are you calling a rat?" Oscar held up a fist.

"You!" Larry swiped at it.

Sally intervened. "Knock it off, guys."

Popcorn and lemonade cost the patrons extra. The girls charged fifteen cents for a bag of popcorn and twenty-five cents for a Dixie cup of lemonade. Because it was so hot, Meredith made a second beverage, a pitcher of lemon-lime Kool-Aid.

The carnival proved to be a big success. The kids had fun, and the three girls split $9.40. Sally stayed true to her word and refused any profits. That meant Melanie, Marlee, and Eloise each earned $3.10. They insisted that Sally take the extra ten cents.

"Gee, thanks," she chuckled.

CHAPTER 13

Not long after Marvin and Meredith wed, they had joined a new church in their diocese, which planned to build on a parcel of land not far from their home. They decided to donate money in memory of their deceased spouses, and because of the larger amount, they were told they could specify how it should be spent.

It took more than a year for the building to be ready, so in the meantime, Masses were held at the Brown County Veterans Memorial Arena. The venue—generally used for hockey games, trade shows, a visiting circus, and various concerts—endured a modest transformation each Sunday morning but still required a healthy imagination from churchgoers to see it as their temporary sacred space.

When they wrote the donation check, Mr. and Mrs. Becket requested that the money be used to purchase a second ambo.

The congregation had been attending Mass in their new modern church for nearly five months, yet there was no second ambo in the sanctuary. Marvin inquired why, and he got the run-around from one of the three parish priests, the one serving as administrator. Nearly three weeks passed before Father Belson politely informed the Beckets at a meeting in his office that their donation had inadvertently been deposited into the general fund. "I regret to tell you the funds went to monthly operating expenses—heat, water, electricity, et cetera."

Marvin and Meredith exchanged glances, frowning at one another. Marvin voiced their joint displeasure. "So, our money will not be buying an ambo? Is that what you're telling us?"

"Yes, I'm afraid so," Father Belson nodded. "I'm deeply sorry for the mix-up."

"Take money from the general fund to purchase the ambo," Marvin suggested.

"It's not a budgeted item."

"I realize that. It didn't need to be a budgeted item because *we* agreed to purchase it. We didn't donate money to the general fund for everyday operating expenses. That's what our weekly contributions are for."

"I'm sorry, Marvin, Meredith." His eyes bravely met each of theirs. "What's done is done. I can't rectify this to your satisfaction."

"I don't understand. Transfer the money from the parish general fund."

"It doesn't work like that, Marvin. Look, I don't know how this happened."

"You're the business administrator here. It's your job to know how it happened." Marvin was not letting Father Belson off easily. "And it's your job to make it right."

"I don't appreciate your tone."

"My tone? You don't appreciate my tone? Well, let me tell you. This is ridiculous! Not to mention utterly disappointing." Marvin shook his head. "We are unfortunately done here." He reached for his wife's hand. She accepted it and hesitated momentarily.

"Thank you for your time, Father."

He nodded, but his eyes were averted.

Marvin waited until they got in the car. "Can you believe him?"

"It is very disappointing."

"I wonder what recourse we have."

To Marvin's surprise, several days later, Father Belson telephoned and invited the couple to dinner with all three parish priests the following Saturday. "We are inviting you, so, of course, it will be our treat."

When Marvin told Meredith of the dinner invitation, he said, "They just want to smooth over this whole thing. This disastrous donation debacle."

"Think positive," Meredith told him. "Maybe they've found a way to make the purchase after all."

They dined with the priests at a local supper club—the popular Victorian House. The evening began pleasantly enough. However, it turned out to be an eye-opening night for the Beckets.

A mistake the couple later made was discussing the evening's conversation with friends within earshot of their children. Marlee tuned in. She heard her parents explain how two of the priests spoke at dinner. Not so much what they said, but how they talked generally.

"I know they're human," Meredith said, "but it wasn't only once. They frequently used foul language."

Marvin nodded. "Clearly, that's how they talk."

Recalling the dinner conversation, Meredith shook her head. "I hate to say it, but it astounded me. It did. I don't know about you, but I hold men of the cloth to a higher standard than the average Joe."

Their friends nodded.

"To top it off," Marvin continued, "they won't be getting a second ambo. 'End of story,' Father Belson told us. I don't believe they ever intended to buy it." Marvin shrugged.

"Wow," their male friend replied. "Are you going to pursue it further up the chain?"

"We've decided to let it drop," Marvin said, disappointed.

As summer edged toward autumn, both Becket girls enjoyed the annual tradition of separate days of shopping for school clothes with their mother, followed by lunch at The Terrace Room.

Meredith first took Melanie. They stopped at a store across the street from Prange's—The Id, a newer shop selling hip clothing for teenagers. Melanie had chosen a bright blue knit dress with three inches of gather on the waist and cuffs. The pattern was of white elephants outlined in black. Thoroughly impressed, Marlee hoped the dress would still be in style when it would inevitably be passed down to her.

"That is the coolest dress!" Marlee exclaimed. "Can I go to Id?"

"Their clothes won't fit you," Melanie told her. "They're for teenagers."

"Is that right, Mom? Don't they have clothes for me?"

"Not really, Marlee. It'll probably be at least a couple more years before you can shop there."

"Aw, dang it."

Marlee did not find anything as fun as the elephant dress, but her choices satisfied her. Most notable was a gray knit jumper with textured front pockets that reminded her of Grandma and Grandpa Simon's dog, Cindy. Marlee thought the pocket fabric resembled Cindy's curly coat of hair. Smiling at the comparison, Meredith agreed.

Marlee entered fourth grade in the fall of 1970. Melanie entered eighth grade, and Todd began his junior year of high school. Troy had one more year at home with their mother to himself.

Miss Cook taught Marlee and a class of twenty-seven energetic youngsters. Marlee knew that, despite her title of *Miss*, her teacher was not young, and she told her mother that Miss Cook looked like a spinster.

Although Meredith held the opinion that Deidre Cook did wear a dowdy bun and could benefit from an updated hairstyle, she didn't care for Marlee's "spinster" reference.

"Do you even know what a spinster is?" Meredith asked her.

"Well, no. Not exactly, but Miss Cook looks like the old spinsters I've seen in movies and books."

"She's not that old, Marlee," Meredith said, and explained that the term was an unfavorable description for older unmarried women.

"But who says a lady has to get married?" Marlee wondered aloud, although she planned to get married herself one day.

"No one," Meredith replied, though it seemed a rhetorical question because Marlee quickly moved off topic.

Miss Cook soon proved more youthful than any adult Marlee had ever known, and she didn't seem so old to Marlee anymore. For one, Miss Cook admitted to liking teen idol Bobby Sherman. And soon after school started, she asked one of her students, Karen Nichols, if she had a boyfriend. Marlee laughed, not because Karen didn't merit one but did Miss Cook really and truly think a nine- or ten-year-old girl could have a boyfriend? Marlee was sure her mother would flip if she heard Miss Cook talking that way.

Karen did, however, spend time with Bobby Dennison, and maybe that is why Miss Cook asked the question in the first place. They played together a lot when fourth grade first began, but it turned out that Karen and Bobby lived next door to one another, and that's all it was. But Miss Cook's question affected their friendship because when Bobby heard about it, he avoided her at school.

After he ditched Karen, it took effort from her to find at least one other friend. She was far more developed on top than her peers and, as a result, intimidated the other girls. Karen eventually found Ava Schneider, who was also ahead in breast development.

As if perfectly planned for Marlee and her female classmates, fourth grade was the year of the *menstruation talk*.

"Mom . . ." Marlee said one day after school. She slid a half sheet of paper across the kitchen counter.

"What's this?"

"It's a permission slip I need you to sign. *You*, not Dad."

"You're going on a field trip?"

"No," Marlee answered meekly.

"Ah, the you-are-becoming-a-woman talk." Meredith smiled.

"I think it'll be embarrassing."

"It doesn't have to be. I'll sign this, but we need to chat first. When is this talk?" She perused the permission slip closer. "It's not until next week. I guess I'll need to know what you already know. Things Melanie may have told you, things you've heard from friends."

"I know girls get a period, and Melanie locks the bathroom door more often now."

Meredith turned away briefly to hide the grin forming.

"Do you know why girls get their period?" She turned back.

"No. I'm not even sure what it is."

"Well," Meredith began, "now is as good a time as any. You and I are alone in the house. We can talk with privacy."

"Okay. So, what is a period exactly?"

Meredith cleared her throat. "Women bleed a bit each month from their vagina—"

"From their bottom?" Marlee interrupted, sounding disgusted and scrunching her nose.

"Yes."

"Why?" she winced.

"I'm trying to tell you. It's not because they're hurt. It's the way God designed the female body to get ready for a baby."

Marlee raised her hand to her forehead and rubbed. Blood and babies? She shuddered, then suddenly remembered the discussion she and her cousins shared after Aunt Lydia's funeral.

Meredith hesitated. "You look like you want to ask me something?"

"Um, yeah. Exactly where do babies come out of their mother?"

"It's all related. A girl's body changes and develops as she matures, or I'll say, grows into a young woman. Her body prepares a special place for a baby to grow one day. It's called a uterus." Meredith patted her belly. "Every month, a woman's uterus gets ready for a baby. If there is no baby, the uterine wall sheds and bleeds a little. The blood comes out and—"

"That's your period?" Marlee asked with her nose still scrunched.

"Yes, and that is also where a baby comes out," Meredith said. "So, this health talk you're scheduled to hear next week should confirm everything I've told you. I believe they may go into more detail. Either way, you'll be better prepared now. If you—"

"Does it hurt when a baby comes out your bottom?"

"Yes, it does."

"I'm never having babies."

"You'll most likely change your mind."

"I don't know about that. It's hard to imagine." Marlee shook her head.

"Well, this is new information for you. It'll take a bit to absorb it, and you can come to me with any questions. I hope you know that."

"The boys thought babies come out of your butt, but we said—"

"What?"

"Never mind," Marlee said.

"Okay, well, here you go. I signed your permission slip. I'm all ears if you have more questions before or after the talk. Okay?"

"Yeah," Marlee said, while squinting and biting the inside of her cheek.

Sam and Bernice asked Marvin and the family to come on Saturday to help rake leaves. "Many hands make light work," Bernice proclaimed. "And we could surely use your help."

The burgeoning red and gold piles beckoned Marlee and Troy. Unable to resist any longer, they dove in. They covered themselves completely with the decaying foliage, pretending they didn't know which pile the other hid under.

"Here I am!" Troy shouted, springing forth from a heap. Marlee chased after him. He turned on her, and she ran. Neither kid was a huge help.

Raking took the better part of the afternoon, and as the sun crept lower in the sky, Sam announced, "I'm gonna let yous finish up out here and put everything away." He mostly meant that for Marvin and Todd. "I'm heading inside to heat the wood stove and start the potato pancakes."

Having been invited to join them for supper, Alvin and Ruby showed up.

On potato pancake days, the women and girls sat at the kitchen table and peeled several pounds of white tubers. Sam always wanted to cook a big batch. Marlee watched Grandma Becket measure the remaining ingredients and got a kick out of the bottom drawer filled with flour. Bernice reached in and partially filled an aluminum cup, not precisely measuring as she and Melanie had learned, nor did Bernice slide a knife flat across the top. Next, she dumped sugar into a large bowl, which astonished Marlee because the pancakes weren't one bit sweet. Not in the least. The girl still found it necessary to smother hers with maple syrup or honey, which barely made them palatable even then.

Sam clamped the potato grinder onto the pull-out, under-counter wood cutting board and fed it quartered potatoes, turning the crank and grinding them nearly into mush. Marlee and Melanie stood close by, observing their grandfather at work, marveling at the amount of potato water or starch left in the pan.

Sam cooked the pancakes in the basement on a woodburning stove, filling the lower level with smoke as thick as fog that snaked up the stairs. The aroma, a familiar mix of earthiness and the autumnal outdoors, wafted through the house. Marlee's stomach rumbled. Finally, when they sat down to eat, she did her best to fill up on the usual side dishes of liverwurst and applesauce while a rectangular enamel pan, heaped with blackened cakes, made its way around the table.

Marvin and Meredith raved whenever Sam made his specialty. So did Alvin and Ruby. Marlee didn't get it. She hated potato pancakes and thought they lacked flavor, always tasting overcooked or burned yet somehow also soggy. It was the worst. However, as she matured into adulthood, she realized it wasn't actually eating the pancakes that had been important to her family but the tradition of making them that was significant. Eventually, she understood, as her fond memories proved, even if her taste buds balked.

On the heels of raking leaves, autumn ushered in deer hunting, but it wasn't the same now that Nancy, Bobbie, and Lisa didn't travel north anymore to their grandparents' place. They worked jobs and had boyfriends they stayed home for in Milwaukee and Sheboygan. Nancy had even gotten engaged to Frank, and they set their wedding date for the upcoming summer in Milwaukee. Todd agreed to be a groomsman, and Meredith was honored that the young couple wanted Troy to be their ring bearer.

Fall also meant high school wrestling, and the team held its home meets in the gymnasium on Thursday evenings. Todd competed at a lower weight class, which he often nearly starved himself to maintain. Cousin Eddie wrestled, too, and the team performed well in the Bay Conference year after year with their winning record.

Marlee enjoyed watching the sport, although the back-and-forth moves could be nerve-wracking. A young man's back might be arching off the floor, an official lying next to him, staring intently with a whistle between his teeth, an arm raised, ready to slap his hand to the mat signifying a pin, when suddenly the boy on the bottom would flip his opponent and score a reversal. The adrenaline rush usually proved enough for him to not only physically come out on top but also be victorious. If a tight competition came down to the final wrestler, that heavyweight match became a guaranteed nail-biter. As much as Marlee liked it when Todd and his teammates won, she always felt bad for the losers who gave it their all.

Marlee and her cousin Katie saw each other at the meets and enthusiastically joined the cheerleaders in their rhythmic cadences. During the brief breaks between matches, they often visited the concession stand in the commons.

"I think I might want to be a cheerleader," Marlee announced, perusing the candy bars.

"It looks kind of fun." Katie changed the subject, "Do you want to split a bag of popcorn? I have a quarter."

"Nah, no, thanks. We can't bring it into the gym, and I want to get back in there."

Marlee picked her head up from the bubbler and wiped her mouth with the back of her hand. She saw a boy about her age watching them. "Why don't you take a picture? It'll last longer."

Katie grabbed Marlee. "I can't believe you just said that."

"Why not? He's rude. My mom says staring at other people is rude."

"Still—"

An uproar in the gymnasium got their attention. The girls ran through the open double doors and saw the crowd on their feet. The Jaguars' Jack Vincent tallied a record-setting pin only thirty-six seconds into the first period. They'd missed an entire match. Understandably, the opposing fans were stunned, though the team score was not close. Mathematically, they could not win, but they did not appreciate one of their own going down like that so quickly.

Most wrestlers went to Big Boy for a bite to eat after. They celebrated their victories and begrudged the occasional loss by indulging in hamburgers, greasy French fries, and even calorie-rich milkshakes. Some of them paid for their high caloric indulgences and needed to diet, workout, and run the entire next week after practice to make weight again, repeating the yo-yo process.

One of the wrestlers was even rumored to have taken a neighbor's water pill she offered him to help eliminate excess water.

Meredith Becket woke the morning after a meet to find a tall, windswept snowdrift out her back kitchen window. She turned the radio on. With almost perfect timing, a disc jockey said, "Stay tuned for local school closings after the commercial break." She walked into the living room and powered on the television. It took several seconds to warm up with a clear picture. A weatherman described the day ahead—eight to ten inches of snow expected to continue blanketing the area, on top of the amount already fallen. He reported that Green Bay's overnight total measured six inches.

"I heard the wind howling last night," Marvin commented, seeing the weatherman on TV.

"I knew they predicted snow, but I didn't hear it would be this significant."

"The kids will be happy with a snow day."

"That's an understatement."

Meredith began to prepare a hearty breakfast for her brood as, one by one, they rousted out of bed. Giddiness erupted when they saw the snow and realized school had been canceled.

"We have the day off!" Marlee exclaimed. "Let's build a snow fort."

"No school!" Todd pumped his fist into the air. "I wonder if I'll have practice."

"It's canceled," his mother said.

"No school? All right!" Melanie cheered. "Long weekend."

"All right!" Troy echoed.

Dampening their enthusiasm, Marvin instructed the kids to pull on their boots and shovel the driveway. One thing he detested was packed-down tire tracks through his snow-covered driveway. They may have wanted to groan in complaint but knew it would be useless. Shoveling was expected of them after any snowfall, any day of the week.

"I'll have a nice, hot breakfast waiting for you," their mother said encouragingly.

"It's so beautiful," Melanie observed aloud as she dressed to go outside. The snow clung to the tree branches and sparkled in the sunshine, creating a stunning winter wonderland.

Todd helped Troy step into his snowsuit and boots.

"Can we have hot cocoa when we come in?" Marlee asked.

"I don't see why not. Maybe you can help make it?"

"I'll help," Melanie offered.

The street was filled with neighbors before and after breakfast as they cleared their driveways. Todd, Chris Curtain, and Kyle White built snow forts with Troy, Devin, Marlee, and Eloise. The Traeger brothers came outside, and a snowball fight ensued. Melanie hauled an old toboggan out of the garage. She and Sally, with Sally's sister Sadie, took turns pulling and pushing one another on the long wooden sled up and down the street.

The town snowplow eventually came through, making the snowbanks taller. Troy and Devin, with several other boys, played King of the Hill until big Curtis Aerts stood atop the highest bank, shouting, "I win. I'm king of the hill!" The others stormed him at the top. A playful shoving match broke out.

Meredith watched the kids from the front living room windows. She chuckled at the roughhousing.

The snowfall eventually trickled to nothing. The front yards spoke volumes of the fun day. A charcoal-smiling snowman greeted folks from across the street.

As always, Todd and Troy celebrated their February birthdays—their seventeenth and fifth. Marlee thought winter birthday celebrations weren't as exciting as her and her sister's spring celebrations, believing the winter parties were less lively. Nonetheless, the boys had fun, especially Troy, the guest of honor for a small party with five little friends: Devin, Oscar, Eric, Curtis Aerts (the opposite of little), and his brother Davey.

Alvin and Ruby Simon gifted their grandsons plenty, yet they promised their youngest a minibike someday.

"Maybe as early as this summer," Ruby suggested.

"Ma, that sounds awfully soon. He'll barely be five and a half."

"You worry too much, Meredith. It'd be fine, but if you're that opposed, I suppose we could hold off until the fall."

Sure. Why not? Meredith thought sarcastically. Troy would be a whopping two or three months older by fall. She left her thoughts unspoken.

An invitation arrived in the mail for Marlee, her first official sleepover, other than, of course, with Eloise. It wasn't even Minnie

Challe's birthday. Her parents allowed her a sleepover for no other reason than for the sheer fun of it.

Five fourth-grade girls unrolled their sleeping bags in the Challes' finished basement. Minnie carefully set the needle to spin 45-rpm records, not wanting to scratch the vinyl discs. The girls danced to "Sugar, Sugar" by The Archies, "Build Me Up Buttercup" by The Foundations, and "Mony Mony" by Tommy James and the Shondells. They held hands, twirling and laughing as they fell atop one another.

Mrs. Challe set out a variety of snacks, and the girls stuffed their bellies with popcorn, candy, cherry pop, and crunchy pork rinds, a personal favorite of the young hostess. When it was lights out, they whispered ghost stories back and forth. Minnie held a flashlight beneath her chin and used her scariest voice. She passed the light to each girl, who, in turn, narrated her own made-up story, beginning with the same half-dozen words: "On a dark and stormy night . . ."

Carrie Alberts learned from her savvy older sister that if you put someone's fingers, better yet their whole hand, in warm water once they've fallen asleep, there's a good chance they'll wet the bed. "Should we try it?" she asked.

"I'll be right back." Minnie flashed an eager smile.

She descended the stairs, carefully transporting a small bowl, the hot water lapping the rim.

The only girl unlucky enough to be fast asleep was Gina Moore. The others quietly gathered around. Since Carrie initiated the prank, she insisted on having the honor of executing it. She gently lifted Gina's hand and placed it into the bowl. The girls scuttled away, stifling their giggles. Gina didn't rustle.

"How will we know if she pees herself?" Minnie asked.

"We might see it come through her sleeping bag," Carrie said.

"Maybe we'll smell it," Diane Taylor said.

"Eww!" Marlee scrunched her nose.

"My mom won't be happy if Gina pees through to our carpet. Maybe I should take the bowl away."

"You're no fun," Carrie scoffed.

Gina woke and tipped the bowl over when she sat up.

"You spilled!" cried Minnie.

"What is it?" Gina screeched. "It's on my sleeping bag!"

"Not so loud!" Minnie covered her friend's mouth.

"What did you guys do?"

"Did you pee your sleeping bag?" Marlee wanted to know.

"No! What was in that bowl?"

Carrie explained the trick. Gina played a good sport, probably because it didn't work on her. Minnie grabbed a towel and sopped up most of the spilled water. A wet circle marked Gina's sleeping bag.

She avoided the damp spot, and the friends sat Indian style, their heads tipped to the middle of the circle they formed. The flashlight lying on Minnie's pillow illuminated the paneled wall behind her. That, and a night-light at the bottom of the stairs, left the room very dark.

"I think Ty is cute," Diane softly admitted.

"Tyler Basten?" Marlee broke out in song, barely above a whisper, "Diane and Ty sittin' in a tree—"

"K-i-s-s-i-n-g," the others chimed in. The girls fell onto their backs and rolled around laughing.

"Shh!" Minnie warned.

Diane asked everyone, "Who do you think is cute?" She looked at each girl in the circle.

"Not Tyler," Carrie said.

"Okay. Who, then?" she demanded.

"Bobby Dennison."

Gina snickered. "Karen has dibs on Bobby."

Marlee snorted and clapped a hand over her nose. Recovering, she said, "Did you know he won't even talk to Karen anymore, ever since Miss Cook asked her if she had a boyfriend?"

"Are they boyfriend and girlfriend?" Minnie asked.

"He won't even give Karen the time of day, at least at school," Marlee said.

"I think Ty's cute, too," Gina said, locking eyes with Diane, wearing a goofy smile, noticeable even in the dim light.

Carrie protested, "No way! What about you, Minnie? Marlee?"

"Boys have cooties," Minnie stated. "I don't want cooties."

Carrie scoffed, "Oh, stop it! You sound like a baby talking about cooties."

The girls roared.

"All of you, be quiet!" Minnie was serious. "You'll wake my parents!"

"You think they're sleeping already?" Carrie looked up at the ceiling as if to find the answer there.

"I don't know, but I surely don't want them coming down."

"Yeah, well, I'm getting tired anyway." Gina crawled into her sleeping bag, careful to avoid the wet spot.

Carrie whispered to Marlee, keeping the topic going, "Who do you think is cute?"

"Um, I don't know. Maybe Danny Moreau."

"Yeah, he is cute," Carrie agreed. "My sister says Danny's brother in sixth grade is cute."

"If he looks anything like Danny, I say your sister has good taste."

"Haven't you ever seen him?"

"I don't know who his brother is. I know his sister, Mary, and they look alike."

"Yeah."

The whispering got softer before it stopped altogether.

By nine the next morning, Marlee, Carrie, Gina, and Diane had rolled up their sleeping bags and tromped upstairs behind Minnie, toting their belongings.

"Good morning, girls," Mrs. Challe smiled. A collective murmur greeted her in return.

"Hi, Mom." Minnie pulled out a chair.

"Yes, girls, grab a seat," the woman instructed. Chocolate chip muffins fresh from the oven on a plate with a paper doily and a mound of orange slices awaited them. A box of Rice Krispies stood next to a pitcher of cold milk and a covered sugar bowl. Five spoons nested in a stack of pastel-colored Tupperware bowls.

The girls ate, rehashing the night, at least the parts they didn't mind Minnie's mother overhearing.

"Thank you for breakfast," Marlee said, wiping her mouth with a napkin. "It was good."

The others echoed similar sentiments.

"You're welcome." Mrs. Challe smiled.

The parents picked up their daughters at 9:30 sharp. Mary Ellen Challe figured most, if not all, of the partygoers would nap that afternoon. She knew the girls lacked sleep and noticed they weren't moving very fast as they walked to the cars parked at the curb.

Spring arrived, and with that, the sisters' birthdays. Melanie turned fourteen, and Marlee entered double digits. They celebrated as they usually did, and that year, Marlee also had a party with friends from the block. She wanted to invite school friends, but Meredith said maybe next year. Eloise was invited, of course, as were Sally VandeGarde and Janice Norton, who rarely played with Marlee but whom Meredith insisted they ask.

"It would be awful to slight her. I often see her with Sally," Meredith explained.

"So?" Marlee challenged.

"It's not up for debate," Meredith stated. "I don't want us to be the cause of any hurt feelings."

"Fine," Marlee gave in. "Janice can come."

"You can have up to three more friends if you'd like. Choose wisely." Meredith didn't want to have to dictate any more guests to her daughter.

Rather quickly, Marlee decided. "How about Penny, Sherry, and, umm, Debbie?"

"Sounds good," she said, confirming Marlee's choices. It didn't surprise Meredith that Marlee opted not to invite the Meyer girls. She'd expected that, and she was not concerned about slighting them. Not only did Marlee not play with them, unless a large group played together, but she didn't care for them either.

Meredith addressed the envelopes in neat cursive handwriting, and Marlee sealed them and licked the stamps. Marvin wondered why they didn't save postage and have Marlee hand-deliver the invitations.

"Two reasons," Meredith explained. "One, it would be poor etiquette, and two, we should not inadvertently advertise to anyone we're excluding."

"Ah." The answer satisfied him.

The guests arrived dressed in their Sunday best. They played party games, including musical chairs and, like a mini art project, frosted and decorated individual cupcakes to eat, crunching on extra sugar pearls. There were plenty of "runaways" under the kitchen table.

Marlee was thrilled to receive a World of Love doll from Eloise. The hippie-like dolls were comparable in size to Barbie dolls. Marlee got the one named Love. She came decked out in a pink top with two different-colored sleeves, purple bell-bottom pants, and lime-green shoes. She wore a green headband over her long blond hair and carried a pink, fringed shoulder bag. The doll was a cheery explosion of color. There were others in the collection named Flower, Peace, Soul, and Music.

Marlee liked all her gifts and wanted a closer look at everything. She was not unhappy when the party ended and everyone went home.

"I'd have to say Eloise knows you pretty well to choose a doll that you especially wanted," Marvin said to Marlee.

"Well, she is my best friend, Dad."

"True." He ruffled her hair.

Once Marlee's birthday rolled around, Meredith felt it signaled the countdown to summer vacation. When the school year ended just after Memorial Day, the Becket children discovered they had earned mostly good grades. Todd, however, had barely eked out a C in Algebra II.

"You got a C in Algebra?" Marvin crinkled his forehead.

Todd sighed. "That class was hard," he said defensively.

"But you had a B+ last quarter."

"I know, but it got harder as we went on."

"You should have asked for help. I'm sure the teachers are open to that."

"I'm sorry, Dad."

"I don't like that there's a C on your report card when I believe you can do better."

"A C is average, Dad, so I'm average in Algebra. I'll probably never use it anyway. Plus, I've met the math requirement for graduation. I'm not taking math in my senior year."

"What kind of attitude is that? Don't ever sell yourself short."

Todd didn't like to disappoint his father, but he couldn't fix it now. Anyway, he didn't quite see what the big deal was.

June 26, 1971, was Frank and Nancy's wedding day. The Beckets traveled to Milwaukee for the weekend and had a hotel room booked near the reception venue.

Nancy wore a beautiful, white, high-necked gown covered in lace. Her bridesmaids wore pastel-colored gowns in soft shades of yellow, pink, lavender, and seafoam green with high lace necklines that matched the bride's. The groom, groomsmen, and ring bearer wore classic black tuxedos with white shirts and black bow ties. Troy was adorable in his little tux.

The wedding Mass and ceremony at St. Philip Neri Catholic Church lasted just under an hour, and as the newlyweds stepped outside, they were showered with rice.

"Why do we throw rice at the bride and groom anyway?" Marlee wanted to know.

Meredith emptied her hand of the starch. "It's tradition and symbolizes fertility, good health, and wealth."

"I know what health and wealth are, but what is fertility?"

"We wish them a family." Meredith smiled.

Melanie cupped her sister's ear. "We hope Nancy gets pregnant."

"Oh! Got it!" Marlee exclaimed too loudly.

The wedding party disappeared for photographs. Other family and friends gathered at Buzzy and Francine's house for appetizers and beverages before heading to the reception hall for dinner and dancing.

"Nancy and Frank are blessed with a gorgeous day," Meredith said to her sister-in-law in the backyard.

"Yes, I'm glad for that. It's one thing you can't control." Francine saw Troy. "My, you did a fine job carrying the ring pillow. I know Nancy was especially proud to have you do it." Troy smiled at his aunt.

"What do you say?" Meredith prompted him.

"Thank you."

"What a handsome little man you are."

"Thank you," Troy said again.

"He did all right, didn't he?" Meredith smiled.

"He certainly did."

The wedding photographer snapped most pictures of Troy before the ceremony, so he didn't have to stick around too long with the wedding party for their photo session.

Earlier that morning, Meredith carefully styled her daughters' hair. It was prearranged for the family to sit for their first professional portrait with the wedding photographer. Weeks before the big day, Meredith talked to Nancy and Francine, and they agreed it was a good idea, saying it would be convenient.

When Marlee saw the eight-by-ten the day it arrived in the mail, she shared her opinion: "It looks like we're all wearing pink lipstick."

Marvin caught his daughter's eye. He shrugged and pursed his lips. Her eyes widened, and she suppressed a giggle. Marlee could tell he agreed with her, but didn't want to say as much to his wife.

"That's part of what makes it professional looking—the colorization," Meredith commented. "I think it turned out nice."

Marvin winked at Marlee.

Meredith was oblivious that the two had shared a moment. It was a little comical.

The portrait hung above the bookcase in the living room, and the family with their pink lips smiled out at all who visited the Becket home. One could say that was a little comical, too.

A rhubarb plant in the corner of the backyard had grown considerably. "Marlee, I need you to go to the grocery store. I'm making a rhubarb cake, and I need buttermilk." Meredith gave her daughter a dollar bill.

Marlee walked a quarter mile south down the grassy median to Super Ron's. The big grocery store had eventually pushed out the mom-and-pop establishment across the street. Bannow's Arena Handi-Mart—known simply as Bannow's—had been frequented by all the locals, including several Green Bay Packers players and a few who, when Tom Bannow was forced to close his business, helped him vacate the building. It didn't seem fair to a lot of the neighbors. And the Bannow family had lived above the store for several years. It was sad when they moved.

Thirteen-year-old Laurie Bannow liked to fall asleep with her bedroom window open, to listen to music as it floated over from the miniature golf course directly south of Super Ron's. "Cecilia" by Simon and Garfunkel lulled her on more than one summer night.

Local kids frequented the mini golf course. It was cheap entertainment. Some golfed while others hung out and talked to whoever was working in the shack. Marlee and Eloise often used allowance money to shoot a round and buy snow cones.

Both girls were always home well before the high schoolers rolled in, where they could be found on sultry summer evenings, dancing in the pea gravel parking lot, kicking up dust to music amplified through, at best, mediocre speakers.

One block east of Super Ron's stood Rola Rena, another more popular spot with kids. Teenagers arrived on Friday evenings for dances featuring live music from local rock bands. The speakers at the golf shack couldn't compete with that. The younger crowd flocked to Rola Rena on Saturday afternoons for open skating. Marlee loved to roller skate, so she went whenever she could and met up with friends. They raced around the rink to the lively "Loco-Motion."

Marlee had wanted her own skates, but her mother said she'd out-grow them too quickly, so she rented them each time for twenty-five cents in addition to the sixty-five-cent price of admission. No knit pom-poms on her toes, like the lucky ones who owned skates. But all the fun Marlee had for less than one dollar was money well spent. Most days, she splurged and bought a treat from the concession stand. Rola Rena's variety of food and treats put the mini-golf shack offerings to shame.

The annual visit to Boulder Lake arrived. And it looked more and more as if it might be the family's last time camping. Marvin and Mer-edith had intensified their search for a cabin or cottage.

The week began differently from previous years. Todd and Melanie took his motorcycle to the campground on Thursday afternoon, a day ahead of the family, to stake out a campsite on the water. They went early because their father had a business meeting scheduled for Friday morn-ing that he couldn't miss, and they didn't want to get a late start and thus lose out on a good site, especially if this was their last hurrah.

Marvin also drove to the lake on Thursday but only to bring sup-plies. He hauled two tents—one a screen tent—and two sleeping bags, as well as miscellaneous items such as flashlights, batteries, a first-aid kit, and food and clothes for the kids. He stayed long enough to help pitch both tents before returning home.

"It makes me nervous," Meredith admitted, "to think of the kids up there alone."

"We've been over this." Marvin pinched the bridge of his nose. "They're fine. It'll be less than twenty-four hours, and we'll join them."

Meredith let the conversation drop. They had discussed this before at length and agreed to the plan. She wondered what she could have pos-sibly been thinking.

After the Friday meeting, Meredith breathed easier when they were finally on their way, knowing they would soon reunite with the older kids. She sat back and relaxed in the car, the tiny lines on her face soften-ing, the placid expression revealing her understated charm.

Todd and Melanie knew when to expect their parents because Mar-vin and Meredith were prompt people. Marvin hoped his children would grow to emulate that quality. He valued punctuality.

"We're here!" Marlee announced, jumping from the car and swing-ing a beach towel above her head like a lasso. Her swimsuit peeked out from beneath her terry cloth cover-up.

"Hello!" Meredith called, stretching her legs.

Todd and Melanie stood with their backs to the screen tent door. Marvin immediately knew something was amiss.

"What's going on?"

"Hi, Dad," Todd said sheepishly.

Melanie half-smiled. She looked uneasy.

The two slowly parted and, in doing so, exposed a long tear in the screen tent, parallel to and about a foot off the zipper.

"How did that happen?" Marvin asked.

"We ripped it moving the bike in last night. I'm sorry, Dad," Todd said.

"I'm sorry, too," Melanie said.

"We should be able to get it repaired," Meredith offered matter-of-factly.

Todd held his breath. He waited for more from his father.

"We must have some duct tape or something along to patch it up until we get home," Marvin said.

"You're not mad?" Todd searched his father's face.

"I'm not over the moon about it, but accidents happen. How did you rip it?"

"I wanted to move the motorcycle inside. So, before Melanie and I went to bed, she held the flap open for me, and I tripped on a tree root." Todd kicked the root. "I caught the side mirror. And it ripped the screen. Sorry."

Marvin sighed and shook his head, "Like your mother said, we'll be able to get it sewn up. Come on. Help us unload."

Todd looked at Melanie, "Boy, I'm glad that's over."

"And he wasn't mad."

"I know, whew!"

Marvin peeled back the boat cover. Everyone pitched in. Troy climbed onto the trailer fender and pulled out swim toys and inflated inner tubes. He made a neat pile on the ground. Marlee set up lawn chairs next to the fire pit.

Soon, Meredith asked, "Who's hungry?" She stood before the camp stove.

"I could eat a horse! What are we gonna have?" Todd wanted to know. He'd had no appetite while waiting to hear whether he was in trouble, but now his stomach rumbled.

"I think I can eat a horse, too," Troy told his mother. She laughed.

"What are we having?" Todd asked again.

"Cold meatloaf sandwiches, potato chips, and fruit. I'm wondering if I should warm up a can of baked beans."

"Nah," muttered Marvin.

"I'll have beans," Todd said, "but I'll eat 'em cold."

"Okay, I'll get going on it."

Novak relatives arrived early at the campsite a couple of days later. The usual routine unfolded. Men carried coolers and lawn chairs from every car. Cousins galore greeted one another. Marlee, Katie, Lori, and Julia squealed with delight.

"Let's go swimming," Marlee said. She knew her cousins were wearing their swimsuits under their clothing. She spotted striped suit straps at the neckline of Katie's top.

Melanie asked, "How long before we eat?"

"You have plenty of time to swim," Meredith nodded. "We'll call you when everything's ready."

Joe and Pete admired Todd's motorcycle. Eddie and Wade had seen it before but waited patiently while the guys took turns going for quick spins.

Troy sidled up to Teddy, and Meredith was pleased that Teddy didn't turn him away. Troy was the youngest boy by four years, and because of that, he didn't always have someone eager to play with him. Trina, considerably younger than the other girls, chose to play with the two boys. That prompted one of the men to brand them "The Triple Ts."

"That sounds X-rated," laughed Uncle Ed.

Melanie, Susan, Bethany, and Linda emerged from the tent wearing bikinis.

"Hey, have you seen the Redmond brothers?" Linda wanted to know.

Bethany nodded, "That's right! You thought one of them was cute."

"I mean, didn't we all think they were cute?" Susan giggled.

"I don't know if they come up anymore. I haven't seen them since that first year," Melanie said, disappointed.

"Too bad," Linda complained.

The cousins made their way into deeper water and crawled on top of one another's shoulders. They vigorously worked to push each other off. There was a lot of playful pulling, shoving, screaming, laughing, and splashing before an aunt summoned everyone to eat.

Immediately, Marlee spotted the potato salad and heaped a big mound onto her plate. All the kids opened bottles of Ting.

"Cream soda is my favorite," Julia said and brought the bottle to her lips.

The boys raided the orange and grape flavors. They took big swigs and burped loudly.

There were too many kids to water-ski, so Marvin treated the ladies to a boat ride around the lake. Betty insisted on retrieving her scarf from the car before climbing aboard.

"I went to the beauty parlor yesterday and had my hair set. I don't want it blown to bits out there."

They circled the lake, admiring the cottages. Meredith told Anne's sisters and sisters-in-law about her and Marvin's quest for a cabin or cottage.

"Does that mean you won't camp anymore?" Carol asked curiously.

"It does, much to the children's dismay."

"Oh, but they are going to love having a place. Will you buy one on the water?" Lorraine inquired.

"We hope to. Did I mention my mother wants to get Troy a minibike?"

"For Troy? Motorized?" Betty shrieked. "Isn't he a little young?"

"Thank you! That's what I keep telling her."

"Well, he is *your* son, Meredith."

"Oh, I know, Alma, but you know how it can be with mothers. Mine seems to be on a mission."

"I wish I knew that feeling," Carol said. "I was fifteen when our mother died of cancer."

"How insensitive of me." Meredith's hand covered her heart. "I'm sorry."

"Not to worry. It is what it is. Such is life."

"It was a long time ago," Alma acknowledged.

Marvin slowed the motorboat and coasted to shore, calling for Todd to assist the ladies with disembarking. After anchoring, Marvin hustled over to the picnic table where the men had a head start making wagers and playing cards.

"Slide over." He sat on the end of the bench and looked momentarily like he had second thoughts because he rose off his butt as if he were going to leave the table but instead reached into his front pants pocket. He produced a worn leather pouch of coins and plunked it onto the table.

He cracked open a cold can of beer, poured it into an insulated mug, and sprinkled it with salt. Marvin believed the salt helped ward off a possible headache. He suffered from headaches easily, and because of that, he did not drink beer often.

"Okay, where are we at?"

Harry discarded. "Next hand, we'll deal you in."

"Gerald took the first trick," George said, bringing Marvin up to speed.

The Beckets brought home a duck given to them by Uncle Bill, Anne's brother-in-law. It was a typical white duck with a yellow beak and orange feet. Marvin fixed a spot on the side of the garage where they kept the animal. Troy named him Donald.

"That's original." Todd rolled his eyes. "Do we know if it's even a male?"

"It's a perfect name," Meredith said.

Marvin patted Troy on the shoulder. "Bill said it's a drake."

"What's a drake?" Troy asked.

"A male duck. A female is a hen," Marvin informed the kids.

"How can you tell what it is?" Marlee wanted to know.

"Uncle Bill could tell." Meredith hoped that would suffice.

Troy's job was to feed their new pet, and he happily scooped corn and provided clean water daily.

Melanie came home from drill team practice one afternoon and peered over the short wooden fence on the side of the garage, but to her surprise, Donald wasn't there.

"Hey, where's Donald?" she asked her mother, who was standing at the kitchen sink.

"Not again. Troy!"

"What do you mean, 'not again'?" Melanie asked.

"He got out earlier today. Troy and Devin brought him back. He was almost to the Meyers' house."

"Troy!" Meredith called.

"What? Oh, hi, Melanie."

"Donald's gone," Meredith said.

"Again?"

"I guess." Meredith didn't sound overly upset.

"I'll help you look for him," Melanie offered.

He wasn't hard to find. Troy ran after the duck, waddling up the middle of the street.

"Donald!" he hollered.

Melanie wondered how far he'd gotten by the time she'd looked in on him.

Troy gathered the approximately seven-pound duck in his arms. Melanie chuckled.

"It's not funny, Melanie. It's the second time today he ran away."

"That duck is almost as big as you."

"Hardly!"

Marlee and Eloise walked down the street on their way home from the park. From near the top of the road, Marlee saw her sister and brother with the duck. She broke into a sprint. Eloise ran after her.

"What are you doing with Donald?"

"He got away," Melanie told her.

"How'd he do that?"

Troy sighed, "I don't know." He sounded exasperated.

"He probably flew over the fence," Melanie said.

"Maybe."

"You found him," Meredith said, peering through the kitchen window.

"Yeah, up the road again." Troy plopped Donald in his pen.

That night's supper conversation centered around Donald getting out and running away.

"I guess I know what I'm doing after supper," Marvin said. "I think I have some chicken wire that I can use to secure the pen."

The sisters were at the sink doing dishes when Troy came in from outside. "Mom!"

"What?" she asked, entering the kitchen.

"Dad doesn't have enough chicken wire."

Meredith met her husband on the driveway. Troy followed behind. "You ran out of wire?"

"Yeah, I'm a little short. I'll get more. But it's good enough for now."

"If you say so."

That darn duck escaped twice more during the week, and unfortunately, the family didn't find him the second time. Four siblings returned home empty-handed.

"We went all the way to the park." Todd shook his head.

"And looked in all the backyards." Troy shrugged.

"It's not good," Marlee said.

"Could Donald come back on his own?" Troy wanted to know.

"I suppose anything's possible," Meredith said.

"What's going to happen to him?" Melanie asked.

"The circle of life," Marvin mumbled.

"What a damn bummer!"

Marlee clapped a hand over her mouth, and her eyes widened. Todd laughed out loud.

"Troy!" Meredith said. "You know not to talk like that."

"I like Donald."

"It's no excuse."

"Sorry," he said halfheartedly.

"He could turn up," Marvin said, patting his son on the shoulder.

"I hope you're right, Dad."

Bernice brought a platter to the table. Alvin and Ruby joined their daughter and family for Sunday supper at Sam and Bernice's house.

Todd picked at his food, barely eating anything. His mother noticed.

"Are you not feeling well, Todd?"

"I'm not very hungry."

"Grandma made chocolate cake for dessert," she said as a way of enticement.

Todd shrugged his shoulders.

Marvin and his wife exchanged a glance.

After eating, the men walked down the path to the garden to look at what was left of the crops. The kids cleared the table, and the girls did the dishes.

Later, in the yard, Todd asked Melanie, "Do you know why I didn't eat much?"

"You weren't hungry."

"That was Donald on the platter."

She squinted at her brother, "What?"

"You ate Donald!"

"I did not!"

"What did you think you were eating?"

"Pheasant."

"Errr!" he made a buzzer sound. "You'd be incorrect."

"You're crazy."

"I'm not, and I'm guessing that was the plan all along. Dad and Mom never meant for us to have a pet duck—at least not for very long."

"Oh gosh!" Melanie buried her mouth in the crook of her arm. Closed her eyes. "I didn't know."

"Well, you do now."

"Did you tell Marlee? Troy?"

"Of course not."

"Why'd you tell me?"

"I thought you'd want to know."

"You should've told me before we ate."

"I didn't know—didn't put it together until they passed the platter. And then Grandma Simon said the duck was moist. That's when I knew for sure."

"I didn't hear that!" Melanie looked as though she might throw up. "I can't believe I ate Donald."

"Me neither."

CHAPTER 14

FIFTH GRADE BEGAN, AND Mrs. Anderson taught Marlee's class. The two popular, pretty Lauras happened to be in her homeroom—Laura Adler and Laura Harding. Both girls had long, dark brown hair parted in the middle and brown eyes to match.

The Lauras had mothers who were younger, hipper, and more lenient than Marlee's. And shy of eleven years old and without an adult, they were allowed to ride the city bus downtown to the movie theater. *Love Story*, starring Ryan O'Neal and Ali MacGraw, played on the big screen.

"I'm sorry," Meredith said to Marlee. "Not only can you *not* ride the bus downtown without an adult, but you cannot see *Love Story*. That is not an age-appropriate film for you in fifth grade."

"Aww, come on, Mom. Laura and Laura can go, and even some of the other girls, too," protested Marlee.

"How many times must your father and I tell you that we don't care what other kids are allowed to do? When we tell you *no* to something, we mean it, and it is not up for discussion."

"But—"

"No buts, Marlee. That's the way it is."

The girl stomped to her bedroom, which she no longer shared with her sister. Marvin had built a second bedroom in the basement and completed it two months prior. Melanie happily joined Todd downstairs in her new digs and relished more privacy.

It wasn't long after Marlee had the room to herself that she invited Eloise for the night. She had Eloise spend the night on many occasions before, but now it felt different.

The friends talked, whispering late into the night. They took turns writing letters and numbers on each other's bare backs, trying to guess what the other had written. Whoever answered correctly the most often earned a three-minute back-scratching—pure heaven if you were the winner.

Troy started school, too—kindergarten. Meredith had mixed emotions, but Troy hadn't. He'd been raring to go. He attended in the afternoon as Marlee had and rode the bus with Devin, Eric, and other boys his age from the block. Surprisingly, there were no girls in the neighborhood exactly Troy's age. Marlee found that fact interesting. And she felt light-years older than her baby brother.

Despite the five-year gap, Marlee believed that their parents—their mother mostly—treated her much like she treated Troy. The mere idea frustrated her, and she thought again about not being allowed to ride the city bus downtown with friends.

The two Lauras not only looked alike but also happened to share a birthday month. How much more alike could two girls be? Marlee wondered. She learned that the Lauras had even received big, identical initial rings for their eleventh birthdays. It was an oval sterling silver piece with the letter *L* in a cursive font on a black background. Marlee thought it was one of the neatest things she'd ever seen and asked her parents if they would get her one for Christmas.

"We would have no idea where to purchase such a ring." Meredith shrugged.

Marlee held that key information. "They got them downtown at Rummele's Jewelers. For thirteen dollars."

"Rummele's, huh?" muttered Meredith.

"Yes. And if I get only one thing for Christmas—but I hope I get more—I want that ring. Please! Pretty please, will you get me that initial ring?"

"You should ask Santa for it," Troy suggested. "He'll know where to get one, or his elves probably can make you one."

Todd snickered.

"What?" Marlee demanded.

"Nothing," Todd said. "I didn't say nothing."

"You didn't say *anything*," corrected their mother.

"So, how about it? Huh, Mom?"

"Put it on your ever-growing Christmas list, Marlee."

That evening, Meredith spoke to Marvin about the two Lauras. "I need to meet these girls," she said.

"Invite them over."

"Under what pretense?"

Marvin laughed. "Marlee likes the girls. Just tell her she can invite a few friends over on Friday after school."

"She's going to want a sleepover."

"Maybe another day," Marvin said.

"How many friends? What will they do?"

"I don't know, three or four, and whatever fifth-grade girls do."

"*That* is potentially the problem. These girls do more than Marlee could ever dream of doing. They are the oldest in their families, and their parents allow them to do things they are not old enough for. They're speedy, Marv. Can you imagine them waltzing into Rummele's?"

"Besides riding the bus downtown and shopping, what else have they been allowed to do?"

"Don't forget they saw a mature movie. And they *buy* clothes without their mothers—at Prange's."

"I don't know," Marvin said. "Ask Marlee what she would like to do."

Meredith decided to wait until morning to tell Marlee she could invite her friends over. If she told her before bed, the girl would likely stay awake too long thinking about it.

Meredith mentioned it at breakfast.

"Are you kidding me?" Marlee asked excitedly. "I get to have friends from school over on Friday night?"

"Yes," confirmed Meredith.

"Why?"

"Your dad and I thought it might be fun for you."

"It's not my birthday."

"No, it's not."

"So, why then?"

"For heaven's sake, Marlee, do you want to invite friends over or not?"

"I do! Yes, I do!" Marlee didn't want the offer retracted, even if she didn't understand why the opportunity came her way in the first place. "How many can I ask?"

"Two or three."

Meredith met her husband's eyes and shrugged.

"Okay. I'll ask Laura and Laura, and . . ."

"Of course you would invite them," Melanie said. "That's all we ever hear about anymore—the two Lauras this and the two Lauras that."

"And Nancy Ninham."

"I don't know Nancy either," Meredith admitted.

"I've known her since last year, in fourth grade. I bet you've seen her, Mom."

"Is she also friends with both Lauras?"

"And me." Marlee smiled.

"Ask them today at school, and they can ask their parents," Meredith said. "If needed, I will call and talk to their mothers."

"What will we do?"

"What do you want to do?" Marvin piped in.

"Play records and dance."

"Games?" Meredith asked.

Marlee turned up her nose. "Games are for babies like Troy. I'm not a baby, you know. We'll want privacy so we can talk."

Meredith rolled her eyes at her husband. "Let's wait and see if they can come before we plan more."

Marlee skipped from the kitchen, humming.

Todd and Melanie helped Marlee amass the music she desired for her little party. Her friends could come, and to describe her as ecstatic would have been an understatement.

Todd owned a Creedence Clearwater Revival album that he agreed Marlee could borrow. It included the song "Lookin' Out My Back Door," which she especially liked. Melanie had 45s of three Bobby Sherman songs Marlee went gaga for: "Little Woman," "Easy Come, Easy Go," and "Julie, Do Ya Love Me."

The sisters walked to Kmart where Marlee used her allowance to purchase several 45-rpm records of her own. She chose "Candida" by Tony Orlando and Dawn, "Love Grows Where My Rosemary Goes" by Edison Lighthouse, "ABC" by the Jackson 5, "Cracklin' Rosie" by Neil Diamond, and "Hey There Lonely Girl" by Eddie Holman. Her family also owned the single of the one-hit wonder "Vehicle" by her cousin Ray's rock band, The Ides of March.

"Now that the music is decided, what would you like to do other than dancing?" Meredith inquired. "And what are you going to want to eat?"

"Do you mean snacks, or will they eat supper here?"

"I guess we could do either."

"What about sloppy joes?"

"I can do that. What time did you tell the girls to come?"

"I don't know if I did."

"Tell them six, and we'll feed them supper. What else besides sloppy joes? Would you like chips or Tater Tots?"

"Tater Tots. How about Jell-O?"

"Any special flavor? What about dessert?"

"Strawberry Jell-O, and um, how about seven-layer bars."

"I don't know about that. Some kids don't like coconut, Marlee. Let's go simpler—cookies or cupcakes?"

"Chocolate cupcakes with vanilla frosting. Can you make those?"

Meredith nodded. "Okay, now that we've set the menu, what else will you girls do?"

"Let me see what Laura and Laura want to do. I'll ask Nancy, too. How long can they stay? Hey, could they sleep over?"

And there it was, thought Meredith. "No. Your dad and I have already discussed that possibility and decided against it. Maybe another day."

"Aww, darn it. Well, can they stay until ten?"

"Can who stay until ten?" Marvin asked as he entered the room.

"My friends. Friday night."

"We're discussing the party."

"Ah, I see."

"Can they?" Marlee asked.

"I'm in favor of nine or nine-thirty." Meredith looked at Marvin.

"Nine-thirty!" Marlee shouted.

Nancy and the two Lauras liked Marlee's new music collection. The girls sang along to the songs but didn't dance much. They hung out in the basement after eating and messed around at the billiard table. They didn't play pool so much as they just ricocheted the balls across the green felt surface.

Nancy set out the Twister mat, and the friends took turns spinning, laughing hysterically when they fell in heaps over one another.

Marlee asked the Lauras what they thought about having the same name, being such good friends, and looking alike.

"You think we look that much alike?" Laura Harding scrunched her nose.

"Totally!"

"It's not a big deal," Laura Adler said.

"It's just, well, I've never met anyone with my first name," Marlee explained. "And if I did, it would be weird if we looked alike."

"Well, your name isn't common," Laura H. said.

"*Laura's* not too common. I didn't know any before I met you guys."

"You've heard of Laura Ingalls Wilder?" Nancy asked.

"Yeah," Marlee said. "I read *Little House in the Big Woods*. But I never met her."

Laura H. laughed.

"You know that story takes place in Wisconsin, don't you?" Nancy told the girls.

"Duh!" Marlee's sarcastic response sparked laughter.

"Laura's the mom on *The Dick Van Dyke Show*," Laura A. said.

The other Laura chuckled. "That's funny you know that."

"My mom says that mom—Laura Petrie—is pretty, and I *think* she named me after her." Laura A. tilted her head and fluttered her thick eyelashes. The others giggled.

Marlee wanted to keep them laughing, so she told the one joke she could remember. "Hey, you guys! I have a joke for you. What did one strawberry say to the other strawberry?"

"Dunno," Laura H. replied. That curt response alone kept them laughing.

Marlee rolled with it. "If you weren't so sweet, we wouldn't be in this jam."

She certainly could've improved on her delivery, but the joke worked anyway. The friends laughed heartily, and Laura Harding fell off the couch, which brought the house down, and their rowdiness was heard upstairs. Meredith couldn't help but smile.

Marlee had, in fact, hosted a successful little get-together. All three guests properly greeted her parents when they met and said goodbye when they left—two biggies in the Becket household.

Lying in bed, Marlee thought the evening had passed far too quickly. Though she lay awake only for a bit, reflecting on all that was said and everything they'd done. Meredith and Marvin peeked in on their youngest offspring before they retired for the night. Troy lay sideways across the mattress, and they righted him. Marlee lay perfectly on her back, hands folded neatly over her stomach with a serene smile. It caught Meredith off guard, and she inhaled sharply.

Crawling in bed, the couple settled in close.

"I'll admit," Meredith spoke softly, "although it was only one meeting, I didn't notice anything I didn't like about the two Lauras. Or Nancy, for that matter."

"Same here." Marvin squeezed his wife's hand. "They were polite."

Marlee received the coveted *M* initial ring for Christmas and felt she would score big with the cool kids at school when they returned after break. She proudly wore her new ring and a new white, furry winter hat with pompoms on the ties.

Rounding the corner outside their classroom, Marlee saw Laura Adler at her locker, surprisingly removing the same furry hat. Then her eyes bugged out when her friend slipped out of warm, outdoor winter boots only to zip up a pair of white faux leather go-go boots. In a surreal moment, Laura Harding walked toward them, wearing the exact hat *and* shiny black go-go boots! Marlee thought she must be hallucinating and shook her head.

Recovering quickly, she said to both Lauras, "Wow! I love your boots. Where'd you get them?"

"Christmas. From my parents." Laura Adler smiled prettily.

"Yeah, me too," Laura Harding nodded.

It didn't escape Marlee's notice that neither girl seemed surprised to see the other's fashion boots. Falling in step behind them, she thought the Lauras looked like sixth—wait, make that seventh—graders! Her head started to spin, and she found it hard to concentrate on the teacher's words.

Mrs. Anderson seemed to be looking directly at Marlee.

"But I trust you're ready to buckle down and get to the business of learning."

A smattering of groans escaped.

"I'll have none of that," she said.

At recess, Jeff Miller, unable to restrain himself, yanked a pompom off Marlee's new hat. She could hardly believe he'd done that and nearly cried. Grabbing it out of his grubby, gloved hand, Marlee tucked it into her jacket pocket and hoped her mother could reattach it, knowing it would never be the same.

Alvin and Ruby Simon bought an Airstream travel trailer and left for Arizona on New Year's Day. They'd sold their last puppy, no longer interested in keeping a dog kennel, and were finally free to go wherever they wanted with Cindy and Sheila. They were expected to be gone until May.

"Will you come out and visit? Bring the kids over Easter break?" Ruby had asked Meredith.

"Don't be silly, Mother."

"I'm serious. But if you think bringing the kids would be too much, you and Marvin come. I'm sure Marlee would be thrilled to have Alice Bogart come and stay again." Ruby cackled.

"Maybe if you and Pa go again next winter, we'll come then. We could plan for it."

"Well, that's something," Ruby conceded.

Just after Alvin and Ruby left, Marvin received notice that his and Meredith's tenants in their other house up the street would be vacating and moving almost immediately.

"So soon and on such short notice? January is an awful month to find someone to move in," Meredith grumbled.

Their renters were a thirty-year-old hockey player, his wife, and their two-year-old son. He played for the Green Bay Bobcats in the United States Hockey League and was traded mid-season to the Marquette Iron Rangers. They would be out of the house before the end of the following week.

"The good news is he's saying here in his notice that he has a teammate interested in taking his place. He's provided a name and phone number. I'll give him a call," Marvin said.

"Wouldn't that be slick?"

It did work out seamlessly. One Bobcat player and his family moved out, and another moved in. Marvin didn't get caught up in the minutia but was thankful for a smooth transition. Whether it was the price, the location, or both, he never thought it difficult to rent out the house. It must have been a good deal. There were, however, a few disappointing one- and two-year turnarounds with tenants, but then the Soukup family moved in and stayed for twelve years.

February arrived, and so did the brothers' birthdays. Todd turned eighteen, became a legal adult, and registered with the Selective Service.

He could now be drafted for military duty. Meredith shuddered at the thought.

Troy turned six and was a happy boy who loved his kindergarten teacher. The brothers were a world apart, but it would not always be that way.

Meredith genuinely worried about Todd being drafted to fight in Vietnam. Marvin told her it did no good to worry about something that may never happen. "You're suffering twice."

"What are you talking about?"

"Like I said, you're worrying about something that may never happen, so there's the first suffering. If Todd is drafted, understandably, you'd worry; hence, a second suffering. Try not to think about it too much, Mer," Marvin pleaded. "It is what it is. It's out of your control."

"I don't know what I would do."

"You're still worrying."

"Oh! You're right, Marvin," she conceded.

It almost crushed Ruby that she couldn't see her grandkids for their birthdays, but she and Alvin sent gifts from Arizona. They sent Todd a card and a crisp one-hundred-dollar bill. Through the mail!

When Todd discovered the large bill, he jubilantly thrust the cash into the air. Despite his excitement, Meredith explained it might be the last birthday gift he received from her folks. Previously, Ruby told Meredith that birthday gift-giving for the kids would likely end when they turned eighteen and graduated from high school.

"I believe you may still get something small for Christmas," Meredith added.

"More cash would be great."

"Todd!"

"What? I can always use cash."

Troy received gifts from his grandparents that Meredith bought using their money. They'd sent a card for her to attach to the top of the wrapped pile: clothes, the cowboy boots her mother insisted on, a pair of cap guns—two silver pistols with red rolls of caps—and a white, silver-studded belt and holster.

Alvin and Ruby called their youngest grandchild long-distance on his birthday. They had tried reaching Todd, too, but never caught him at home. Ruby got emotional when she heard Troy's sweet voice. She listened to him talk about school, and he also told her a story about Crisco. It sounded like the dog chewed a hole in Marlee's Mrs. Beasley doll, but

Ruby couldn't understand the whole story. When Meredith got the phone back, she explained that Crisco had suffered a false pregnancy, and Mrs. Beasley was collateral damage.

Ruby felt sick. She hated to think about what Crisco must have gone through. "I told you, a long time ago, that you should have spayed that dog."

"I know, Ma. We're working with the vet now to take care of that."

"Poor Crisco," Ruby lamented.

Meredith felt terrible about the whole thing, but it hadn't been a picnic for them either.

No sooner had Meredith hung up the phone than she realized that her mother never mentioned a word about a minibike for Troy, which she was perfectly okay with. She preferred it that way, wanting him to be older before receiving a gift like that. Meredith wondered if her mother had meant to say something but was distracted by thoughts of Crisco.

In catechism class, Marlee was learning about confession. The instructors referred to it as "Celebrating the Sacrament of Penance." She listened, aghast. Celebrating? Who were they trying to kid? You celebrate birthdays, not confession. Marlee did not like the idea, let alone *celebrate* the thought of telling a priest what she had done wrong, and she informed her mother of that.

"It is an important sacrament in the Catholic Church," Meredith insisted. "God's forgiveness of sins and absolution are vital," she explained. "That's what we celebrate—mercy and forgiveness."

"What's absolution?" Marlee frowned.

"It frees you of blame or guilt for your sins."

Marlee sighed. "And you say that's vital?"

"It's necessary for healing to take place."

"I'm not doing it," Marlee said matter-of-factly.

"Oh, yes, you are," her mother said.

"I don't believe in it."

"You think you're perfect? You don't believe you need God's forgiveness?"

"Well, I'm not talking to *our* priests," Marlee said.

"Why not?" Meredith asked and just as quickly offered her daughter an alternative. "Then I will take you somewhere else—another church—to make your First Confession."

"No!" Marlee was emphatic.

"Marvin!" Meredith summoned her husband.

"What's going on?" He appeared in the kitchen.

"Marlee tells me she won't make her First Confession."

"Is that so? And why not?"

"Because our priests are sinners," she said, sounding righteous.

"We all are, Marlee, hence the need for confession," Meredith said.

"Well, I know they swear, and um, they talk badly about people."

Meredith looked at Marvin and raised her eyebrows. "How do you know that?" she asked Marlee.

"I heard you talking once."

Meredith brought her hand to her face in embarrassment. She'd suspected the kids may have overheard that unfortunate conversation and felt awful and remorseful.

"Well, Marlee, that was sinful behavior on *my* part. I should not have talked about our priests like that, and I'm sorry for having done so. You know, priests are human, too, and they go to confession just like we do."

"They go to confession? I didn't know that. Well, I'm still not going."

"This discussion is not over, young lady, but I will let it drop for now," Meredith said.

"Can I go?"

"Yes, go! Get out of here." Meredith shook her head in exasperation but waited until she heard Marlee close her bedroom door. She glared at her husband. "You were zero help. Thanks for nothing."

"Well, the girl had some valid points."

"Really, Marvin?"

"When did you last walk into a confessional?" He tried not to sound judgmental.

Meredith stiffened, "I made my First Confession. I went for years. I partake in general absolution now."

"You know it's not the same as going to individual confession."

Meredith breathed a deep sigh. "Fine. Let me get in touch with someone at church. Maybe I can talk to her religion teacher."

"Good idea," Marvin said.

There wasn't much time before Marlee's class was scheduled for confession, so Meredith didn't procrastinate. She made an appointment and met with Sister Rose, the director of religious education. Meredith explained the situation, conveniently leaving out her role and the specifics as to why Marlee was being obstinate.

"I am sympathetic to your dilemma, Mrs. Becket; however, you must attempt again to impart to Marlee the importance of receiving the sacrament."

"How am I—how are we, her father and I, to do that?" Meredith paused. "Would you be willing to talk to her, or maybe her teacher could?"

"Her catechist is a volunteer, a parent just like you. I can inquire, but the children have been learning about the sacrament for several weeks. If her instructor has something additional, something she thinks she could tell Marlee to aid her, and of course, if Mrs. Brown is willing, then maybe."

"Would *you* talk to Marlee? It may mean more coming from a religious sister."

Sister Rose thought before she spoke. "I suppose I can give it a go."

"Oh, thank you, Sister! My husband and I appreciate it."

"I am not guaranteeing results."

"I understand."

Meredith may have appreciated Sister Rose agreeing to talk to Marlee; however, the girl certainly did not appreciate Sister corralling her before religion class, making her tardy. Marlee told her parents she was embarrassed to walk into the classroom late, with everyone gawking at her, wondering what happened. She chose not to share what she and Sister Rose had discussed but agreed to make her First Confession.

To their credit, neither parent pressed their daughter for more information. Meredith danced a triumphant jig in her head. Marvin winked at his wife.

"Don't expect this to be a regular thing," Marlee interrupted their brief, silent reverie.

Marvin disliked her tone.

"In fact," she added, "I won't ever go again."

"Hey! I do *not* appreciate your attitude."

"Marlee," Meredith interrupted, "you may feel differently after you cross this hurdle. Who knows, it may be a good experience. Freeing."

The girl decided against saying anything more. She just wanted this whole confession thing over with.

Four days later, lines with nervous fifth graders formed outside the confessionals. Marlee observed the kids ahead of her. Most left the tiny rooms looking somber. One girl was in tears. Chewing on her bottom lip, Marlee reached the front of the line. Taking hold of the doorknob, she quietly pulled it closed behind her. She dropped to her knees on the padded kneeler in the dimly lit space and stared into a thick-woven screen that separated her from the priest. Relief washed over her, for she could not see him and he could not see her. His identity was known only because his name had been engraved on a placard outside the door. It was not Father Belson.

Marlee said nothing. She knew the priest waited for her to speak the familiar words: "Forgive me, Father, for I have sinned. This is my First Confession." But she remained mute.

"Is anyone there?"

Marlee held her breath.

"Is anyone there?" he asked again.

Silence.

A third time, more assertively, "Hello? Are you there?"

Marlee dared to wait a few more seconds, trying to stay in the room for as long as she felt the other kids had. The priest rustled in his chair behind the screen. A slight panic rose in her. It was time. Defiantly, she exited the confessional. Looking straight ahead, she walked to the front of the church, taking her place in a pew, like those before her. She knelt, bowed her head in feigned penance, and pretended to pray. Her heart thumped wildly in her chest. A tinge of regret flickered.

Later, back at home, Meredith congratulated Marlee and said, "I'm proud of you." Smiling, she added, "And it wasn't so bad, was it?"

Marlee shrugged, her eyes on the floor, studying the linoleum, unwilling to meet her mother's scrutiny.

CHAPTER 15

THE BECKET SISTERS' BIRTHDAYS came and went—their fifteenth and eleventh—and there was nothing remarkable about them, except that Marlee felt genuinely older since she "made" her First Confession.

Todd looked forward to graduation. After the algebra debacle in junior year, he set out in his senior year to graduate with honors. He told no one of his plans, and when he learned his final grades, he was almost certain he'd earned a spot on the honor roll and took the time to verify it with his guidance counselor. He kept it to himself, knowing his report card would soon come in the mail. To his surprise, it arrived the same day his mother showed him the newspaper with the Ashwaubenon High School honor roll, and sure enough, there was his name. It leapt off the printed page at him. It made him feel proud. And Meredith was almost giddy. She left the *Green Bay Press-Gazette* spread open across the table, taking up nearly half of it. When Marvin returned home from work, he took the bait.

"What's this?" he asked.

"It's for you to read," she said cheerily.

Marvin scanned the pages and saw Todd's name among the other honorees listed. A smile filled his face, and he met his wife's gaze.

"This is fantastic."

"I know."

"Todd!"

"Hey, Dad."

Marvin watched his firstborn son enter the kitchen, realizing he was no longer a boy. He'd thought Todd looked more like a man since filling out after the wrestling season ended. "The honor roll, way to go!"

"Yeah," Todd smiled humbly.

"I think I can speak for your mother when I say we're proud of you, Todd, for *all* your high school accomplishments."

Meredith piped in, "We talked about this, your dad and I did, last year. You could have gone either way," she said, "had you not cared about . . . Well, let's just say your dad and I are very proud you chose to buckle down and finish high school academically strong."

Todd beamed. "Thanks."

The Beckets hosted a celebratory graduation party. Relatives and friends gathered outside under a large tent, tables and coolers offering food and beverage options.

Because Todd and Nita Fischer were dating, some of her girlfriends wandered into the backyard. From next door, the Whites walked over. Together, Marlee and Eloise hovered near the teenagers. They listened to their conversations and found the recent grads weren't very interesting. They discussed boring summer jobs, going away to college and what that might be like, or staying home for technical school. One guy droned on about his full-time employment in one of the mills and bragged about how much he made. Boring! The girls thought.

After wrestling wrapped up, Todd had worked as a part-time janitor in the evenings at, of all places, the high school. Although he accepted a full-time custodial position at the school after graduation, with a nice pay increase, he still planned to attend Northeast Wisconsin Technical Institute in the fall. Todd would work and go to school. NWTI offered a nine-month program for woodworking and cabinetry, where he would earn an associate degree. Several friends joined Todd on that path and enrolled at NWTI for other specialized vocational training.

While some classmates were excited to head to state colleges, others eagerly entered the workforce. But with the conflict in Vietnam lingering, Todd and his friends, along with their parents, desperately hoped to avoid it. As a result, none of his buddies enlisted in the military.

Not long after graduation, Marvin and Meredith closed on an offer-to-purchase and bought a small cabin tucked in the woods in Marinette County. Thunder Lake was a short walk through the woods, across the rural highway, and down a steep hill. The kids could swim and water-ski there.

The two-bedroom cabin sat in the middle of a clearing, and straight out from the front windows was a man-made salt lick they used to lure deer. An outside floodlight mounted next to the front door brightly illu-minated the spot. Marvin and his family never hunted on their property. Instead, they enjoyed observing the majestic creatures during the mostly nighttime visits.

Buying a cabin was bittersweet as it meant no more camping at Boulder Lake, though it paved the way for new adventures. The week the family usually went tenting, they now planned to spend at the cabin.

When Alvin and Ruby heard their daughter and son-in-law had de-cided on a little place in the woods, they made good on their promise and gifted Troy with a shiny 40-cc Honda minibike. He was six-and-a-half years old, had wide open space to ride, and, according to Ruby, the boy was plenty old enough.

Everyone, including Meredith, took the bike for a spin, and Troy was always willing to share it, which was great for Marlee. She liked the little motorized vehicle.

For the most part, the cabin came furnished. Marvin replaced the mattresses, which included those for a double-sized bunk bed in the kids' small bedroom that was shoved tight into a corner and thus a total pain to make. Meredith freshened up the couch with a new slipcover. Metal cabinets hung on the kitchen walls and sat on either side of the enamel sink. The drawers and cupboards came stocked with mismatched silver-ware, cups, plates, bowls, and just about anything a person would need to cook a meal. Meredith brought extra kitchen and bathroom towels and bed sheets from home. Marlee happily helped her mother organize the cupboards and the mirrored medicine chest hanging above the bathroom sink.

"This place is great!" she'd said after walking through the cabin the first time, and let the wooden screen door bang shut behind her as she leaped onto a sandy patch of ground where grass never grew. For Marlee, the creaking noise of the screen door became synonymous with the cabin.

"Are you kids going to like it here?" their father asked.

"Boy, am I ever!" Troy said.

"Yeah," Marlee agreed.

"Sure," Melanie said.

Marvin hung a tire swing in a sturdy oak near the side door. The family never used the front door for anything other than airflow that breezed through the screen and straight out the bathroom window above the tub, in the shower.

And Marvin also hauled up an old, heavy swing set from Green Bay that he had gotten from who knows where, spray-painted it black, and plunked it down behind the cabin, along with a new metal shed he'd assembled. He filled it with three old bicycles, a lawn mower, a metal garbage can, rakes, inner tubes, and miscellaneous tools.

Best of all was a rock-encircled fire pit surrounded by halved logs, serving as benches.

On that first day, when they toured the property, Marvin drove Meredith and the three kids to the boat landing at Thunder Lake.

"Here is where you'll swim," he announced.

The children scrambled to the edge of the water. It wasn't a clear lake with a sandy bottom like they were used to. Melanie reached down to swish her hand in the water. Marlee slipped off a sandal and dipped her toes in.

"Holy cow, that's cold!" she exclaimed.

"Well, it is spring fed," their father informed them.

"What does that mean?" Troy wanted to know.

"It means groundwater flows into the lake. Spring-fed lakes are generally colder," Marvin explained.

The Beckets regularly went north to their cabin on Fridays in the summer of 1972, as often as their schedule allowed. But for one week at the end of June, the Town of Ashwaubenon came together to celebrate its centennial—seven days packed with activities planned for all ages to mark its one hundredth birthday. Some events were held at the community center, while others took place at fancier venues.

Men grew beards and mustaches, started months in advance, and women shopped for fabric and sewed ruffled dresses in styles reminiscent of a hundred years ago. Facial hair and couples' attire were judged and trophies awarded.

An old-fashioned barn dance took place in the parking lot, where they auctioned off traditional box lunches with a three-dollar limit. There was a Miss Ashwaubenon Centennial Pageant, carnivals, donkey baseball, a battle between polka bands, and nightly dancing with live music for adults, among other activities.

Saturday afternoon featured a Marine aircraft flyover, and that evening, a teen dance was held in the parking lot. The Centennial Ball took place at the Brown County Veterans Memorial Arena, where folks danced to the music of The Glenn Miller Orchestra until the wee hours of the morning.

Sunday's parade showcased many marching bands, including the impressive United States Naval Band and ten high school units, representing much of the state.

The week-long festivities required many volunteers to invest copious hours on various committees to plan and execute the milestone celebration. President Richard Nixon even signed a letter commemorating the momentous occasion.

Marlee and Troy discovered a lot together on the property up north and rode bicycles to the lake. The relics had tires not filled with air but made from hard, hollow rubber. While a flat tire was impossible, some bike tires were so worn in places that their hollow insides were freakishly exposed. It didn't matter to the kids.

They wore swimsuits and draped beach towels around their necks and pedaled barefoot to the top of the steep hill, bravely flying down to the lake. As they got close to the water, they yanked the towels free and let them sail through the air, landing on the grass near the shore. They coasted straight into the lake, bike and all. The first time Marlee suggested it, Troy looked wide-eyed but grinned. It soon became their modus operandi.

Thunder Lake never seemed to warm up, and the further one swam out, the darker and colder the water got. Marlee often imagined scary sea creatures lurking below as she floated on top. And it was a little creepy if she fell while water-skiing across the middle of the lake. She rarely tried to get up on skis again from the deep, dark water, choosing instead to pass them to someone in the boat and climb over the edge for a safe ride back to shore.

Melanie water-skied, but she did not swim much in Thunder Lake. She preferred to stay at the cabin, lie in a hammock, and read a good book.

One weekend, Eloise and Devin White accompanied the Beckets up north. Marvin pitched the tent, and the kids rolled out their sleeping bags.

They played Jarts—boys against girls—and launched the missile-like lawn darts back and forth. Eloise lofted one high in the air. It came down and struck Marlee, piercing her right thigh, just above the knee.

"Ow!" she screamed and fell back onto her butt, the Jart in her flesh.

"I'm sorry!" cried Eloise. "I didn't mean to hit you."

Marlee pulled the Jart from her thigh, which hadn't penetrated the skin deeply yet took a bit of flesh with it.

"Get your mom or dad!" Eloise ordered Troy.

Marlee winced. There wasn't much blood to speak of, but it hurt.

"What happened?" Meredith asked, seeing the kids next to Marlee on the ground.

"Eloise hit Marlee with a Jart," Devin told her.

"It was an accident," Eloise said.

"I know, honey." Meredith patted her shoulder. "I'm sure Marlee will be okay; don't you worry."

They helped Marlee into the cabin, and Meredith cleaned and disinfected the small wound and covered it with a butterfly bandage. Marlee's thigh gradually stiffened throughout the afternoon, but it didn't hinder her activity.

That night in the tent, Marlee lay on her back inside her sleeping bag atop an air mattress. The others were fast asleep. She ran her hand over the tender spot, which wasn't unpleasant. It was a soreness she didn't mind, and it reminded her of the ache of sore muscles that she enjoyed stretching out or the tenderness in your upper arm after a vaccination. Marvin once shared that he, too, didn't mind that mild type of soreness.

"I guess you and I are a little weird," he'd told her.

Summer began to fade, and the shorter days meant the streetlights popped on earlier in the evenings. Marlee grumbled when called inside for the night but obeyed. She dutifully brushed her teeth and washed her face and feet before climbing into bed.

One afternoon, she sat on the side porch pulling the sturdy husks off sweet corn, filling a metal garbage can with layers of green. Summer suppers were undoubtedly some of the best meals, although they were often meatless due to the bounty of fresh vegetables harvested from Grandpa Becket's large garden.

Meredith prepared a mayonnaise dressing and poured it over thinly sliced cucumbers. She quartered ruby red tomatoes, arranging them on a plate. Water came to a rolling boil in a large stockpot to cook the corn, but the tastiest of all the garden variety was the zucchini coins dredged in flour, generously salted, and fried in butter until golden brown. They sizzled and crisped up deliciously on an electric skillet.

Marlee's mouth watered just thinking about it. She believed she could eat a whole zucchini by herself if her mother allowed it. Just like Marlee, the entire family clamored for fried zucchini.

Eloise strolled around the front of the Becket house and found her friend on the porch, her back to her, diligently picking shiny threads of corn silk off her fingers.

"Hi, Marlee!"

"Oh, hey, hi, Eloise."

"Guess what? My mom says you can sleep over tonight."

"Really? Be right back. I'll see if I can." Marlee climbed the porch with one giant step and quickly returned. "She said I can," referring to her mother. "When do you want me to come over?"

"I'll come get you when we're done eating. It looks like you're having corn on the cob."

"And fried zucchini. They're my favorites." Eloise had never tried fried zucchini.

"I'll see you in a little while, Marlee."

"Hold on." Marlee went into the house again and this time asked her mother if Eloise could eat over.

"Another time. You're sleeping over there. That's enough for one night."

Marlee accepted Meredith's answer and reappeared on the porch without explaining to her best friend. "I'll see you after supper."

"Okay, see you later." Eloise skipped across the lawn.

Marlee was waiting when Eloise came. A canvas bag packed with a toothbrush, pajamas, and a change of clothes sat on a kitchen chair, ready to go.

"Bye, Mom! Bye, Dad!" Marlee hollered.

"Whoa, whoa, whoa," Meredith said. "How about a kiss good night. And one for your father, too. You'll find him in the garage."

"Mind your manners," Marvin said.

Marlee tossed her canvas bag on the twin bed in Eloise's bedroom, and they ventured outside to play night games.

Joanna White let the kids play until after dark, calling them in about nine-thirty. She made popcorn, and after the girls changed into pajamas, they were allowed to bring the bowl into Eloise's bedroom, along with glasses of fruit punch and a warning not to spill.

The two sat on the blue carpeted floor playing Mystery Date, both hoping to avoid the dud. Joanna poked her head in and said they had ten minutes before lights out at ten-thirty.

"Okay, Mom," Eloise said.

She snapped off the bedside lamp and whispered to Marlee, "We can stay up and talk and scratch backs if you want." Marlee thought that was a given.

Soft moonlight cascaded across the floor onto the bed and climbed the wall, showcasing Eloise's porcelain birthday girl figurines. Marlee always thought they were neat and tried to decide on a favorite. The shades partially covered two open windows in the corner bedroom. The chirp of crickets hidden outdoors wafted in on the gentle breeze.

The girls sat on one another, straddling their lower backs, guessing letters and numbers traced over their bare skin. They took turns giving one another amateur back massages that were more like running their nails up and down than anything else. No matter. It all felt good.

The Colton family lived at the top of Stadium Drive. Tim and Tom Colton gathered with a few friends in their parents' garage and made music. They banged on drums, hammered a keyboard, and strummed electric guitars, and the sound was heard partway down the block and all the way to the park and back. The Becket sisters and several others wandered the street following the music.

Neither Marlee nor Melanie knew the guys in the band, other than the Colton brothers, but they agreed that the one singing—Donny, they heard him called—was pretty darn cute. His wild brown hair nearly touched his shoulders, and his piercing blue eyes mesmerized them from across the garage. He wore a plain black T-shirt with cuffed blue jeans and sported black penny loafers, minus the pennies. He moved his head from side to side, singing and swaying to the music, sometimes briefly closing his beautiful eyes.

Marlee leaned against an old chest of drawers just inside the overhead garage door. Her stomach flipped. In a good way. A great way. She didn't know all of the songs, but most sounded familiar. Girls danced in place, moving their hips in rhythm. Others tapped their feet or kept time, patting their thighs. The small crowd clapped and cheered between songs. Marlee was fascinated. She glanced at her sister. Melanie flashed a bright, giddy smile. The music continued for twenty glorious minutes.

Eleven-year-old Marlee may have been too young to understand the curious feelings she experienced that day, but she liked how the music made her feel. And she liked what she saw.

Years later, talking with girlfriends about boys from their youth, Marlee shared her memories from that warm, carefree afternoon and used the verb *swoon* to best describe the lightheaded giddiness she happily recalled. Wearing a goofy smile, she admitted, "Man, did I swoon hard over that rugged, handsome, teenage neighborhood rock star. And I remember the feeling like it was yesterday." Marlee smiled just like she'd probably done all those years ago. Her friends chuckled. She giggled. One wondered what happened to the mysterious Donny with the great hair and gorgeous eyes.

"Wow! They were something, huh?" Marlee exclaimed to Melanie when the band stopped playing and the spectators dispersed.

"Yeah, they were great! That was fun!"

"I like Donny," Marlee said, her face flushed.

"Yeah, you and me and probably every girl in that garage."

"How old is he?"

Melanie laughed heartily. "I don't know, but get real, he's way too old for you!"

"Well, maybe when I'm older," Marlee suggested.

"Keep dreaming."

CHAPTER 16

IN THE FALL OF 1972, the local school district implemented a split-shift schedule at the high school, affecting grades six through twelve and directly impacting the Becket sisters.

Due to persistent overcrowding and the need to accommodate the students while a new middle school was under construction, the powers that be deemed the split shift the best solution. Melanie and the sophomore class began their five-hour academic day at seven and continued until noon. Marlee and her fellow sixth graders went from 12:30 to 5:30 p.m.—the whole of it, less than ideal. All second-shift students, no matter their proximity, were bused at no cost to their families.

Marlee attended classes at the high school for the second time in her young educational life before becoming an actual high school student. Her kindergarten class had also occupied space there during the building of a third elementary school. Ashwaubenon, that small suburb of Green Bay, experienced rapid growth.

The later start suited Marlee and afforded her the option to sleep in or not; either way, she did not have to change out of her pajamas straight away, which was a bonus because she loved lounging.

One lazy morning, Marlee sat at the kitchen counter on the red vinyl step stool, talking to her mother. She took full advantage of any opportunity to ask questions about her first mom. A convenient opening presented itself via a health history form that Meredith had helped Todd complete earlier.

"So, because my first mom died in a car accident, her health history isn't important?" Marlee asked.

"I did not say that. I told Todd there isn't much health history for your mother because she died so young."

"Oh, I get it now." Marlee blurted out another curious inquiry, "Did my mom die right away? Did Duane?"

Meredith closed her eyes momentarily. "Yes, they did."

"Gosh." Marlee hesitated before her next question. "What did you do after Duane died?"

"What do you mean? I had a funeral for him, of course. I had injuries I needed to heal from. I had all that to deal with."

"Well, yeah, but besides that? Did you have a job?"

"I did. Don't you remember? I worked at Gateway."

"What did you do when you came home from work?"

"I found you on my porch," Meredith said, hoping to lighten the mood. Effectively end the conversation.

"I remember that. But you must have missed Duane because you loved him, right?"

"Absolutely. I missed him dearly. I still do."

"But you love my dad?"

"Of course, I love your dad. Differently," Meredith added, instantly regretting her add-on. She hoped Marlee missed it. Not a chance.

"You love my dad differently?"

"We married out of a tragedy that happened, a shared tragedy. You have to understand. Oh, what am I saying? I don't expect you to understand this. How could you?" Meredith bit her bottom lip. Exhaled.

"That's just it. I don't understand. Melanie and I talk about this. All the time. We don't understand!"

"I know, Marlee. I'm sorry. No one does."

"But you love my dad?"

"Yes, I love your dad dearly. It's just that . . . well, we started differently, that's all. We didn't have that starry-eyed love, you know."

Marlee waited. She wanted more.

Meredith took a deep breath. She tried to explain in terms that an eleven-year-old child might grasp. "I saw three kids who needed a mother, and I felt guilty." She did it again. Offered more than she should have.

"Yeah. Me and Todd and Melanie. But why did you feel guilty?"

Meredith wanted to scream. "Why do you make me talk about this?"

Her mother's words and tone caught Marlee, but the girl didn't miss a beat. "Because I *need* to know," she pleaded.

"It was our car. Duane was driving, okay?" Meredith said, louder and clearly annoyed.

"But he didn't do it on purpose. He died, too."

Meredith's volume returned to normal, but her frustration simmered. "No, he most certainly did not do it on purpose."

"Say!" Meredith said, abruptly shifting gears. "You ought to get your teeth brushed and change clothes. You've been lounging in your pj's long enough."

"Oh, fine." Marlee folded the steps into the stool. Left her mother with the conversation's shrapnel.

Marlee was meeting new classmates almost daily. Greg Kampo kept catching her attention, mostly because of his nice smile. He seemed to reciprocate her interest—or maybe he'd been the one to spark it in her first.

One day, Greg asked if she could meet him at Smith Park sometime.

"Yeah, probably," Marlee nodded.

"Do you know how to French kiss?" His bold question surprised her.

"What do you think?" She hoped she didn't sound flustered. But she couldn't be expected to know how to do something if she didn't even know what that something was. Kiss? Yeah, but French—what did that even mean? Marlee had no intention of letting on.

"That's cool because—I like to. French kiss, I mean," Greg stammered, that nice smile suddenly looking idiotic.

"Okay," she said flatly, but a creepy sensation bristled up her back.

Marlee and two school friends, Carrie Alberts and Gina Moore, biked to Smith Park on Saturday to meet up with Greg. When they didn't see him by the picnic tables, they waited, and when, ultimately, the girls could not find him anywhere in the park, Carrie suggested they bike to his house.

"I know where he lives. His house is just across the street and up the hill a little. Come on, follow me."

Carrie was right. The Kampo house was close to the park. Marlee and Gina stayed out front on their bicycles, waiting at the curb. Carrie bravely walked to the door and rang the bell when, suddenly, a woman appeared in a second-story window, shouting down at them.

"What do you want?" she hollered, all mean-like.

Carrie stepped back from the front door and looked up to find Mrs. Kampo. "Is Greg home?"

"No! You little hussies stay away from here. Stay away from Greg! Do you hear me? Stay away!" she ranted.

Carrie bolted for her bike. She raced after Marlee and Gina and caught up to them by the tennis courts. They roared with laughter.

"Wow, was she cranky or what?" Carrie shook her head.

Marlee needed to catch her breath. "That was so dang funny!"

"It was embarrassing!" Carrie stated. "And how embarrassing for Greg if he heard his mom. What a lunatic! What'd she call us—hussies?"

"Yeah," Gina snickered. "Can you believe her? I would die if my mom ever acted like that."

"I'm not sure Greg Kampo is worth all that." Carrie met Marlee's eyes.

"Me neither," Gina agreed.

"I know." Marlee felt foolish.

The girls got on their bikes and rode to Carrie's house.

Marlee dressed in a hand-me-down Halloween costume that Melanie had worn more than once. It wasn't exactly a witch but certainly witchy-looking. The plastic mask had long, slightly matted black hair streaked with a swath of white. Marlee wished her family would update their costume choices because the kids wore the same tired stuff year after year.

Troy got to wear Casper the Friendly Ghost, a get-up that, sadly, Marlee had outgrown. At least she liked that one; the old witch—new to her—not so much.

Neighborhood girls, including Marlee and Eloise, trick-or-treated together. They tromped three or four streets to the south, crossing the park, before turning back, their orange plastic jack-o'-lanterns full, a bit heavy.

A day or two before, Marlee heard on the television news a warning to folks to beware of needles and other sharp, harmful objects hidden in Halloween candy, including razor blades in apples! They reported that the hospitals were X-raying candy free of charge, and police advised parents to check their children's treats.

Once home, Marlee sorted her candy and took a piece with her to her bedroom. She fished a single silver stick pin from a glass dish atop her dresser and looked at it before setting it down. Unwrapping a thin, blue chewy candy roll, she folded the piece in half, careful not to break it, then inserted the pin. She didn't plan it. Gave no thought to the repercussions. Molding it back together, she rolled it into its original clear wrapper and twisted the ends closed.

Walking into the kitchen, opening it again, Marlee scrunched her nose with feigned innocence. "There's something in my candy." She held the blue chewy piece out to her mother.

"Let me see that. Marvin!" Meredith called. "Marlee's got a pin in her candy!"

"What? You've got to be kidding." He looked closely at the candy his wife handed him. "What the—"

"We've got to notify the police," Meredith stated.

Marlee froze.

She couldn't let them do that!

But didn't stop them. Marvin hung up the phone. "A Brown County Sheriff's deputy will be here to take a report."

The girl stood speechless and mortified, though not enough to admit to what she'd just done. Marlee waited silently, and worse, lied to the police officer.

"Tell me what happened," he said, studying the chewy roll.

"I just found it in my pumpkin after trick-or-treating."

"And where did you trick-or-treat?"

Marvin interjected, "They went a few streets south, past Skyline Park. They hit plenty of houses."

The sheriff's deputy looked at Marlee. "Do you have any idea, any idea at all, who could have given you this candy?"

"No," she trembled, which ironically was not a lie.

"It's a good thing she broke it in half before trying to eat it," Meredith noted.

"Can you believe people?" The officer didn't hide his disappointment. "It's alarming what some do to get their kicks. I'm going to take this with me. I'm guessing you don't want to eat it."

Marlee shook her head, "No, sir."

"Well, thanks for letting us know," the deputy said. "Unfortunately, there's not much we can do, but we like to be aware and let the public know what's happening out there."

"We understand," Marvin said. "Thank you for your time." He extended his right hand, and the two shook firmly.

Meredith echoed her husband's sentiments, "Yes, thank you for coming out."

"Well, good night, folks." The deputy turned, his hand on the doorknob, "Don't let this get to you."

Marvin nodded, then closed and locked the door.

Marlee burst into tears.

Meredith hugged her daughter. "Oh, honey, it's all right now. Scary, though, huh? Here's your candy. I've checked all of it. It's fine."

"Thank you. But I don't want any," Marlee cried and retreated to her bedroom, having lost her sweet tooth.

Meredith frowned at Marvin.

Marlee never told anyone about the unfortunate incident. Not her friends, not anyone. If her sister or brothers did, she never heard a word about it. For that, she was grateful.

Sixth grade hummed along. Marlee flourished under the split-shift schedule and enjoyed middle school, meeting new kids from the other elementary schools. She earned good grades and kept her nose clean after the Halloween incident, even leaving Greg Kampo behind, agreeing with Carrie Alberts that Greg had a wacky mom and it was probably best to stay clear. Besides, Marlee had never kissed a boy, let alone French kissed one. She asked around and learned about the open-mouthed kiss and the whole tongue thing, but she wanted no part of it. It sounded gross.

The weather turned colder, and after the festive holiday celebrations, the Becket family spent their winter weekends on snowmobiles. They owned two, which they trailered to Chute Pond for an ice-fishing derby.

Melanie learned how to operate the machines and offered to take her sister for a spin around the frozen lake. Marlee sat behind her, worked to adjust her helmet chin strap, and fell backward onto the ice with an unexpected acceleration.

"I wasn't ready!"

Melanie laughed.

Scrambling up, Marlee wrapped her arms around her sister's waist. "Now you can go," she shouted.

They lurched forward and circled the anglers, carefully winding their way back to their family huddled around holes they'd drilled in the ice.

Watching his tip-up, Troy drank hot cocoa from a plaid thermos.

Melanie stepped off the snowmobile and removed her helmet. "What a blast!" She elbowed her sister. "Didn't you just love it?"

Marlee elbowed back. The two laughed.

Meredith and Bernice exchanged a curious glance. Bernice shrugged. "Kids," she said.

"Kids," Meredith echoed.

For reasons Marvin didn't understand, Marlee wanted to trade bedrooms with Troy, saying she preferred the smaller, cozy bedroom to the one she occupied. Since Troy agreed, Marvin allowed them the switch.

"I won't paint the rooms until the snowmobiling season's over," he said.

"I can wait."

Marvin pointed out that the smaller bedroom had only one window and a much smaller closet. Marlee assured her folks that neither would be an issue.

Meredith welcomed the opportunity to deep-clean both bedrooms and weed out clothes the kids had outgrown. She sneakily discarded random trinkets and toys no one would miss.

Marvin painted her ceiling white, but Marlee finally got the hot pink walls she'd longed for. He balked a bit about the bright color she chose and tried, to no avail, to convince her to pick a lighter shade. Neither could her mother dissuade her.

"Ah, it's only paint," Marvin conceded.

Meredith purchased pink and yellow curtains from Kmart with a big, bold flower pattern and found a twin bedspread at Montgomery Ward that matched well enough.

Troy didn't care what color his walls were, so Marvin gladly painted them off-white. It took the better part of two weekends to complete the project and make the switch, but it was worth it. Meredith appreciated the early spring cleaning and the fresh new looks, and both kids were pleased.

They slept in their new digs for approximately a month when, one evening, Marlee crept into Troy's room while he occupied the bathroom, getting ready for bed. She lay on the floor between the side of his double bed and the wall and silently, patiently, waited for him. Hearing the bathroom door open, she stifled a giggle. Troy went to the living room to say good night to his parents and finally crawled into bed. He lay on his back, pulled the covers to his chin, and settled in.

Slowly, quietly, Marlee moved onto the mattress next to her brother and deeply exhaled. Troy shot out of bed as if fired out of a cannon and practically flew down the hall to his mother, crying hysterically, and landed in her lap.

"What happened?" she asked, knowing the boy hadn't been in bed long enough to have experienced a nightmare.

Marlee could be heard down the hall, belly laughing.

Flicking on the light switch, Marvin found her atop the bed, wriggling about and laughing uncontrollably.

"What did you do to your brother?"

"I scared him."

"Nearly to death!"

Marlee sat up. Looming in the doorway stood her mother, scowling, and Troy clinging to her quilted housecoat.

"She deliberately scared him," Marvin stated.

"*That*, young lady, was not very nice of you." Meredith was angry.

"Yeah, and it wasn't funny either!" Troy shouted.

"No, it wasn't. It was a mean thing to do to your brother."

"Oh, c'mon," Marlee complained. "I was just joking."

"How would you like it?" Marvin asked.

"What possessed you to do that?" Meredith frowned. "You scared him half to death."

Hearing those words again, Marlee swallowed a remnant of rising laughter. Neither parent shared her humor. She sighed. "It was just for fun. I'm sorry, geez." She looked away from Troy so as not to laugh or feel bad. Regret wormed in anyway.

Troy, a softie at heart, told his sister, "It's okay, I guess. But don't scare me like that again. I didn't know you were there," he added, stating the obvious.

Marvin understood his oldest son was a prankster and wondered if it rubbed off on his youngest daughter. "You know, Marlee," he said, "not many people appreciate pranks like that."

The truth was, Marlee knew that, in fact, all too well and had a pretty good idea of how Troy felt. Todd had once waited in the bathtub behind the shower curtain for her when she was about eight years old and scared her half to death while sitting on the toilet. She remembered being mad at Todd. And embarrassed. She also recalled checking behind the curtain and all shower curtains for *months* after that. Maybe even a year. Marlee thought Troy might feel the same and would probably check the side of his bed and under it before hopping in at night. A smidge of remorse washed over her.

"I know," Marlee replied. "I'm sorry."

"Okay, no more of that," Marvin spoke sternly. "Got it?"

"Got it," she said.

"Get to bed." Marvin lightly pushed her out of the room, toward her own bedroom.

CHAPTER 17

IN 1973, THE BECKET siblings turned nineteen, seven, sixteen, and twelve—in that order, and such different phases of life. Todd pulled double duty, attending school and working, while the rest of the family traveled to Arizona over an extended spring break to visit Alvin and Ruby and see the sights.

The family bunked with the Simons in tight quarters in their travel trailer at a mobile home park, first in Tucson, Arizona.

On a day trip, they crossed the border into Mexico to see a little bit of the country and shop for souvenirs. Marlee watched a woman, with a baby strapped to her back and a young girl clinging to her long skirt, bury her head in a rusty, foul-smelling garbage can. Rummaging for something useful, she resurfaced with three shriveled oranges. Perspiring, she peeled the fruit and gave several dry slices to the pitiable child at her side. The girl greedily shoved them into her mouth.

"Grandpa." Marlee stopped walking hand in hand with him. "I want to give her some of my money."

"I know," he replied, "but you can't because just on the other side of these tourists will unfortunately be more just like her, needing food. Your money won't go far, and we can't help them all, Marlee."

"But I could help her," she pleaded.

"She's moved on already, Marlee." Alvin patted her shoulder. He didn't say as much, but if you're hungry, possibly starving, dried-up oranges probably aren't half bad. There were plenty of times as a kid when he hungered for more food than his good mama could muster up for himself and his brothers.

The girl's mood turned somber until she noticed individual booths where people were hawking their wares.

Ruby approached. "Now, Marlee, you're going to see plenty of stuff here that you'll likely want to buy."

"And I have my own money, Grandma. I brought my allowance that I've saved ever since I found out we were coming to visit you."

"That's all well and good, but you need to know that you never pay full price."

"How come?"

"Because they expect you to haggle with them—negotiate what you're willing to pay."

"How do I do that?"

"I'll show you. Tell me when you see something you want to buy."

Three booths away, Marlee spotted a small, navy blue suede purse with embroidered edging. She pointed, "I want to see that purse."

"Let's check it out; see what she'll take for it."

Ruby took the purse, about the size of a five-by-seven-inch picture frame, off the nail and inspected it. Marlee stood beside her.

"Fi dollar," the seller said.

"Oh, that's too much." Ruby set the purse down and perused other items for sale.

"Grandma," Marlee whispered. "What are you doing? I want that. I have five dollars."

"Shh."

Ruby looked again at the blue suede purse without removing it from the nail.

The woman spoke, "Four dollar for you."

"Ah, I don't know," Ruby grimaced. She hesitated. "I—I can give you three dollars."

"You take it," the woman said, shoving it toward them.

"Okay, you have a deal. Thank you." Ruby smiled. Turning to her granddaughter, she said, "Pay the lady."

Marlee gave her three one-dollar bills. "Thank you. It's pretty."

"*Gracias*," the woman nodded.

"That was great!" Marlee exclaimed as the two moved toward the next booth.

"That's how you do it," Ruby said proudly.

Marlee haggled with her grandma nearby and bought a pair of green maracas. They had pink and purple painted flowers carved into the shellacked wood. A man wanted six dollars for the pair and drove a hard bargain. Marlee ended up parting with four dollars. It proved a good purchase since they survived the years in her possession.

A couple of days later, the family moved on to Flagstaff. The kids hung out at the swimming pool in the trailer park, and Marlee liked how she could frolic about in the water under the hot sun and look up and see skiers slalom down a tall snowy peak. It was a scene she believed she would never forget, and therefore she loved that city nestled in the mountains.

From there, the family visited the colorful Painted Desert—the multihued badlands—and the Petrified Forest National Park. The thought of trees turning into stone over millions of years blew Marlee's mind. Unable to resist, she swiped the tiniest piece of petrified wood. The square-shaped fossil looked like an ordinary stone. Possessing a healthy fear that somewhere, somehow, a ranger might have seen her, Marlee pretended to throw it back. Eventually, she pocketed the pilfered piece.

When arriving at the Grand Canyon, Marvin stood on the precipice in awe, taking it in. "What an amazing sight to behold."

"It is breathtaking," Meredith agreed—and nerve-wracking, but she kept that to herself. The unwelcome thought pushed in, and she wondered if a child had ever slipped into a deep gorge. Despite the stunning beauty, relief washed over her when they left the vast national park. It was more comfortable for her to admire from afar.

Upon returning home, Melanie resumed her driver education classes, including behind-the-wheel training. She could hardly wait to take her driving test, and unlike Todd, she passed on the first try.

Since Melanie and her friends were obtaining their licenses one by one, some sought employment that required transportation. As a result, Marlee started babysitting more, taking over some of their jobs. Melanie hung on to two of her favorite gigs while volunteering as a candy striper at St. Vincent Hospital. She planned to go into nursing after high school, and being a candy striper was a way to see if she might like it.

Marlee regularly sat for the Stump family up the street, who moved in a year ago. They had three children. The oldest was Troy's age. One evening, the eleven-month-old had an ugly diaper blowout that soiled the crib sheet. In a panic, Marlee called home, fully expecting her mother to come bail her out, but there was no such luck. Meredith methodically coached her daughter through the stinky situation.

"Leave the baby in his crib; locate a fresh sleeper and a clean fitted crib sheet. Then get some wet paper towels—use warm water—and grab a bucket or something for the soiled items. Clean him thoroughly, and after you've dressed him, strap him safely into his highchair so you can change the crib sheet. You can do this, Marlee."

She took a deep breath. "Okay. Thanks."

"Good luck."

Marlee hung up the phone. "Mandy!" she called. "Is there a bucket I can use?"

"I'll get it," replied the seven-year-old.

Marlee broke out in a sweat, doing exactly as Meredith instructed. The two older kids watched her bustle about.

About a month later, it was Marlee's second time that week babysitting for the Stumps, and she helped the four-year-old tie his shoes so he could play outside on the driveway. After tightening the laces, she looked up and saw the baby toddling two feet away from the open basement door. Hard, wooden steps descended before him to a bare concrete floor. Instinctively, Marlee knew not to shout or frighten the child, and she didn't even say his name. Quickly, yet cautiously, she reached him, scooping him into her arms, her heart beating wildly. Immediately, she closed her mind to what could have happened.

That babysitting job was by far the most difficult one she'd ever had, and she deserved the seventy-five cents per hour it paid, which was better than any of her other jobs at a whopping fifty cents per hour.

Report cards were released, which brought unexpected cash to Marlee because, to her surprise, she'd earned straight As while tallying perfect attendance. She'd never achieved either before. The girl had made wonderful progress since first grade, when early learning had frustrated her. In some ways, getting paid for good grades was easier than watching kids.

Her parents rewarded her with five dollars, amounting to one dollar for each of her core subjects. Instrumental Music, or band, as it was more commonly called, and Physical Education and Art were not letter-graded. However, she earned a CM for commendable performance in each of those subjects.

Meredith delighted in Marlee playing saxophone, though, when introduced to the instruments, the girl would have preferred to try the flute. She chose the alto sax solely to please her mother, which may in part explain why she never played better than mediocre.

The Little League baseball season was in full swing, and Troy loved playing. One weeknight game, when Marvin and Meredith could not attend due to a business function, the sisters accompanied their brother to the ball diamond directly behind his grade school.

The evening was hot, and the infield parched. A mother wearing a sleeveless shift dress sat at the end of the bleachers, fanning herself with a folded newspaper, her eyes lazily on the game. The sun inched toward the horizon, slanting in on the spectators. A large oak offered partial shade.

Troy came up to bat, and Melanie and Marlee snapped to attention. The first pitch fell short of the plate, kicking up dust. The second pitch came straight down the pike, and Troy connected. The girls clapped as the ball sailed over the second baseman's head, landing between the outfielders. Rounding second base and on his way to third, Troy saw his coach sending him—windmilling his arm, signaling him to run for home plate. Shifting his legs into high gear, the realization hit him—a home run was possible! Crossing home plate, the boy's face twisted with emotion. Tears spilled over, streaking his dusty skin. The girls jumped up, cheering wildly with other fans. The coaches playfully slapped his backside, and teammates celebrated by mobbing him. Troy felt like a hero, grinning from ear to ear.

Later, the trio recalled Troy's first home run for their parents.

"I'm sorry we missed it," Meredith grumbled.

"Yeah, Troy was great!" Marlee reiterated.

"Oh my gosh," Melanie gushed, "he was so dang cute, coming across the plate bawling."

"What every dad longs to hear," Marvin chuckled. "But I'm with your mother, son. I'm sorry we missed your first home run. That would have been fun to see."

"Yeah, Dad," Troy said, still beaming. "I knew when I got to third and saw my coach that I could probably score." Everyone laughed. Marvin proudly patted his boy on the shoulder.

Todd had completed his studies at NWTI and earned an associate degree. He found a job with a cabinet company and accepted a small pay cut, making less than he earned as a night custodian with the school district. The new position would eventually pay more and be more fulfilling. He just had to bide his time.

To celebrate, Todd offered to treat his siblings and suggested a trip to Bay Beach before going out with friends for the evening. The popular amusement park sat near the mouth of the Fox River. The City of Green Bay owned and operated the family-friendly park, where rides were only ten cents.

Todd appreciated a little-known historical fact that almost forty years ago, in 1934, President Franklin D. Roosevelt visited Bay Beach. He did so to commemorate French explorer Jean Nicolet, who landed at the site three hundred years earlier in 1634. Todd thought it was neat that FDR showed up.

"What about Jean Nicolet?" his father probed.

"What do you mean?"

"Well, it wasn't a park then, it was just undeveloped, probably over-grown, land," Marvin said.

"I suppose."

"Do you think Nicolet envisioned an amusement park along the bay?"

"Probably not."

"Would he have even known what an amusement park was?" Melanie wondered aloud.

"That's a good point," Marvin nodded. "It's anyone's guess."

After supper, the kids found the park less crowded than during the day and were thankful that the heat had subsided. A pleasant breeze blew in off the water. Fewer people meant shorter lines for rides; and for the slippery slide, nonexistent. They welcomed that. Trekking up the high stairs to slide down on burlap bags, they raced, four across, with their arms aloft, reaching for the sky, the wind blowing their hair. The Ferris wheel tickled their bellies, and they chased and banged into one another riding the bumper cars. Troy and Marlee hopped on a few kiddie rides. But the giant slide proved a favorite for all. Before heading home, they slowed down by circling the park riding on the open-air miniature train.

Todd splurged and bought treats for everyone. The girls chose cotton candy. Troy opted for a snow cone that turned his tongue blue, and Todd ordered an ice cream sandwich that Marlee pointed out he could have gotten at home. It was a rare occasion for the siblings to be together without their parents, and Melanie commented that it was a great way to jump-start the weekend.

The youngest kids went north with their folks to the cabin on Friday afternoon. Melanie stayed home with Todd to volunteer at the hospital and hang out with friends. Todd was dating a new girl, Rhonda Welling, and planned to go out with her, his buddies, and their girlfriends.

Nita Fischer had gone away to college last fall and had a good job working off campus, so she remained there year-round. Meredith didn't like it when the girl left but understood it was the natural progression of life. She disliked it even more when the young couple decided not to continue their relationship because of the distance separating them. Again, she understood. But when pressed, Todd did admit that Nita's leaving left a void in his heart. That is the part Meredith didn't care for.

Troy and Marlee spent most of their time up north, outdoors. They swam, went boating and water-skiing, took turns riding the minibike, and pushed one another on the tire swing.

Marlee savored her time on the minibike, exploring the forest trails surrounding their cabin. The wind whipping through her hair was exhilarating. And the time spent alone in nature prompted daydreaming and thoughtful reflection. More than once, Marlee wondered if she could get lost riding down a wrong path that might not circle back around to the cabin.

In the middle of the night, Marlee woke and reached under the covers to scratch her ankle. Feeling something unusual, she called for her mother.

"What is it?" Meredith asked, refraining from turning on a light.

Marlee flipped back the covers. "There's something on my ankle."

Meredith turned on the bedside lamp. "You've got a cluster of wood ticks," she said.

"Eww," Marlee shuddered.

"I'll take care of it. Don't pull at them. I'll be right back," Meredith told her.

Troy leaned down from the upper bunk. "What's going on?" he asked groggily.

"I've got three wood ticks on my ankle."

Meredith returned with an odd plethora of things—a magnifying glass, tweezers, matches, an ashtray, a cotton ball, and rubbing alcohol.

"Hold still," she said, after looking through the lens. Lighting a match and holding it close to the wood ticks but not touching them, she hoped they'd back out of Marlee's flesh. "They're not embedded. See that," Meredith said and, with the tweezers, grabbed the ticks one by one and dropped them into the ashtray. "I'll flush these down the toilet. Put rubbing alcohol on that cotton ball and clean your ankle. They came out easily. See their heads. They probably weren't on you too long."

"They're creepy," Marlee told her mother.

"Wash your hands," Meredith instructed, looking inside the sheets to check for more pesky ticks.

"Thanks, Mom," Marlee said.

"You're welcome. See you in the morning."

The kids went to the lake but didn't ride bicycles because Troy wanted to fish from the shore and needed both hands to carry his equipment. Marlee walked with him, helped lug gear, and rolled a huge black inner tube for herself.

Troy cast his line from the dock, about forty yards from where his sister floated. Frustrated because he twice snagged the weeping willow branches behind him, he stepped off the short wooden pier and waded into deeper water. Holding the rod and reel, he flicked his wrist to let out more line. He did that several times before he yelped.

"My back! Marlee! I hooked my back! Help me!"

She spun her tube around and squinted into the sun.

"What?" she hollered. Sliding off the inner tube, she waded over to Troy, wondering what the commotion was about.

He turned his back to her. Marlee gasped. Clapped a hand over her mouth. The hook had caught his bare skin.

"Get it out!"

"I don't know how!" Her voice suddenly became high-pitched.

Troy gently tugged the line he'd reeled in. Marlee winced.

"It's that bad?"

"I don't know what to do. I'm gonna run and get Dad and Mom."

"I'm coming with."

"You can't! Just sit still. Wait on the dock. We'll be back fast."

"No, I'm going with you," Troy insisted.

Marlee winced again. "Oh, Troy."

"Let's go. Grab my tackle box. Leave the rest."

The siblings headed up the steep incline. Troy held the fishing pole straight up in the air, tight against his chest, as still as he could manage.

"How bad does it hurt?" Marlee wanted to know.

"It's okay."

"Really?"

"It hurt when I caught my skin. It hurts if it pulls," he admitted. "How bad did it tear?"

"I don't know. I mean, yeah, the hook is in, but I can't see that it tore your skin. There's barely any blood," she explained, trying to sound hopeful.

The kids got to the top of the hill and waited for a few cars to pass before crossing the road. They didn't run across like normal, not wanting to jiggle the hook. They walked the short distance on the worn path through the woods, and as they approached the clearing where the cabin stood, Marlee started to yell.

"Mom! Dad!" Louder, "Dad!"

Both parents came running, their mother from inside the cabin and their father from somewhere behind it.

Meredith had a head start and reached the kids first. "What happened?"

"Troy's got a hook in his back."

He turned to show his folks.

"What!" Meredith's hand flew to her forehead.

"How did that happen?" Marvin asked.

"I cast my line and snagged myself."

"Oh, my goodness!" Meredith moved toward the cabin. "I'm getting my jackknife and rubbing alcohol."

Marvin cut the fishing line, freeing Troy, using fingernail clippers he always carried in his front pants pocket, and took the pole from his son. In the kitchen, he swung a chair out from under the table and instructed Troy to sit backward, straddling the chair back.

Meredith removed her glasses and looked closer at the hook. "The barb is buried. We're going to have to cut it out."

Troy closed his eyes.

"You can't do that," Marvin told his wife. "We've got to take him somewhere."

"Where would we take him?"

"I'm going over to Muralski's. I'm taking the minibike. Jerry should know who to call. Put your knife away, Meredith."

Jerry Muralski owned the tavern on the corner of the main road where the kids crossed. It never occurred to them to stop there and ask for help.

Meredith slid a chair next to Troy. "Tell me again how this happened."

He recalled the details for her.

"Okay. Well, sit tight. Dad will be back soon."

It wasn't long before they heard the hum of the minibike motor.

"All right, let's go," Marvin said. "Jerry called and talked to a guy he knows, a retired doctor who has a place not far from us, less than twenty minutes from here. I've got directions. He knows we're coming. He'll be ready for us."

Troy breathed a sigh of relief. He did not want his mother and her jackknife anywhere near his back.

Marvin hustled to the bedroom and grabbed the car keys and his wallet from the top of the dresser.

Meredith placed a soft pillow behind Troy in the car as a cushion against the seat.

Marlee slid in next to Troy. She remained quiet but kept her eyes on her brother, trying to imagine how he felt.

Eighteen minutes later, they pulled into the driveway of a year-round home on a lake with amazing views. A man with a mop of silver hair exited the house, and a woman trailed behind him.

"You found us. Come on in. I'm Ned Baker. This is my wife, June." June smiled.

"I'm Marvin; this is my wife, Meredith, and two of our kids. This here is Troy, whom Jerry told you about on the phone. Boy, I'm glad you're home."

The retired physician ushered everyone inside. He lowered his bi-focals from the top of his head. "Well, Troy, let me have a look-see. How old are you?"

Wearing only cut-off jean shorts and a ragged pair of rubber thongs on his dirty feet, Troy turned to show his back to Dr. Baker. "I'm seven and a half, going into second grade."

"Second grade, huh? Do you like school?" he asked, surveying the boy's back.

"I guess."

Ned chuckled. "Okay, this doesn't look too bad. I'm going to numb the area with a topical ointment." His next question was directed to Meredith. "Is Troy up to date with Tetanus?"

"He is."

"Good, good," Ned nodded. "We need to wait a few minutes for this to take effect. Did you give the boy any aspirin?"

"No, we didn't." Marvin turned to Meredith.

"I never thought about it," she admitted.

"Not a problem. Troy? How about we give you two chewable aspirin?"

"Okay."

The doctor sat down. "We're ready," he soon said. "You'll feel this a little, but I know you can handle it, Troy. You're going into second grace, after all. You look tough." Using a sharp, scalpel-type instrument, he cut into the boy's skin. "You feel that?"

"Barely."

"Good, good. I've almost got it. There. The worst is over." He held the hook for Troy to see. "It was deep. I'll clean the spot and put a stitch or two in to be on the safe side."

Marlee watched, recalling an earlier occasion, the day of Aunt Lydia's funeral, when the family paid a similar visit to a country doctor who treated Melanie's blood poisoning.

"Two was the magic number," the doctor said. "You were a trooper."

"You're done?" Troy asked, rounding his shoulders, slightly stretching, feeling almost nothing. "Thanks!"

"You're welcome. It'll be tender for a couple of days. Watch the area, Mom, for any drainage. If you notice any signs of infection, call your family doctor immediately to get an antibiotic. You should call him anyway to remove the stitches."

Meredith nodded. "Thank you, Doctor." Marvin felt certain she would want to remove them herself.

"Yes, thank you." Marvin reached into his back pocket for his billfold. "What do I owe you?"

"Twenty bucks will cover it."

Marvin pulled a twenty out. "Thank you very much."

"You're welcome. Say, I didn't even ask. Did you catch any fish, Troy?"

"I was just getting started."

Ned chuckled. "Well, next trip out, I hope you catch a big one."

"Thank you again," Meredith smiled.

Troy and Marlee waved to Ned and June Baker.

Marlee dressed for a Novak family reunion, choosing her favorite bell-bottoms and a white-and-pink polka-dotted top with flowing short sleeves. A cold front rolled through northeastern Wisconsin overnight, dropping late-summer temperatures below average. The day before, it hovered at ninety degrees, and the air was sticky with humidity. In this part of the Midwest, it is often said that if you don't like the weather, wait a few minutes because it will likely change. Such is life so near the Great Lakes.

"Remember, it's always a tad cooler at their house on the river," Meredith reminded the kids. "Why don't you bring a sweater or a sweatshirt?" she suggested.

The family traveled thirty minutes south to the home of one of Anne's sisters. Mary and Bill hosted the large gathering.

All the best foods indicative of the Novak family's Czech heritage filled the long tables outside under a canopy. Among them, roasters filled with pork, dumplings, and tangy sauerkraut, as well as large sheet pans of colorfully filled kolaches—raspberry, blackberry, blueberry, and apricot—nature's rainbow—beckoned. Meredith brought a humongous bowl of potato salad as her contribution. It wasn't of Czech origin, but neither was she.

It was a perfect day to be outdoors. The temperature held steady at a pleasant seventy-four degrees with no trace of humidity and a minimal breeze rolling in off the Fox River. Bright sunshine penetrated the trees, smiling down upon nearly one hundred relatives.

Marlee and the many cousins her age ran about on the sprawling lawn, playing tag and hide-and-seek. Later, following the consumption of plentiful food, the men settled in to play cards, throw horseshoes, and, for many of them, consume a matching amount of beer and alcohol. The women walked about the property, praising Mary as they admired her flower gardens. They sipped cold beverages while relaxing in lawn chairs.

"Harry and I are taking the kids on a day trip to see the new Sears Tower," Alma announced.

"That's in Chicago?" Betty asked.

"It is. Harry says it's the tallest building in the world. It's something like fourteen hundred feet high and has over a hundred floors. He's fascinated with skyscrapers, although he says he'd never want to live in a big city."

"That'll be a nice family getaway," smiled Carol.

"And interesting," commented Meredith. "I would like to visit the Sears Tower." She continued, albeit off-topic, when she added, "I always look forward to receiving their big catalogs in the mail. Marlee loves to cut up the Sears books when I've finished with them. She essentially makes cut-out dolls."

"Is there a Sears store in the Tower?" Mary inquired.

"Not that I'm aware of," Alma chuckled.

"Oh, sorry. Talk of the Sears Tower reminds me that Marlee and a friend always clamor for the Sears catalogs. They often chose a whole family—husband, wife, a few kids, wardrobes for all of them, and furniture for their dream home." Meredith smiled. "Do your girls do that?"

Lorraine raised her hand. "Mine have done that."

"I look forward to the catalogs arriving, too," Carol said. "And the kids mark it all up, circle items they want for Christmas. Too many things, I'm afraid."

The women laughed. Each could relate.

The Becket family ventured home before dark. Marvin and Meredith talked, trading news and gossip they heard from the in-laws. The kids were mostly quiet. Melanie and Todd turned to look out their respective windows. Looking straight ahead, over her brother's head, Marlee pondered the day.

Meredith sighed as they arrived home. "You may as well get ready for baths and bed," she said to Troy and Marlee. "There's not much daylight left, and we have church tomorrow."

Behind the closed bathroom door, Troy played with his bath toys. His lips made the sound of boat motors, and small, plastic cowboys and Indians dove from tall cliffs, splashing into the water below.

Next up was Marlee, but she had something else entirely on her mind. She knocked apprehensively on her parents' bedroom door.

"Who's there?" Marvin called.

"Me."

"What do you want?"

"Can I come in?"

Marvin exchanged glances with his wife.

"Ah, give us a minute," he said. Meredith grabbed a lightweight summer robe and threw it over her nightgown. Marvin opened the bedroom door, still dressed in the pants he'd worn all day, his top half stripped to a white ribbed tank-top undershirt. "What's going on?"

Marlee looked at the open bedroom door. Marvin picked up her cue and motioned her in, closing the door behind her.

"What's on your mind?"

"Well, today, um . . . today I, ah . . . went with Lori and Katie, Julia, Johnny, Grant, and well, all of us went behind the boat shed and we umm . . ."

"What?" Marvin prompted.

"We um," Marlee cleared her throat. "We smoked."

"Cigarettes?"

"Yes." She looked down at the floor.

Meredith exhaled, not realizing she'd been holding her breath.

"Why are you telling your mother and me this now?"

"Because, um, I know we shouldn't have been, and I'm, ah, I'm sorry."

"Where did you get the cigarettes?"

"Johnny got them from his dad."

"Bill gave Johnny cigarettes?" Meredith sounded skeptical.

"No. Johnny told us he swiped them from his dad's workbench."

"I see," Marvin nodded. "What did you think about smoking? Aside from the fact you shouldn't have done it and you're sorry you did."

"It burned."

"Your throat?"

"And my eyes," Marlee admitted. She began to feel a weight lift from her shoulders. The admission wasn't going badly.

"What do you think we should do about this?"

"I guess I should be punished." Marlee looked down again. She put her arms behind her back and crossed her fingers.

"What's a fair punishment?" Meredith asked.

"I don't know."

Marvin folded his arms, rubbed his chin, and remained quiet for several seconds. "It was brave of you to tell us, Marlee, and by the looks of it, not very easy."

"No," she agreed.

"Thank you for telling us."

She nodded, looked at the carpeted floor once more, and tightened her crossed fingers.

"Do you promise never to smoke again?"

"Yeah, I promise."

"Smoking's not good for you," Meredith added.

"We're going to hold you to that, Marlee." Marvin took hold of her shoulders. "Look at me."

Her eyes met his. She still waited for the hammer to fall.

"Don't *ever* smoke again."

"I won't. I promise."

Her father's gaze bore into her. "Okay." Finally, he opened the door.

"I'll take my bath now," she said, anxious to leave, and thankful for no punishment.

Marlee soaked in the tub and shed a few tears. She didn't know why she cried, nor did she understand what prompted her to come clean about smoking. She'd never admitted to the Halloween incident. Maybe that was why she came clean about smoking—for the very fact that she hadn't with the candy. Perhaps a clear conscience now would feel good because when she thought back on that autumn night, that didn't. Whatever inspired her, Marlee felt right with the world as she lay in the bathtub, washing away the day's dirt.

CHAPTER 18

THE INAUGURAL SEVENTH-GRADE CLASS, including Marlee, took residence in the brand-new, modern Parkview Middle School. It housed grades six through eight in clusters of three open-concept classrooms referred to as pods. Local academia had high expectations.

"*Please*, can I wear jeans to school?" Twelve-year-old Marlee begged her mother.

"The school district didn't allow young ladies to wear slacks to school until last year, which you barely did, and now you want to wear *blue jeans*?" Meredith sounded almost disgusted. "Blue jeans are for the farm, Marlee, not school."

"Everyone wears them!"

"And if everyone jumped off a cliff, would you?"

"There are no cliffs anywhere near here," she muttered under her breath.

"What was that? What did you say?" Meredith demanded.

"Just that we don't have any cliffs around."

"Don't be a smart aleck. My answer isn't changing, so stop asking me. You can't wear jeans to school, Marlee. End of discussion."

Meredith generally enjoyed her youngest daughter's company. But when Marlee Joan Becket wanted something, she could be relentless. No one enjoyed that.

After saying good night, Marlee shuffled down the hall to bed and closed the bedroom door tightly. She flopped on the mattress and just as quickly popped up. The curtains were open, and the shade was pulled only halfway, exposing the open window. The evening was slow to cool, and Marlee rested her arms on the window ledge. The few stars above the trees twinkled brightly. The moon was just a sliver.

She couldn't help but wonder if her other mom would have let her wear jeans to school. That was how she always thought about and referred to Anne—her other mother or her first mom—never her birth mom. And no one in the family ever referred to Meredith as a stepmother. Marlee liked to think of Meredith as her mom now, or her second mom. And one thing was certain: Marlee would always be grateful she got another mom. She didn't hate God for letting her mother die that awful night, but she suffered plenty for it, and she tried very hard to understand why he let her die.

For Marlee, it seemed innate from the beginning to be happy that she had Meredith. She didn't know any kids who didn't have a mom, and she wanted one. It was important, even vital, to have one of her own, and so Marlee was always thankful for Meredith, whom she dearly loved. She just missed her other mother sometimes, often wondering what life would have been like had Anne not died. Melanie experienced the same feelings, and together, the sisters occasionally commiserated over their mother's death, more so as they grew to be young women. Losing their mother as children was a heavy cross to carry.

Fall brought middle school football, and Marlee found the games captivating. Everything about them was new and fun and spirited. The Warriors competed against other local schools, and students traveled on fan buses to cheer for their team. The weather for the weekly contests always seemed perfect—crisp and invigorating. Marlee delighted in milling about, talking to friends behind the sidelines, and joining in to echo the cheerleaders' chants, adding to the raucous atmosphere. She truly reveled in all the excitement. It helped that the Warriors were a winning team, and the girl didn't miss a single game that first season.

First quarter report cards were released, and the word *mortified* immediately came to mind when Marlee saw that she'd earned herself two big, fat Ds! They jumped off the paper. Slapped her in the face. Science and Social Studies were the two subjects Mr. Herman taught. How could she have let that happen? Sure, she didn't like Mr. Herman, not in the least. But did he know? It was tough to wrap her brain around two below-average marks. And what about her parents? This would not go over well.

The rest of her report card wasn't exceptional either. She got an A in Reading but Cs in Math and Communication Skills. The other subjects were non-letter graded. Satisfactory marks were earned in Physical Education and Art, but an ugly, unsatisfactory mark for "Personal/Group

Behavior." What would her parents say? Especially since she'd finished sixth grade on such a high note, having earned straight As. Marlee dreaded handing over her report card.

Meredith and Marvin reacted much the way she'd anticipated. Her mother blew her top, threatening, "Wait until your father sees this."

He didn't blow his top but instead asked, calmly and straightforwardly, as was his way, albeit with a curse word, "What the hell happened here, Marlee?" He rarely swore.

"I—don't know. I was just as surprised as you were."

"Is that so?"

"You know, Marv, maybe this open-concept pod thing isn't working for Marlee?" Meredith suggested. She'd never liked the idea of open classrooms. There was too much opportunity for distraction.

"Yeah, that's it!" Marlee glommed onto the suggestion. "That's got to be it!"

"Hmm," muttered Marvin, not completely sold. "Is there any other reason you can think of for such poor grades here?"

"No," Marlee shook her head.

"How about if I make an appointment to talk with this, ah, Mr. Herman, and see what he can tell us?" Meredith offered.

"That's a good idea," Marvin agreed. Looking at his daughter, he added, "These grades are unacceptable, Marlee. Do you get that?"

"Yes."

"I'm not entirely sure you do. But we'll discuss this again after your mother meets with your teacher."

Marlee understood she had to quickly improve her grades in almost all subjects, although her parents didn't say much about the two Cs. After seeing Ds, they probably thought they weren't half bad. The girl realized she must try harder to like Mr. Herman, too. It could only help her case.

Meredith met with Neil Herman and learned that Marlee socialized during class and that her work had been inconsistent. Mr. Herman agreed that the open-concept setting may not be best for Marlee, but he was clear in stressing that it was not the crux of her problem. She talked too much when she ought to be listening.

Marvin restated his and Meredith's earlier stance on the matter. "As we've said before, Marlee, Ds are unacceptable for you. You can do better. School is important, and you are there to learn. You *must* buckle down and pay attention, keep your mouth shut, and listen when your teachers are talking. It's simple. You need to work harder and do better. Don't be afraid to ask me or your mother for help with your homework if you don't understand something. It's the same with your teachers. My gosh, ask for help."

"I will."

"Did I make myself clear?"

"Yes."

"Mr. Herman will send home mid-quarter progress reports," Meredith stated.

"So, if you're not showing marked improvement, your mother and I will reevaluate."

"Reevaluate?"

"I think it's also best if your mother reviews your homework assignments with you each night."

Marlee's jaw dropped. "For how long?"

"Well, at least until we see a progress report."

"Crap."

"Marlee," Meredith warned.

"You put yourself in this position with your choices," Marvin stated.

The girl did buckle down and tried hard to be nicer to Mr. Herman. He was, though, not an easy man for her to like. She couldn't pinpoint why, but he irritated her.

After a few weeks into the second quarter, Marlee brought home her first progress report. Her effort had improved, and it showed in her daily work. But Science and Social Studies test scores weren't where Mr. Herman thought they should be. Marlee was capable of more, he'd said.

Marvin and Meredith commended their daughter on her progress and encouraged her to continue working hard.

"Try to get your test scores up. I'll study with you if you want," offered Marvin.

"You will?"

"I like Science. Social Studies—I'm not as sure about."

"See," Marlee said.

"See what? All I'm saying is I'm not as interested in Social Studies, but I certainly can help you study."

"Maybe."

Meredith religiously monitored homework.

Marlee wanted a change in more ways than her grades and decided a haircut was the answer.

When Troy saw her, he said, "It's not much different."

"Hello! I got, like, three inches cut off!"

Meredith defended Troy's observation, "But your style's the same, just shorter, is all."

"It's probably healthier," Melanie commented. "I read in *Seventeen* that it's best to cut off a good amount of length occasionally. Get rid of split ends, you know?"

"Are you gonna get your hair cut?" Troy asked Melanie.

"Me? Gosh, no."

"Good. I like it long."

"Thanks, Troy. Me, too."

The Christmas school break was waiting around the corner. In just over twenty-four hours, Marlee would be free of school and homework until after the new year. First, she had to survive end-of-semester report cards.

Walking with two friends, she giggled as they approached their pod classrooms after lunch. Mr. Herman stepped out into the corridor.

Marlee straightened up. Smiled obsequiously, "Hi, Mr. Herman."

It sounded like he grunted, and his face confirmed it. "Grades are already submitted."

The two friends failed in their attempt at suppressing laughter.

"Knock it off!" Marlee swatted them.

One mocked Marlee with an overly sweet, cloying voice, "Hi, Mr. Herman." The two roared.

"Cut it out!"

"Next time, maybe don't be such an obvious brownnoser. You've never said hi to him before."

"Be quiet." She walked off in a huff.

After clearing the supper table, Marlee handed her parents a sealed report card. That's what she immediately noticed when they were distributed just before the bell rang. She wondered why it was sealed. It wasn't sealed before. A fingernail went into her mouth. She started chewing while her dad read. His expression gave nothing away. Then he smiled.

"You're going in the right direction, Marlee. Keep it up." He passed the report card to Meredith.

She nodded, "Nice job."

Marlee breathed a sigh of relief. It did reflect her earlier progress report. Science and Social Studies had climbed to a C and B, respectively, and Communication Skills improved to a B. Math held steady at a C, but Reading slipped to a B. Sorting it all out, her parents were pleased. No Ds! No As either, she realized.

"Will you go to the Rola Rena to celebrate your success?" Meredith inquired.

"That's a great idea! I think I will." Marlee was happy, but it bothered her that she hadn't earned at least one A.

Rola Rena remained a popular hangout on Saturday afternoons. And not only did Marlee skate and hold hands with Mark McGregor, but afterward, he walked her halfway home. Where she turned right onto Oneida Street, he continued straight across the intersection to his house.

The two started meeting after school, and sometimes they walked partway home together. One day, as the winter wind blew and nipped at their skin, they sought refuge at the nearby Valley View Elementary School, huddling together outside in the corner of the south entrance. Mark leaned in and pressed his cold, closed lips to Marlee's mouth. Her belly did a weird little flip. Her first kiss! Instinctively, she snuggled into his shoulder, a smile against his scratchy wool peacoat.

"Are you freezing?" he asked her.

"It's pretty cold."

He kissed her again before they parted. "See you tomorrow, Marlee."

"Bye, Mark." She practically floated home.

Later that night, after eating, completing homework, and watching a little TV, Marlee went to her bedroom and climbed onto her bed to look out the frosted bedroom window. Wow! she thought when she found the hazy orb of night. How pretty. Aided by the fluffy white snow cover, she could see into the darkness. The moonlight cast long, creepy shadows off the leafless, skeletal trees and over the snow-covered lawns; it looked as if many arms reached out, their fingers ready to snatch whatever tried to scuttle away.

No one was outside at nine at night, and Marlee savored the still-ness and the mystery she sensed. Mark McGregor popped into her head, although he had never been far away since they kissed that afternoon. Her belly did an encore flip. A smile graced her lips.

Deciding not to tell even Melanie about Mark or what happened after school, Marlee considered calling a friend. Thinking better of it, she dared not risk being overheard. Her parents would certainly disapprove, and while this wasn't a date, dating in her family was forbidden before the age of sixteen. Melanie herself had begun dating only months prior. The more Marlee thought about it, the more she knew it was best to keep this to herself, not wanting anyone to ruin its sweetness. She reached up and pulled the shade down, hesitant to abandon the night sky. Her mother often reminded the kids that their bedrooms would stay warmer at night if they drew the shade against the cold winter weather. Marlee fell back onto her bed.

A poster of Bobby Sherman on the opposite wall kept her mind on Mark. She could barely see it but knew it well enough. Bobby and Mark wore their brown hair similarly long, almost to their chins, parted on the side, and swept low across their foreheads. Bobby's adorable smile brought the corners of her mouth up. Mark's smile had the same effect on her.

Mr. Herman ushered Marlee and her class into the planetarium. They'd been studying the solar system for weeks, and he often bragged about the fascinating room, eager to share the astronomy experience. He told his students they should be grateful for the planetarium. "The high school doesn't even have one," he pointed out, "and here you are with one in your new middle school. You ought to consider yourselves lucky. Take a seat on the floor," he said.

Mr. Herman explained what to expect—a completely dark room, the dome-shaped ceiling twinkling above, littered with stars. "Prepare to be dazzled!" He flashed a rare smile. "I will show you different stars and constellations, so buckle up," he chuckled. His festive mood was infectious.

As soon as the room went black, the class oohed and aahed. A smattering of comments could be heard: "This is so cool!" "Wow!" and "Amazing" were just a few.

Mr. Herman used a laser pointer to circle Polaris, the North Star. "And here you see Ursa Minor, which is Latin for *Little Bear*, as opposed to Ursa Major, meaning *Great Bear*. You may know them better as the Little Dipper and the Big Dipper."

Giggling surfaced, and sounds of scuffling ensued.

"Stop it!" he warned.

The muffled whispers continued. A single scream escaped.

Suddenly, the lights popped on. Mr. Herman thundered, "What is going on?"

Five surly preteens in a heap—two boys and three girls, Marlee included—looked up guiltily at their teacher.

"Well, I might've known! Mr. Martin, get off of her!" he boomed. Turning a deep crimson, he aggressively pointed, stabbing the air in front of the five. "You, you, you—all of you—I will see you after school!" Marlee feared the man's head might explode. He was as angry a person as she'd ever seen.

The dismissal bell rang at the end of the day, and after another lengthier, more controlled chewing-out by Mr. Herman, Marlee walked home with Gina Moore. The two carried notes that needed their parents' signatures.

"They're not going to like this," Gina complained.

"Mine either! What'll happen to you?"

"I've no idea. What do you think yours will say?"

"I don't even want to think about it. But how would you like to be Bet?" Marlee asked, "Or Chad Martin? Mr. Herman was totally ticked when he saw Chad on top of her."

"I know! But it wasn't Bet's fault. She was so embarrassed." Gina frowned.

"Still," Marlee muttered.

The girls reached the bottom of the street where Gina lived and said goodbye. Marlee plodded on.

She immediately gave the note to her mother. "Here, this is for you and Dad. It's from Mr. Herman."

Meredith raised her eyebrows. As expected, she and Marvin were not pleased. Marlee listened to a lecture about proper behavior and had to write an apology to her teacher. Also, Saturday's roller skating privileges were revoked for that week.

Before homeroom the next day, Mr. Herman read Marlee's note while she stood by. He kept his head lowered until he'd finished reading, then glared at her above his glasses that sat low on his long nose.

"From now on, mind your p's and q's."

"I will."

"And a bit of advice: choose your friends wisely."

"Okay."

"You may go. But watch yourself!" Mr. Herman warned.

Spring had sprung with an unusually warm day, an early weather teaser, and after school, Stadium Drive came alive with a kickball game in the middle of the street. Kyle White and Larry Traeger acted as self-appointed captains. They chose teams and divided the boys and girls evenly.

Brett Zelinski pitched a big, red rubber ball straight to Oscar Traeger. Oscar booted it over the head of the third baseman into Johnson's front yard. Kyle ran to back up Eloise, but she didn't need help. Suddenly, someone yelled, "Car!" Everyone scattered as the vehicle parted the field of play to proceed up the street. An argument started over how far Oscar could have gotten before he might have been tagged out. They had not settled it before Marlee and Troy were called home to eat. Sally Vande-Garde bowed out then because of the bickering.

Meredith wanted to know who had homework. Since Marlee had brought the note home from Mr. Herman about the shenanigans in the planetarium, her mother seemed to be monitoring her more closely.

"I feel like a little kid when you always have to check everything I do," Marlee grumbled. "Can't we be done with this?"

"Stop!" Marvin interjected. "You need to prove that you're towing the mark."

"Well, I am," she huffed.

"Excellent. Then it's all good."

Gina Moore found Marlee at school first thing in the morning and pulled her into the restroom.

"What's going on?" Marlee asked.

Gina checked under all the stalls. "Something terrible happened last night."

"What happened?"

"Chad Martin and Darin Boekman went to Bet's house and *depantsed* her!" Gina enunciated her strange word choice.

"What exactly does that mean?"

"They took her pants and underwear off!"

"What? Oh my gosh! How did that happen?"

"Chad and Darin went to Bet's house. Her parents weren't home. No one was except Bet. She told me she got away from them after they pulled her pants off. Locked herself in the bathroom. I guess the guys left then. Bet called me crying."

"How—" Marlee stared incredulously at her friend.

"Bet said she didn't want Chad or Darin even at her house. Didn't know why they came."

"Is she here today?"

"Yeah, but she didn't tell her parents what happened."

"She didn't?"

"I guess not."

"I hate those guys!" Marlee said. Fire in her eyes.

"I do, too."

"Does Bet know you're telling me?"

"I think so, but don't tell anyone."

"I can't believe she's here today. And has to see those dumb jackasses!"

"She's going to ignore them."

"We can't let them get away with this!" Marlee scowled.

"What are we supposed to do? If she didn't even tell her parents?" Gina frowned.

"Damn."

"I know."

Marlee turned thirteen years old.

"You're a teenager!" Melanie cheered. "Welcome to the club."

Meredith handed Marlee a few cards that arrived in the mail. She received cash from her grandparents and godparents.

The new teen chose fried venison, green beans cooked in salt pork, mashed potatoes, and freshly baked dinner rolls for her special meal. Angel food cake topped it off, decorated with her mother's signature white lamb frosting—not too sweet—and she'd written in pink script, *Happy Birthday Marlee*. Thirteen candles flickered before they were blown out with an unspoken wish.

Marvin and Meredith gifted Marlee clothes, an owl necklace, and a book, *The Charmed Circle* by Dorothea J. Snow. But the best part was knowing she could finally get her ears pierced, which Marlee had begged to do since turning nine. Her mother and sister joined her, and the three got their ears pierced on the same day.

Ruby was puzzled by it. "I can't believe you paid someone to punch holes in your perfectly good ears," she groused. "It reminds me of the time, Meredith, when you and Marvin bought a dishwasher and then rinsed the dishes so thoroughly you practically washed them before loading the darn thing! For it to supposedly do its job. It didn't make any sense!"

"Don't be ridiculous, Ma. Those two things aren't even remotely the same."

"They're both senseless."

"You sound like my brother, Buzzy," Marvin joked. "He couldn't understand why I had air conditioning installed in the car. He told me, 'Just roll down the windows and drive seventy down the highway—presto—air conditioning!' That's Buzzy," he laughed.

"You get my point, though, don't you?" Ruby waggled her finger. "And you know what? I probably have a hundred pairs of beautiful clip earrings. Who will want those someday, now that all of you have *pierced* ears?" She seemed genuinely sad.

"I'm sorry to disappoint you, Mother."

Marlee looked at Melanie. Did Grandma think they would wear her gaudy, outdated clip earrings? Sure, they looked good on her. But Marlee had a new pair of sterling silver hoops, plus her allowance and babysitting money, ready to be spent on all kinds of cute earrings.

"I just don't understand you kids," Ruby said, unable to let it go, shaking her blacker-than-night wig-covered head.

The Becket women cleaned their earlobes nightly with cotton swabs soaked in rubbing alcohol. And at least three times a day, they diligently turned the small gold posts as instructed. Seeing one do it reminded the others. And Marlee didn't dare remove the earrings before the piercings had healed.

Now, she thought, if somehow she could convince her mom to let her wear jeans to school, everything would be perfect. Seventh grade was only days from ending, so it seemed fitting to delay that all-important request until summer, maybe just before the start of eighth grade.

Marlee finished her academic year with four Bs and one C in her core subjects, similar to the grades she'd earned at the end of the third quarter. And still no As. The C came in Science—no surprise there.

Most summer weekends were spent at the cabin, and the family, minus Todd, took a vacation to Niagara Falls and New York City. According to Marlee, Niagara Falls was spectacular. She liked the cascading waters better than she'd liked the gorges of the Grand Canyon.

"They're both incredible," Marvin stated.

"I don't even know how you can compare them. Or choose. They're so different," Melanie balked. "Both unique."

"I agree," Meredith nodded. Waiting in line for the sightseeing boat tour, she was captivated by the sheer beauty before her. "Breathtaking," she muttered.

"Do you think it looks different from the other side?" Troy asked.

"From the Canadian side?" Marvin clarified. "I don't know, but I hear it's more of a panoramic view from over there."

"So, that's a yes," Marlee stated. "It looks different from the other side."

"Wiseacre," Marvin smiled.

"Maybe someday you can check it out," he suggested to Troy.

"I'd like that," Troy admitted.

The family donned full rain suits and boarded the *Maid of the Mist*. Up close, they saw the green-blue rushing waters, heard the thunderous roar of several hundred thousand gallons of water, and felt the mist pelt their faces. Marlee smiled at her father.

"Niagara Falls is my favorite!" she declared. "This is so cool!"

"You've never seen anything quite like it, huh, Marlee?" Marvin asked.

"Never! I love it!"

They took a ferry to see the Statue of Liberty, which afforded them a view of the New York City skyline with the new Twin Towers of the World Trade Center. Lady Liberty was undergoing maintenance and painting for the Bicentennial celebration in 1976. But you could still climb the two-hundred-plus steps up the pedestal, and then climb another 162 steps to the crown. No one relished the narrow, spiral staircase, which was more claustrophobic than Marlee cared for. Not to mention hot. She barely stepped onto the landing to look outside the tiny windows.

"Why can't we go all the way up her arm? Into the torch?"

"Like you could handle that!" Melanie guffawed.

"They stopped allowing that long ago, during the First World War, if I remember correctly," Marvin informed them.

After sandwiches at a crowded New York deli, Marvin announced, "On to the Empire State Building."

Gazing upward, the family was grateful to skip the nearly two thousand stairs, opting instead for a long elevator ride to the top, where they enjoyed even more impressive views of the sprawling city.

"I'd like to come back at night," Troy said.

"Yeah," agreed Marlee. She was more comfortable stepping close to the window than she'd been in the tight space of the Statue of Liberty.

The sights from both were far grander than those from the rooftop pool of their hotel. They witnessed a man straddling an open window in a high-rise apartment building, one leg dangling eighteen stories above the rock-hard pavement below. He wore only his skimpy underwear. No shirt. Just bottoms. They probably were ordinary Fruit of the Loom briefs. Today, someone might call them "tighty-whities."

Meredith ordered the kids to look away. "That's disturbing," she said.

Marvin chuckled. Surprisingly, so did Meredith.

However, she disliked that the "damage" had already been inflicted—imagining the scandalous image forever seared in the kids' brains. Yet there they were, snagging a few more stolen glances in that direction.

"Stop looking," Meredith scoffed.

Everyone laughed. Meredith threw up her hands.

Marvin carried most of his money in his shoes while they toured the Big Apple. "No one is going to pick-pocket me and get away with it," he stated.

"I hope your feet don't stink," Troy kidded his dad.

"Oh boy. That's something I'd expect from your brother," Marvin said.

Marlee sent Eloise a postcard of Niagara Falls. She also secretly wanted to send one to Mark McGregor but didn't have his address memorized like her best friend's. She'd have to tell him about it.

A week or two after the Beckets returned home, Marlee and a friend met Mark and a buddy at the mini-golf course behind Super Ron's grocery store. They putted around the obstacles for eighteen holes and afterward sat at a picnic table, licking soft-serve ice cream cones. Marlee shared details from the trip, and they got a kick out of the guy in his undies.

Mark added the golf scores. "I won," he announced.

"How did I do?" his buddy asked.

"I beat you by three."

Marlee and Sherry were unconcerned with their scores.

"I can hardly believe next weekend is Labor Day," Marlee said.

"Are you going up north?" Sherry asked her.

"You know it. What are you guys going to do?"

Mark and his buddy shrugged.

"I have a family cookout at my aunt and uncle's house on Sunday," Sherry offered. "They have a pool, so, yeah."

"Sounds fun." Marlee smiled.

"We gotta get to practice," Mark stated. "Come on, dude." He swung his leg over his bike. The Warriors had football practice at four every weekday afternoon.

"See ya, Marlee," Mark winked.

A faint sensation pleasantly tossed her insides. "Bye," she waved.

Marlee liked spending time with Mark, but it hadn't been easy. Her family went up north most weekends, and often during the week, either her mother or Mrs. White dropped the kids off at Colburn Park for an afternoon of swimming. Marlee told Mark he could find her at the pool most weekdays, but he never showed up.

With most of the summer reflected in the rearview mirror, Marlee steeled herself to broach with her mother again the idea of wearing jeans to school.

"You have corduroy pants. Be happy with that," Meredith breathed a deep sigh.

"Come on, Mom! Corduroys aren't jeans. Everyone but me wears jeans," Marlee griped.

"I'm certain that's not true."

"Except for a few dorks, it is *so* true," she argued.

"You're being dramatic."

"Will you think about it some more?"

"No."

"I don't get what the big deal is," Marlee said.

"I've told you my position on this more times than I care to count. We're done. My answer is no," Meredith said emphatically.

Marlee huffed, stormed out of the kitchen, and stomped to her bedroom, careful not to slam her door.

A few days later, the girl almost fell over when her mother surprised her with a new pair of Wranglers. "Why did you—"

"Hold on," Meredith interrupted. "You can't wear them to school," she quickly explained, "but I thought you would like them for football games."

"Oh." Well, that's something Marlee thought. "Thank you! I don't have to wear my dumb cords anymore."

"To school, you do."

Despite Marlee's disappointment, she knew from the get-go that eighth grade in the fall of 1974 would surely be an improvement over the previous year; for one, she liked all her teachers.

Another reason, ranking equally high, was Bet Riley's willingness to bring a pair of jeans to school for Marlee to wear. She didn't dare sneak her pair to school, as her mother would undoubtedly have noticed. But the two hatched a plan, and immediately after the denim exchanged hands, Marlee bolted to the nearest bathroom to slip them on. She shoved her unwanted pants into her locker, only to pull them back out after the final bell rang. And, at the end of the school week, Marlee gave Bet the coveted jeans, and her trusted friend returned with them on Monday morning, freshly laundered. This charade continued, almost without interruption, for the better part of the school year.

"I don't know what I would do without you," Marlee often told Bet. "I'm sorry I can't take the jeans home and wash them."

"Don't worry about it. I would hate it if I couldn't wear jeans, and I have, like, five pairs."

"You are so lucky!" Marlee could hardly fathom that.

The second year of Warrior football proved as much fun as the first. Again, Marlee loudly cheered with friends from the sidelines: "Hold 'em, defense, don't let 'em through!" Clap, clap. The kids went wild when, as usual, the defense held the other team, forcing a change of possession by making them punt. They yelled and cheered, jumping up and down, rumbling the bleachers. When the team scored, it was more of the same rowdy response. Sometimes, Marlee returned home hoarse.

Basketball tryouts took place after school over two afternoons. Although Marlee knew nothing more about the sport than how to dribble and shoot free throws—both of which she did in the driveway—she tried out. Her effort didn't merit a spot on either team, but she wasn't terribly disappointed.

Almost like a consolation prize, she settled for leading cheers for one of the boys' four basketball teams, where they played only against their classmates. Any eighth-grade girl who wanted to cheer was allowed. Marlee realized it wasn't the real deal—nothing like the esteemed Warrior cheerleaders who tried out amid dozens, earning a place on the squad.

Adding insult to injury, the basketball cheerleaders had to purchase their own "uniforms." They decided what to wear and got approval from the principal. Marlee's group of seven shopped, deciding on gold turtleneck sweaters, short black full skirts they rolled at the waistline to make even shorter, and gold knee-high socks. Some girls lobbied for saddle shoes, but when they couldn't get them in everyone's size, they opted for black canvas tennis shoes.

Their cheerleading was weak, and they struggled to cheer in sync. They practiced some but received no help or guidance from any parent or teacher. An underwhelming bunch they were. For the most part, it was the same with the other three squads.

Laura Adler and Laura Harding were girls mostly from Marlee's past, mainly because they hung out in different groups. Marlee still liked the girls, and the groups regularly meshed at events such as pep rallies and sporting events.

One day, Laura Harding caught Marlee after gym class.

"Hey, Marlee, are you going to the eighth-grade dance on Saturday?"

"I think so. Are you?"

"Yeah, I'm going. I'll see you there."

"Okay," she smiled.

Truth be told, Marlee hadn't yet asked her parents for permission to attend the dance.

They said she could go. Lucky for her, they didn't go up north much in fall and winter.

The girl bebopped in her stockinged feet, even slow dancing with a couple of the more popular guys. Mark hadn't gone to the dance: his mother wouldn't let him. Laura Harding found Marlee in the crowd, and they bounced around until they were sweaty before taking a break to guzzle water near the concession stand, where it was cooler.

After she got home and lay in bed, Marlee struggled to fall asleep, her mind abuzz. It was the most fun she'd ever had. Peeling back the covers, she hopped to her knees, raised the window shade, and briefly peered across the street. Looking up to study the starlit sky proved useless. Unable to focus, she flopped onto her back and replayed the entire evening in her head, eventually dozing off with a goofy grin frozen in place.

Marlee thought she heard a car in the driveway and yanked open the floor-length sheers. Seeing an evergreen tree tied to the car's roof, she panicked.

"I don't have the living room done yet!"

"It's not the end of the world," Meredith tried to assure Marlee, knowing that for the past few years, her youngest daughter had wanted the living room cleaned and everything perfect before the Christmas tree went up. She'd vacuumed that day but still had furniture to dust.

At first, Meredith could not understand why Marlee valued that kind of thing so much, but eventually, she recognized that her daughter *needed* to do it, yearning for the idyllic setting. That was long before Hallmark became the king of holiday movies, portraying picture-perfect Christmas settings.

It was also about then that Meredith noticed Marlee taking it upon herself to clean and organize cupboards and closets. One day, she pulled everything out of the bathroom vanity. She even cut new shelf-lining paper and wiped the contents down before organizing them neatly. Meredith did not object.

Marlee also began rewriting her class notes each night. Meredith initially thought it was her way of studying until she learned her daughter did it because she wanted her notes to be immaculate, as neat as Laura Harding's.

"Laura takes the neatest, cleanest notes. I wish you could see them, Mom," she said. "I want my notes as neat as Laura's."

"Then why don't you work on doing that the first time? You're going through spiral notebooks like they're, oh, I don't know, toilet paper. What's going on, Marlee? Why the perfectionism lately?"

Marlee glared at her mother. "What's wrong with trying to be neat?"

"Nothing unless it becomes an obsession. You seem obsessed with it."

"I'm not obsessed," she snapped.

Changing the subject, Marlee calmly and purposefully offered a tidbit of information, "Speaking of Laura, Laura *Adler* is going steady. So is Amy Andrews." The only reason Marlee even mentioned it was to get her mother's take. She got it all right.

"That's ridiculous. If their mothers allow that, they ought to have their heads examined."

Marlee continued, "Amy Andrews even goes on dates with Bobby Dennison. Their parents take them to the movies and pick them up afterward. They even went to Kroll's for a milkshake."

"Marvin?" Meredith called. "Do you hear your daughter?" Now she was *his* daughter. "Is this what we're up against? Eighth-grade girls have no business dating boys."

"I think waiting until I'm sixteen is too long."

"Has someone asked you out on a date, Marlee?" Marvin wanted to know.

"No. Who would ask me out?"

Meredith interjected, "Maybe letting Marlee go to that middle school dance wasn't the best idea after all."

"Crap!" Marlee muttered.

"What?" Marvin asked.

"Nothing," Marlee shook her head.

Fortunately, neither parent pushed the issue, which was good because another dance was scheduled for February, in time for Valentine's Day. Marlee prayed that her folks, especially her mother, would forget that this conversation ever happened. She hoped that with all her mother had to do to prepare for the holidays—reminding the kids at every turn—it might very possibly slip her mind.

Todd wanted to build something special for his parents for Christmas, so he presented them with a pair of octagon-shaped oak end tables with doors. You would have thought Meredith had died and gone to heaven. She was beyond excited.

"You built these? Wow! When? Oh my, they're beautiful," she gushed. "This extra storage space is great!"

"Yeah, nice work, Todd." Marvin admired his son's craftsmanship. "They let you use their equipment?" he asked, referring to his employer.

"Yeah. There are certain nights after business hours when we can stay and use any machines we want. The guys design and build a lot of cool furniture and other stuff. I just had to pay for materials," he explained.

"Can you make me a jewelry rack?" Marlee asked.

"These are wonderful, Todd. I can't wait to move them in." Meredith hugged her son, but he brushed her kiss away.

"There's no time like the present." Marvin started to clear the floor. Move everything out of the way.

"What! Are you sure?" Meredith rubbed her palms together. She watched with her fingertips pressed to her mouth, relishing her good fortune.

"Where do you want these?" Todd patted the top of the old end tables.

"In the basement for now," Marvin replied. "Your mother can decide later what she wants to do with those."

Marlee leaped over a pile of moving blankets Todd had used to disguise the tables then scampered after him. "Can you make me a jewelry rack? Something to hang my necklaces on?"

"Sure. You'll have to tell me what you want."

"You can?"

"It'll be easy."

"Cool!"

"I might want you to build me a rack for fishing poles," Troy told his brother.

"I was thinking we need a rack for pool cues instead of standing them in the corner," Todd suggested.

Marvin agreed with both of his sons. "I like that—racks for pool cues and fishing poles."

CHAPTER 19

MARLEE TIED HER GYM shoes with one foot atop a bench. Betty Fuller swiped her hand over her classmate's shin. "How about you shave those hairy things?" she snickered.

Embarrassed, Marlee lowered her foot and tried to quickly think of an excuse for why she hadn't shaved but offered nothing. The idea had never occurred to her before. Betty pushed open the locker-room door toward the gymnasium. Her deep-throated, almost manly laughter sent a shiver up Marlee's spine.

Eager to get home after school and take care of the matter, Marlee holed up in the bathroom. Having borrowed a razor from Melanie without asking, she carefully scraped the peach fuzz from her legs. It surprised her how shiny they looked and how smooth they felt. She hadn't so much as nicked her skin. Fortunately, it hadn't taken too long, and no one had tried to get into the bathroom or asked what she was doing. Marlee didn't know if her mother would have approved but didn't want to chance being told she couldn't shave her legs. Her attitude was such that what her mother didn't know wouldn't hurt her.

The girl pondered what else she may have missed and what other grown-up things she probably should be doing. The first thing that popped into her head was that she hadn't started her period yet. Nothing obviously could be done about that, but frankly, she was more than okay with it. Several friends, though, had begun menstruating—some literally for years already. Gina Moore started a few months ago, and although she tried to be covert, Marlee noticed her taking a purse to the restroom. She had never done that previously. Practically every middle school girl knew that when another girl carried a purse, Aunt Flo had officially begun her monthly visits. Marlee filed a mental note to one day hide her supplies in her socks.

Next, she thought about her eyebrows, mostly concealed under her long bangs. She wondered if they needed attention.

The following day at school, Marlee confirmed her suspicion that girls her age plucked their eyebrows. Laura Harding, Amy Andrews, and even Minnie Challe appeared to have thinned and shaped eyebrows. Marlee played it cool, asking no questions. Then, on her walk home, she thought about Melanie, wondering if her sister plucked her eyebrows. It surprised her that she didn't know the answer.

All through supper, Marlee watched Melanie. She couldn't tell if she plucked. Afterward, standing side by side doing dishes, Marlee reached to turn on the radio. From the living room, their parents probably overheard everything the two ever discussed at the kitchen sink. She didn't want to risk being overheard.

Leaning close to Melanie, she kept her voice low, "Hey, do you pluck your eyebrows?"

"Not really." Melanie looked at her sister funny. "I've plucked a few strays here and there, but that's about it. They're so light, it just doesn't matter. Why do you want to know?"

"Keep your voice down," Marlee whispered. "Mine are darker than yours, and I want to pluck them. Will you help me?"

"When we finish here, get the magnifying mirror and tweezers," Melanie instructed.

The last dish was dried and put away, and Marlee ran the wet towels to the basement. Melanie put out fresh ones and swept the kitchen quickly. The girls met in Marlee's room.

Melanie closed the door. "Put the mirror on your dresser and pull up a chair. Or try lying on your bed, maybe."

Marlee chose the bed. Lying on her belly and leaning on her elbows, she raised the magnifying mirror to her face. "Whoa!" she groaned.

Melanie chuckled. "I once read in *Seventeen* magazine that you're supposed to pluck in the direction the hair grows."

Marlee honed in on her right brow first, pinching the tweezers. "Yow, wow!" she yelped, pressing her fingers to her brow. Her right eye watered. "Dang! That stings." She studied the tweezers. Two tiny brown hairs were caught.

"You'll get used to it," Melanie giggled. "Do you think you know what you're doing?"

"Yeah, I got it. Thanks."

About an hour later, after Marlee showered, she wrapped her head in a towel and exited the bathroom. She joined her parents in the living room, where they sat, sharing the evening newspaper, fully absorbed in their reading.

Marlee sat on the carpet with her smooth legs to the side, near her dad, and petted Crisco, who lay curled up in the chair next to him.

Marvin asked his wife, "Did you see what the mayor of Green Bay is trying to get passed?"

"No, I've not read that section yet," Meredith muttered, lowering the newspaper out of consideration. "What's he working on?"

"Marlee!" she gasped. "What did you do to your eyebrows? Did you pluck them?"

Marvin looked up. Raised his eyes over the paper.

Marlee instinctively brought her fingertips to her brows. "Yeah. Why?" she asked meekly. "What's wrong?"

"There's nothing left! Oh, Marvin . . ."

"What?" Marlee asked.

"They'll grow back," Marvin said, more for his wife's sake than his daughter's.

"You don't like them?"

"Whatever possessed you to do such a thing? Why didn't you ask me?"

"I asked Melanie."

"Melanie helped you. And she thinks that looks good?"

Tears threatened. "Well, I didn't show her when I finished. She just helped me get started."

"Oh," Meredith groaned. "Go comb your hair. You'd better hope they're not noticeable under your bangs."

Marlee ran to the bathroom, closed the door, and thrust her index finger into the knob, locking it. She pulled the towel off her head and, with tearful eyes blurring her vision, did her best to see her reflection in the mirror. She liked her eyebrows. The tears spilled over anyway. She sobbed.

Meredith frowned. "That girl gives me a run for my money."

"It's not so bad, Mer," Marvin said.

"Did you see her?"

"They'll grow back."

The newspaper went up in front of Meredith's face. She sighed heavily.

Marvin gingerly brought his paper up, too.

Marlee celebrated her fourteenth birthday, and three weeks later, the school year wound to a close. She had successfully navigated eighth grade, earning a solid B average without the hijinks of the previous year. She briefly thought ahead to high school, already anticipating her freshman year.

The family busied themselves with preparations for Melanie's graduation party, which, not surprisingly, turned out to be a near–carbon copy of Todd's party three years earlier. The same relatives and neighbors came; only the friends were different.

Carolyn Jacobs, a former tenant and good friend of the Beckets, quizzed Melanie on her plans.

"I'm enrolled at NWTI for the fall medical assistant program," she said proudly. "It's a one-year program. After that, I would like to work either in Marshfield or at the Mayo Clinic. You know, somewhere like that."

"Well, you seem motivated." Mrs. Jacobs smiled. "I wish you all the success in the world."

"Thank you." Melanie continued making the rounds, talking with all the guests as her parents had instructed.

The week ahead was chock-full of graduation parties all over town, and Melanie liked the idea of attending other celebrations away from the spotlight of her own. She had always been uncomfortable when too much attention turned her way.

Melanie rarely went up north to the cabin anymore. Instead, in the summer of 1975, she worked full time at a cafeteria inside one of the large paper mills, and because she was eighteen, she went out with friends to the bars on Friday and Saturday nights. She was also sweet on a guy named Steve. And he was sweet on her.

Troy befriended some boys whose families also owned cabins in the woods or cottages on the lake, and they often fished together. As a result, he and Marlee were no longer attached at the hip up north.

Marlee often felt isolated at the cabin. Swimming or floating alone was boring, so she read more while lying in the hammock or stretched out on a webbed chaise longue. And she rode the minibike down the trails, reflecting on the stories she'd read. It was easy to insert herself into the characters' lives; she lived vicariously through them, whether it was Nancy Drew or *Julie of the Wolves*.

The song "Seasons in the Sun" by Terry Jacks played on the battery-operated radio sitting atop a stump in the yard. Marvin listened while he puttered about doing odd jobs. The song had a somber effect on Marlee. She tossed her book aside and hopped on the minibike. Tears came. She didn't know why she cried. She did nothing to stop the waterworks but, instead, gave in to the overwhelming emotion, choosing not to analyze it. Sometimes a good cry was needed, and it felt cleansing. And then it was over. Whatever prompted it.

That summer, Marlee found herself contemplating life more. She used to want to invite a school friend up north but ultimately decided against asking her parents. She began to crave the solitude of the woods surrounding the cabin, maybe even needing it. It most likely was the calm before the high school storm.

One sultry afternoon, beneath the shaded cover of trees, Meredith and Marlee picked wild raspberries that grew near the cabin. A warm breeze blew gently through the trees.

"You know," Marlee started. "I'll be in high school soon, and I . . ."

Meredith waited to hear what was on her daughter's mind. She continued to fill her pail with the red berries.

"I—I really . . . I'm hoping I can wear jeans to school this year."

"This again?" Meredith said, though not angrily. She had thought about it, knowing she'd not heard the last of it. If Marlee was anything, she was persistent.

"This may come as a surprise to you, but I think you can wear jeans to school once a—"

Marlee interrupted, hearing what she desperately longed to hear. "I can? I can wear jeans my freshman year! Oh, Mom!" She squealed.

"You didn't let me finish," Meredith said, and reading her daughter's expression, she knew Marlee's heart sank. "Yes, you can wear jeans to school. But only once a week."

"Once a week?" Marlee repeated. "What made you finally change your mind?" She regretted the word *finally*.

"I talked it over with Dad, and I've observed kids at the high school whenever I had the opportunity. I *still* see many girls wearing skirts and dresses. And nice slacks."

"I know, Mom." Marlee sounded almost breathless. "But thank you! Thank you so much!" She hugged her mother, jostling their buckets.

"Careful, you'll spill our raspberries."

Marvin and Meredith began to treat their children, at least the two who traveled with them to the cabin, to dinner out most Saturday evenings at Rene's Dining Room, next door to Popp's Resort in the Twin Bridge area of Crivitz, Wisconsin.

That is where Marlee discovered fried shrimp, which became her absolute favorite meal. When she eventually learned it was customary to allow death-row inmates a last meal of their choice before execution, she liked to say that fried shrimp, without a doubt, would be her last meal.

"What? You plan to kill someone or burn down a city somewhere?" Todd had joked.

Marlee laughed. "Hardly. I'm just saying . . . I like me some shrimp!"

Those fabulous dinners out were always topped off with after-dinner drinks made with ice cream, nonalcoholic versions for the kids matching the alcoholic choices of their parents, either a Golden Cadillac or a Grasshopper. Marlee believed it was the perfect dessert, capping off the perfect meal.

Toward the end of August, Meredith took Marlee school shopping, and afterward, they sat across from one another at a table at The Terrace Room, awaiting their lunch. Marlee briefly perused the menu, quickly deciding on her choice. She rested her hands in her lap and gazed out the bank of windows overlooking the Fox River. She relaxed in the comfort of the familiar restaurant, pleased to see that Mrs. Curtain still worked there. Marlee immediately noticed that she had changed her hair, wearing it short instead of styled in a smooth French twist that she'd come to think of as her signature look. The woman approached their table.

"My, my," Jean Curtain exclaimed. "It's that time of year already. Boy, didn't the summer go fast? How are you gals doing?"

"We're fine," Meredith smiled. "How are you and Floyd? And the family?"

"Same, we're all doing well. That's a good thing, I guess. Did you gals have a chance to look at the menu?"

"We did," Meredith nodded and gestured to her daughter.

"Well, what can I get you?" Jean turned to Marlee.

"I would like a Reuben sandwich and a root beer, please."

"That's served with fries, and for you, Meredith?"

"The Reuben sounds good. I'll do that, too. However, I'd like a decaf coffee, please."

"All righty, I'll put that in. It shouldn't be too long."

"Thank you, Jean."

The restaurant was busy. All the waitresses bustled about.

Meredith extracted a piece of paper from her purse and reviewed her shopping list. With a ballpoint pen, she crossed out most things. It had been a productive morning. She muttered something her daughter either failed to hear or didn't acknowledge.

Marlee sat content, having just purchased a pair of Lee jeans with her hard-earned money. Meredith told her that she preferred to buy other, more sensible clothing, and Marlee was okay with that. She had no problem using babysitting and allowance money to buy jeans. She'd waited a long time to be able to wear denim "legally" to school, so whatever it took, it worked for her.

She also bought a nice pair of tan, flared corduroy pants from Nau's, an upscale clothing store. The high-waisted pants featured a decorative brushed gold adornment. It looked like a tiny buckle.

"Those are expensive," Meredith remarked as she rifled through the sale racks. "If you want those, you'll have to pay for them. Or I'll tell you what—I'll pay half." Marlee's half totaled thirteen dollars before tax. Her mother covered that.

The night before school began, Marlee tossed and turned every which way on her mattress before finally kneeling to look out her bedroom window. She sighed. Then prayed her hair would look okay the next day after a night of sleeping on it, since showers were forbidden in the morning. She hated the rule—her hair always looked best freshly blown dry. She'd chopped it short—just covering her ears—so it could be parted in the middle and feathered back. The more feathered, the better.

"There are simply too many people needing to get ready all at once," her mother had explained. Marvin often left that kind of dirty work to his wife.

Marlee balked, "Are you serious? You can't be serious!"

That was when her father stepped in and spoke sternly, "Marlee. You heard your mother. You *cannot* shower in the morning. That is all there is to it. Everyone needs to get in and out of the bathroom. We all have places to go and things to do."

"Not mom," she'd muttered under her breath. Luckily for her, no one heard.

Despite a fitful start to sleep, Marlee woke early, feeling excited. After eating a piece of peanut butter toast, she used every minute of her allotted time in the bathroom. Marlee then eagerly dressed in her new tan flared corduroys and an orange-and-yellow long-sleeved nylon blouse. She assessed herself in a full-length mirror mounted on her closet door. Her hair looked okay.

"I'm a freshman," she said out loud to no one other than herself.

"Time to go," Marvin called. He drove Marlee to school that first day and dropped her off at the main entrance.

"See you later," he said.

"See you later, and thanks for the ride, Dad." She took a deep breath.

Marlee walked into her new high school wearing stylish brown wedge heels and breezed through the large foyer with a confidence she had not yet earned. The lunch commons to her left buzzed with students. She hesitated for the tiniest amount of time and caught a fleeting thought—more of a feeling, really—before continuing in the direction of her homeroom for the next four years. Her stomach flipped. She grinned.

CHAPTER 20

MARLEE RECLINED IN THE cushioned rocker on the back patio and gazed upward into the night sky. The nearly full moon flickered behind clouds drifting slowly past. Her husband had joined her moments earlier and lit a fire in the round, iron pit, the brisk fall evening a welcome respite on the heels of a hot summer. He realized that her mind was someplace else once again. By now, he was used to it, finding it part of the intrigue and charm that attracted him all those years ago.

An announcer's voice for the high school homecoming football game permeated the autumn air. His words floated over the sound system, just a quarter mile away. Marlee's thoughts were interrupted by the roar of the crowd. The running back had scored a touchdown for the home team.

A deep sigh escaped her. She shifted in her chair to face her husband. "Wow, totally lost in my thoughts."

"I see that. Reliving history for the millionth time?"

"I guess, but you know what? I've been thinking of writing my story. Get it all down on paper. It could be freeing, you know, and a tribute to my mother. Mothers," she corrected herself, "and my dad, all of us."

Marlee smiled lovingly at her husband of thirty-five years, her life partner, her rock. He didn't dismiss or challenge her but met her smile with one of his own. His genuine smile could still melt her heart.

"You've always said you had a story to tell. Maybe now's the time."

"Yes," she said, the very thought tingling her whole body. "It just might be the extraordinary story of an ordinary girl."